Jack Vance

The World-Thinker
and Other Stories

Jack Vance

The World-Thinker
AND OTHER
STORIES

John Holbrook Vance

Spatterlight Press Signature Series, Volume 1

The World-Thinker © 1945, 2005
I'll Build Your Dream Castle © 1947, 2005
The Ten Books © 1951, 2005
The God and the Temple Robber © 1951, 2005
Telek © 1952, 2005
Noise © 1952, 2005
Seven Exits from Bocz © 1952, 2005
DP! © 1953, 2005
The Absent Minded Professor © 1954, 2005
The Devil on Salvation Bluff © 1955, 2005
The Phantom Milkman © 1956, 2005
Where Hesperus Falls © 1956, 2005
A Practical Man's Guide © 1957, 2005
The House Lords © 1957, 2005
The Secret © 1966, 2005
by Jack Vance

Published by Spatterlight Press

Cover art by Howard Kistler

ISBN 978-1-61947-148-1

Spatterlight Press LLC

Spatterlight
P R E S S
340 S. Lemon Ave #1916
Walnut, CA 91789

www.jackvance.com

CONTENTS

Foreword: *Jack Vance: The World-Thinker* i

The World-Thinker 1

I'll Build Your Dream Castle 28

The Ten Books. 46

The God and the Temple Robber 67

Telek 82

Noise 151

Seven Exits from Bocz 164

DP! 174

The Absent Minded Professor 196

The Devil on Salvation Bluff 212

The Phantom Milkman 235

Where Hesperus Falls 248

A Practical Man's Guide 258

The House Lords 267

The Secret 283

JACK VANCE: THE WORLD-THINKER

A BIOGRAPHICAL SKETCH AND LITERARY ASSESSMENT
by David B. Williams

> *"I have this theory that the titles of first published stories are symbolic. They seem to intimate the direction of a career."*
>
> — Barry Malzberg, introduction to *The Best of Jack Vance*

JACK VANCE's first published story was entitled "The World-Thinker" and appeared in the Summer 1945 issue of *Thrilling Wonder Stories*. Its title was blazoned on the cover, unusual recognition for a first-time author.

Sam Merwin, editor of *Thrilling Wonder*, later recalled having received several "fascinating but, alas, unpurchasable, pseudo-Cabell fantasies." These were the stories that were later to become *The Dying Earth*. But his initial failure to sell them taught Vance the first rule of a successful freelancer: write what sells. He turned to science fiction and, after attempting an epic space opera in the spirit of E. E. "Doc" Smith, he tried shorter lengths and sold "The World-Thinker" to *TWS*.

Robert Silverberg recalled: "Magazine science fiction in 1945 was pretty primitive stuff, and so too was 'The World-Thinker', a simple and melodramatic chase story; but there was a breadth of vision in it, a philosophic density, that set it apart from most of what was being published then, and the novice author's sense of color and image, his power to evoke mood and texture and sensory detail, was already as highly developed as that of anyone then writing science fiction, except perhaps C. L. Moore and Leigh Brackett."

In Peter Close's assessment, Vance's first published story "stands as an impressive debut flawed by formula plot, characterization, and pacing, but it revealed Vance's extraordinary imagination, gift for dialogue, and narrative skill.... Studded with exotic detail and elegant dialogue, powerfully vivid and fast-moving, disappointing and flat in resolution, 'The World-Thinker' foreshadows the best and worst of Vance's writing."

It was the last year of World War II and Vance was serving in the Merchant Marine. Writing on shipboard in wartime, Vance overcame one further editorial challenge in getting his first story into print: the FBI agent stationed on board. "He seems to be especially suspicious of me, and held up 'The World-Thinker' for some weeks, turning the copy in to the censors, who got it well rumpled and spotted with lipstick, but finally released it as harmless," Vance informed his editor.

Vance wanted to establish himself as a successful freelance writer because he yearned for the independence that profession offered. His continued efforts resulted in a further two published stories in 1946. He later deprecated his early stories as apprentice work, but they were colorful, inventive, and met the basic requirements of pulp fiction. "As a pulp writer there were two things which set Vance apart from the herd," according to Malcolm Edwards. "There was his style, exotic and strangely mannered; and there was his apparently inexhaustible ability to devise odd and attractive cultural milieux." Vance became a regular contributor to *Startling Stories* and *TWS* with his stories often featured on the covers.

James Blish, writing in 1952, opined that Vance was "a fascinating study in the technical development of a freelance writer. He began with three apparently natural gifts: a free, witty, unmannered style; an almost frighteningly fertile imagination; and a special talent for the visualization of physical color and detail. Any one of these gifts in excess in a young writer can prove fatal, since they can be and often have been used to mask or substitute for the essential construction problems of story-telling. Exactly this happened to Vance in his early work: He tossed off ideas, wisecracks, splashes of color and exotic proper names like a Catherine wheel, while his plotting remained rudimentary or non-existent."

With experience, Vance gained control of his gifts, eventually mastering the difficult trick of achieving vivid effects with a minimum of adverbs and adjectives.

Vance published only one story in 1947, but it was a coup. "I'll Build

Your Dream Castle" sold to editor John Campbell at *Astounding Science Fiction*, the premier SF magazine of the era. "Its appearance in this demanding market at such an early stage of Vance's career was no mean achievement," according to Peter Close.

Vance submitted all his early stories to Campbell first, but he managed to place only five other stories in *Astounding*: "The Potters of Firsk" in 1950, "Telek" in 1952, "The Gift of Gab" in 1955, "The Miracle Workers" in 1958, and "Dodkin's Job" in 1959. "The Narrow Land", published in *Fantastic Stories* in 1967, was written for Campbell as the first of a three-story sequence. "But Campbell didn't like it very much," Vance said. "In fact, he was rather unreasonable. Since it didn't sell in a good market, I never completed the sequence." (Those who have seen the Vance–Campbell correspondence in the Mugar Library at Boston University report that it makes interesting reading.)

"John Campbell couldn't see me for sour owl spit," Vance said many years later. "Although that's not quite true, as soon as I wrote a story for Campbell that involved telepathy, or something similar, he went for it…. Campbell was engrossed with things like telepathy, telekinetics, extra-sensory perception of all kinds…. I knew I could always sell him something, as long as I threw in something of that sort. Some of my worst stories — just hack writing, some of the worst I've ever written, I sold it to him; he loved it."

Eventually, Vance would define his literary independence in terms of editor Campbell: He got tired of writing to please Campbell and began writing to please himself.

Vance's single sale in 1947 did not indicate that he wasn't working hard. But after his initial success in science fiction, he turned his attentions to the mystery genre. Between 1946 and 1948 he worked on three mystery novels: a first chapter and outline for a novel titled *Cat Island* in 1946; novel *Bird Isle* in 1947, published ten years later as *Isle of Peril*; and *The Flesh Mask*, also published in 1957 as *Take My Face*.

In 1948, hoping to increase his production and income, Vance tried first-draft writing and launched the Magnus Ridolph series in *Startling Stories*. The first two stories were written in a single weekend. The series continued for several years and was popular with readers, but the plan to write copiously and sell the first drafts didn't pan out.

Nonetheless, "these wretched stories," as Vance described them, proved rewarding beyond all intentions. In 1951 Twentieth Century Fox bought film rights to "Hard-Luck Diggings" (*Startling Stories*, July 1948), the very first and, in Vance's opinion, the very worst Ridolph story, and hired Vance as scriptwriter. Jack and Norma moved to Hollywood. Then within a few weeks the producer changed jobs, the project was dropped, and Vance took the money and ran. Magnus Ridolph helped finance the Vances' first sojourn in Europe.

Robert Silverberg is charitable toward the Ridolph stories: "There was nothing very memorable among them...but it was clear that a remarkable imagination was at work producing these trifles, for even the most minor story had its flash of extraordinary visual intensity and its moments of unexpected ingenuity.

Another way to accommodate higher production was to adopt pseudonyms, as when Vance used John Holbrook for "Ultimate Quest" (*Super Science Stories*, September 1950) and Jack Van See for "First Star I See Tonight" (*Malcolm's Magazine*, March 1954). "The plan was to have lots of names, to do varied stuff, so as to sell more of it," Vance explained, "but it didn't work out. I couldn't deliver."

The concept survived only in his later use of his full name, John Holbrook Vance, for mystery titles and the less formal Jack Vance for SF and fantasy. Vance later regretted using his nickname for his SF and fantasy. "I've often thought that maybe, if I were starting all over again, I probably wouldn't use Jack Vance as a byline. John Vance would be somewhat more dignified perhaps."

In 1950, Damon Knight became editor of a new magazine, *Worlds Beyond*, and bought three Vance stories. The publisher, Hillman Periodicals, was also launching a paperback line, and Knight asked Vance whether he had anything for a book. Vance reworked the unsold fantasy manuscripts he had written at sea, included narrative links to tie them together, and *The Dying Earth* became Hillman No. 41, an instant collectible because of poor distribution. A teenaged Robert Silverberg ransacked Brooklyn for the book and despaired until a friend gave him a copy.

The Dying Earth made a tremendous impression in the field and established Vance as a first-rank fantasy writer. The opening scene, in which Mazirian the Magician strolls in his garden, leaves an indelible impression in the memory of every reader. (That is, the opening scene in the Hillman edition; the Mazirian story appeared first in that edition, even though it breaks the continuity of the episodes featuring T'sais. Mazirian was placed second in all later editions but was placed first again in the Vance Integral Edition at the author's insistence.)

Peter Close assessed *The Dying Earth* as "often brilliant, occasionally crass, bejeweled with splendid descriptive passages, exotic invention, polished dialogue, vivid metaphor, rare vocabulary. In its range of themes and settings, it displays almost all of Vance's talents and weaknesses." James Blish agreed: "exuberant, chaotic, colorful and shapeless." Decades later, Gene Wolfe assessed *The Dying Earth*: "If it is true, as some say, that the wonder has departed from science fiction, this is where it went."

But the Hillman paperback was a fluke, an unexpected chance to publish unsold material in book form. It would be years before Vance wrote fantasy again or produced stories in the full "Vancean style," the characteristic mode of expression that was first displayed, vividly but imperfectly, in the *Dying Earth* stories — what Jack Rawlins called "Vance's ability to capture subtle, evocative, emotively rich ambiances on paper". He continued writing for the SF pulps and the growing number of new digest-size magazines in the early 1950s, advancing to longer lengths as his skills developed.

1950 was a breakout year for Vance. During the previous two years, he had published only Ridolph stories. But "1950 saw the publication of work more sophisticated in verbal surface, narrative structure, and characterization than the early Ridolph stories," according to Russell Letson.

In addition to *The Dying Earth*, 1950 saw publication of "The Potters of Firsk" in *Astounding*, the novelette "New Bodies for Old" (*Thrilling Wonder Stories*, August) and *The Five Gold Bands* (*Startling Stories*, November) his first story to be published as a novel (though actually only 36,000 words).

To make 1950 even more memorable, "The Potters of Firsk" was adapted and broadcast as an episode of *Dimension X* on the NBC Radio Network, July 28, 1950. The story "contains some effective pictorial writing — for example, the extended opening description of the pottery bowl," Russell Letson wrote. "What makes the story work, though, is the sense of place with which Vance invests the world of Firsk. The other Vance hallmark is the treatment of alien psychology as simply different rather than evil."

Robert Silverberg considered "New Bodies for Old [Chateau d'If]" a conventional adventure story in form but added, "the prose was rich with dazzling descriptive passages, sometimes to the point of purpleness, and the science fiction inventions — the Chateau d'If, the Empyrean Tower, the technology of personality transplants — were brilliantly realized."

Peter Close considered this novelette "a critical turning point in Vance's career. It was his longest, most ambitious, most accomplished story to date.... It is probably the earliest published story in which Vance demonstrated the depth of his potential as a major stylistic talent in the field."

Silverberg found *The Five Gold Bands* even more conventional, "a simple tale of interstellar treasure hunt, but it was made notable by its unflagging pace, the lively assortment of alien beings with which Vance had stocked it, and the light, sensitive style."

Some of Vance's early works also initiated his major contribution to the SF form known as the planetary romance, which, according to John Clute in *The Encyclopedia of Science Fiction,* is an SF tale "whose primary venue (excluding contemporary or near-future versions of Earth) is a planet, and whose plot turns to a significant degree upon the nature of that venue. In the true planetary romance, the world itself encompasses — and generally survives — the tale which fitfully illuminates it."

Terry Dowling proposed a more academic term for the planetary romance, the xenographical novel, which he defined as "the portrayal of alien worlds in sufficient detail for that portrayal to have been a major reason for the story or novel." Just as Doc Smith and Edmond Hamilton were pioneers of the space opera, so Vance is recognized as perhaps the preeminent practitioner of the planetary romance.

Set in the remote future, *The Dying Earth* has been called "the first full-fledged modern planetary romance." Vance wanted to title the book *Mazirian the Magician* (and so it is in the Vance Integral Edition) but the Hillman editor correctly recognized that the setting was at least as significant as the characters and titled the book accordingly. Gene Wolfe put his finger on the matter when he asked, "Did Vance…realize that The Dying Earth itself was to be his greatest character?"

But The Dying Earth is fantasy and a suite of stories, not a true novel. A more apt example is Vance's second major work in this form, Big Planet (Startling Stories, September 1952). The novel's title again indicates the central importance of the setting.

James Blish wrote that in Big Planet Vance "has gone back to basics, as he was going to have to do sooner or later. Big Planet has the simplest possible construction a long story can have — it is a saga, the primary narrative form of all cultures in the first stages of development. Its sole trace of narrative sophistication is in the circularity of its plot, that is, its return at the crisis to the essential situation with which the story began…. By taking himself back to this primitive a narrative form, Vance has found…a story structure suitable to his talents and one which he can control. The result is quite striking and completely satisfying, where earlier long stories of Vance's were not, because for once the technique and the material are wedded to each other."

Blish didn't realize that, according to the chronology presented in Volume 44 of the Vance Integral Edition, Big Planet may have been written as early as 1948 and was therefore Vance's first successful attempt at a novel. If true, this means that Vance adopted the simple saga narrative form for his first long work and didn't "take himself back" to it.

Damon Knight gave the novel a rave review: "Big Planet shows this brilliant writer at the top of his form. Big Planet is as vividly compelling as the dream-world of Eddison's The Worm Ouroboros: and that's the highest praise I know." Knight also perceived the story's character as a planetary romance: "Big Planet itself dominates the book. Like Burroughs' Pellucidar, it colors every landscape with its own overhanging presence…. In Vance, as in Eddison, the background is the story."

Why did Vance write such an extended epic? "Oh, I just felt in the mood." But for the next three decades, Vance as a practical freelance writer would produce long works in commercially viable segments: the five Demon Princes books, the four novels of the Planet of Adventure, the three Durdane books. Each of these "series" is a single long story, designed and plotted to break into sections to suit the magazine serial and paperback book markets of the era.

When Vance traveled to Europe in 1951, he had a commission from the John C. Winston Company to write an SF juvenile, *Vandals of the Void*, his sole effort in the youth market and, coincidentally, his first hardcover book (and first contract for an original work). *Vandals* was written in Positano, Italy, in an apartment overlooking the water. It has become a much-sought collector's item, most copies having been sold to libraries and therefore defaced.

Vance fans don't rate the story very highly. "The opening paragraph is Vancean in tone," according to Richard Tiedman, "but he is scarcely recognizable elsewhere." But *Vandals* impressed some readers. In childhood, John Vance II read the book and liked it. "The rascal won't read any of my other books," Vance said at the time. "I think he finds them too grown up. But he thinks I'm a good writer on the basis of *Vandals of the Void*."

In 1953, Vance earned additional income for the first time from a paperback reprint of earlier magazine work when Toby Press published *The Space Pirate*, a reprint of *The Five Gold Bands* with a new title. This was important to Vance as a working writer. As the paperback industry expanded, he attracted a growing income stream from publication of his old magazine novels and stories as paperback books. Indeed, at this time the pulp magazines were dying, and the rapidly growing paperback market replaced them.

In 1956, Ballantine published both hardcover and paperback editions of *To Live Forever*, Vance's first book contract for an original adult novel. Vance defined a new stage in his career with the later remark that *To Live Forever* was "the first of the type of stories I write today."

The origins of *To Live Forever* (Betty Ballantine's choice for the title, not the author's) date back to 1953. According to Tim Underwood, "One night, while on a writing retreat in Mexico, Frank Herbert and Jack tossed around an idea for a novel and afterward flipped a coin to see who would write it. Jack won the toss and the book became *To Live Forever*."

Richard Tiedman rated *To Live Forever*, "the most brilliant and important of Vance's early works. In ingenuity of plot and mastery of prose, it is probably the quintessential assertion of sheer individuality among his novels of this period." He continued: "This novel is, even for Vance, extremely elaborate and embroidered; hardly any detail is touched on without an embellishmental flourish. Here the full Vancean orchestra is displayed in a way that exhibits his baroque tendencies at their apogee."

Anthony Boucher didn't think the novel was wholly successful, "but when it does succeed it's as exciting as anything this none-too-rewarding year has brought forth in this field. This is SF in the grand manner: intricate melodrama rousingly played against the elaborate background of a curiously conceived future society. Logic and characterization falter at moments, and the book's self-consistency does not always bear close examination; but the action is forceful, the ideas and visualization vivid."

Also in 1957, Vance directly linked the magazine, hardcover, and paperback markets with publication of *The Languages of Pao,* first in *Satellite Science Fiction* and then as an Avalon hardcover and Ace paperback. This pattern of magazine serialization prior to hardcover and/or paperback release would continue during the next two decades for many novels, including various titles from the Demon Princes, Durdane, and Alastor series as well as singletons *The Blue World, Emphyrio, The Gray Prince* and many of the stories featuring Cugel the Clever.

Pao initially disappointed Richard Tiedman: "Vance's prose, usually so facile, is strangely ineffective here, its normally bright colors diluted into gray halftones…. While there can be no doubt that this is second-order Vance, the novel will retain reader interest for the originality of its conceptions." Fifteen years later, he revised his opinion: "I was not fully aware in 1964 of the tendency toward what Peter Close calls the sociological and anthropological elements in Vance's fiction."

Vance's first mystery novels were also published in 1957, but his entry into this genre was far from auspicious. As noted earlier, Vance wrote these novels in 1947–48, and they remained unsold until Mystery House bought them for the derisory sum of $100 each. Mystery House published these two mysteries under pseudonyms, *Isle of Peril* as by Alan Wade and *Take My Face* as by Peter Held. But then, Pyramid

Books purchased paperback rights for *Take My Face*. This sale to a major publisher encouraged Vance to give the mystery genre another try.

The concealed authorship of these novels was fortuitous, because it made Vance eligible for an Edgar Award from the Mystery Writers of America as best "new" writer in 1961 for *The Man in the Cage*, published by Random House in 1960 under his own name in full form, John Holbrook Vance. The novel was also adapted for television and broadcast on *Thriller* on January 17, 1961, with Boris Karloff as host.

In 1958, Vance published the novella "Parapsyche" in *Amazing Stories* (August 1958). Richard Tiedman was puzzled and considered it "the novel furthest removed from the main sequence of Vance's development. It shows that, with him, content and style are not inseparably fused, for his usual identifying touches are almost completely absent.... Perhaps a more conventional mode was chosen because of the contemporary Earthbound setting." This conclusion is well founded; Vance has stated, "I am aware of using no inflexible or predetermined style. Each story generates its own style, so to speak." Vance's narrative style is most subdued in his here-and-now mysteries, more evident in his science fiction, especially in far-future settings, and most extravagant in his fantasies.

Also in 1958, Vance began a decade in which he demonstrated his mastery of the novelette form, a length particularly suited to a Vance story. The short story is too cramped to allow him to display all his talents to advantage; the greater length of the novelette provides the necessary scope to fully establish the setting and circumstances of the story, without the extended complications and developments required by a full novel.

"The Miracle Workers" appeared in *Astounding* in 1958, earning Vance his first Hugo Award nomination, followed the next year by "Dodkin's Job," his last appearance in *Astounding*.

Amazing SF provided a venue for "I-C-A-BEM [The Augmented Agent]" in 1961 and "Gateway to Strangeness [Sail 25, Dust of Far Suns]" in 1962. These stories were commissioned by editor Cele Goldsmith, who invited Vance and Frank Herbert to a meeting at Poul Anderson's house. She displayed a number of SF-style paintings purchased in bulk and invited each writer to select one or two and write a story to match each illustration. (Such commissions usually paid a higher word rate and, of course, guaranteed the writer a cover story.) Vance was no stranger to this kind of assignment. "Ecological Onslaught," the cover story for the May 1953 issue of *Future SF*, was also written, or adapted, to include the scene in the cover painting.

Galaxy published "The Moon Moth" in 1961, "The Dragon Masters" in 1962 (Hugo Award for short fiction 1963), and "The Last Castle" in 1966 (Hugo and Nebula awards 1967).

Terry Dowling designated "The Moon Moth" as "the definitive xenographical work.... In 'The Moon Moth,' we encounter that blend of the arcane and the commonplace, that balance of the alien and the exotic with the familiar and the mundane, that is so vital a part of Vance's writing."

Regarding "The Dragon Masters", Lawrence Person has written: "What most impresses is the cleverness of the setup, the way in which Vance has crafted ever-widening circles of mirror-imaged antagonists, like a yin-yang symbol which turns out to be the eye of a larger yin-yang symbol, which, in turn, is the eye of a still larger one."

Interestingly, "The Miracle Workers", "The Dragon Masters", and "The Last Castle" share a characteristic Vancean concept, a remnant human population in the far future of Earth or isolated and lost to history on a remote planet, a "last days" situation reminiscent of *The Dying Earth*.

This string of successful novelettes was the tip of the iceberg. Indeed, the 1960s were an enormously productive decade for Vance. For much of the decade he was writing full time, markets were proliferating, and he had attained full mastery of his craft.

The era of the great novelettes was coming to a close, however. As a professional writer, Vance needed to maximize income for each hour of labor. Novelettes and short stories could only be sold to magazines for pennies per word, then earn modest additional income if chosen for an anthology or included in one of his own collections. In 1967 Vance told Guy Lillian "only novels now are financially profitable for me."

In the early 1960s, Vance continued his sideline in mysteries by contracting to write three "Ellery Queen" novels. *The Four Johns* was published in 1964, *A Room to Die In* in 1965, and *The Madman Theory* in 1966. The books were published under the shop name Ellery Queen, and Vance was contractually obligated not to reveal his authorship. In later years, after the word got out, Vance honored the agreement by sometimes autographing these books as "Ellery Queen" with his own initials appended.

Vance didn't regret his name's absence from the covers of these novels; they were extensively and badly edited, no doubt to make them conform to the Ellery Queen brand, and Vance disowned the results. It was gainful employment, however; he was paid $3,000 per book, substantially more than the typical advance for an SF paperback at that time.

Vance hadn't published any fantasy since *The Dying Earth* in 1950. His return to this genre was probably precipitated in 1962 when Avram Davidson, then editor of *The Magazine of Fantasy & Science Fiction*, visited California on honeymoon and met Vance. *F&SF* was one of only two magazines (and the best paying) then publishing fantasy, and Davidson must have asked Vance if he had anything the magazine could use. As a result, "Green Magic" appeared in the June 1963 issue of *F&SF*. It's probably no coincidence that two years later, the Cugel stories began appearing in the same magazine.

Vance's first great SF novel series also began in 1964 when Berkley published *The Star King*, first of the Demon Princes books. All in all, this may be Vance's most popular SF series. (The series name "Demon Princes" came later, as the publisher's marketing tag when DAW Books reissued the novels.)

Then in 1965, with the first two Demon Princes books in print, Vance finally returned to fantasy at full throttle with a series of stories in *F&SF*, assembled as *The Eyes of the Overworld* (Ace 1966). The story sequence features Cugel the Clever and returns to the haunted landscapes of *The Dying Earth*. A second series, *Cugel's Saga*, would follow in 1983, making Cugel Vance's longest running character and perhaps his favorite. Vance confessed that Cugel "surprised me. I think I rather admire myself for having invented him."

As indicated by first publication as a series of magazine stories, *Eyes of the Overworld* is episodic. The novel is a picaresque adventure, a dark comedy set in a world of constant menace, avarice, deception, and betrayal, projecting "a singularly bleak world-view," according to Robert Silverberg, "made more palatable only by the elegance of the prose in which it is set forth and the unfailing courtliness with which the murderous beings of the dying Earth address one another."

Jack Dann and Gardner Dozois assessed the Cugel stories in glowing terms: "Although almost quintessential 'sense of wonder' stuff, marvelously evocative, the Cugel stories are also elegant and intelligent, full of sly wit and subtle touches, all laced with Vance's typical dour irony and deadpan humor."

Considering the two Cugel books together, the double circular plot is an effective advance over the perfunctory linking of stories in *The Dying Earth*. Each Cugel story is truly sequential. Each adventure can stand alone, but altogether they comprise a grand novel with a beginning and an end, containing "a rigid skeleton beneath its picaresque surface," noted Silverberg.

The Eyes of the Overworld earned a Hugo Award nomination for best novel in 1966, and the concluding episode, "The Manse of Iucounu", earned a Nebula Award nomination in 1967 for best novelette.

Vance published more comedy in 1965 with *Space Opera*. As an editorial joke for SF fans, Berkley Books asked for a book titled "space opera" and Vance accepted the assignment with predictable results (in the same spirit, Philip K. Dick agreed to write a book called *The Zap Gun*). *Space Opera* is another *Gold Bands*, a series of interplanetary encounters, this time featuring a rather passive protagonist and his domineering aunt, oddly echoed almost four decades later in *Ports of Call*.

The Blue World, published by Ballantine in 1966, was expanded from a shorter magazine version, "The Kragen" (*Fantastic Stories*, July 1964). The novel earned Vance another Hugo Award nomination. Vance identified *The Blue World* as "my last gadget story," his break with the traditional concept of science fiction as stories with plots derived from, or resolved by, a scientific premise. In this case, the hero triumphs by extracting copper from blood on a water-world bereft of metals.

The water-world setting is also something of a homage to Frank Herbert's desiccated planet Dune. While writing his long novel, Herbert had regaled Vance with details of the Dune setting, and

Vance wrote *The Blue World* as a kind of counterpoint to his friend's planetary romance. When *Dune* proved to be a phenomenal success, Herbert often told interviewers that he owed it all to Jack Vance's encouragement — much to Vance's surprise, since he hadn't thought much of the idea when Herbert first described the story and setting.

More than one Vance fan believes *The Blue World* is an underrated work. Writing in 1978, Malcolm Edwards declared *The Blue World* to be one of the two stories in which Vance had shown his talents at full stretch (the other was "The Moon Moth"). Richard Tiedman called it "a tale of initiative, ordeal, and change, with a magical, fairy-tale atmosphere — altogether one of Vance's most beautiful books."

When *The Blue World* was reissued by Gollancz in 2003, Joan Montserrat was less fulsome: "The book begins promisingly but, as sometimes happens with Vance's novels, as the plot unfolds it seems to lose dramatic energy...." She also faults a lack of real surprises or character development. Nonetheless, "The novel's real strength is Vance's quasi-sociological description of the way social rules operate in an extreme situation so as to generate a kind of order, albeit often at the expense of truth.... This is vintage Vance: light, but not entirely light, reading, and in any case highly entertaining."

The Brains of Earth appeared in 1966 as half of an Ace Double with *The Many Worlds of Magnus Ridolph*. *Brains* is the only first-publication work among Vance's Ace Double titles. It seems stylistically old-fashioned for the author who had already published "The Moon Moth", "The Dragon Masters", and *Eyes of the Overworld*, and Vance himself doesn't rate it highly. But Richard Tiedman disagreed: *The Brains of Earth* is a fascinating study on some of the same themes of parapsychological phenomena [that Vance featured in "Parapsyche"] and is an underrated work."

In 1966, just as the third Ellery Queen novel appeared, Vance resumed mystery writing under his own name with *The Fox Valley Murders*, published by Bobbs-Merrill. This was the first Sheriff Joe Bain novel, to be followed by *The Pleasant Grove Murders* in 1967. The Joe Bain novels are California regionals, set in the imaginary San Rodrigo County of central California. Both books were reprinted as Ace paperbacks in 1969. An outline for a third Joe Bain novel, *The Genesee Slough*

Murders, appears in Hewett and Mallett's *The Work of Jack Vance*. But Vance's editor at Bobbs-Merrill died, and the new editor wasn't interested in continuing the series.

As the third Demon Princes novel, *The Palace of Love*, was seeing print in 1967, Vance was writing his second SF series, the four Planet of Adventure or Tschai novels. These books were commissioned by Ace as paperback originals. "They enticed me with talk of big promotion, million-copy sales," Vance recalled a few years later. "I had fun writing these things, although I never made much money out of them." The Ace editors apparently thought there was big sales potential in mentor–protégé stories along the lines of Obi-wan and Luke in *Star Wars* or Batman and Robin. Vance, of course, wasn't interested in writing to formula and added the sly and sardonic Anacho the Dirdirman to form a trio with Adam Reith and Traz.

City of the Chasch, Servants of the Wankh, The Dirdir, and *The Pnume* appeared in rapid succession between 1968 and 1970 (*The Pnume* garnered a Hugo Award nomination for best novel in 1970). The series was later reissued by DAW and enjoyed several foreign editions as well as omnibus editions from Grafton (trade paperback 1985), Tor (hardcover 1992, Orb trade paperback 1993), and the Science Fiction Book Club, so the series' ultimate earning power far exceeded the initial advance.

As the collective Planet of Adventure title indicates, these four novels comprise a quintessential planetary romance. Jack Rawlins rates the Planet of Adventure series as "the most sophisticated expression of a myth first used in *Big Planet*, in which a culturally neutral Earthman wanders through a series of small cultural enclaves, constantly facing anew the challenge of decoding and surviving a fresh set of cultural mores and shibboleths."

Vance recalled that he began writing the series with a definite mood about the planet Tschai (which Vance, inexplicably, chose to pronounce as "chay" while all his readers pronounce it "chy"). A few readers have speculated that Vance received some inspiration from Edgar Rice Burroughs' Barsoom novels when he wrote the Tschai books, and Vance was indeed an avid Burroughs fan as a boy.

"I read *Tarzan* and was fascinated by it," Vance recalled. "I got all the other books from the library. Barsoom, I thought, was wonderful; Burroughs had a knack for creating this wonderful atmosphere… and the atmosphere of Barsoom got into me when I was seven or eight years old and never left me." But he denies any conscious influence in his Tschai novels: "I had no intention of emulating Burroughs' Barsoom books in Tschai; I never even thought of Barsoom while I was writing Tschai; totally separate, brand new." What Vance may have gained from Barsoom was a life-long love for the planetary romance.

In the same year that the second and third Tschai novels appeared, Vance published one of his finest works, *Emphyrio* (Arthur Jean Cox: "in my opinion, the best SF novel of 1969"). Joanna Russ assessed *Emphyrio* as "not an adventure story but a Bildungsroman (a novel of the formation of a character, of the process of passing from childhood to adulthood, making oneself into a person) that describes a perfect curve from beginning to end."

According to Stuart Carter: "The depiction of an over-attentive, restricting and ultimately self-serving welfare system struck me as a very American invention. That it is overseen by 'Lords and Ladies' is an even more emphatically republican statement. *Emphyrio* isn't otherwise a political novel. The overthrow of the welfare system is of only cursory interest, it is rather the road to truth against tradition and ignorance that is the major theme…."

In Terry Dowling's analysis, "*Emphyrio* conforms perfectly to the selective-and-expanding focus — exotic travelogue — mystery format Vance has devised." *Emphyrio* also has been called "dark," perhaps because this is a rare novel in which Vance has suppressed his usual humor.

The year 1969 also saw publication of Vance's last conventional mystery, *The Deadly Isles*, again from Bobbs-Merrill in hardcover and Ace as a paperback (1971). This novel draws on Vance's sojourn in the South Pacific in the mid-1960s and his love for blue-water sailing.

The 1960s had been a prodigious decade for Vance. The 1970s began quietly. No new Vance books appeared in 1971 or 1972 (except for magazine serializations of books to come), but this was the lull before the storm. From 1973 to 1976, Vance published eight SF novels plus his last non-genre work, *Bad Ronald* (Ballantine paperback, 1973). *Bad Ronald* is not so much a mystery as a psychological thriller. If proof is needed that Vance does not fit his stories to a consistent style but adapts his style to each story, *Bad Ronald* is Exhibit A, starkly different from anything else he has written. The story of a 17-year-old rapist and murderer is bleak and disturbing, being written from Ronald's point of view. In 1974, the novel was adapted for television as an *ABC Wednesday Night Movie of the Week*.

The first draft of *Bad Ronald* was written as early as 1955 and revised for publication in 1973. Ed Winskill believes this early novel previewed better-known characters to come: the Demon Princes' Viole Falushe and especially Howard Alan Treesong. "Ronald Wilby is in many ways the direct ancestor of Howard Hardoah: the murder of the first girl who rejected his advances and the Book of Dreams-like fantasy writings in his hideout, in particular."

Dell published the Durdane trilogy as a paperback series following serialization in *F&SF* (*The Anome* 1973, *The Brave Free Men* 1973, and *The Asutra* 1974). According to Malcolm Edwards: "What Vance is doing in these three novels is to set up a series of levels of opposition: each time Etzwane defeats one antagonist, he finds he has to face a new and more difficult opponent," first the Chilites, then the Anome, then the Roguskhoi, then the Asutra and their Ka opponents.

Edwards rates *The Anome* "among Vance's best half-dozen novels" but thinks the series declines progressively through the subsequent two books. The hero, Mur, begins as an insider, growing up and struggling within the society in which he was born, but as Mur becomes Gastel Etzwane and struggles against progressively higher levels of opposition, he becomes more and more an outsider in his own world. Edwards thinks *The Anome* is "Vance at the top of his form…unfortunately, the story starts to emerge from its background about two-thirds of the way through the first book, and the remainder of the trilogy never recaptures that early magic." Vance's fellow SF writers were not as dismayed, and *The Brave Free Men* earned a Nebula Award nomination for best novel. In 1973, Vance launched a new kind of series with *Trullion: Alastor 2262*, followed by *Marune: Alastor 933* (1975) and *Wyst: Alastor 1716* (1978). These are stand-alone novels sharing the common background of the Alastor Cluster and the Connatic, ruler of the cluster's 3,000 inhabited

Worlds. *Trullion* and *Marune* are planetary romances, *Wyst* a satire on egalitarianism.

A fourth Alastor Cluster novel, to be titled *Pharism: Alastor 458*, was contemplated but never written. Vance may have been deflected by his return to the Demon Princes series.

Something else happened in 1976 that made a significant contribution to Jack Vance's career. Tim Underwood and Chuck Miller decided to form a company to publish deluxe, limited, hardcover editions of works by important SF and fantasy writers, and they chose *The Dying Earth* as their first project. After the Hillman edition in 1950, Lancer had brought *The Dying Earth* back into print with a paperback edition in 1962 (reissued 1969, 1972), but Vance's most acclaimed work had never appeared in a durable binding. Underwood-Miller printed 1,100 handsome hardcover copies, including 111 signed and numbered. All the copies were sold in five months, demonstrating there was a good market for limited, quality, hardcover editions of Vance books.

Over the following two decades, Underwood-Miller would publish hardcover editions of more than 50 Vance novels and collections, eventually gathering all of his short stories (a few never before reprinted) into the more permanent hardcover form. These Underwood-Miller editions lent a note of dignity to Vance's works, earned reviews in major newspapers, and stimulated library sales, putting Vance books where more readers could discover him. Last but not least, over time they also represented a modest but cumulatively significant income stream for the author.

Then in 1977, more than a quarter century after Vance became a recognized name in the science fiction field and a decade after he won Hugo and Nebula awards, *Maske: Thaery* became his first selection from the Science Fiction Book Club. Part of the delay might be explained by the fact that very few of Vance's previous adult SF/F books had appeared first in hardcover editions. Nonetheless, it is remarkable that a novel as fine as *Emphyrio*, first published by Doubleday (owner of the SFBC!) in hardcover in 1969, did not make the SFBC list.

In the following quarter century, the SFBC published club editions of the three Lyonesse and the three Cadwal novels, *Night Lamp*, and the combined *Ports of Call/Lurulu*. The club also made up for missed opportunities by issuing omnibus editions of the Planet of Adventure and Demon Princes series and *The Compleat Dying Earth*.

Vance's second career as a mystery writer lacked the momentum of his SF and fantasy work and essentially ended in 1973. As a practical freelance writer, Vance found that he simply earned more from his SF/F writing, and the commercial publishers weren't clamoring for more Vance mysteries. In fact, when Underwood-Miller began printing limited editions of Vance's SF and fantasy, they learned that he had four unsold mystery manuscripts. Underwood-Miller published these novels in limited editions: *The House on Lily Street* and *The View from Chickweed's Window* in 1979 (450 copies each) and *The Dark Ocean* and *Strange Notions* in 1985 (500 copies).

For almost 30 years, Vance stories had appeared regularly in SF magazines, but in the 1970s the SF magazine market was contracting sharply and Vance was concentrating on novels. His last story published in a magazine was "The Seventeen Virgins" (*F&SF* 1974). First publication in original anthologies replaced magazines for a few remaining stories, as Vance phased out shorter forms to concentrate on novels. "Morreion" appeared in *Flashing Swords 1*, 1973, "The Dogtown Tourist Agency" in *Epoch*, 1975, "The Bagful of Dreams" in *Flashing Swords 4*, 1977, and "Freitzke's Turn" in *Triax*, 1977. The short novel *Fader's Waft* and "The Murthe" appeared as original works with the reprint "Morreion" in Vance's own volume, *Rhialto the Marvelous* (1984).

In 1967 Vance had left his Demon Princes series unfinished, to the lamentations of his fans. But a decade later, opportunity knocked a second time. As Vance was finishing *Wyst*, DAW Books acquired reprint rights to the first three Demon Princes titles and gave Vance a contract to complete the series (paying the author $30,000 for the package, a handsome sum for a five-book paperback deal at that time). *The Face* appeared in 1979 and *The Book of Dreams* in 1981. The paperback industry had changed and longer books were now favored, so the last two Demon Princes novels are substantially longer than the first three.

Critics have sometimes claimed that Vance's series seem to lose energy as they progress, but even if that is true in some cases, the Demon Princes series is an exception. The final two novels demonstrate Vance's ability to take up a series after a long hiatus and recapture the original tone and spirit of the first volumes (with one minor slip-up in continuity — Gersen's grandfather in the first three installments briefly becomes his uncle in *The Face*). Perhaps the long break in the series allowed Vance to take it up again with fresh vigor.

As Steven Sawicki wrote when reviewing Tor's two-volume reprint of the five Demon Princes books, "There are Vance books which better represent his plotting and there are Vance books which showcase his language manipulation and word creation and there are Vance books which shine with his talent at naming. The Demon Princes books are perhaps the best example of Vance running on all cylinders."

Not every reviewer was convinced. Tom Easton, reviewing *The Face* in Analog, wrote: "As always, Vance displays great originality in names and incidents, but his characters seem oddly dreamlike, arbitrary, and both hero and villain lack luster. The hero's feats are the product of fortune rather than prowess, and the villain, for all his omniscience, dies in impotent triumph. All writers stack the deck, but Vance does so more than most. This irritates me, even though I recognize that it is a hallmark of his style and presumably one root of his popularity."

Vance also revisited an earlier stage in his career in 1981 with publication of *Galactic Effectuator* as an Ace paperback, a collection of his two Miro Hetzel adventures. The novella "The Dogtown Tourist Agency" (1975) and the novelette "Freitzke's Turn" (1977) had first appeared in anthologies of original stories. Together, these tales of an interstellar detective appear to represent Vance's second take on Magnus Ridolph with a quarter-century's additional skill and experience. Vance might easily have extended this series, but he was now focused on novels.

The year 1983 was an annus mirabilis for Vance's fantasy fans. Eighteen years after *Eyes of the Overworld*, Vance brought back Cugel the Clever in *Cugel's Saga* (Baen 1983, not Vance's title). This second Cugel outing had a long incubation with two of the component novelettes appearing in 1974 and 1977. Vance may have been encouraged to complete a book's worth of new adventures after "The Seventeen Virgins" (*F&SF*, October 1974) won a Jupiter Award for best novelette in 1975 and "The Bagful of Dreams" (*Flashing Swords!* #4, SFBC) garnered a 1978 World Fantasy Award nomination for best short fiction. *Cugel's Saga* tied with Le Guin's *The Farthest Shore* in the best-novel category for Spain's Gilgamesh Awards.

Also in 1983, Vance launched a major fantasy trilogy with publication of *Lyonesse, Book I, Suldrun's Garden*, to be followed in 1985 by *The Green Pearl* and concluding in 1989 with *Madouc*. Vance told a correspondent that he was contemplating "a large medieval fantasy" as early as 1978 while he was writing *The Face*. Later, he told the SF newsmagazine *Locus* that, after completing the Demon Princes series with *The Book of Dreams*, "I wanted to write a large book — three large books. As far as I know, no one has written about Lyonesse before, and it seemed high time to do it."

Unlike the remote future setting of the Dying Earth fantasies, Lyonesse is set in pseudo-historical times, after the collapse of the Roman Empire and a generation or two before King Arthur. Vance explained that this more conventional fantasy setting was chosen "to do something to sell to the general public, a broader audience. These particular situations and characters, I think, will have a wider appeal than some of the other stuff I've written."

Reviewing *Suldrun's Garden*, Baird Searles admired the way Vance wrote SF in the mode of fantasy. But "there lies the problem — here is Vance's extravagant, fantastical style at the service of an extravagant, fantastical fantasy. What a farrago results! What a mass of characters, places, races, events are thrown at the reader!"

Searles appears to lack the kind of fanciful literary ear for which Vance was writing. But he had to admit: "Much of it is a lot of fun, certainly.... The continuous invention is staggering, and there is an odd satisfaction in the fact that most of the characters, despite the dizzy people, places, and things they encounter, act with a certain sensibility and intelligence (another sustained quality in Vance's stories). But it all does seem to be too much of a muchness; the reader ends up struggling in an Olympic-sized bubble bath."

One the other hand, Kirkus Review praised the same qualities that confounded Searles: "Dazzlingly imaginative, fascinatingly intricate, delicately controlled, engagingly peopled, and set forth in the inimitable Vance prose style. Fantasy at its brilliant best."

Publication of *Suldrun's Garden* in 1983 marked a tectonic shift in Vance's career. Up to then he had written stand-alone novels or series composed of short paperback novels (Demon Princes, Tschai, Durdane, Alastor). But for the next decade, Vance's creative energies would be invested in the long and elaborate installments of the Lyonesse trilogy and the Cadwal Chonicles.

Vance still had some shorter works in the pipeline. In addition to the new Cugel adventures, and perhaps counterbalancing the intended broader market appeal of the Lyonesse series, Vance published *Rhialto the Marvellous* in 1984, his last venture into the remote future of the Dying Earth and the ultimate Vancean fantasy in style and content. The book includes novelettes "Morreion" and "The Murthe" and the short novel *Fader's Waft*.

Never before or since has Vance been more droll, whimsical, mordant. His matchless imagination soars, his view of human (and sandestin) nature has never been more sardonic, his dialogs are like knife fights. According to Joe Schwab, "*Rhialto the Marvellous* presents the ultimate demonstration of Vance's skills and shows that forty years of experience have truly elevated his prose style to a masterful level."

By this time, however, the first symptoms of glaucoma were diminishing Vance's already poor vision. Over the next decade, Vance's glaucoma progressed, finally leading to surgery. "The doctor who tried to repair my eyes did so using the laser, and every time he operated on me my eyes got worse. He finally just gave up."

Eventual loss of eyesight also caused Vance to abandon his active participation in classic jazz, "one of the great interests in my life." Music has always been important to Vance. "In fact, I think of myself more as a musician half the time than a writer." He played cornet and banjo in bands occasionally, but "nobody tried to get in touch with me when they needed somebody to play, only as a last resort. I enjoyed it tremendously... but when my eyes went out I kind of hung it up."

Before concluding the Lyonesse trilogy, Vance returned to science fiction with a similarly expansive work, the three-volume Cadwal Chronicles: *Araminta Station, Ecce and Old Earth, Throy*.

"*Araminta Station* is a biggie, over five hundred pages long," wrote Baird Searles in *Asimov's SF Magazine*. "And given the whimsical nature of Vance's writing, and the curiously coy quality of the dialogue —

clever and stilted in equal parts — there are times when the reader feels s/he is drowning in a vat of marshmallow fluff.

"But s/he keeps reading. Or at least this one did. Things get pretty exciting and much is resolved to the reader's satisfaction (Vance has a neat habit of letting the good guys win in a direct and agreeable manner)."

When *Throy* appeared in 1992, Vance was 76 and nearly blind, but his abilities were undiminished. That year he was named Guest of Honor at the World Science Fiction Convention in Orlando (MagiCon), the SF field's highest popular accolade, the genre equivalent of a Roman triumph.

After completing the vast Lyonesse and Cadwal trilogies, Vance returned to the one-volume novel with *Night Lamp* in 1996. This is another rare example of a "dark" Vance novel, the story propelled by horrid crimes and tragedies. The new book earned good reviews (*New York Times*: "Vance at the top of his form").

L. R. C. Munro, reviewing the novel online for *Science Fiction Weekly,* called it "a somewhat rambling novel, written with an eye for fanciful detail, a poetic turn of phrase and a dry sense of humor…. If Charles Dickens and Dr. Seuss teamed up to write a space opera, they might manage to come up with something as imaginative, whimsical and entertaining as *Night Lamp*."

Till Noever found *Night Lamp* "a profoundly satisfying book, despite its grim tone. When all is done there is a sense of completion; that things happened as they must have, and that, despite a note of wistful sadness, all is well; and that, when you have friends, the universe — though often dangerous, twisted, morbid, and evil — is not a bad place to be; and that there are things to do, places to go, and wonders to behold."

To cap his Worldcon Guest of Honor selection in 1992, Vance's professional colleagues in the Science Fiction Writers of America named him a Grand Master in 1997. He had long expected to be named. "I think it was something I'd been waiting for for many years," he told an interviewer on the Sci-Fi Channel, "and when it came I was properly, uh, not thankful, or grateful or anything, but I kind of took it for granted. I went to Kansas City, and I was polite; I got up and made a little speech, said thank you, accepted the award, came home and put it somewhere,

I don't know where it is." (Vance couldn't see it, but in 2004 his Grand Master trophy was on display in the central dining/living room of the Oakland hills house beside a World Fantasy Award.)

The fact that Vance long expected to be named a Grand Master indicates that he recognized his high status in the field; yet typically, he distanced himself from the honor, disclaiming gratitude or special satisfaction in the achievement. Paul Rhoads has pondered on this trait: "I am intrigued by Jack's ambiguous relationship to his success/non-success. I think he knows who he is (an exceptionally great artist) but that his life experience and character are such that his natural exuberance and combativeness have become hidden so that he practices a modesty and detachment not fully representative of his deeper character."

One important element of that life experience was the years Vance spent writing for the cheap, gaudy SF pulp magazines for as little as half a cent per word, followed by many more years as a novelist whose work appeared almost exclusively in paperback editions without serious critical attention.

One part of that Vance character is a highly self-critical nature. He didn't reread his old stories; once a manuscript was mailed to his agent, it was no longer his concern. He readily dismissed his early stories as "apprentice work" and referred to his later writing as "my stuff" or "my junk." He assumed no airs as a writer and explained that writing was just his job, what he did for a living.

Vance never expatiated on the artistic aspects of his writing; indeed, he generally declined any analytical discussion of his work. When asked what aspect of his work had given him the most satisfaction, Vance replied: "Getting the check. I'm not fooling! But to be not quite as sardonic, I could say: writing the words 'The End'."

Nonetheless, son John has testified that his father did derive satisfaction from the creative process: "Growing up, when I was fooling around, running around the house while Dad was writing, occasionally out of nowhere he'd chuckle to himself. It was very clear that he was enjoying what he was doing—that the writer was having a good time."

Ports of Call appeared in 1998. To the dismay of some readers, the novel ends abruptly, without resolution. It is, in fact, only the first part of a larger work completed by publication of *Lurulu* in 2004.

"When I was writing *Ports of Call,*" Vance said, "I wound up with a long book, but still had a lot of material I wanted to use. So freely, unconventionally, I said, 'Ladies and Gentlemen, I've got to stop this story here, and continue in the next volume. And so I ended *Ports of Call.*" Unfortunately, the publisher didn't label the book "Volume 1" or print "to be continued" on the last page.

Ports is another of Vance's episodic novels, in this case a series of situations and incidents that has a beginning but lacks conventional plot development. The novel is a "tour de force" of Vance's "fervid and boundless imagination," wrote reviewer Brooks Peck in *SF Weekly*. But "what *Ports of Call* lacks is a central plot to carry it from port to exotic port, adventure to adventure."

Paul Rhoads is unconcerned. *Ports* "might seem a mere improvisation without plan or purpose. In fact it is a subtly structured meditation upon no less a subject than mortality. In admirable order each episode casts a light on life as seen from the various limits imposed by time and death. For the reader who can take hints the book's casual charm is supplanted by a growing mood of poignant urgency which could be neither generated nor sustained should the theme be stated less quietly."

Finishing the story begun in *Ports of Call* was a slow and arduous task for the sightless author, who had to compose it using a voice synthesizer to read back his words. When Till Noever visited in 2002, he could hear the peculiar robotic voice through the workroom door.

Finally, publication of *Lurulu* in 2004 completed the tale, bringing the combined work to 140,000 words (and published in a single volume by the Science Fiction Book Club in 2005). As a continuation of *Ports, Lurulu* is equally episodic and lacks a central plot, though story elements begun in *Ports* are brought to a conclusion by the final pages. Myron does finally return home, and he has learned things about himself and the meaning of life; but he has not won the girl, achieved revenge on his enemies, or demolished a calcified society as so many protagonists do in earlier Vance novels.

Lurulu is "a story that reveals a truth that is no less profound for being simple: Life is a voyage whose significance is in the going, not in the arrival," says Matt Hughes. "So the tale is not about a beginning, a middle and an end, connected by an arc of character, but is instead a celebration and an urging to live this fleeting moment to the full."

Vance explained lurulu as "a special word from the language of myth." Patrick Hudson noted that "Lurulu is the name of the mischievous troll befriended by Prince Orion in *The King Of Elfland's Daughter* by Lord Dunsany, who was a popular fantasist around the time that Vance was a boy — *The King Of Elfland's Daughter* was first published in 1924. Much of Dunsany's book concerns Orion's search for the ineffable Elfland, which seems to taunt him with its closeness yet torment him with its remoteness. Similarly, Myron and friends find lurulu is both impossibly distant and paradoxically close at hand."

Once again demonstrating that Vance discards nothing in story ideas or words, Lurulu is also the name he gave to the eponymous character in his story "Golden Girl", published in 1951 (*Marvel Science Stories*) but written as early as 1946.

Considering *Ports of Call* and *Lurulu* together, Russell Letson classes the work not as "a plot-driven adventure but a 'Vancean Ramble'.... It does not have anything like the unifying force of the quests that run through *Emphyrio*, *The Blue World*, or *Durdane*. It is closer kin to the Dying Earth or Cugel stories — that is, it is picaresque, a tradition in which being episodic is not a bug but a feature."

When he delivered the manuscript of Lurulu to his editor at Tor, Vance declared himself "semi-retired." He began a new work but without contract, deadline, or certain expectation of ever finishing it. He continued writing, he explained, because "that's what I do" and, after writing continuously for sixty years, he would feel restless if he didn't have a work in progress, something to occupy his mind.

A few years earlier, Jack and Norma had traded houses with son John, whose family was occupying a small house nearby while the two elder Vances were living alone in their very large house. *Lurulu* was written in the small house. Then in July 2004, the elder Vances moved back to the big house, to occupy rooms on the ground floor. This move may have marked Vance's final retirement from fiction writing. His work station was set up in a corner of the great hall, but Norma lamented that she couldn't coax him into resuming regular work.

Over a career spanning six decades, Vance wrote 4.6 million published words. His works have been translated into a dozen languages (even Esperanto). He achieved his childhood goal of becoming a writer and enjoyed his work, which gave him the independence he craved and which he was able to perform in many locales while exploring the world.

Vance has received the highest honors in all three of the genres to which he gave his attention, the respect of his professional colleagues, and a worldwide readership so admiring that many collaborated over a period of years to publish his collected works in a handsome edition with corrected texts. He had the time and acquired the means to pursue his avocations — ceramics, cooking, sailing, jazz — and built an elaborate home with his own hands.

In Jack Vance's own estimation, "I've had a lot of fun in my life without too much hardship or tragedy."

"An original author always invents an original world, and if a character or an action fits into the pattern of that world, then we experience the pleasurable shock of artistic truth."

— Vladimir Nabokov

The World-Thinker

I

THROUGH THE OPEN WINDOW came sounds of the city — the swish of passing air-traffic, the clank of the pedestrian-belt on the ramp below, hoarse undertones from the lower levels. Cardale sat by the window studying a sheet of paper which displayed a photograph and a few lines of type:

FUGITIVE!

Isabel May — Age 21; height 5 feet 5 inches; medium physique.
Hair: black (could be dyed).
Eyes: blue.
Distinguishing characteristics: none.

Cardale shifted his eyes to the photograph and studied the pretty face with incongruously angry eyes. A placard across her chest read: *94E-627*. Cardale returned to the printed words.

Sentenced to serve three years at the Nevada Women's Camp,
in the first six months of incarceration Isabel May accumulated
22 months additional punitive confinement. Caution is urged
in her apprehension.

The face, Cardale reflected, was defiant, reckless, outraged, but neither coarse nor stupid — a face, in fact, illuminated by intelligence and sensitivity. Not the face of a criminal, thought Cardale.

He pressed a button. The telescreen plumbed into sharp life. "Lunar Observatory," said Cardale.

The screen twitched to a view across an austere office, with moonscape outside the window. A man in a rose-pink smock looked into the screen. "Hello, Cardale."

"What's the word on May?"

"We've got a line on her. Quite a nuisance, which you won't want to hear about. One matter: please, in the future, keep freighters in another sector when you want a fugitive tracked. We had six red herrings to cope with."

"But you picked up May?"

"Definitely."

"Keep her in your sights. I'll send someone out to take over." Cardale clicked off the screen.

He ruminated a moment, then summoned the image of his secretary. "Get me Detering at Central Intelligence."

The polychrome whirl of color rose and fell to reveal Detering's ruddy face.

"Cardale, if it's service you want —"

"I want a mixed squad, men and women, in a fast ship to pick up a fugitive. Her name is Isabel May. She's fractious, unruly, incorrigible — but I don't want her hurt."

"Allow me to continue what I started to say. Cardale, if you want service, you are out of luck. There's literally no one in the office but me."

"Then come yourself."

"To pick up a reckless woman, and get my hair pulled and my face slapped? No thanks…One moment. There's a man waiting outside my office on a disciplinary charge. I can either have him court-martialed or I can send him over to you."

"What's his offense?"

"Insubordination. Arrogance. Disregard of orders. He's a loner. He does as he pleases and to hell with the rule-book."

"What about results?"

"He gets results — of a sort. His own kind of results."

"He may be the man to bring back Isabel May. What's his name?"

"Lanarck. He won't use his rank, which is captain."

"He seems something of a free spirit…Well, send him over."

Lanarck arrived almost immediately. The secretary ushered him into Cardale's office.

"Sit down, please. My name is Cardale. You're Lanarck, right?"

"Quite right."

Cardale inspected his visitor with open curiosity. Lanarck's reputation, thought Cardale, was belied by his appearance. He was neither tall nor heavy, and carried himself unobtrusively. His features, deeply darkened by the hard waves of space, were regular and dominated by a cold directness of the gray eyes and a bold jutting nose. Lanarck's voice was pleasant and soft.

"Major Detering assigned me to you for orders, sir."

"He recommended you highly," said Cardale. "I have a ticklish job on hand. Look at this." He passed over the sheet with the photograph of Isabel May. Lanarck scrutinized it without comment and handed it back.

"This girl was imprisoned six months ago for assault with a deadly weapon. She escaped the day before yesterday into space — which is more or less trivial in itself. But she carries with her a quantity of important information, which must be retrieved for the economic well-being of Earth. This may seem to you an extravagant statement, but accept it from me as a fact."

Lanarck said in a patient voice: "Mr. Cardale, I find that I work most efficiently when I am equipped with facts. Give me details of the case. If you feel that the matter is too sensitive for my handling, I will retire and you may bring in operatives better qualified."

Cardale said crossly: "The girl's father is a high-level mathematician, at work for the Exchequer. By his instruction an elaborate method of security to regulate transfer of funds was evolved. As an emergency precaution he devised an over-ride system, consisting of several words in a specific sequence. A criminal could go to the telephone, call the Exchequer, use these words and direct by voice alone the transfer of a billion dollars to his personal account. Or a hundred billion."

"Why not cancel the over-ride and install another?"

"Because of Arthur May's devilish subtlety. The over-ride is hidden in the computer; it is buried, totally inaccessible, that it might be protected from someone ordering the computer to reveal the over-ride.

The only way the over-ride can be voided is to use the over-ride first and issue appropriate orders."

"Go on."

"Arthur May knew the over-ride. He agreed to transfer the knowledge to the Chancellor and then submit to a hypnotic process which would remove the knowledge from his brain. Now occurred a rather sordid matter in regard to May's remuneration, and in my mind he was absolutely in the right."

"I know the feeling," said Lanarck. "I've had my own troubles with the scoundrels. The only good bursar is a dead bursar."

"In any event there follows an incredible tale of wrangling, proposals, estimates, schemes, counter-proposals, counter-schemes and conniving, all of which caused Arthur May a mental breakdown and he forgot the over-ride. But he had anticipated something of the sort and he left a memorandum with his daughter: Isabel May. When the authorities came for her father, she refused to let them in; she performed violent acts; she was confined in a penal institution, from which she escaped. Regardless of rights and wrongs she must be captured, more or less gently, and brought back — with the over-ride. You will surely understand the implications of the situation."

"It is a complicated business," said Lanarck. "But I will go after the girl, and with luck I will bring her back."

Six hours later Lanarck arrived at Lunar Observatory. The in-iris expanded; the boat lurched through.

Inside the dome Lanarck unclamped the port, stepped out. The master astronomer approached. Behind came the mechanics, one of whom bore an instrument which they welded to the hull of Lanarck's spaceboat.

"It's a detector cell," the astronomer explained. "Right now it's holding a line on the ship you're to follow. When the indicator holds to the neutral zone, you're on her track."

"And where does this ship seem to be headed?"

The astronomer shrugged. "Nowhere in Tellurian space. She's way past Fomalhaut and lining straight out."

Lanarck stood silent. This was hostile space Isabel May was entering.

In another day or so she would be slicing the fringe of the Clantlalan System, where the space patrol of that dark and inimical empire without warning destroyed all approaching vessels. Further on opened a region of black stars, inhabited by nondescript peoples little better than pirates. Still farther beyond lay unexplored and consequently dangerous regions.

The mechanics were finished. Lanarck climbed back into the boat. The out-iris opened; he drove his craft through, down the runway, and off into space.

A slow week followed, in which distance was annihilated. Earth empire fell far astern: a small cluster of stars. To one side the Clantlalan System grew ever brighter, and as Lanarck passed by the Clantlalan space-spheres tried to close with him. He threw in the emergency bank of generators and whisked the warboat far ahead. Someday, Lanarck knew, he would slip down past the guard ships to the home planet by the twin red suns, to discover what secret was held so dear. But now he kept the detector centered in the dial, and day by day the incoming signals from his quarry grew stronger.

They passed through the outlaw-ridden belt of dark stars, and into a region of space unknown but for tales let slip by drunken Clantlalan renegades — reports of planets covered with mighty ruins, legends of an asteroid littered with a thousand wrecked spaceships. Other tales were even more incredible. A dragon who tore spaceships open in its jaws purportedly wandered through this region, and it was said that alone on a desolate planet a godlike being created worlds at his pleasure.

The signals in the detector cell presently grew so strong that Lanarck slackened speed for fear that, overshooting his quarry, the cell would lose its thread of radiation. Now Isabel May began to swing out toward the star-systems which drifted past like fireflies, as if she sought a landmark. Always the signals in the detector cell grew stronger.

A yellow star waxed bright ahead. Lanarck knew that the ship of Isabel May was close at hand. Into that yellow star's system he followed her, and lined out the trail toward the single planet. Presently, as the planet globed out before him, the signals ceased entirely.

The high clear atmosphere braked the motion of Lanarck's spaceboat. He found below a dun, sun-baked landscape. Through the telescope the surface appeared to be uniformly stony and flat. Clouds of dust indicated the presence of high winds.

He had no trouble finding Isabel May's ship. In the field of his telescope lay a cubical white building: the only landmark visible from horizon to horizon. Beside the building sat Isabel May's silver spaceboat. Lanarck swooped to a landing, half-expecting a bolt from her needle-beam. The port of the spaceboat hung open, but she did not show herself as he came down on his crash-keel close by.

The air, he found, was breathable. Buckling on his needle-beam, he stepped out on the stony ground. The hot gale tore at him, buffeting his face, whipping tears from his eyes. Wind-flung pebbles bounding along the ground stung his legs. Light from the sun burned his shoulders.

Lanarck inspected the terrain, to discover no sign of life, either from the white building or from Isabel May's spaceboat. The ground stretched away, bare and sundrenched, far into the dusty distances. Lanarck looked to the lonely white structure. She must be within. Here was the end of the chase which had brought him across the galaxy.

II

Lanarck circled the building. On the leeward side, he found a low dark archway. From within came the heavy smell of life: an odor half-animal, half-reptile. He approached the entrance with his needle-beam ready.

He called out: "Isabel May!" He listened. The wind whistled by the corner of the building; little stones clicked past, blowing down the endless sun-dazzled waste. There was no other sound.

A sonorous voice entered his brain.

"The one you seek is gone."

Lanarck stood stock-still.

"You may come within, Earthman. We are not enemies."

The archway loomed dark before him. Step by step he entered. After the glare of the white sun the dimness of the room was like a moonless night. Lanarck blinked.

Slowly objects about him assumed form. Two enormous eyes peered through the gloom; behind appeared a tremendous domelike bulk. Thought surged into Lanarck's brain. "You are unnecessarily truculent. Here will be no occasion for violence."

Lanarck relaxed, feeling slightly at a loss. Telepathy was not often practised upon Earth. The creature's messages came like a paradoxically silent voice, but he had no knowledge how to transmit his own messages. He hazarded the experiment.

"Where is Isabel May?"

"In a place inaccessible to you."

"How did she go? Her spaceboat is outside, and she landed but a half-hour ago."

"I sent her away."

Keeping his needle-beam ready, Lanarck searched the building. The girl was nowhere to be found. Seized by a sudden fearful thought, he ran to the entrance and looked out. The two spaceboats were as he had left them. He shoved the needle-beam back into the holster and turned to the leviathan, in whom he sensed benign amusement.

"Well, then — who are you and where is Isabel May?"

"I am Laoome," came the reply. "Laoome, the one-time Third of Narfilhet — Laoome the World-Thinker, the Final Sage of the Fifth Universe... As for the girl, I have placed her, at her own request, upon a pleasant but inaccessible world of my own creation."

Lanarck stood perplexed.

"Look!" Laoome said.

Space quivered in front of Lanarck's eyes. A dark aperture appeared in midair. Looking through, Lanarck saw hanging apparently but a yard before his eyes a lambent sphere — a miniature world. As he watched, it expanded like a toy balloon.

Its horizons vanished past the confines of the opening. Continents and oceans assumed shape, flecked with cloud-wisps. Polar ice-caps glinted blue-white in the light of an unseen sun. Yet all the time the world seemed to be but a yard distant. A plain appeared, rimmed by black, flinty mountains. The color of the plain, a ruddy ocher he saw presently, was due to a forest-carpet of rust-colored foliage. The expansion ceased.

The World-Thinker spoke: "That which you see before you is matter as real and tangible as yourself. I have indeed created it through my mind. Until I dissolve it in the same manner, it exists. Reach out and touch it."

Lanarck did so. It was actually only a yard from his face, and the red forest crushed like dry moss under his fingertips.

"You destroyed a village," commented Laoome, and caused the world to expand once more at a breathtaking rate, until the perspectives were as if Lanarck hung a hundred feet above the surface. He was looking into the devastation which his touch had wrought a moment before. The trees, far larger than he had supposed, with boles thirty or forty feet through, lay tossed and shattered. Visible were the ruins of rude huts, from which issued calls and screams of pain, thinly audible to Lanarck. Bodies of men and women lay crushed. Others tore frantically at the wreckage.

Lanarck stared in disbelief. "There's life! Men!"

"Without life, a world is uninteresting, a lump of rock. Men, like yourself, I often use. They have a large capacity for emotion and initiative, a flexibility to the varied environments which I introduce."

Lanarck gazed at the tips of his fingers, then back to the shattered village. "Are they really alive?"

"Certainly. And you would find, should you converse with one of them, that they possess a sense of history, a racial heritage of folklore, and a culture well-adapted to their environment."

"But how can one brain conceive the detail of a world? The leaves of each tree, the features of each man —"

"That would be tedious," Laoome agreed. "My mind only broadly conceives, introduces the determinate roots into the hypostatic equations. Detail then evolves automatically."

"You allowed me to destroy hundreds of these — men."

Curious feelers searched his brain. Lanarck sensed Laoome's amusement.

"The idea is repugnant? In a moment I shall dissolve the entire world... Still, if it pleases you, I can restore it as it was. See!"

Immediately the forest was unmarred, the village whole again, secure and peaceful in a small clearing.

Awareness came to Lanarck of a curious rigidity in the rapport he had established with the World-Thinker. Looking about, he saw that the great eyes had glazed, that the tremendous black body was twitching and jerking. Now Laoome's dream-planet was changing. Lanarck leaned forward in fascination. The noble red trees had become gray rotten stalks and were swaying drunkenly. Others slumped and folded like columns of putty.

On the ground balls of black slime rolled about with vicious energy pursuing the villagers, who in terror fled anywhere, everywhere.

From the heavens came a rain of blazing pellets. The villagers were killed, but the black slime-things seemed only agonized. Blindly they lashed about, burrowed furiously into the heaving ground to escape the impacts. More suddenly than it had been created, the world vanished. Lanarck tore his gaze from the spot where the world had been. He looked about and found Laoome as before.

"Don't be alarmed." The thoughts came quietly. "The seizure is over. It occurs only seldom, and why it should be I do not know. I imagine that my brain, under the pressure of exact thought, lapses into these reflexive spasms for the sake of relaxation. This was a mild attack. The world on which I am concentrating is usually totally destroyed."

The flow of soundless words stopped abruptly. Moments passed. Then thoughts gushed once more into Lanarck's brain.

"Let me show you another planet — one of the most interesting I have ever conceived. For almost a million Earth years it has been developing in my mind."

The space before Lanarck's eyes quivered. Out in the imaginary void hung another planet. As before, it expanded until the features of the terrain assumed an earthly perspective. Hardly a mile in diameter, the world was divided around the equator by a belt of sandy desert. At one pole glimmered a lake, at the other grew a jungle of lush vegetation.

From this jungle now, as Lanarck watched, crept a semi-human shape. A travesty upon man, its face was long, chinless and furtive, with eyes beady and quick. The legs were unnaturally long; the shoulders and arms were undeveloped. It slunk to the edge of the desert, paused a moment, looking carefully in both directions, then began a mad dash through the sand to the lake beyond.

Halfway across, a terrible roar was heard. Over the close horizon bounded a dragon-like monster. With fearsome speed it pursued the fleeing man-thing, who outdistanced it and gained the edge of the desert by two hundred feet. When the dragon came to the limits of the sandy area, it halted and bellowed an eery mournful note which sent shivers along Lanarck's spine. Casually now, the man-thing loped to the lake, threw himself flat and drank deeply.

"An experiment in evolution," came Laoome's thought. "A million years ago those creatures were men like yourself. This world is oddly designed. At one end is food, at the other drink. In order to survive, the 'men' must cross the desert every day or so. The dragon is prevented from leaving the desert by actinic boundaries. Hence, if the men can cross the desert, they are safe.

"You have witnessed how admirably they have adapted to their environment. The women are particularly fleet, for they have adjusted to the handicap of caring for their young. Sooner or later, of course, age overtakes them and their speed gradually decreases until finally they are caught and devoured.

"A curious religion and set of taboos have evolved here. I am worshipped as the primary god of Life, and Shillal, as they call the dragon, is the deity of Death. He, of course, is the basic concern of their lives and colors all their thoughts. They are close to elementals, these folk. Food, drink, and death are intertwined for them into almost one concept.

"They can build no weapons of metal against Shillal, for their world is not endowed with the raw materials. Once, a hundred thousand years ago, one of their chiefs contrived a gigantic catapult, to hurl a sharp-pointed tree-trunk at Shillal. Unluckily, the fibers of the draw-cord snapped and the chief was killed by the recoil. The priests interpreted this as a sign and —

"Look there! Shillal catches a weary old woman, sodden with water, attempting to return to the jungle!"

Lanarck witnessed the beast's great gulping.

"To continue," Laoome went on, "a taboo was created, and no further weapons were ever built."

"But why have you forced upon these folk a million years of wretched existence?" asked Lanarck.

Laoome gave an untranslatable mental shrug. "I am just, and indeed benevolent," he said. "These men worship me as a god. Upon a certain hillock, which they hold sacred, they bring their sick and wounded. There, if the whim takes me, I restore them to health. So far as their existence is concerned, they relish the span of their lives as much as you do yours."

"Yet, in creating these worlds, you are responsible for the happiness of the inhabitants. If you were truly benevolent, why should you permit disease and terror to exist?"

Laoome again gave his mental shrug. "I might say that I use this universe of our own as a model. Perhaps there is another Laoome dreaming out the worlds we ourselves live on. When man dies of sickness, bacteria live. Dragon lives by eating man. When man eats, plants and animals die."

Lanarck was silent, studiously preventing his thoughts from rising to the surface of his mind.

"I take it that Isabel May is upon neither of these planets?"

"That is correct."

"I ask that you make it possible for me to communicate with her."

"But I put her upon a world expressly to assure her safety from such molestation."

"I believe that she would profit by hearing me."

"Very well," said Laoome. "In justice I should accord to you the same opportunity that I did her. You may proceed to this world. Remember, however, the risk is your own, exactly as it is for Isabel May. If you perish upon Markavvel, you are as thoroughly dead as you might be upon Earth. I can not play Destiny to influence either one of your lives."

There was a hiatus in Laoome's thoughts, a whirl of ideas too rapid for Lanarck to grasp. At last Laoome's eyes focused upon him again. An instant of faintness as Lanarck felt knowledge forced into his brain.

As Laoome silently regarded him, it occurred to Lanarck that Laoome's body, a great dome of black flesh, was singularly ill-adapted to life on the planet where he dwelt.

"You are right," came the thoughts of Laoome. "From a Beyond unknown to you I came, banished from the dark planet Narfilhet, in whose fathomless black waters I swam. This was long ago, but even now I may not return." Laoome lapsed once more into introspection.

Lanarck moved restlessly. Outside the wind tore past the building. Laoome continued silent, dreaming perhaps of the dark oceans of ancient Narfilhet. Lanarck impatiently launched a thought.

"How do I reach Markavvel? And how do I return?"

Laoome fetched himself back to the present. His eyes settled upon a point beside Lanarck. The aperture which led into his various imaginary spaces was now wrenched open for the third time. A little distance off in the void, a spaceboat drifted. Lanarck's eyes narrowed with sudden interest.

"That's a 45-G — my own ship!" he exclaimed.

"No, not yours. One like it. Yours is still outside." The craft drew nearer, gradually floated within reach.

"Climb in," said Laoome. "At present, you will find Isabel May in the city which lies at the apex of the triangular continent."

"But how do I get back?"

"Aim your ship, when you leave Markavvel, at the brightest star visible. You will then break through the mental dimensions into this universe."

Lanarck reached his arm into the imaginary universe and pulled the imagined spaceboat close to the aperture. He opened the port and gingerly stepped in as Laoome's parting thoughts reached him.

"Should you fall into danger, I cannot modify the natural course of events. On the other hand, I will not intentionally place dangers in your way. If such befall you, it will be due solely to circumstance."

III

Lanarck slammed shut the port, half-expecting the ship to dissolve under his feet. But the ship was solid enough. He looked back. The gap into his own universe had disappeared, leaving in its place a brilliant blue star. He found himself in space. Below glimmered the disk of Markavvel, much like other planets he had approached from the void. He tugged at the throttle, threw the nose hard over and down. Let the abstracts take care of themselves. The boat dropped down at Markavvel.

It seemed a pleasant world. A hot white sun hung off in space; blue oceans covered a large part of the surface. Among the scattered land masses he found the triangular continent. It was not large. There were mountains with green-forested slopes and a central plateau: a not un-Earthlike scene, and Lanarck did not feel the alien aura which surrounded most extra-terrestrial planets.

Sighting through his telescope Lanarck found the city, sprawling and white, at the mouth of a wide river. He sent his ship streaking down through the upper atmosphere, then slowed and leveled off thirty miles to sea. Barely skimming the sparkling blue waves, he flew toward the city.

A few miles to the left an island raised basalt cliffs against the ocean. In his line of sight there heaved up on the crest of a swell a floating black object. After an instant it disappeared into the trough: a ramshackle raft. Upon it a girl with tawny golden hair desperately battled sea-things which sought to climb aboard.

Lanarck dropped the ship into the water beside the raft. The wash threw the raft up and over and down on the girl.

Lanarck slipped through the port and dived into clear green water. He glimpsed only sub-human figures paddling downward, barely discernible. Bobbing to the surface, he swam to the raft, ducked under, grasped the girl's limp form, pulled her up into the air.

For a moment he clung to the raft to catch his breath, while holding the girl's head clear of the water. He sensed the return of the creatures from below. Dark forms rose in the shadow cast by the raft, and a clammy, long-fingered hand wound around his ankle. He kicked and felt his foot thud into something like a face. More dark forms came up from the depths. Lanarck measured the distance to his spaceboat. Forty feet. Too far. He crawled onto the raft, and pulled the girl after him. Leaning far out, he recovered the paddle and prepared to smash the first sea-thing to push above water. But instead, they swam in tireless circles twenty feet below.

The blade of the paddle had broken. Lanarck could not move the unwieldy bulk of the raft. The breeze, meanwhile, was easing the spaceboat ever farther away. Lanarck exerted himself another fifteen minutes, pushing against the water with the splintered paddle, but the gap increased. He cast down the paddle in disgust and turned to the girl who, sitting cross-legged, regarded him thoughtfully. For no apparent reason, Lanarck was reminded of Laoome in the dimness of his white building, on the windy world. All this, he thought, looking from clear-eyed girl to heaving sun-lit sea to highlands of the continent ahead, was an idea in Laoome's brain.

He looked back at the girl. Her bright wheat-colored hair frothed around her head in ringlets, producing, thought Lanarck, a most pleasant effect. She returned his gaze for a moment, then, with jaunty grace, stood up.

She spoke to Lanarck who found to his amazement that he understood her. Then, remembering Laoome's manipulation of his brain, extracting ideas, altering, instilling new concepts, he was not so amazed.

"Thank you for your help," she said. "But now we are both in the same plight."

Lanarck said nothing. He knelt and began to remove his boots.

"What will you do?"

"Swim," he answered. The new language seemed altogether natural.

"The Bottom-people would pull you under before you went twenty feet." She pointed into the water, which teemed with circling dark shapes. Lanarck knew she spoke the truth.

"You are of Earth also?" she asked, inspecting him carefully.

"Yes. Who are you and what do you know of Earth?"

"I am Jiro from the city yonder, which is Gahadion. Earth is the home of Isabel May, who came in a ship such as yours."

"Isabel May arrived but an hour ago! How could you know about her?"

"'An hour'?" replied the girl. "She has been here three months!" This last a little bitterly.

Lanarck reflected that Laoome controlled time in his universes as arbitrarily as he did space. "How did you come to be here on this raft?"

She grimaced toward the island. "The priests came for me. They live on the island and take people from the mainland. They took me but last night I escaped."

Lanarck looked from the island to the city on the mainland. "Why do not Gahadion authorities control the priests?"

Her lips rounded to an O. "They are sacred to the Great God Laoome, and so inviolate."

Lanarck wondered what unique evolutionary process Laoome had in progress here.

"Few persons thus taken return to the mainland," she went on. "Those who win free, and also escape the Bottom-people, usually live in the wilderness. If they return to Gahadion they are molested by fanatics and sometimes recaptured by the priests."

Lanarck was silent. After all, it concerned him little how these people fared. They were beings of fantasy, inhabiting an imaginary planet. And yet, when he looked at Jiro, detachment became easier to contemplate than to achieve.

"And Isabel May is in Gahadion?"

Jiro's lips tightened. "No. She lives on the island. She is the Thrice-Adept, the High Priestess."

Lanarck was surprised. "Why did they make her High Priestess?"

"A month after she arrived, the Hierarch, learning of the woman whose hair was the color of night, even as yours, tried to take her to Drefteli, the Sacred Isle, as a slave. She killed him with her weapon. Then when the lightnings of Laoome did not consume her, it was known that Laoome approved, and so she was made High Priestess in place of the riven Hierarch."

The philosophy, so Lanarck reflected, would have sounded naive on Earth, where the gods were more covert in their supervision of human affairs.

"Is Isabel May a friend of yours — or your lover?" asked Jiro softly.

"Hardly."

"Then what do you want with her?"

"I've come to take her back to Earth." He looked dubiously across the ever-widening gap between the raft and his spaceboat. "That at least was my intention."

"You shall see her soon," said Jiro. She pointed to a long black galley approaching from the island. "The Ordained Ones. I am once more a slave."

"Not yet," said Lanarck, feeling for the bulk of his needle-beam.

The galley, thrust by the force of twenty long oars, lunged toward them. On the afterdeck stood a young woman, her black hair blowing in the wind. As her features became distinct, Lanarck recognized the face of Cardale's photograph, now serene and confident.

Isabel May, looking from the silent two on the raft to the wallowing spaceboat a quarter-mile distant, seemed to laugh. The galley, manned by tall, golden-haired men, drew alongside.

"So Earth Intelligence pays me a visit?" She spoke in English. "How you found me, I cannot guess." She looked curiously at Lanarck's somber visage. "How?"

"I followed your trail, and then explained the situation to Laoome."

"Just what is the situation?"

"I'd like to work out some kind of compromise to please everyone."

"I don't care whether I please anyone or not."

"Understandable."

The two studied each other. Isabel May suddenly asked, "What is your name?"

"Lanarck."

"Just Lanarck? No rank? No first name?"

"Lanarck is enough."

"Just as you like. I hardly know what to do with you. I'm not vindictive, and I don't want to handicap your career. But ferrying you to your spaceboat would be rather quixotic. I'm comfortable here, and I haven't the slightest intention of turning my property over to you."

Lanarck reached for his needle-beam.

She watched him without emotion. "Wet needle-beams don't work well."

"This one is the exception." Lanarck blasted the figurehead from the galley.

Isabel May's expression changed suddenly. "I see that I'm wrong. How did you do it?"

"A personal device," replied Lanarck. "Now I'll have to request that you take me to my spaceboat."

Isabel May stared at him a moment, and in those blue eyes Lanarck detected something familiar. Where had he seen eyes with that expression? On Fan, the Pleasure Planet? In the Magic Groves of Hycithil? During the raids on the slave-pens of Starlen? In Earth's own macropolis Tran?

She turned and muttered to her boatswain, a bronzed giant, his golden hair bound back by a copper band. He bowed and moved away.

"Very well," said Isabel May. "Come aboard."

Jiro and Lanarck clambered over the carven gunwale. The galley swept ahead, foaming up white in its wake.

Isabel May turned her attention to Jiro, who sat looking disconsolately toward the island Drefteli. "You make friends quickly," Isabel told Lanarck. "She's very beautiful. What are you planning for her?"

"She's one of your escaped slaves. I don't have any plans. This place belongs to Laoome; he makes all plans. I'm interested only in getting you out. If you don't want to come back to Earth, give me the document which you brought with you, and stay here as long as you like."

"Sorry. The document stays with me. I don't carry it on my person, so please don't try to search me."

"That sounds quite definite," said Lanarck. "Do you know what's in the document?"

"More or less. It's like a blank check on the wealth of the world."

"That's a good description. As I understand this sorry affair, you became angry at the treatment accorded your father."

"That's a very quiet understatement."

"Would money help soothe your anger?"

"I don't want money. I want revenge. I want to grind faces into the mud; I want to kick people and make their lives miserable."

"Still…don't dismiss money. It's nice to be rich. You have your life ahead of you. I don't imagine you want to spend it here, inside Laoome's head."

"Very true."

"So name a figure."

"I can't measure anger and grief in dollars."

"Why not? A million? Ten million? A hundred million?"

"Stop there. I can't count any higher."

"That's your figure."

"What good will money do me? They'll take me back to Nevada."

"No. I'll give you my personal guarantee of this."

"Meaningless. I know nothing about you."

"You'll learn during the trip back to Earth."

Isabel May said: "Lanarck, you are persuasive. If the truth be known, I'm homesick." She turned away and stood looking over the ocean.

Lanarck stood watching her. She was undeniably attractive and he found it difficult to take his eyes from her. But as he settled on the bench beside Jiro, he felt a surge of a different, stronger, feeling. It irritated him, and he tried to put it aside.

IV

Wallowing in the swells, the spaceboat lay dead ahead. The galley scudded through the water at a great rate, and the oarsmen did not slacken speed as they approached. Lanarck's eyes narrowed; he jumped upright shouting orders. The galley, unswerving, plowed into the spaceboat, grinding it under the metal-shod keel. Water gushed in through the open port; the spaceboat shuddered and sank, a dark shadow plummeting into green depths.

"Too bad," remarked Isabel. "On the other hand, this puts us more on an equal footing. You have a needle-beam, I have a spaceboat."

Lanarck silently seated himself. After a moment he spoke. "Where is your own needle-beam?"

"I blew it up trying to recharge it from the spaceboat generators."

"And where is your spaceboat?"

Isabel laughed at this. "Do you expect me to tell you?"

"Why not? I wouldn't maroon you here."

"Nevertheless, I don't think I'll tell you."

Lanarck turned to Jiro. "Where is Isabel May's spaceboat?"

Isabel spoke in a haughty voice: "As High Priestess to Almighty Laoome, I command you to be silent!"

Jiro looked from one to the other. She made up her mind. "It is on the plaza of the Malachite Temple in Gahadion."

Isabel was silent. "Laoome plays tricks," she said at last. "Jiro has taken a fancy to you. You're obviously interested in her."

"Laoome will not interfere," said Lanarck.

She laughed bitterly. "That's what he told me — and look! I'm High Priestess. He also told me he wouldn't let anyone come to Markavvel from the outside to molest me. But you are here!"

"My intention is not to molest you," said Lanarck curtly. "We can as easily be friends as enemies."

"I don't care to be a friend of yours. And as an enemy, you are no serious problem. Now!" Isabel called, as the tall boatswain came near.

The boatswain whirled on Lanarck. Lanarck twisted, squirmed, heaved, and the golden-haired boatswain sprawled back into the bilge, where he lay dazed.

A soft hand brushed Lanarck's thigh. He looked around, smoothing his lank black hair, and found Isabel May smiling into his face. His needle-beam dangled from her fingers.

Jiro arose from the bench. Before Isabel could react, Jiro had pushed a hand into her face, and with the other seized the needle-beam. She pointed the weapon at Isabel.

"Sit down," said Jiro.

Weeping with rage, Isabel fell back upon the bench.

Jiro, her young face flushed and happy, backed over to the thwart, needle-beam leveled.

Lanarck stood still.

"I will take charge now," said Jiro. "You — Isabel! Tell your men to row toward Gahadion!"

Sullenly Isabel gave the order. The long black galley turned its bow toward the city.

"This may be sacrilege," Jiro observed to Lanarck. "But then I was already in trouble for escaping from Drefteli."

"What do you plan in this new capacity of yours?" Lanarck inquired, moving closer.

"First, to try this weapon on whomever thinks he can take it away from me." Lanarck eased back. "Secondly — but you'll see soon enough."

White-tiered Gahadion rapidly drew closer across the water.

Isabel sulked on the bench. Lanarck had little choice but to let matters move on their own momentum. He relaxed against a thwart, watching Jiro from the corner of his eye. She stood erect behind the bench where Isabel sat, her clear eyes looking over the leaping sparkles of the ocean. Breeze whipped her hair behind and pressed the tunic against her slim body. Lanarck heaved a deep sad sigh. This girl with the wheat-colored hair was unreal. She would vanish into oblivion as soon as Laoome lost interest in the world Markavvel. She was less than a shadow, less than a mirage, less than a dream. Lanarck looked over at

Isabel, the Earth girl, who glared at him with sullen eyes. She was real enough.

They moved up the river and toward the white docks of Gahadion. Lanarck rose to his feet. He looked over the city, surveyed the folk on the dock who were clad in white, red and blue tunics, then turned to Jiro. "I'll have to take the weapon now."

"Stand back or I'll —" Lanarck took the weapon from her limp grasp. Isabel watched in sour amusement.

A dull throbbing sound, like the pulse of a tremendous heart, came down from the heavens. Lanarck cocked his head, listening. He scanned the sky. At the horizon appeared a strange cloud, like a band of white-gleaming metal, swelling in rhythm to the celestial throbbing. It lengthened with miraculous speed, until in all directions the horizon was encircled. The throb became a vast booming. The air itself seemed heavy, ominous. A terrible idea struck Lanarck. He turned and yelled to the awestruck oarsmen who were trailing their oars in the river.

"Quickly — get to the docks!"

They jerked at their oars, frantic, yet the galley moved no faster. The water of the river had become oily smooth, almost syrupy. The boat inched close to the dock. Lanarck was grimly aware of the terrified Isabel on one side of him, Jiro on the other.

"What is happening?" whispered Isabel. Lanarck watched the sky. The cloud-band of bright metal quivered and split into another which wabbled, bouncing just above.

"I hope I'm wrong," said Lanarck, "but I suspect that Laoome is going mad. Look at our shadows!" He turned to look at the sun, which jerked like a dying insect, vibrating through aimless arcs. His worst fears were realized.

"It can't be!" cried Isabel. "What will happen?"

"Nothing good."

The galley lurched against a pier. Lanarck helped Isabel and Jiro up to the dock, then followed.

Masses of tall golden-haired people milled in panic along the avenue.

"Lead me to the spaceboat!" Lanarck had to shout to make himself heard over the tumult of the city. His mind froze at a shocking thought: what would happen to Jiro?

He pushed the thought down. Isabel pulled at him urgently. "Come, hurry!"

Taking Jiro's hand, he ran off after Isabel toward the black-porticoed temple at the far end of the avenue.

A constriction twisted the air; down came a rain of warm red globules: small crimson jellyfish which stung naked flesh like nettles. The din from the city reached hysterical pitch. The red plasms increased to become a cloud of pink slime, now oozing ankle-deep on the ground.

Isabel tripped and fell headlong in the perilous mess. She struggled until Lanarck helped her to her feet.

They continued toward the temple, Lanarck supporting both girls and keeping an uneasy eye on the structures to either side.

The rain of red things ceased, but the streets flowed with ooze.

The sky shifted color — but what color? It had no place in any spectrum. The color only a mad god could conceive.

The red slime curdled and fell apart like quicksilver, to jell in an instant to millions upon millions of bright blue manikins three inches high. They ran, hopped, scuttled; the streets were a quaking blue carpet of blank-faced little homunculi. They clung to Lanarck's garments, they ran up his legs like mice. He trod them under, heedless to their squeals.

The sun, jerking in small spasmodic motions, slowed, lost its glare, became oblate. It developed striations and, as the stricken population of Gahadion quieted in awe, the sun changed to a segmented white slug, as long as five suns, as wide as one. It writhed its head about and stared down through the strange-colored sky at Markavvel.

In a delirium, the Gahadionites careened along the wide avenues. Lanarck and the two girls almost were trod under as they fought past a cross-street.

In a small square, beside a marble fountain, the three found refuge. Lanarck had reached a state of detachment: a conviction that this experience was a nightmare.

A blue man-thing pulled itself into his hair. It was singing in a small clear baritone. Lanarck set it upon the ground. His mind grew calmer. This was no nightmare; this was reality, however the word could be interpreted! Haste! The surge of people had passed; the way was relatively open. "Let's go!" He pulled at the two girls who had been watching the slug which hung across the sky.

As they started off, there came the metamorphosis Lanarck had been expecting, and dreading. The matter of Gahadion, and all Markavvel, altered into unnatural substances. The buildings of white marble became putty, slumped beneath their own weight. The Malachite Temple, an airy dome on green malachite pillars, sagged and slid to a sodden lump. Lanarck urged the gasping girls to greater speed.

The Gahadionites no longer ran; there was no destination. They stood staring up, frozen in horror by the glittering slug in the sky. A voice screamed: "Laoome, Laoome!" Other voices took up the cry: "Laoome, Laoome!"

If Laoome heard, he gave no sign.

Lanarck kept an anxious eye on these folk, dreading lest they also, as dream-creatures, alter to shocking half-things. For should they change, so would Jiro. Why take her to the spaceboat? She could not exist outside the mind of Laoome...But how could he let her go?

The face of Markavvel was changing. Black pyramids sprouted through the ground and, lengthening tremendously, darted upward, to become black spikes, miles high.

Lanarck saw the spaceboat, still sound and whole, a product of more durable mind-stuff, perhaps, than Markavvel itself. Tremendous processes were transpiring beneath his feet, as if the core of the planet itself were degenerating. Another hundred yards to the spaceboat! "Faster!" he panted to the girls.

All the while they ran, he watched the folk of Gahadion. Like a cold wind blowing on his brain, he knew that the change had come. He almost slowed his steps for despair. The Gahadionites themselves knew. They staggered in unbelieving surprise, regarding their hands, feeling their faces.

Too late! Unreasonably Lanarck had hoped that once in space, away from Markavvel, Jiro might retain her identity. But too late! A blight had befallen the Gahadionites. They clawed their shriveling faces, tottered and fell, their shrunken legs unable to support them.

In anguish Lanarck felt one of the hands he was holding become hard and wrinkled. As her legs withered, he felt her sag. He paused and turned, to look sadly upon what had been Jiro.

The ground beneath his feet lurched. Around him twisted dying Gahadionites. Above, dropping through the weird sky, came the slug. Black spikes towered tremendously over his head. Lanarck heeded none of these. Before him stood Jiro — a Jiro gasping and reeling in exhaustion, but a Jiro sound and golden still! Dying on the marble pavement was the shriveled dream-thing he had known as Isabel May. Taking Jiro's hand, he turned and made for the spaceboat.

Hauling back the port, he pushed Jiro inside. Even as he touched the hull, he realized that the spaceboat was changing also. The cold metal had acquired a palpitant life of its own. Lanarck slammed shut the port, and, heedless of fracturing cold thrust-tubes, gushed power astern.

Off careened the spaceboat, dodging through the forest of glittering black spines, now hundreds of miles tall, swerving a thousand miles to escape the great slug falling inexorably to the surface of Markavvel. As the ship darted free into space, Lanarck looked back to see the slug sprawled across half a hemisphere. It writhed, impaled on the tall black spikes.

Lanarck drove the spaceboat at full speed toward the landmark star. Blue and luminous it shone, the only steadfast object in the heavens. All else poured in turbulent streams through black space: motes eddying in a pool of ink.

Lanarck looked briefly toward Jiro, and spoke. "Just when I decided that nothing else could surprise me, Isabel May died, while you, Jiro the Gahadionite, are alive."

"I am Isabel May. You knew already."

"I knew, yes, because it was the only possibility." He put his hand against the hull. The impersonal metallic feel had altered to a warm vitality. "Now, if we escape from this mess, it'll be a miracle."

Changes came quickly. The controls atrophied; the ports grew dull and opaque, like cartilage. Engines and fittings became voluted organs; the walls were pink moist flesh, pulsing regularly. From outside came a sound like the flapping of pinions; about their feet swirled dark liquid. Lanarck, pale, shook his head. Isabel pressed close to him.

"We're in the stomach of — something."

Isabel made no answer.

A sound like a cork popped from a bottle, a gush of gray light. Lanarck had guided the spaceboat aright; it had continued into the sane universe and its own destruction.

The two Earth-creatures found themselves stumbling on the floor of Laoome's dwelling. At first they could not comprehend their deliverance; safety seemed but another shifting of scenes.

Lanarck regained his equilibrium. He helped Isabel to her feet; together they surveyed Laoome, who was still in the midst of his spasm. Rippling tremors ran along his black hide, the saucer eyes were blank and glazed.

"Let's go!" whispered Isabel.

Lanarck silently took her arm; they stepped out on the glaring wind-whipped plain. There, the two spaceboats, just as before. Lanarck guided Isabel to his craft, opened the port and motioned her inside. "I'm going back for one moment."

Lanarck locked the power-arm. "Just to guard against any new surprises."

Isabel said nothing.

Walking around to the spaceboat in which Isabel May had arrived, Lanarck similarly locked the mechanism. Then he crossed to the white concrete structure.

Isabel listened, but the moaning of the wind drowned out all other sounds. The chatter of a needle-beam? She could not be sure.

Lanarck emerged from the building. He climbed into the boat and slammed the port. They sat in silence as the thrust-tubes warmed, nor did they speak as he threw over the power-arm and the boat slanted off into the sky.

Not until they were far off in space did either of them speak.

Lanarck looked toward Isabel. "How did you know of Laoome?"

"Through my father. Twenty years ago he did Laoome some trifling favor — killed a lizard which had been annoying Laoome, or something of the sort."

"And that's why Laoome shielded you from me by creating the dream Isabel?"

"Yes. He told me you were coming down looking for me. He

arranged that you should meet a purported Isabel May, that I might assess you without your knowledge."

"Why don't you look more like the photograph?"

"I was furious; I'd been crying; I was practically gnashing my teeth. I certainly hope I don't look like that."

"How about your hair?"

"It's bleached."

"Did the other Isabel know your identity?"

"I don't think so. No, I know she didn't. Laoome equipped her with my brain and all its memories. She actually was I."

Lanarck nodded. Here was the source of the inklings of recognition. He said thoughtfully: "She was very perceptive. She said that you and I were, well, attracted to each other. I wonder if she was right."

"I wonder."

"There will be time to consider the subject…One last point: the documents, with the over-ride."

Isabel laughed cheerfully. "There aren't any documents."

"No documents?"

"None. Do you care to search me?"

"Where are the documents?"

"Document, in the singular. A slip of paper. I tore it up."

"What was on the paper?"

"The over-ride. I'm the only person alive who knows it. Don't you think I should keep the secret to myself?"

Lanarck reflected a moment. "I'd like to know. That kind of knowledge is always useful."

"Where is the hundred million dollars you promised me?"

"It's back on Earth. When you get there you can use the over-ride."

Isabel laughed. "You're a most practical man. What happened to Laoome?"

"Laoome is dead."

"How?"

"I destroyed him. I thought of what we just went through. His dream-creatures — were they real? They seemed real to me, and to themselves. Is a person responsible for what happens during a nightmare? I don't know. I obeyed my instincts, or conscience, whatever it's called, and killed him."

Isabel May took his hand. "My instincts tell me that I can trust you. The over-ride is a couplet:

> *Tom, Tom, the piper's son*
> *Stole a pig and away he run.*

V

Lanarck reported to Cardale. "I am happy to inform you that the affair is satisfactorily concluded."

Cardale regarded him skeptically. "What do you mean by that?"

"The over-ride is safe."

"Indeed? Safe where?"

"I thought it best to consult with you before carrying the over-ride on my person."

"That is perhaps over-discreet. What of Isabel May? Is she in custody?"

"In order to get the over-ride I had to make broad but reasonable concessions, including a full pardon, retraction of all charges against her, and official apologies as well as retributive payments for false arrest and general damage. She wants an official document, certifying these concessions. If you will prepare the document, I will transmit it, and the affair will be terminated."

Cardale said in a cool voice: "Who authorized you to make such far-reaching concessions?"

Lanarck spoke indifferently. "Do you want the over-ride?"

"Of course."

"Then do as I suggest."

"You're even more arrogant than Detering led me to expect."

"The results speak for themselves, sir."

"How do I know that she won't use the over-ride?"

"You can now call it up and change it, so I'm given to understand."

"How do I know that she hasn't used it already, to the hilt?"

"I mentioned compensatory payments. The adjustment has been made."

Cardale ran his fingers through his hair. "How much damages?"

"The amount is of no great consequence. If Isabel May had chosen to make intemperate demands, they would only partially balance the damage she has suffered."

"So you say." Cardale could not decide whether to bluster, to threaten, or to throw his hands in the air. At last he leaned back in his chair. "I'll have the document ready tomorrow, and you can bring in the over-ride."

"Very well, Mr. Cardale."

"I'd still like to know, unofficially, if you like, just how much she took in settlement."

"We requisitioned a hundred and one million, seven hundred and sixty-two dollars into a set of personal accounts."

Cardale stared. "I thought you said that she'd made a temperate settlement!"

"It seemed as easy to ask for a large sum as a small."

"No doubt even easier. It's a strange figure. Why seven hundred and sixty-two dollars?"

"That, sir, is money owing to me for which the bursar refuses to issue a voucher. It represents expenses in a previous case: bribes, liquor and the services of a prostitute, if you want the details."

"Any why the million extra?"

"That represents a contingency fund for my own convenience, so that I won't be harassed in the future. In a quiet and modest sense it also reflects my annoyance with the bursar."

Lanarck rose to his feet. "I'll see you tomorrow at the same time, sir."

"Until tomorrow, Lanarck."

I'll Build Your Dream Castle

When Farrero first met Douane Angker, of Marlais and Angker, Class III Structors, something in his brain twisted, averted itself; and, looking down at the curl on Angker's tough mouth, he knew the feeling flowed in both directions. Angker, short and solid, had concentrated in him a heavy unctuous vitality, the same way a cigar stub holds the strongest juices.

Farrero did not, on this occasion, meet Leon Marlais, the other half of the firm, nor did he during the entire length of his job. He would not have recognized him face to face on the pedestrip — because Marlais chose not to be known. His mania for privacy transcended an ordinary taste for seclusion and approached obsession.

Angker held to no such aloofness. The panel to his office stood always wide. All day technicians in the adjoining workroom could look in to see him shouldering, driving, battering through his work; watch him barking orders into the telescreen, flourishing a clenched hand for emphasis.

Farrero stayed away from the office, appearing only for new assignments. He assumed his work was satisfactory. If not, he felt sure Angker would have fired him, and with gusto. However, the day he knocked at Angker's door to report on the Westgeller job, he knew he was in for trouble.

"Come in!" called Angker, not looking up. Farrero, who was somewhat deaf, turned up his hearing-aid and sauntered forward.

"Good morning," said Farrero.

Angker responded only with a brief glance upward.

Farrero dropped two strips of microfilm on the desk. "Ready for execution. I've shown them to Westgeller, got his O.K."

"Westgeller? I suppose he can pay for the place." Angker tipped the strips down the slot in his desk.

"Your credit office likes him," said Farrero. From where he stood, Angker's lowered and foreshortened face looked like a rudely molded mask. "He makes heavy glass," said Farrero. "The stuff tourist submarines are built from. He's also got a finger in Moon Mining."

The screen on the far wall glowed, projected the holographic image of a large solid house backed by a gloomy wall of fir trees. It was an old-fashioned house, with high gables and many chimneys, as if it were intended to fight year after year of winter snow. Its colors were a dark red, with gray and white trim, and the sun-cells of the roof glowed a rich burnished copper. Behind, the great fir trees marched almost up to the house; the trunks of many others could be seen dwindling off through the dim aisles. At the front a lawn rolled gently down to banks of bright flower-beds. It was clearly a Class III house.

"Ah...ah," Angker grunted. "Nice piece of work, Farrero. Where's the site?"

"Fifty miles from Minusinsk, on the Yenisei." Farrero dropped into a chair, crossed his legs. "Fifty-four degrees latitude."

"Take him hours to get there," commented Angker sourly.

"He says he likes it. Winter — snow — solitude. The untouched forests, wild-life, wolves, peasants, things like that. He's got a lifetime lease on three hundred acres."

Angker grunted again, leaned back in his chair. "What are the numbers?"

Farrero laid his head back against the cushion. "Our cost is a hundred thousand, add five thousand contingency cushion and fifteen percent profit comes to about a hundred twenty-one thousand. That's our bid."

Angker leveled a sudden under-eyebrow glance at Farrero, squared up in his seat. He pressed a button. A cutaway section of the first floor flicked upon the screen. He pressed again. The second floor. Again. Detailed wall plans. He looked up and the lines from his nostrils down seemed to gather, purse his mouth, pull it out into a hard lump.

"How do you fix on that figure?" He jerked a pencil toward the screen. "My guess is that you're fifty or sixty thousand low. That's a big house, with considerable detail."

"I really don't think so," said Farrero politely.

"What is the basis for your estimate?" inquired Angker, as gently.

Farrero clasped his hands around his knee. "There's a philosophical background to the figure."

"Philosophy?" cried Angker, in such a voice that Farrero turned down the volume on his hearing-aid. "But continue, if you will."

"Certainly. One of the shortcomings of modern civilization — ancient civilization too, for that matter — is that the average man never gets all he wants of the most desirable products, never makes his life fit his dreams. In the competent Type A man this lack creates incentive to earn more money: hence high productivity. In the incompetent inefficient Type B man it breeds resentment, dissatisfaction and low productivity. There are far more Type B's than Type A's; therefore, in the longest view we help ourselves by providing so-called 'dream'-merchandise at an affordable cost."

"I'm a Type X man," said Angker. "To me this all sounds like flapdoodle. Explain how I can fulfill my dreams and gain fifteen thousand profit from a house which I sell at sixty thousand dollars below cost."

"Certainly. We use new methods. I've explored the system carefully. It works."

"How?"

Farrero paused. "I, personally, am a Type A man. I want, and I hereby request, a five percent royalty in all houses built using my materials."

"Continue."

"First, please sign this memorandum."

Angker barely glanced at it. "Sure." He scrawled his name across the bottom.

"Fine," said Farrero. "Excellent. I'll give construction the go-ahead." He started to rise to his feet.

"Not so fast. How is all this accomplished?"

Farrero said: "Well, first of all, in North Siberia, land is inexpensive. We shoot carbolon piles into the permafrost — using a machine I've developed. We erect carbolon poles, tie on plumbing, wiring and ducts, pour a slab of coagulated mud. I can't reveal the exact nature of the binder just yet, but it's highly efficient. The slab is immediately finished with tile or hardwood. That's the first day's work. Next — and here is one of my innovations — the walls and partitions are formed around pre-standing doors, windows and fireplaces, rather than cutting them in and setting them after. We save three days here. On the third day the roof is dropped in place. This is, naturally, a pre-fab. Fixtures are installed, insulation is applied and the outer shell sprayed on. The fourth day sees the plot landscaped; a details crew takes over for a day or two. Then Westgeller moves in."

"If all goes well."

"No reason otherwise, except inclement weather."

Angker leaned abruptly forward, pointed a pencil at Farrero. "You shouldn't have given Westgeller the estimate till you checked with the office."

"That's what you're paying me for," said Farrero, with the glibness of forethought. "Designing, estimating, selling."

"Wrong. You are paid to work and also to represent the company's best interests. Assume that the system works. You've cost us a lot of money, all in order to finance your theories. I have theories of my own I want to finance and since I run the company, I get first choice."

"Your point is well-taken," said Farrero politely. "Still, it is a short-sighted view. When the human race as a whole benefits, we all benefit. I am a member of the League of Hope, and this is our basic doctrine."

"And you think it wise to finance this doctrine with my money?"

Farrero considered a moment. "There are two answers I could make to this, 'Yes' and 'No'. If I answered 'Yes', I could point out that you have wealth far more than ample for your needs. However, I will answer 'No'. My instructions are explicit: I am to quote prices which allow the company a fifteen percent profit, this is precisely what I have done."

When Angker was aroused, his dog-brown eyes glowed with russet lights. Now he put his hands on the edge of the desk, and Farrero, with an inward quiver, gazing deep into Angker's eyes, saw the russet flicker.

"Fifteen percent," said Angker, "is a rough basis for operation. However, you're supposed to exercise judgement. We guarantee our customers quality, nothing else. If our price suits 'em, fine. If it doesn't, there are thirty-nine other outfits with the same kind of license we've got."

"You forget," said Farrero, getting to his feet, "that what makes this saving is *my* private idea. I worked it out."

"On company time."

Farrero flushed. "I built a small-scale section with company equipment, for company protection — to check the idea, and see whether it was a lemon or not. The scheme was completely formulated before I even left the Institute. In any event, the patent is in my name."

"Well," said Angker heavily, "you'll have to sign it over to Marlais and Angker."

Farrero thrust his hands into his pockets. "Surely you're not serious."

"Farrero, how old are you?"

"Twenty-eight."

"You've put in four years at the Institute, studying Class III technique, right?"

"Exactly so."

"So it would be just four years wasted if you couldn't get a job with any Class III contractor."

"That's an odd thing to say," remarked Farrero. "It seems quite irrelevant. What do the other companies of the association have to do with this?"

"They are concerned in two ways. If Marlais and Angker suddenly cut prices, we dislocate the entire industry. They don't care how much money we make so long as we maintain the price structure."

"Short-sighted, to the extreme."

"Secondly, assume that you were no longer associated with Marlais and Angker. You would naturally apply for employment to another member of the association. Why? We are the only agencies licensed world-wide for Class III construction. When you applied, they would call me and ask: 'What about this chap Farrero?'"

"I would say, 'He is a very philosophical fellow. He belongs to the League of Human Decency —'"

"League of Hope."

"' — and wherever he sees a way to save money, he rushes out and grants these benefits to the customer without consulting the home office. A dear kind fellow, but also a pain in the head.' So the thirty-nine would tear up your application and that is the second reason why they are involved in this conversation."

"I see."

"Now, as to your process, it clearly has been developed while you worked for us; therefore it becomes our property. There are a thousand legal precedents to this effect."

"I devised this method, and dozens of others, while I was still at Tek."

"Where's the proof?"

"In the patent office."

"How old are the patents?"

Farrero waved his hand. "Irrelevant. My basic idea is to bring Class III homes down to the Class II price level, which is of course not a patentable process."

"It's not even sensible. If anyone wants to pay Class II prices, let 'em buy Class II houses — from our affiliate XAB Company."

Farrero held out his hands. "Does public welfare mean anything to you, at all? Do you want to take money without giving anything? That's the code of the pickpocket!"

Angker touched a button on his desk. "Dave? Ernest Farrero will shortly be passing by your office, on his way out. Have his termination check ready. He is, as of now, fired."

"Very good, sir."

Farrero said hotly: "That is a foolish and spiteful act! If you can't discuss abstract ideas without resorting to such crude tactics, you are in sorry shape, and deserve to lose money! In fact, I shall make it my business to see that you do so."

"Oh? You won't find a job anywhere around the association, I assure you of that."

"An idle threat. I plan to go into business for myself."

"Have you forgotten the little detail of the license? You haven't got one. You can't get one. There's none being issued. Without a license you can't build and sell a doghouse anywhere on Earth, Mars, or the Moon."

Farrero smilingly shook his head. "If you were right — which isn't always the case, as witness your attitude toward the League of Hope — that would seem definite and very discouraging."

"You can bet your dirty lavender socks it's definite and discouraging! Go back to Tek and grow up!"

"Your insults and threats are childish, Mr. Angker. I will now make a prediction, which you can regard as a counter-threat, if you choose. You have just heard one of my innovative concepts. I have several others, and before I'm done I'll have cost you so much money, you'll wish you'd taken me in as a partner. Remember that, Mr. Angker."

Farrero turned off his hearing-aid and departed the office.

Angker touched another button. A soft voice said "Yes?"

"Did you hear this last interview?"

"No," said Marlais.

"I'll run it back for you — quite a lot in it." He adjusted the recorder and replayed the interview.

"What do you think?" Angker asked the unseen Marlais.

"Well, Douane," presently came Marlais' soft voice, "you probably could have handled him more subtly…" His voice trailed off to a whisper. Then: "We'll have a hard time proving ownership of any patents. Still, it may be for the best. The industry is stable. We're all making money. No telling where disruption might take us. Perhaps we'd better call a meeting of the association, lay our cards on the table. I think everyone will contract neither to hire Farrero nor use his process."

Angker made a doubtful noise. "I said so, but I'm not so sure."

Marlais spoke with a gentle edge to his voice. "There are forty companies in the association. The chance of Farrero's approaching any given firm is one in thirty-nine. Consequently, every operator, to protect himself, will obligate himself."

"Very well. I'll get the meeting set up."

The next day Angker instructed his secretary: "Get me Westgeller."

"Yes, sir…There's a call coming in for you right now, Mr. Angker. In fact, it's Mr. Westgeller himself."

"Put him on."

Laurin Westgeller's face appeared on Angker's screen — fat, friendly, with twinkling blue eyes. "Mr. Angker," said Westgeller, "I've decided to have you go no further with my job. You can send me a bill for your work to date."

Angker sat glowering at the image. "What's the matter? Price too high?"

"No," replied Westgeller. "Price doesn't enter into the picture. In fact, I plan to spend rather more — perhaps a million."

Angker's jaw slacked. "Who... I mean, shall I send out a consultant?"

"No," said Laurin Westgeller, "I've already signed — with one of your late employees, Mr. Farrero. He now is in business for himself, as I guess you know."

Angker stared. "Farrero? He has no license to build! The minute he drives a stake into the ground, he's liable for prosecution."

Westgeller nodded. "So he informed me. Thank you, however, for your advice. Good day." The screen blurred, sank through the pink after-image to blank ground-glass.

Angker blurted the news through to Marlais.

"There's nothing we can do until Farrero tries to fulfill the contract," said Marlais. "When and if he makes an illegal move, then we'll file charges."

"He's got something up his sleeve. Farrero's only part crazy."

"Nobody who gets a contract for a million is crazy," said the soft voice. "All we can do is wait. You might put an investigator on him."

"I've already done so."

Two hours later, Angker's telescreen buzzer sounded.

"Yes?" snarled Angker.

"A Mr. Lescovic, sir."

"Put him on."

The face of the investigator appeared.

"Well?"

"Farrero's slipped us."

"How did this happen?"

"He walked through the Transport Union, and into a public lavatory. I waited across the lobby, watching the detector. He showed very positive. When he didn't move after ten minutes, I got suspicious and went to look. His clothes were hung on a hook, with the radiator attached. Farrero gave us the clean slip."

"Find him!"

"There are four operatives on the case now, sir."

"Call me as soon as you get anything."

✳

Six months later Angker's call-button sounded. Angker hardly looked up from a model of a Caribbean island. "Yes?"

"Mr. Lescovic calling."

"Put him through."

The detective's face appeared on the screen. "Farrero's back in town."

"When did he get back?"

"Well, evidently during the week."

"Did you find out where he's been?"

"No word on that."

"What's he doing now?"

"He's calling on Franklin Kerry, of Kerry Armatures. He's been there now about two hours."

"Kerry! He's one of our clients! At least he's looking over our bid… Anything more on Farrero?"

"He's got plenty of money — registered at the Gloriana."

Angker said, "Hold on a minute." He flipped a switch, reported to Marlais.

Marlais was noncommittal. "We've nothing to go on. We'll have to wait, see what happens."

Angker brought back Lescovic's face. "Watch him. Report everything he does. Find out what he wants with Kerry."

"Yes, sir." The screen faded.

Angker slammed into Marlais' office. "Well, he's done it again."

Marlais had been sitting in half-darkness, gazing out across the many-tiered city. He slowly turned his head.

"I presume you mean Farrero."

Angker stomped back and forth. "Glochmeinder this time. Last month it was Crane. Before that, Haggarty. He doesn't go near the small ones, but just let us get wind of a big account —"

"What did Glochmeinder say?"

"Just what Kerry and Crane and Haggarty and Desplains and Churchward and Klenko and Westgeller said. He's given his contract to Farrero, and that's all he'll say."

Marlais rose to his feet, rubbed his chin. "There's a leak in the office. Somewhere."

The muscles roped around Angker's mouth. "I've been trying to find it." He slowly clenched and unclenched his hands.

Marlais turned back to the window. "No word from the detective?"

"I gave you his last report. Farrero's been ordering all over the world — construction materials and landscaping supplies. There's not a job going anywhere that isn't legitimate and licensed."

"Clever," mused Marlais, toying with the massive blue spinel he used for a paper-weight.

"He made a threat and he made it good," gloomed Angker. "He's cost us millions."

Marlais smiled wanly. "Just so."

For a moment there was silence. Angker paced the floor heavily. Marlais stared through the window.

"Well," said Marlais, "something must be done."

Farrero found himself an office, a two-room suite in the Sky-rider Tower, facing west across Amargosa Park, with the Pylon of All Nations thrusting high in the distance. He also found himself a receptionist: Miss Flora Gustafsson, who claimed Scandinavian ancestry, and for evidence displayed birch-blonde hair, eyes blue as Geiranger Fjord. She was hardly bigger than a kitten, but everything about her matched, and she was efficient with detectives.

The teleview buzzed. Flora reached over, screened the caller. "Oh, good afternoon, Mr. Westgeller." Indeed, Mr. Westgeller's round and ruddy features occupied the screen. "I'll put you through to Mr. Farrero."

"Thank you," said Westgeller. Flora looked sharply at the image, buzzed Farrero.

"Hello, Mr. Westgeller," said Farrero. "What can I do for you?"

"Farrero, an old friend of mine, John Etcheverry, wants to build, and I'm sending him around to see you."

"Ah, fine, Mr. Westgeller. I'll try to accommodate him, though we're pretty busy."

"Good day, Farrero," and Westgeller abruptly left the screen. Farrero sat stroking his chin, smiling faintly. Then he went into the outer room, kissed Flora.

✳

John Etcheverry was about sixty, tall, thin, pale as raw dough. He had a large egg-shaped head, sparse white hair that wandered across his scalp in damp unruly tendrils. His eyes, set in dark concavities, never seemed to blink. He had large ears, with long pale lobes and a long pale nose that twitched when he spoke.

"Have a seat," said Farrero. "I understand you're planning to build."

"That's right. May I smoke?"

"Definitely not."

Etcheverry gave Farrero a startled glance, shrugged in not the best of grace.

"What do you have in mind? I might as well warn you that my prices are high. I deliver, but it costs a lot of money."

Etcheverry made a brief gesture with his fingers. "I want a country place, with absolute seclusion and quiet. I'm prepared to pay for it."

Farrero tapped the desk with a pencil once or twice, laid it down, sat back, quietly watched Etcheverry.

Etcheverry went on. "Westgeller tells me you've satisfied him very well. In fact, that's all he'll say."

Farrero nodded. "It's in the contract. I needed time to protect myself, especially from my ex-employers Marlais and Angker: a pair of scoundrels."

"Oh? I've heard that they were most reputable."

"To the contrary. Angker is a surly stupid lummox, with the morals of a hyena. Marlais is atrociously ugly, and is ashamed to show himself. Neither trusts the other; they quarrel like lunatics. Their company is on the teetering verge of bankruptcy. They do shoddy work, disregard warranties and pad their bills."

"Hm," said Etcheverry. "That is a far-reaching denunciation."

"It's only the tip of the iceberg." Farrero adjusted his hearing-aid. "Speak up, Mr. Etcheverry, if you please. You speak softly and I find it hard to hear you."

"Well, back to why I'm here. I'd like to see an example of your work. Is your secrecy so total that —"

Farrero interrupted. "The time for secrecy is about over. At the moment I'm only trying to protect myself from new houses. Class III builders won't see much new business for a long time, until I sell eleven hundred and thirty-two more estates."

"Curious! How do you arrive at that number?"

"No matter, not just now. Assuming that I'm right you can appreciate my need for secrecy. Marlais and Angker are the worst. They went so far as to hire detectives. They are capable of any underhanded trick. In fact — Flora! Get me Westgeller at his office."

Etcheverry pulled reflectively at his nose.

A moment passed. Flora's face appeared on the screen. "Mr. Westgeller hasn't been in his office today."

Farrero turned back to Etcheverry. "It's a habit left over from the early stages of the game. Endless caution, endless foresight. It was necessary then. Now I can relax."

Etcheverry delicately inspected the tips of his shoes. "Before we continue, may I see your contractor's license?"

"I don't have any."

"Then you build illegally?"

"Naturally not."

Etcheverry pursed his lips. "You'll have to explain."

Farrero stared thoughtfully out the window. "Why not? How much time can you spare?"

"You mean — ?"

"Right now."

"Well … There are no important demands on my time."

"If you can give me the rest of the day, I'll do better than explain — I'll demonstrate."

"Fine." Etcheverry rose to his feet. "I'll admit that you've aroused my curiosity."

Farrero called a cab. "County Field," he told the driver.

At County Field, Farrero took Etcheverry to a small space-boat. "Jump in." He followed the stooped figure into the cabin.

Etcheverry adjusted himself gingerly to the cushions. "If you haven't a license to build, I hope at least you have a license to fly."

"I have. Check it if you care to. It's under the aerator."

"I'll take your word for it."

They rode up off the seared field: a hundred, two hundred miles, and earth blurred below. A thousand, five thousand, ten thousand miles — twenty, thirty thousand miles, and Farrero kept a close watch on his radar screen. "Should be about here now." A pip showed yellow-green. "There it is." He swerved the boat, jetted off in the new direction. After a minute: "You can see it below, off to the left."

Etcheverry, craning his gaunt neck, saw a small irregular asteroid, perhaps a mile in diameter. Farrero edged down the boat, lowered with hardly a jolt on a patch of white sand.

Etcheverry grabbed Farrero's arm. "Are you crazy? Don't open that port! That's space out there!"

Farrero shook his head. "It's air, at fifteen pounds pressure, twenty percent oxygen. Look at the barometer."

Etcheverry looked, watched numbly as Farrero flung open the port and jumped out of the boat. Etcheverry followed. "But…There's gravity here."

Farrero climbed to the top of a little hillock, waved an arm to Etcheverry. "Come on up."

Etcheverry stalked slowly up the slope.

"This is Westgeller's estate," said Farrero. "His private world. Look, there's his house."

Westgeller's house sat on a wide flat field covered with emerald-green turf. A lake glistened in the sunlight; a white crane stood fishing among the rushes. Trees lined the plain, and Etcheverry heard birds singing across the distance.

The house was a long single-story structure, built of timber planks. There were many windows, and below each a window-box overflowing with geraniums. Beach umbrellas stood like other, larger, flowers beside a swimming pool.

Farrero squinted across the field. "Westgeller is at home. I see his space-boat. Like to call on him? Might like to talk things over with your old friend, eh, Mr. Etcheverry?"

Etcheverry gave him a sharp side-glance, then said slowly: "Perhaps it would be just as well if —"

Farrero laughed. "Save your excuses. They are no good. You probably don't know I read lips. I was stone deaf the first ten years of my life.

When you flashed Westgeller's picture on my screen, his voice saying, 'I'm sending over my dear old friend Etcheverry,' and his lips saying, 'I've decided to have you stop work on my job, Mr. Angker,' I smelled a rat — a very large rat by the name of Marlais."

The thin man gave Farrero a quick side-glance. Realizing his lack of options, he said, "Yes, I'm Marlais. Impressive operation you've got."

"I'm making money," said Farrero.

Marlais looked around the toy world. "You're spending it too." He stamped his foot on the ground. "You've got me beat. How do you lick gravity? Why doesn't the air all blow away? Seems as if I'm — oh, about normal weight."

"You're a little lighter. Gravity here is three per cent less than on Earth."

"But," and Marlais looked from horizon to close horizon, calculated. "A half-mile in diameter to eight thousand for Earth, and the gravity is the same. Why?"

"For one thing," said Farrero, "you're closer to the center of gravity — by almost four thousand miles."

Marlais reached down, plucked a blade of grass, inspected it curiously.

"All new," said Farrero. "The trees were brought here at no slight effort by Lindvist — he's a Danish ecologist — and me. He figures out how many bees I need to fertilize the flowers, how many earthworms, how many trees to oxygenate the air."

Marlais nodded his head. "A most appealing concept."

"There won't be a millionaire living on Earth in another twenty years," said Farrero. "I'll have sold them all private planets. Some will want big places. I can furnish them."

"Incidentally, where did you get this one?"

"Out in space a ways."

Marlais nodded sagely. "That's probably where Marlais and Angker will go to find theirs."

Farrero turned his head slowly. Marlais met his gaze blandly.

"So — you think you'll cut in?"

"Of course. Why not?"

"You think," Farrero went on meditatively, "that you'll cash in on my idea. You've got all the equipment, all the technicians necessary for a quick skim at the cream. Maybe you'll even get some law barring non-licensees from the game."

"I'd be a fool if I didn't."

"Maybe yes. Maybe no. Like to see another of my jobs? This is Westgeller's. I'll show you Desplains'."

They re-entered the space-boat. Farrero clamped the port, pulsed power through the jets. Westgeller's world fell away beneath them.

They reached Desplains' world half an hour later. "Eventually," said Farrero, "space around Earth will be peppered thick with these little estates. There'll be laws regulating their orbits, minimum distances set for their spacing." He touched the controls; the space-boat drifted across Desplains' sky and settled on a rocky outcrop.

Marlais unsealed the port, angled his skinny legs to the ground. "*Phew*," he grunted, "Desplains must intend to raise orchids — positively dank."

Farrero grinned, loosened his jacket. "He hasn't moved in yet. We're having a little trouble with the atmosphere. He wants clouds, and we're experimenting with the humidity." He looked up. "It's easy to get a muggy high overcast — but Desplains wants big fluffs of cumulus. Well, we'll try. Personally I don't think there's enough total volume of air."

Marlais looked into the sky too, where Earth hung as a huge bright crescent. He licked his pale old lips.

Farrero laughed. "Makes a man feel naked, doesn't it?" He looked across the little world to the queerly close horizon — barely a stone's throw off, so it seemed — then back to the sweep of sky, with the crescent of Earth dominating a new moon behind. "Out here," he said, "beauty — grandeur, whatever you choose to call it — comes a lot at a time."

Marlais gingerly perched himself on a slab of rock. "Exotic place, certainly."

"Desplains is an exotic man," said Farrero. "But he's got the money, and I don't care if he wants the rocks upholstered with rabbit fur." He hopped up beside Marlais, and indicated a clump of trees. "That's his bayou. Flora from Africa and the Matto Grosso. Fauna from here and there, including a very rare Tasmanian ibis. It's pretty, and certainly wild enough — connecting ponds, with overhanging trees. The moss hasn't got a good start yet, and there isn't quite the authentic smell, but give it time. Behind there's a jungle — well, call it a swamp — cut with a lot of waterways. When the flowers all start blooming, it'll be quite pleasant."

"Individual worlds to suit any conceivable whim," murmured Marlais.

"That's it exactly," said Farrero. "We've got our largest world — about ten miles in diameter — sold to a Canadian yachtsman."

"Fred Ableman," said Marlais dryly. "He canceled his contract with us about two months ago."

"I wanted to reserve it for a League of Hope headquarters, but they wouldn't pay the price. People of this sort are always the most careful with their money."

"When you worked for Marlais and Angker, I recall that you advocated a different philosophy."

"That's true. Circumstances have changed, and have dictated a different philosophy. It's easiest to be generous with someone else's money. It's one of the great luxuries of the public administrator; his generosity with public money knows no bounds. In any event, Fred Ableman wants his world all ocean, with plenty of wind to sail his boats. He wants islands here and there, with beaches, coral banks, pretty fish."

"Coconut palms too, I expect."

"Right — but no sharks. We won't have it completed for another year and a half. It's heavy and unwieldy — difficult to bring out and get established in an orbit. And we need a great deal of water."

"Where do you get the water? You can't bring it out from Earth."

Farrero shook his head. "We mine the Hipparchus ice floe. Every time the moon comes in apposition we shoot across a few big chunks. Slow but sure. It costs a lot, but Ableman makes too much money for his own good. Anyway, how could he spend the money to better purpose?"

Marlais pursed his lips. "I expect you get some strange specifications."

"There's a man named Klenko, who made his money in fashion design. He's responsible for those whirling things women were wearing a year or two ago on their heads. Strange man, strange world. The air is full of thirty-foot glass bubbles, floating loose. Glass bubbles everywhere — topaz, blue, red, violet, green — high and low. It's a hazard trying to land a space-boat. He's got a fluorescent forest — activators in the sap. When he turns ultraviolet on it, the leaves glow — silver, pale-green, orange. We built him a big pavilion overhanging a lake. Luminous fish in the lake."

"He evidently plans a lot of night life."

"He wants nothing but night. His world won't have any axial spin at all, when we get it trued in its orbit. He's planning some rather odd entertainments."

Marlais shrugged. "If a man owns his world, I suppose he makes the laws."

"That is Klenko's theory."

"So far, so good. But how do you beat gravity? Artificial gravity has never been discovered."

Farrero nodded. "True."

"Well — whatever the system is, I imagine it will work for Marlais and Angker too."

"So it would," said Farrero. "Only Marlais and Angker have come to the party late. I don't especially want to drive them into bankruptcy; I don't imagine I could. There'll always be a few oddments of Class III construction on Earth for the cautious and conventional. But I'll be licking cream off the top for a long time to come."

Marlais shook his head, and a spark appeared back in the depths of his eyes. "You have not quite grasped the idea, my friend. We don't plan to take the back seat. We have the connections, the equipment, the staff. We can bring the asteroids out here cheaper than you can, and undersell you four ways from Sunday. We'll even take losses if we need to. However you handle gravity, our engineers can duplicate the conditions."

"My dear Mr. Marlais," said Farrero, "do you think I'd leave a loop-hole for you and the other bandits? Have you ever heard of the Space Claims Act?"

"Certainly. It defines and authorizes mining development of the asteroids."

"Under this act I've filed on eleven hundred and thirty-two asteroids — of a peculiar nature. The little black pebble by your right foot: that shiny one, like flint. Pick it up."

Marlais reached, grasped, strained. His mouth slacked in amazement. He pulled again, till his skinny old arms quivered, creaked. He glanced up at Farrero. "It's glued down!"

"It weighs several tons, I expect," said Farrero. "It's star stuff. Matter crystallized at tremendous pressure in the heart of a star. A little bit turns on a lot of gravity. Somehow or other, eleven hundred and thirty-two chunks of the stuff drifted into an orbit around the sun — not too far out from Earth. They're small and dark and not heavy enough to cause any noticeable perturbations. But when you stand on their surface, the center of gravity is close enough to give you Earth weight. I've filed on every one of those chunks. Some I'll have to lump together, others I'll have to crust over with a few miles of ordinary matter to reduce gravity. It diminishes, you know, as the square of the distance from the center of mass." Farrero opened the port of his space-boat, motioned Marlais in. "I know where you can get all the heavy matter you can use."

Marlais wordlessly climbed into the boat. He eyed Farrero lambently. "Where?"

Farrero clamped the port, swung the power-arm, and Desplains' world fell off below.

"If I were you, I'd try the Alpha Centauri System first. There's sure to be all sorts of debris floating around. If you're lucky it won't be hot."

"Never mind the jokes," said Marlais. "Let's get back to Earth. I've got much to tell Angker. I don't suppose you want to work for us again, at a raise in salary?"

"No."

"I thought not."

Ten minutes later Marlais brought out his check-book and wrote. He handed the check to Farrero. "Half a million deposit on one of your worlds, about like Westgeller's. I'd be a fool not to get in on the ground floor."

THE TEN BOOKS

THEY WERE AS ALONE as it is possible for living man to be in the black gulf between the stars. Far astern shone the suns of the home worlds — ahead the outer stars and galaxies in a fainter ghostly glimmer.

The cabin was quiet. Betty Welstead sat watching her husband at the assay table, her emotions tuned to his. When the centrifuge scale indicated heavy metal and Welstead leaned forward she leaned forward too in unconscious sympathy. When he burnt scrapings in the spectroscope and read *Lead* from the brightest pattern and chewed at his lips Betty released her pent-up breath, fell back in her seat.

Ralph Welstead stood up, a man of medium height — rugged, tough-looking — with hair and skin and eyes the same tawny color. He brushed the whole clutter of rock and ore into the waste chute and Betty followed him with her eyes.

Welstead said sourly, "We'd be millionaires if that asteroid had been inside the Solar system. Out here, unless it's pure platinum or uranium, it's not worth mining."

Betty broached a subject which for two months had been on the top of her mind. "Perhaps we should start to swing back in."

Welstead frowned, stepped up into the observation dome. Betty watched after him anxiously. She understood very well that the instinct of the explorer as much as the quest for minerals had brought them out so far.

Welstead stepped back down into the cabin. "There's a star ahead —" he put a finger into the three-dimensional chart "— this one right here, Eridanus two thousand nine hundred and thirty-two. Let's make a quick check — and then we'll head back in."

Betty nodded, suddenly happy. "Suits me." She jumped up, and together they went to the screen. He aimed the catch-all vortex, dialed the hurrying blur to stability and the star pulsed out like a white-hot coin. A single planet made up the entourage.

"Looks about Earth-size," said Welstead, interest in his voice, and Betty's heart sank a trifle. He tuned the circuit finer, turned up the magnification and the planet leapt at them. "Look at that atmosphere! *Thick!*"

He swiveled across the jointed arm holding the thermocouple and together they bent over the dial.

"Nineteen degrees Centigrade. About Earth-norm. Let's look at that atmosphere. You know, dear, we might have something tremendous here! Earth-size, Earth temperature..." His voice fell off in a mutter as he peered through the spectroscope, flipping screen after screen past the pattern from the planet. He stood up, cast Betty a swift exultant glance, then squinted in sudden reflection. "Better make sure before we get too excited."

Betty felt no excitement. She watched without words as Welstead thumbed through the catalogue.

"*Whee!*" yelled Welstead, suddenly a small boy. "No listing! It's ours!" And Betty's heart melted at the news. Delay, months of delay, while Welstead explored the planet, charted its oceans and continents, classified its life. At the same time, a spark of her husband's enthusiasm caught fire in her brain and interest began to edge aside her gloom.

"We'll name it 'Welstead'," he said. "Or, no — 'Elizabeth' for you. A planet of your own! Some day there'll be cities and millions of people. And every time they write a letter or throw a shovelful of dirt or a ship lands — they'll use your name."

"No, dear," she said. "Don't be ridiculous. We'll call it 'Welstead' — for us both."

They felt an involuntary pang of disappointment later on when they found the planet already inhabited, and by men.

Yet their reception astonished them as much as the basic discovery of the planet and its people. Curiosity, hostility might have been expected...

They had been in no hurry to land, preferring to fall into an orbit just above the atmosphere, the better to study the planet and its inhabitants.

It looked to be a cheerful world. There were a thousand kinds of forest, jungle, savannah. Sunny rivers coursed green fields. A thousand lakes and three oceans glowed blue. To the far north and far south snowfields glittered, dazzled. Such cities as they found — the world seemed sparsely settled — merged indistinguishably with the countryside.

They were wide low cities, very different from the clanging hives of Earth, and lay under the greenery like carvings in alabaster or miraculous snowflakes. Betty, in whose nature ran a strong streak of the romantic, was entranced.

"They look like cities of Paradise — cities in a dream!"

Welstead said reflectively, "They're evidently not backward. See that cluster of long gray buildings off to the side? Those are factories."

Betty voiced a doubt which had been gradually forming into words. "Do you think that they might — resent our landing? If they've gone to the trouble of creating a secret — well, call it Utopia — they might not want to be discovered."

Welstead turned his head, gazed at her eye to eye. "Do you want to land?" he asked soberly.

"Why, yes — if you do. If you don't think it's dangerous."

"I don't know whether it's dangerous or not. A people as enlightened as those cities would seem to indicate would hardly maltreat strangers."

Betty searched the face of the planet. "I think it would be safe."

Welstead laughed. "I'm game. We've got to die sometime. Why not out here?"

He jumped up to the controls, nosed the ship down.

"We'll land right in their laps, right in the middle of that big city down there."

Betty looked at him questioningly.

"No sense sneaking down out in the wilds," said Welstead. "If we're landing we'll land with a flourish."

"And if they shoot us for our insolence?"

"Call it Fate."

They bellied down into a park in the very center of the city. From the observation dome Welstead glimpsed hurrying knots of people.

"Go to the port, Betty. Open it just a crack and show yourself. I'll stay at the controls. One false move, one dead cat heaved at us, and we'll be back in space so fast they won't remember we arrived."

Thousands of men and women of all ages had surrounded the ship, all shouting, all agitated by strong emotion.

"They're throwing flowers!" Betty gasped. She opened the port and stood in the doorway and the people below shouted, chanted, wept. Feeling rather ridiculous, Betty waved, smiled.

She turned to look back up at Welstead. "I don't know what we've done to deserve all this but we're heroes. Maybe they think we're somebody else."

Welstead craned his neck through the observation dome. "They look healthy — normal."

"They're beautiful," said Betty. "All of them."

The throng opened, a small group of elderly men and women approached. The leader, a white-haired man, tall, lean, with much the same face as Michelangelo's Jehovah, stood forth.

"Welcome!" he called resonantly. "Welcome from the people of Haven!"

Betty stared, and Welstead clambered down from the controls. The words were strangely pronounced, the grammar was archaic — but it was the language of Earth.

The white-haired man spoke on, without calculation, as if delivering a speech of great familiarity. "We have waited two hundred and seventy-one years for your coming, for the deliverance you will bring us."

Deliverance? Welstead considered the word. "Don't see much to deliver 'em from," he muttered aside to Betty. "The sun's shining, there's flowers on all the trees, they look well fed — a lot more enthusiastic than I do. Deliver 'em from what?"

Betty was climbing down to the ground and Welstead followed.

"Thanks for the welcome," said Welstead, trying not to sound like a visiting politician. "We're glad to be here. It's a wonderful experience, coming unexpectedly on a world like this."

The white-haired man bowed gravely. "Naturally you must be

curious — as curious as we are about the civilized universe. But for the present, just one question for the ears of our world. How goes it with Earth?"

Welstead rubbed his chin, acutely conscious of the thousands of eyes, the utter silence.

"Earth," he said, "goes about as usual. There's the same seasons, the same rain, sunshine, frost and wind." And the people of Haven breathed in his words as devoutly as if they were the purest poetry. "Earth is still the center of the Cluster and there's more people living on Earth than ever before. More noise, more nuisance..."

"Wars? New governments? How far does science reach?"

Welstead considered. "Wars? None to speak of — not since the Hieratic League broke up. The government still governs, uses lots of statistical machinery. There's still graft, robbery, inefficiency, if that's what you mean.

"Science — that's a big subject. We know a lot but we don't know a lot more, the way it's always been. Everything considered it's the same Earth it's always been — some good, a lot of bad."

He paused, and the pent breath of the listeners went in a great sigh. The white-haired man nodded again, serious, sober — though evidently infected with the excitement that fired his fellows.

"No more for the present! You'll be tired and there's much time for talk. May I offer you the hospitality of my house?"

Welstead looked uncertainly at Betty. Instinct urged him not to leave his ship.

"Or if you'd prefer to remain aboard..." suggested the man of Haven.

"No," said Welstead. "We'll be delighted." If harm were intended — as emphatically did not seem likely — their presence aboard the ship would not prevent it. He craned his neck, looked here and there for the officialdom that would be bumptiously present on Earth.

"Is there anyone we should report to? Any law we'll be breaking by parking our ship here?"

The white-haired man laughed. "What a question! I am Alexander Clay, Mayor of this city Mytilene and Guide of Haven. By my authority and by common will you are free of anything the planet can offer you. Your ship will not be molested."

He led them to a wide low car and Betty was uncomfortably conscious of her blue shorts, rumpled and untidy by comparison with the many-colored tunics of the women in the crowd.

Welstead was interested in the car as providing a gauge of Haven's technics. Built of shiny gray metal it hung a foot above the ground, without the intervention of wheels. He gave Clay a startled look. "Antigravity? Your fortune's made."

Clay shook his head indulgently. "Magnetic fields, antipathetic to the metal in the road. Is it not a commonplace on Earth?"

"No," said Welstead. "The theory, of course, is well-known but there is too much opposition, too many roads to dig up. We still use wheels."

Clay said reflectively, "The force of tradition. The continuity which generates the culture of races. The stream we have been so long lost from..."

Welstead shot him a sidelong glance. Clay was entirely serious.

The car had been sliding down the road at rather high speed through vistas of wonderful quiet and beauty. Every direction showed a new and separate enchantment — a glade surrounded by great trees, a small home of natural wood, a cluster of public buildings around a plaza, a terrace checkered with trees and lined with many-colored shops.

Occasionally there were touches of drama, such as the pylon at the end of a wide avenue. It rose two hundred feet into the air, a structure of concrete, bronze and black metal, and it bore the heroic figure of a man grasping vainly for a star.

Welstead craned his neck like a tourist. "Magnificent!"

Clay assented without enthusiasm. "I suppose it's not discreditable. Of course, to you, fresh from the worlds of civilization —" He left the sentence unfinished. "Excuse me, while I call my home." He bent his head to a telephone.

Betty said in Welstead's ear, "This is a city every planner on Earth would sell his soul to build."

Welstead grunted. "Remember Halleck?" he muttered. "He was a city planner. He wanted to tear down a square mile of slums in Lanchester, eighteen stories high on the average, nothing but airless three-room apartments.

"First the real estate lobby tore into him, called him a Chaoticist. A rumor circulated among his friends that he was morally degenerate. The poor devils that lived there tried to lynch him because they'd be evicted. The Old Faithfuls read him out of the party because they pulled the votes of the district. The slums are still there and Halleck's selling farm implements on Arcturus Five."

Betty looked off through the trees. "Maybe Haven will turn out to be an object lesson for the rest of the cluster."

Welstead shrugged. "Maybe, maybe not. Peace and seclusion are not something you can show to a million people — because it isn't peace and seclusion any more."

Betty sat up straighter in her seat. "The only way to convince the unbelievers is by showing them, setting them an example. Do you think that if the Lanchester slum-dwellers saw this city they'd go back to their three-room apartments without wanting to do something about it?"

"If they saw this city," said Welstead, "they'd never leave Haven. By hook or crook, stowaway or workaway, they'd emigrate."

"Include me in the first wave!" said Betty indignantly.

The car turned into a leafy tunnel, crossed a carpet of bright green turf, stopped by a house built of dark massive wood. Four high gables in a row overlooked a terrace, where a stream followed its natural bed. The house looked spacious, comfortable — rather like the best country villas of Earth and the garden planets without the sense of contrived effect, the strain, the staging.

"My home," said Clay. He slid back a door of waxed blond wood, ushered them into an entry carpeted with golden rattan, walled with a fabric the color of the forest outside. A bench of glowing dark wood crossed a wall under a framed painting. From no apparent source light flooded the room, like water in a tank.

"One moment," said Clay with a trace of embarrassment. "My home is poor and makeshift enough without exposing it to your eyes at its worst." He was clearly sincere; this was no conventional deprecation.

He started away, paused and said to his half-comprehending guests, "I must apologize for our backwardness but we have no facilities for housing notable guests, no great inns or embassies or state-houses such as must add to the dignity of life on Earth. I can only offer you the hospitality of my home."

Welstead and Betty both protested. "We don't deserve as much. After all we're only a pair of fly-by-night prospectors."

Clay smiled and they could see that he had been put more at his ease. "You're the link between Haven and civilization — the most important visitors we've ever had. Excuse me." He departed.

Betty went to the picture on the wall, a simple landscape — the slope of a hill, a few trees, a distant range of mountains. Welstead, with small artistic sensibility, looked around for the source of the light — without success. He joined Betty beside the picture. She said half-breathlessly, "This is a — I'm afraid to say it — a masterpiece."

Welstead squinted, trying to understand the basis of his wife's awe and wonderment. Indeed the picture focused his eyes, drew them in and around the frame, infused him with a pleasant exhilaration, a warmth and serenity.

Clay, returning, noticed their interest. "What do you think of it?" he asked.

"I think it's — exceedingly well done," said Betty, at a loss for words which would convey her admiration without sounding fulsome.

Clay shook his head ruefully, turned away. "You need not praise an inconsequentiality out of courtesy, Mrs. Welstead. We know our deficiencies. Your eyes have seen the Giottos, the Rembrandts, the Cézannes. This must seem a poor thing."

Betty began to remonstrate but halted. Words evidently would not convince Clay — or perhaps a convention of his society prompted him to belittle the works of his people and it might be discourteous to argue too vehemently.

"Your quarters are being prepared," Clay told them. "I've also ordered fresh clothing for you both as I see yours are stained with travel."

Betty blushed, smoothed the legs of her blue shorts. Welstead sheepishly brushed at his faded blouse. He reached in his pocket, pulled out a bit of gravel. "From an asteroid I prospected a few weeks ago." He twisted it around in his fingers. "Nothing but granite, with garnet inclusions."

Clay took the bit of rock, inspected it with a peculiar reverence. "May I keep this?"

"Why, of course."

Clay laid the bit of stone on a silver plate. "You will not understand what this small stone symbolizes to us of Haven. Interstellar travel — our goal, our dream for two hundred and seventy-one years."

The recurrence of the period two hundred and seventy-one years! Welstead calculated. That put them back into the Era of the Great Excursives, when the over-under space-drive had first come into use, when men drove pell-mell through the galaxy like bees through a field of flowers and human culture flared through space like a super-nova.

Clay led them through a large room, simple in effect, rich in detail. Welstead's vision was not analytical enough to catch every particular at first. He sensed overall tones of tan, brown, mellow blue, watery green, in the wood, fabric, glass, pottery — the colors combined to marvellous effect with the waxy umber gleam of natural wood. At the end of the room a case held ten large books bound in black leather and these, by some indefinable emphasis, seemed to bear the significance of an icon.

They passed through a passage open along one side into a garden filled with flowers, low trees, tame birds. Clay showed them into a long apartment streaming with sunlight.

"Your bath is through the door," said Clay. "Fresh clothes are laid out on the bed. When you are rested I shall be in the main hall. Please be at leisure — the house is yours."

They were alone. Betty sighed happily, sank down on the bed. "Isn't it wonderful, dear?"

"It's queer," said Welstead, standing in the middle of the room.

"What's queer?"

"Mainly why these people, apparently gifted and efficient, act so humble, so self-deprecating."

"They look confident."

"They *are* confident. Yet as soon as the word Earth is mentioned it's like saying Alakland to an exiled Lak. There's nothing like it."

Betty shrugged, began to remove her clothes. "There's probably some very simple explanation. Right now I'm tired of speculating. I'm for that bath. Water, water, water! *Tons* of it!"

✳

They found Clay in the long hall with his pleasant-faced wife, his four youngest children, whom he gravely introduced.

Welstead and Betty seated themselves on a divan and Clay poured them small china cups of pale yellow-green wine, then settled back in his own seat.

"First I'll explain our world of Haven to you — or have you surmised our plight?"

Welstead said, "I guess a colony was planted here and forgotten — lost."

Clay smiled sadly. "Our beginnings were rather more dramatic. Two hundred and seventy-one years ago the passenger packet *Etruria*, en route to Rigel, went out of control. According to the story handed down to us the bus-bars fused inside the drive-box. If the case were opened the fields would collapse. If it were not, the ship would fly until there was no more energy."

Welstead said, "That was a common accident in the old days. Usually the engineer cut away the thrust-blocks on one side of the hull. Then the ship flew in circles until help arrived."

Clay made a wry sad grimace. "No one on the *Etruria* thought of that. The ship left the known universe and finally passed close to a planet that seemed capable of sustaining life. The sixty-three aboard took to the life-boats and so landed on Haven.

"Thirty-four men, twenty-five women, four children — ranging in age from Dorothy Pell, eight, to Vladimir Hocha, seventy-four, with representatives of every human race. We're the descendants of the sixty-three — three hundred million of us."

"Fast work," said Betty, with admiration.

"Large families," returned Clay. "I have nine children, sixteen grandchildren. From the start our guiding principle has been to keep the culture of Earth intact for our descendants, to teach them what we knew of human tradition.

"So that when rescue came — as it must finally — then our children or our children's children could return to Earth, not as savages but as citizens. And our invaluable source has been the Ten Books, the only books brought down from the *Etruria*. We could not have been favored with books more inspiring…"

Clay's gaze went to the black bound books at the end of the room, and his voice lowered a trifle.

"The *Encyclopedia of Human Achievement*. The original edition was in ten little plastrol volumes, none of them larger than your hand — but in them was such a treasury of human glory that never could we forget our ancestry, or rest in our efforts to achieve somewhere near the level of the great masters. All the works of the human race we set as our standards — music, art, literature — all were described in the *Encyclopedia*."

"Described, you say," mused Welstead.

"There were no illustrations?" asked Betty.

"No," said Clay, "there was small compass for pictures in the original edition. However —" he went to the case, selected a volume at random "— the words left little to the imagination. For example, on the music of Bach — 'When Bach arrived on the scene the toccata was tentative, indecisive — a recreation, a *tour de force,* where the musician might display his virtuosity.

"'In Bach the toccata becomes a medium of the noblest plasticity. The theme he suggests by casual fingering of the keyboard, unrelated runs. Then comes a glorious burst into harmony — the original runs glow like prisms, assume stature, gradually topple together into a miraculous pyramid of sound.'

"And on Beethoven — 'A God among men. His music is the voice of the world, the pageant of all imagined splendor. The sounds he invokes are natural forces of the same order as sunsets, storms at sea, the view from mountain crags.'

"And on Leon Bismarck Beiderbecke — 'His trumpet pours out such a torrent of ecstasy, such triumph, such overriding joys that the heart of man freezes in anguish at not being wholly part of it.'" Clay closed the book, replaced it. "Such is our heritage. We have tried to keep alive, however poorly, the stream of our original culture."

"I would say that you have succeeded," Welstead remarked dryly.

Betty sighed, a long slow suspiration.

Clay shook his head. "You can't judge until you've seen more of Haven. We're comfortable enough though our manner of living must seem unimpressive in comparison with the great cities, the magnificent palaces of Earth."

"No, not at all," said Betty, but Clay made a polite gesture.

"Don't feel obliged to flatter us. As I've said, we're aware of our deficiencies. Our music for instance — it is pleasant, sometimes exciting, sometimes profound, but never does it reach the heights of poignancy that the *Encyclopedia* describes.

"Our art is technically good but we despair of emulating Seurat, who 'out-lumens light', or Braque, 'the patterns of the mind in patterns of color on the patterns of life', or Cézanne — 'the planes which under the guise of natural objects march, merge, meet in accord with remorseless logic, which wheel around and impel the mind to admit the absolute justice of the composition.'"

Betty glanced at her husband, apprehensive lest he speak what she knew must be on his mind. To her relief he kept silent, squinting thoughtfully at Clay. For her part Betty resolved to maintain a noncommittal attitude.

"No," Clay said heavily, "we do the best we can, and in some fields we've naturally achieved more than in others. To begin with we had the benefit of all human experience in our memories. The paths were charted out for us — we knew the mistakes to avoid. We've never had wars or compulsion. We've never permitted unreined authority. Still we've tried to reward those who are willing to accept responsibility.

"Our criminals — very few now — are treated for mental disorder on the first and second offense, sterilized on the third, executed on the fourth — our basic law being cooperation and contribution to the society, though there is infinite latitude in how this contribution shall be made. We do not make society a juggernaut. A man may live as integrally or as singularly as he wishes so long as he complies with the basic law."

Clay paused, looking from Welstead to Betty. "Now do you understand our way of living?"

"More or less," said Welstead. "In the outline at least. You seem to have made a great deal of progress technically."

Clay considered. "From one aspect, yes. From another no. We had the lifeboat tools, we had the technical skills and most important we knew what we were trying to do. Our main goal naturally has been the conquest of space. We've gone up in rockets but they can take us nowhere save around the sun and back. Our scientists are close on the secret of the space-drive but certain practical difficulties are holding them up."

Welstead laughed. "Space-drive can never be discovered by rational effort. That's a philosophical question which has been threshed back and forth for hundreds of years. Reason — the abstract idea — is a function of ordinary time and space. The space-drive has no qualities in common with these ideas and for this reason human thought can never consciously solve the problem of the over-drive. Experiment, trial and error can do it. Thinking about it is useless."

"Hm," said Clay. "That's a new concept. But now your presence makes it beside the point, for you will be the link back to our homeland."

Betty could see words trembling on her husband's tongue. She clenched her hands, willed — willed — *willed*. Perhaps the effort had some effect because Welstead merely said, "We'll do anything we can to help."

All of Mytilene they visited and nearby Tiryns, Dicte and Ilium. They saw industrial centers, atomic power generators, farms, schools. They attended a session of the Council of Guides, both making brief speeches, and they spoke to the people of Haven by television. Every news organ on the planet carried their words.

They heard music from a green hillside, the orchestra playing from under tremendous smoke black trees. They saw the art of Haven in public galleries, in homes and in common use. They read some of the literature, studied the range of the planet's science, which was roughly equivalent to that of Earth. And they marveled continually how so few people in so little time could accomplish so much.

They visited the laboratories, where three hundred scientists and engineers strove to force magnetic, gravitic and vortigial fields into the fusion that made star-to-star flight possible. And the scientists watched in breathless tension as Welstead inspected their apparatus.

He saw at a single glance the source of their difficulty. He had read of the same experiments on Earth three hundred years ago and of the fantastic accident that had led Roman-Forteski and Gladheim to enclose the generatrix in a dodecahedron of quartz. Only by such a freak — or by his information — would these scientists of Haven solve the mystery of space-drive.

And Welstead walked thoughtfully from the laboratory, with the disappointed glances of the technicians following him out. And Betty had glanced after him in wonder, and the rest of the day there had been a strain between them.

That night as they lay in the darkness, rigid, wakeful, each could feel the pressure of the other's thoughts. Betty finally broke the silence, in a voice so blunt that there was no mistaking her feeling.

"Ralph!"

"What?"

"Why did you act as you did in the laboratory?"

"Careful," muttered Welstead. "Maybe the room is wired for sound."

Betty laughed scornfully. "This isn't Earth. These people are trusting, honest…"

It was Welstead's turn to laugh — a short cheerless laugh. "And that's the reason I'm ignorant when it comes to space-drive."

Betty stiffened. "What do you mean?"

"I mean that these people are too damn good to ruin."

Betty relaxed, sighed, spoke slowly, as if she knew she was in for a long pull. "How — 'ruin'?"

Welstead snorted. "It's perfectly plain. You've been to their homes, you've read their poetry, listened to their music…"

"Of course. These people live every second of their lives with — well, call it exaltation. A devotion to creation like nothing I've ever seen before!"

Welstead said somberly, "They're living in the grandest illusion ever imagined and they're riding for an awful fall. They're like a man on a glorious wine drunk."

Betty stared through the dark. "Are you crazy?"

"They're living in exaltation now," said Welstead, "but what a bump when the bubble breaks!"

"But why should it break?" cried Betty. "Why can't —"

"Betty," said Welstead with a cold sardonic voice, "have you ever seen a public park on Earth after a holiday?"

Betty said hotly, "Yes — it's dreadful. Because the people of Earth have no feeling of community."

"Right," said Welstead. "And these people have. They're knit very tightly by a compulsion that made them achieve in two hundred-odd years what took seven thousand on Earth. They're all facing the same direction, geared to the same drive. Once that drive is gone how do you expect they'll hold on to their standards?"

Betty was silent.

"Human beings," said Welstead dreamily, "are at their best when the going's toughest. They're either at their best or else they're nothing. The going's been tough here — these people have come through. Give them a cheap living, tourist money — then what?"

"But that's not all. In fact it's only half the story. These people here," he stated with emphasis, "are living in a dream. They're the victims of the Ten Books. They take every word literally and they've worked their hearts out trying to come somewhere near what they expect the standards to be.

"Their own stuff doesn't do half the things to them that the Ten Books says good art ought to do. Whoever wrote those Ten Books must have been a copywriter for an advertising agency." Welstead laughed. "Shakespeare wrote good plays — sure, I concede it. But I've never seen 'fires flickering along the words, gusty winds rushing through the pages'.

"Sibelius I suppose was a great composer — I'm no expert on these things — but whoever listened and became 'part of Finland's ice, moss-smelling earth, hoarse-breathing forest', the way the Ten Books said everyone did?"

Betty said, "He was merely trying to express vividly the essence of the artists and musicians."

"Nothing wrong in that," said Welstead. "On Earth we're conditioned to call everything in print a lie. At least we allow for several hundred percent overstatement. These people out here aren't immunized. They've taken every word at its face value. The Ten Books is their Bible. They're trying to equal accomplishments which never existed."

Betty raised herself up on an elbow, said in a voice of hushed triumph. "And they've *succeeded*! Ralph, they've *succeeded*! They've met the challenge, they've equaled or beaten anything Earth has ever produced! Ralph, I'm proud to belong to the same race."

"Same species," Welstead corrected dryly. "These people are a mixed race. They're all races."

"What's the difference?" Betty snapped. "You're just quibbling. You know what I mean well enough."

"We're on a sidetrack," said Welstead wearily. "The question is not the people of Haven and their accomplishments. Of course they're wonderful — *now*. But how do you think contact with Earth will affect them?

"Do you think they'll continue producing when the challenge is gone? When they find the Earth is a rookery — nagging, quarreling — full of mediocre hacks and cheap mischief? Where the artists draw nothing but nude women and the musicians make their living reeling out sound, sound, sound — any kind of sound — for television soundtracks? Where are all their dreams then?

"Talk about disappointment, staleness! Mark my words, half the population would be suicides and the other half would turn to prostitution and cheating the tourists. It's a tough proposition. I say, leave them with their dreams. Let them think we're the worst sort of villains. I say, get off the planet, get back where we belong."

Betty said in a troubled voice, "Sooner or later somebody else will find them."

"Maybe — maybe not. We'll report the region barren — which it is except for Haven."

Betty said in a small voice, "Ralph I couldn't do it. I couldn't violate their trust."

"Not even to keep them trusting?"

Betty said wildly, "Don't you think there'd be an equal deflation if we sneaked away and left them? We're the climax to their entire two hundred and seventy-one years. Think of the listlessness after we left!"

"They're working on their space-drive," said Welstead. "Chances are a million to one against their stumbling on it. They don't know that. They've got a flicker of a field and they think all they have to do is adjust the power feed, get better insulation. They don't have the Mardi Gras lamp that Gladheim snatched up when the lead tank melted."

"Ralph," said Betty, "your words are all very logical. Your arguments stay together — but they're not satisfying emotionally. I don't have the feeling of rightness."

"Pish," said Welstead. "Let's not go spiritual."

"And," said Betty softly, "let's not try to play God either."

There was a long silence.

"Ralph?" said Betty.

"What?"

"Isn't there *some* way..."

"Some way to do what?"

"Why should it be *our* responsibility?"

"I don't know whose else it is. We're the instruments —"

"But it's *their* lives."

"Betty," said Welstead wearily, "here's one time we can't pass the buck. We're the people who in the last resort say yes or no. We're the only people that see on both sides of the fence. It's an awful decision to make — but I say no."

There was no more talking and after an unmeasured period they fell asleep.

Three nights later Welstead stopped Betty as she began to undress for bed. She gave him a dark wide-eyed stare.

"Throw whatever you're taking into a bag. We're leaving."

Betty's body was rigid and tense, slowly relaxing as she took a step toward him. "Ralph..."

"What?" And she could find no softness, no indecision in his topaz eyes.

"Ralph — it's *dangerous* for us to go. If they caught us, they'd execute us — for utter depravity." And she said in a murmur, looking away, "I suppose they'd be justified too."

"It's a chance we'll have to take. Just what we said the day we decided to land. We've got to die sometime. Get your gear and let's take off."

"We should leave a note, Ralph. Something..."

He pointed to an envelope. "There it is. Thanking them for their hospitality. I told them we were criminals and couldn't risk returning to Earth. It's thin but it's the best I could do."

A hint of fire returned to Betty's voice. "Don't worry, they'll believe it."

Sullenly she tucked a few trinkets into a pouch. "It's a long way to the ship you know," she warned him.

"We'll take Clay's car. I've watched him and I know how to drive it."

She jerked in a small bitter spasm of laughter. "We're even car thieves."

"Got to be," said Welstead stonily. He went to the door, listened. The utter silence of honest sleep held the rest of the house. He returned to where Betty stood waiting, watching him coldly with an air of dissociation.

"This way," said Welstead. "Out through the terrace."

They passed out into the moonless night of Haven and the only sound was the glassy tinkle of the little stream that ran in its natural bed through the terrace.

Welstead took Betty's hand. "Easy now, don't walk into that bamboo." He clutched and they froze to a halt. Through a window had come a sound — a gasp — and then the relieved mutter a person makes on waking from a bad dream.

Slowly, like glass melting under heat, the two came to life, stole across the terrace, out upon the turf beside the house. They circled the vegetable garden and the loom of the car bulked before them.

"Get in," whispered Welstead. "I'll push till we're down around the bend."

Betty climbed into the seat and her foot scraped against the metal. Welstead stiffened, listened, pierced the darkness like an eagle. Quiet from the house, the quiet of relaxation, of trust... He pushed at the car and it floated easily across the ground, resisting his hand only through inertia.

It jerked to a sudden halt. And Welstead froze in his tracks again. A burglar alarm of some sort. No, there were no thieves on Haven — except two recently-landed people from Earth. A trap?

"The anchor," whispered Betty.

Of course — Welstead almost groaned with relief. Every car had an anchor to prevent the wind from blowing it away. He found it, hooked it into place on the car's frame and now the car floated without hindrance down the leafy tunnel that was Clay's driveway. Around a bend he ran to the door, jumped in, pressed his foot on the power pedal, and the car slid away with the easy grace of a canoe. Out on the main road he switched on the lights and they rushed off through the night.

"And we still use wheels on Earth," said Welstead. "If we only had a tenth of the guts these people have —"

Cars passed them from the other direction. The lights glowed briefly into their faces and they cringed low behind the windscreen.

They came to the park where their ship lay. "If anyone stops us," Welstead said in Betty's ear, "we've just driven down to get some personal effects. After all we're not prisoners."

But he circled the ship warily before stopping beside it and then he waited a few seconds, straining his eyes through the darkness. But there was no sound, no light, no sign of any guard or human presence.

Welstead jumped from the car. "Fast now. Run over, climb inside. I'll be right behind you."

They dashed through the dark, up the rungs welded to the hull, and the cold steel felt like a caress to Welstead's hot hands. Into the cabin; he thudded the port shut, slammed home the dogs.

Welstead vaulted to the controls, powered the reactors. Dangerous business — but once clear of the atmosphere they could take time to let them warm properly. The ship rose, the darkness and lights of Mytilene fell below. Welstead sighed, suddenly tired, but warm and relaxed.

Up, up — and the planet became a ball, and Eridanus two thousand nine hundred and thirty-two peered around the edge and suddenly, without any noticeable sense of boundary passed, they were out in space.

Welstead sighed. "Lord, what a relief! I never knew how good empty space could look."

"It looks beautiful to me also," said Alexander Clay. "I've never seen it before."

Welstead whirled, jumped to his feet.

Clay came forward from the reaction chamber, watching with a peculiar expression Welstead took to be deadly fury. Betty stood by the bulkhead, looking from one to the other, her face blank as a mirror.

Welstead came slowly down from the controls. "Well — you've

caught us in the act. I suppose you think we're treating you pretty rough. Maybe we are. But my conscience is clear. And we're not going back. Looks like you asked for a ride, and you're going to get one. If necessary —" He paused meaningfully.

Then, "How'd you get aboard?" and after an instant of narrow-eyed speculation, "And why? Why tonight?"

Clay shook his head slowly. "Ralph — you don't give us any credit for ordinary intelligence, let alone ordinary courage."

"What do you mean?"

"I mean that I understand your motives — and I admire you for them. Although I think you've been bull-headed putting them into action without discussing it with the people most directly concerned."

Welstead lowered his head, stared with hard eyes. "It's basically my responsibility. I don't like it but I'm not afraid of it."

"It does you credit," said Clay mildly. "On Haven we're used to sharing responsibility. Not diluting it, you understand, but putting a dozen — a hundred — a thousand minds on a problem that might be too much for one. You don't appreciate us, Ralph. You think we're soft, spiritless."

"No," said Welstead. "Not exactly —"

"Our civilization is built on adaptability, on growth, on flexibility," continued Clay. "We —"

"You don't understand just what you'd have to adapt to," said Welstead harshly. "It's nothing nice. It's graft, scheming sharp-shooters, tourists by the million, who'll leave your planet the way a platoon of invading soldiers leaves the first pretty girl they find."

"There'll be problems," said Clay. His voice took on power. "But that's what we want, Ralph — problems. We're hungry for them, for the problems of ordinary human existence. We want to get back into the stream of life. And if it means grunting and sweating we want it. We're flesh and blood, just like you are.

"We don't want Nirvana — we want to test our strength. We want to fight along with the rest of decent humanity. Don't you fight what you think is unjust?"

Welstead slowly shook his head. "Not any more. It's too big for me. I tried when I was young, then I gave up. Maybe that's why Betty and I roam around the outer edges."

"No," said Betty. "That's not it at all, Ralph, and you know it. You explore because you like exploring. You like the rough and tumble of human contact just as much as anyone else."

"Rough and tumble," said Clay, savoring the words. "That's what we need on Haven. They had it in the old days. They gave themselves to it, beating the new world into submission. It's ours now. Another hundred years of nowhere to go and we'd be drugged, lethargic, decadent."

Welstead was silent.

"The thing to remember, Ralph," said Clay, "is that we're part of humanity. If there's good going, fine. But if there are problems we want to help lick them. You said you'd given up because it was too big for you. Do you think it would be too big for a whole planet? Three hundred million hard honest brains?"

Welstead stared, his imagination kindled. "I don't see how —"

Clay smiled. "I don't either. It's a problem for three hundred million minds. Thinking about it that way it doesn't seem so big. If it takes three hundred brains three days to figure out a dodecahedron of quartz —"

Welstead jerked, looked accusingly at his wife. "Betty!"

She shook her head. "I told Clay about our conversation, our argument. We discussed it all around. I told him everything — and I told him I'd give a signal whenever we started to leave. But I never mentioned space-drive. If they discovered it they did it by themselves."

Welstead turned slowly back to Clay. "*Discovered* it? But — that's impossible."

Clay said, "Nothing's impossible. You yourself gave me the hint when you told me human reason was useless because the space-drive worked out of a different environment. So we concentrated not on the drive itself but on the environment. The first results came at us in terms of twelve directions — hence the dodecahedron. Just a hunch, an experiment and it worked."

Welstead sighed. "I'm licked. I give in. Clay, the headache is yours. You've *made* it yours. What do you want to do? Go back to Haven?"

Clay smiled, almost with affection. "We're this far. I'd like to see Earth. For a month, incognito. Then we'll come back to Haven and make a report to the world. And then there's three hundred million of us, waiting for the bell in round one."

The God and the Temple Robber

In the nip-and-tuck business of keeping himself alive, Briar Kelly had not yet been able to shed his disguise. The adventure had turned out rather more ruggedly than it had started. He had not bargained for so much hell.

Up to the moment he had entered the queer dark temple at North City, the disguise had served him well. He had been one with the Han; no one had looked at him twice. Once inside the temple he was alone and disguise was unnecessary.

It was an oddly impressive place. A Gothic web of trusses supported the ceiling; alcoves along the walls were crammed with bric-a-brac. Red and green lamps cast an illumination which was stifled and absorbed by black drapes.

Walking slowly down the central nave, every nerve tingling, Kelly had approached the tall black mirror at the far end, watching his looming reflection with hypnotic fascination. There were limpid depths beyond, and Kelly would have looked more closely had he not seen the jewel: a ball of cool green fire resting on a black velvet cushion.

With marvelling fingers Kelly had lifted it, turned it over and over — and then tumult had broken loose. The red and green lights flickered; an alarm horn brayed like a crazy bull. Vengeful priests appeared in the alcoves as if by magic, and the disguise had become a liability. The tubular black cloak constricted his legs as he ran — back along the aisle, down the shabby steps, through the foul back alleys to his air-boat. Now as he crouched low over the controls sweat beaded up under the white grease-paint and his skin itched and crawled.

Ten feet below, the salt-crusted mud-flats fleeted astern. Dirty yellow rushes whipped the hull. Pressing an elbow to his hip Kelly felt the hard shape of the jewel. The sensation aroused mixed feelings, apprehension predominating. He dropped the boat even closer to the ground. "Five minutes of this, I'll be out of radar range," thought Kelly. "Back at Bucktown, I'm just one among fifty thousand. They can't very well locate me, unless Herli talks, or Mapes…"

He hazarded a glance at the rear-vision plate. North City could still be seen, an exaggerated Mont St. Michel jutting up from the dreary salt marsh. Misty exhalations blurred the detail; it faded into the sky, finally dropped below the horizon. Kelly eased up the nose of the boat, rose tangentially from the surface, aiming into Magra Taratempos, the hot white sun.

The atmosphere thinned, the sky deepened to black, stars came out. There was old Sol, a yellow star hanging between Sadal Suud and Sadal Melik in Aquarius — only thirty light years to home —

Kelly heard a faint swishing sound. The light changed, shifting white to red. He blinked, looked around in bewilderment.

Magra Taratempos had disappeared. Low to the left a giant red sun hulked above the horizon; below, the salt marshes swam in a new claret light.

In amazement Kelly gazed from red sun to planet, back up across the heavens where Magra Taratempos had hung only a moment before.

"I've gone crazy," said Kelly. "Unless…"

Two or three months before, a peculiar rumor had circulated Bucktown. For lack of better entertainment, the sophisticates of the city had made a joke of the story, until it finally grew stale and was no more heard.

Kelly, who worked as computer switchman at the astrogation station, was well-acquainted with the rumor. It went to the effect that a Han priest, dour and intense under his black cloak, had been tripped into the marsh by a drunken pollen-collector. Like a turtle the priest had shoved his white face out from under the hood of his cloak, and rasped in the pidgin of the planet: "You abuse the priest of Han; you mock us and the name of the Great God. Time is short. The Seventh Year is at hand, and you godless Earth-things will seek to flee, but there will be nowhere for you to go."

Such had been the tale. Kelly remembered the pleased excitement which had fluttered from tongue to tongue. He grimaced, examined the sky in new apprehension.

The facts were before his eyes, undeniable. Magra Taratempos had vanished. In a different quarter of the sky a new sun had appeared.

Careless of radar tracing, he nosed up and broke entirely clear of the atmosphere. The stellar patterns had changed. Blackness curtained half the sky, with here and there a lone spark of a star or the wisp of a far galaxy. To the other quarter a vast blot of light stretched across the sky, a narrow elongated luminosity with a central swelling, the whole peppered with a million tiny points of light.

Kelly cut the power from his engine; the air-boat drifted. Unquestionably the luminous blot was a galaxy seen from one of its outer fringes. In ever-growing bewilderment, Kelly looked back at the planet below. To the south he could see the triangular plateau shouldering up from the swamp, and Lake Lenore near Bucktown. Below was the salt marsh, and far to the north, the rugged pile where the Han had their city.

"Let's face it," said Kelly. "Unless I'm out of my mind — and I don't think I am — the entire planet has been picked up and taken to a new sun... I've heard of strange things here and there, but this is it..."

He felt the weight of the jewel in his pocket, and with it a new thrill of apprehension. To the best of his knowledge the Han priests could not identify him. At Bucktown it had been Herli and Mapes who had urged him into the escapade, but they would hold their tongues. Ostensibly he had flown to his cabin along the lakeshore, and there was no one to know of his comings and goings... He turned the boat down toward Bucktown, and a half hour later landed at his cabin beside Lake Lenore. He had scraped the grease-paint from his face; the cloak he had jettisoned over the swamp; and the jewel still weighed heavy in his pocket.

The cabin, a low flat-roofed building with aluminum walls and a glass front, appeared strange and unfamiliar in the new light. Kelly walked warily to the door. He looked right and left. No one, nothing was visible. He put his ear to the panel of the door. No sound.

He slid back the panel, stepped inside, swept the interior with a swift glance. Everything appeared as he had left it.

He started toward the visiphone, then halted.

The jewel.

He took it from his pocket, examined it for the first time. It was a sphere the size of a golf-ball. The center shone with a sharp green fire, decreasing toward the outer surface. He hefted it. It was unnaturally heavy. Strangely fascinating, altogether lovely. Think of it around the neck of Lynette Mason…

Not now. Kelly wrapped it in paper, tucked it into an empty pint jar. Behind the cabin, an old shag-bark slanted up out of the black humus and overhung the roof like a gray and tattered beach-umbrella. Kelly dug a hole under one of the arched roots, buried the jewel.

Returning to the cabin, he walked to the visiphone, reached out to call the station. While his hand was yet a foot from the buttons, the buzzer sounded… Kelly drew his hand back.

Better not to answer.

The buzzer sounded again — again. Kelly stood holding his breath, looking at the blank face of the screen.

Silence.

He washed the last of the grease-paint from his face, changed his clothes, ran outside, jumped into his air-boat and took off for Buck-town.

He landed on the roof of the station, noting that Herli's car was parked in its wonted slot. Suddenly he felt less puzzled and forlorn. The station with its machinery and solid Earth-style regulations projected reassurance, a sense of normality. Somehow the ingenuity and aggressive attack which had taken men to the stars would solve the present enigma.

Or would it? Ingenuity could take men through space, but ingenuity would find itself strained locating a speck of a planet a hundred thousand light-years in an unknown direction. And Kelly still had his own problem: the jewel. Into his mind's-eye came a picture: the cabin by the lake, the dilapidated gray parasol of the shag-bark, and glowing under the root, the green eye of the sacred jewel. In the vision he saw the black-robed figure of a Han priest moving across the open space before the cabin, and he saw the flash of the dough-white face…

Kelly turned a troubled glance up at the big red sun, entered the station.

The administration section was vacant; Kelly climbed the stair to the operations department.

He stopped in the doorway, surveyed the room. It covered the entire square of the upper floor. Work-benches made a circuit of the room, with windows above. A polished cylinder, the cosmoscope, came down through the ceiling, and below was the screen to catch the projection.

Four men stood by the star-index, running a tape. Herli glanced up briefly, turned back to the clicking mechanism.

Strange. Herli should have been interested, should at least have said hello.

Kelly self-consciously crossed the room. He cleared his throat. "Well — I made it. I'm back."

"So I see," said Herli.

Kelly fell silent. He glanced up through the window at the red sun. "What do you make of it?"

"Not the least idea. We're running the star-tapes on the off chance it's been registered — a last-gasp kind of hope."

There was more silence. They had been talking before he had entered the room; Kelly sensed this from their posture.

At last Mapes said with a forced casualness, "Seen the news?"

"No," said Kelly. "No, I haven't." There was more in Mapes' voice, something more personal than the shift of the planet. After a moment's hesitation he went to the visiphone, pushed the code for news.

The screen lit, showed a view of the swamp. Kelly leaned forward. Buried up to their necks were a dozen boys and girls from the Bucktown High-school. Crawling eagerly over them were the small three-legged salt-crabs; others popped up out of the slime, or tunnelled under toward the squirming bodies.

Kelly could not stand the screams. He reached forward —

Herli said sharply, "Leave it on!" — harder than Kelly had ever heard him speak. "The announcement is due pretty soon."

The announcement came, in the rasping toneless pidgin of the Han priests.

"Among the outsiders is a wicked thief. He has despoiled us of the

Seven-year Eye. Let him come forward for his due. Until the thief has brought the Seven-year Eye in his own hand to the sacred temple of Han, every hour one of the outsiders will be buried in the crab-warren. If the thief hangs back, all will be so dealt with, and there will be an end to the Earth-things."

Mapes said in a tight voice, "Did you take their Seven-year Eye?"

Kelly nodded numbly. "Yes."

Herli made a sharp sound in his throat, turned away.

Kelly said miserably, "I don't know what came over me. There it was — glowing like a little green moon…I took it."

Herli said gutturally, "Don't just stand there."

Kelly reached out to the visiphone, pushed buttons. The screen changed, a Han priest stared forth into Kelly's face.

Kelly said, "I stole your jewel…Don't kill any more people. I'll bring it back to you."

The priest said, "Every hour until you arrive one of the Earth-things dies a wicked death."

Kelly leaned forward, slammed off the screen with a sudden furious sweep of his hand. He turned in anger.

"Don't stand there glaring at me! You, Herli, you told me I wouldn't even make it into the temple! And if any of you guys had been where I was and saw that jewel like I saw it, you'd have taken it too."

Mapes growled under his breath. Herli's shoulders seemed to sag; he looked away. "Maybe you're right, Briar."

Kelly said, "Are we helpless? Why didn't we fight when they took those twelve kids? There's maybe a million Han, but there's fifty thousand of us — and they have no weapons that I know of."

"They've seized the power station," said Herli. "Without power we can't distill water, we can't radiate our hydroponics. We're in a cleft stick."

Kelly turned away. "So long, fellows."

No one answered him. He walked down the stairs, across the parking strip to his air-car. He was conscious of their eyes looking down from the window.

In, up, away. First to his cabin by the lake, under the shag-bark for the Seven-year Eye, then the arc over the planet, south to north.

Then the gray fortress of North Settlement, and the dark temple in the center.

Kelly dropped the air-car directly in front of the temple. No reason now for stealth.

He climbed to the ground, looked about through the strange purple twilight which had come to the ramshackle city. A few Han moved past, and Kelly saw the flash of their faces.

He walked slowly up the steps to the temple, paused indecisively in the doorway. There was no point in adding further provocation to his offenses. No doubt they planned to kill him; he might as well make it as easy as possible.

"Hello," he called into the dark interior, in a voice he tried to keep firm. "Any priests in there? I've brought back the jewel…"

There was no response. Listening intently, he could hear a distant murmur. He took a few steps into the temple, peered up the nave. The muffled red and green illumination confused rather than aided his vision. He noticed a curious irregularity to the floor. He took a step forward — another — another — he stepped on something soft. There was the flash of white below him. The floor was covered by the black-robed priests, lying flat on their faces.

The priest he had trod on made no sound. Kelly hesitated. Time was passing… He crammed all his doubts, fears, vacillations into a corner of his mind, strode forward, careless of where he stepped.

Down the center of the nave he walked, holding the green jewel in his hand. Ahead he saw the sheen of the tall black mirror, and there on the black cushion was a second jewel identical to the one he carried. A Han priest stood like a ghost in a black robe; he watched Kelly approach without movement. Kelly laid the jewel on the cushion beside its twin.

"There it is. I've brought it back. I'm sorry I took it. I — well, I acted on a wild impulse."

The priest picked up the jewel, held it under his chin as if feeling the warmth from the green fire.

"Your impulse has cost fifteen Earth lives."

"Fifteen?" faltered Kelly. "There were but twelve —"

"Two hours delay has sent two to the crab warren," said the Han. "And yourself. Fifteen."

Kelly said with a shaky bravado, "You're taking a lot on yourself—these murders—"

"I am not acquainted with your idiom," said the priest, "but it seems as if you convey a foolish note of menace. What can you few Earth-things do against Great God Han, who has just now taken our planet across the galaxy?"

Kelly said stupidly, "Your god Han—moved the planet?"

"Certainly. He has taken us far and forever distant from Earth to this mellow sun; such is his gratitude for our prayers and for the tribute of the Eye."

Kelly said with studied carelessness, "You have your jewel back; I don't see why you're so indignant—"

The priest said, "Look here." Kelly followed his gesture, saw a square black hole edged with a coping of polished stone. "This shaft is eighteen miles deep. Every priest of Han descends to the coomb once a week and carries back to the surface a basket of crystallized stellite. On rare occasions the matrix of the Eye is found, and then there is gratification in the city... Such a jewel did you steal."

Kelly took his eyes away from the shaft. Eighteen miles..."I naturally wasn't aware of the—"

"No matter; the deed is done. And now the planet has been moved, and Earth power is unable to prevent such punishments as we wish to visit upon you."

Kelly tried to keep his voice firm. "Punish? What do you mean?"

Behind him he heard a rustling, the shuffle of movement. He looked over his shoulder. The black cloaks merged with the drapes of the temple, and the Han faces floated in mid-air.

"You will be killed," said the priest. Kelly stared into the white face. "If the manner of your going is of any interest to you—" The priest conveyed details which froze Kelly's flesh, clabbered the moisture in his mouth. "Your death will thereby deter other Earth-things from like crimes."

Kelly protested in spite of himself. "You have your jewel; there it is... If you insist on killing me—kill me, but—"

"Strange," said the Han priest. "You Earth-things fear pain more than anything else you can conceive. This fear is your deadliest enemy.

We Han now, we fear nothing —" he looked up at the tall black mirror, bowed slightly "— nothing but our Great God Han."

Kelly stared at the shimmering black surface. "What's that mirror to do with your god Han?"

"That is no mirror; that is the portal to the place of the gods, and every seven years a priest goes through to convey the consecrated Eye to Han."

Kelly tried to plumb the dark depths of the mirror. "What lies beyond? What kind of land?"

The priest made no answer.

Kelly laughed in a shrill voice he did not recognize. He lurched forward, threw up his fist in a blow which carried every ounce of his strength and weight. He struck the priest at a point where a man's jaw would be, felt a brittle crunch. The priest spun around, fell in the tangle of his cloak.

Kelly turned on the priests in the nave, and they sighed in fury. Kelly was desperate, fearless now. He laughed again, reached down, scooped both jewels from the cushion. "Great God Han lives behind the mirror, and moves planets for jewels. I have two jewels; maybe Han will move a planet for me…"

He jumped close to the black mirror. He put out his hand and felt a soft surface like a curtain of air. He paused in sudden trepidation. Beyond was the unknown…

Pushing at him came the first rank of the Han priests. Here was the known.

Kelly could not delay. Death was death. If he died passing through the black curtain, if he suffocated in airless space — it was clean fast death.

He leaned forward, closed his eyes, held his breath, stepped through the curtain.

Kelly had come a tremendous distance. It was a distance not to be reckoned in miles or hours, but in quantities like abstract, irrational ideas.

He opened his eyes. They functioned; he could see. He was not dead…Or was he?…He took a step forward, sensed solidity under his feet. He looked down, saw a glassy black floor where small sparks burst, flickered, died. Constellations? Universes? Or merely — sparks?

He took another step. It might have been a yard, a mile, a light-year; he moved with the floating ease of a man walking in a dream.

He stood on the lip of an amphitheater, a bowl like a lunar crater. He took another step; he stood in the center of the bowl. He halted, fought to convince himself of his consciousness. Blood made a rushing sound as it flowed through his veins. He swayed, might have fallen if gravity had existed to pull him down. But there was no gravity. His feet clung to the surface by some mysterious adhesion beyond his experience. The blood-sound rose and fell in his ears. Blood meant life. He was alive.

He looked in back of him, and in the blurring of his eyes could not distinguish what he saw. He turned, took a step forward —

He was intruding. He felt the sudden irritated attention of gigantic personalities.

He gazed about the glassy floor, and the faintest of watery gray lights seeping down from above collected in the concavity where he stood. Space was vast, interminable, without perspective.

Kelly saw the beings he had disturbed — felt rather than saw them: a dozen giant shapes looming above.

One of these shapes formed a thought, and a surge of meaning permeated space, impinged on Kelly's mind, willy-nilly translating itself into words:

"What is this thing? From whose world did it come?"

"From mine." This must be Han. Kelly looked from shape to shape, to determine which the god might be.

"Remove it quickly —" and to Kelly's mind came a jumble of impressions he had no words to express. "We must deal with the matter of…" Again a quick listing of ideas which refused to translate in Kelly's mind. He felt Han's attention focussing on him. He stood transfixed, waiting for the obliteration he knew to be imminent.

But he held the jewels, and their green glow shone up through his fingers. He cried out, "Wait, I came here for a purpose; I want a planet put back where it belongs, and I have jewels to pay —"

He felt the baleful pressure of Han's will on his mind — increasing, increasing; he groaned in helpless anguish.

"Wait," came a calm thought, transcendently clear and serene.

"I must destroy it," Han protested. "It is the enemy of my jewel-senders."

"Wait," came from yet another of the shades, and Kelly caught a nuance of antagonism to Han. "We must act judicially."

"Why are you here?" came the query of the Leader.

Kelly said, "The Han priests are murdering people of my race, ever since the planet we live on was moved. It's not right."

"Ah!" came a thought like an exclamation from the Antagonist. "Han's jewel-senders do evil and unnatural deeds."

"A minor matter, a minor matter," came the restless thought of still another shape. "Han must protect his jewel-senders."

And Kelly caught the implication that the jewel-sending was of cardinal importance; that jewels were vital to the gods.

The Antagonist chose to make an issue of the matter. "The condition of injustice which Han has effected must be abated."

The Leader meditated. And now came a sly thought to Kelly, which he sensed had been channelled to his mind alone. It came from the Antagonist. "Challenge Han to a..." The thought could only be translated as 'duel'. "I will aid you. Relax your mind." Kelly, grasping at any straw, loosened his mental fibers, and felt something like a damp shadow entering his brain, absorbing, recording... All in an instant. The contact vanished.

Kelly felt the Leader's mind wavering over in favor of Han. He said hurriedly, improvising as best he could: "Leader, in one of the legends of Earth, a man journeyed to the land of the giants. As they came to kill him, he challenged the foremost to a duel with his life at stake." "*Of three trials,*" came a thought. "Of three trials," added Kelly. "In the story, the man won and was permitted to return to his native land. After this fashion let me duel in three trials with Han."

The surge of thoughts thickened the air — rancorous contempt from Han, sly encouragement from the Antagonist, amusement from the Leader.

"You invoke a barbaric principle," said the Leader. "But by a simple yet rigorous logic, it is a just device, and shall be honored. You shall duel Han in three trials."

"Why waste time?" inquired Han. "I can powder him to less than the atoms of atoms."

"No," said the Leader. "The trial may not be on a basis of sheer potential. You and this man are at odds over an issue which has no fundamental right or wrong. It is the welfare of his people opposed to the welfare of your jewel-senders. Since the issues are equal, there would be no justice in an unequal duel. The trial must be on a basis which will not unwontedly handicap either party."

"Let a problem be stated," suggested the Antagonist. "He who first arrives at a solution wins the trial."

Han was scornfully silent. So the Leader formulated a problem — a terrific statement whose terms were dimensions and quasi-time and a dozen concepts which Kelly's brain could in no wise grasp. But the Antagonist intervened.

"That is hardly a fair problem, lying as it does entirely out of the man's experience. Let me formulate a problem." And he stated a situation which at first startled Kelly, and then brought him hope.

The problem was one he had met a year previously at the station. A system to integrate twenty-five different communication bands into one channel was under consideration, and it was necessary to thrust a beam of protons past a bank of twenty-five mutually inter-acting magnets and hit a pin-point filter at the far end of the case. The solution was simple enough — a statement of the initial vector in terms of a coordinate equation and a voltage potential — yet the solution had occupied the station calculator for two months. Kelly knew this solution as he knew his own name.

"Hurry!" came the Antagonist's secret thought.

Kelly blurted out the answer.

There was a wave of astonishment through the group, and he felt their suspicious inspection.

"You are quick indeed," said the Leader, non-plussed.

"Another problem," called the Antagonist. Once more he brought a question from Kelly's experience, this concerning the behavior of posi-trons in the secondary layer of a star in a cluster of six, all at specified temperatures and masses. And this time Kelly's mind worked faster. He immediately stated the answer. Still he anticipated Han by mere seconds.

Han protested, "How could this small pink brain move faster than my cosmic consciousness?"

"How is this?" asked the Leader. "How do you calculate so swiftly?"

Kelly fumbled for ideas, finally strung together a lame statement: "I do not calculate. In my brain is a mass of cells whose molecules form themselves into models of the problems. They move in an instant, the problem is solved, and the solution comes to me."

Anxiously he waited, but the reply seemed to satisfy the group. These creatures — or gods, if such they were — were they so naïve? Only the Antagonist suggested complex motives. Han, Kelly sensed, was old, of great force, of a hard and inflexible nature. The Leader was venerable beyond thought, calm and untroubled as space itself.

"What now?" came from the Antagonist. "Shall there be another problem? Or shall the man be declared the victor?"

Kelly would have been well pleased to let well enough alone, but this evidently did not suit the purposes of the Antagonist; hence his quiet jeer.

"No!" The thoughts of Han roared forth almost like sound. "Because of a ridiculous freak in this creature's brain, must I admit him my superior? I can fling him through a thousand dimensions with a thought, snap him out of existence, out of memory —"

"Perhaps because you are a god," came the Antagonist's taunt, "and of pure —" another confusing concept, a mixture of energy, divinity, force, intelligence. "The man is but a combination of atoms, and moves through the oxidation of carbon and hydrogen. Perhaps if you were as he, he might face you hand to hand and defeat you."

A curious tenseness stiffened the mental atmosphere. Han's thoughts came sluggishly, tinged for the first time with doubt.

"Let that be the third trial," said the Leader composedly. Han gave a mental shrug. One of the towering shadows shrunk, condensed, swirled to a man-like shape, solidified further, at last stood facing Kelly, a thing like a man, glowing with a green phosphorescence like the heart of the Seven-year Eye.

The Antagonist's secret thought came to Kelly: "Seize the jewel at the back of the neck."

Kelly scanned the slowly advancing figure. It was exactly his height and heft, naked, but radiating an inhuman confidence. The face was blurred, fuzzy, and Kelly could never afterward describe the countenance. He tore his gaze away.

"How do we fight?" he demanded, beads of sweat dripping from his body. "Do we set any rules — or no holds barred?"

"Tooth and nail," came the calm thoughts of the Leader. "Han now has organic sensibilities like yours. If you kill this body, or render it unconscious, you win. If you lose this trial, then we shall decide."

"Suppose he kills me?" objected Kelly, but no one seemed to heed his protest.

Han came glaring-eyed at him. Kelly took a step backward, jabbed tentatively with his left fist. Han rushed forward. Kelly punched furiously, kneed the onrushing body, heard it grunt and fall, to leap erect instantly. A tingle of joy ran down Kelly's spine, and more confidently he stepped forward, lashing out with rights and lefts. Han leapt close and clinched his arms around Kelly's body. Now he began to squeeze, and Kelly felt a power greater than any man's in those green-glowing arms.

"The jewel," came a sly thought. Sparks were exploding in Kelly's eyes; his ribs creaked. He swung a frenzied hand, clawing at Han's neck. He felt a hard protuberance, he dug his nails under, tore the jewel free.

A shrill cry of utmost pain and horror — and the god-man puffed away into black smoke which babbled in a frenzy back and forth through the darkness. It surged around Kelly, and little tendrils of the smoke seemed to pluck at the jewel clenched in his hand. But they had no great force, and Kelly found he could repel the wisps with the power of his own brain.

He suddenly understood the function of the jewel. It was the focus for the god. It centralized the myriad forces. The jewel gone, the god was a welter of conflicting volitions, vagrant impulses, insubstantial.

Kelly felt the Antagonist's triumphant thoughts. And he himself felt an elation he had never known before. The Leader's cool comment brought him back to himself:

"You seem to have won the contest." There was a pause. "In the absence of opposition we will render any requests you may make." There was no concern in his thoughts for the decentralized Han. The black smoke was dissipating, Han was no more than a memory. "Already you have delayed us long. We have the problem of —" the now familiar confusion of ideas, but this time Kelly understood vaguely. It seemed that there was a vortex of universes which possessed consciousness, as mighty or mightier than these gods, which was driving on a course that would be incommoding. There were qualifications, a host of contributory factors.

"Well," said Kelly, "I'd like you to move the planet I just came from back to its old orbit around Magra Taratempos. If you know what planet and what star I'm talking about."

"Yes." The Leader made a small exertion. "The world you mention moves in its previous orbit."

"Suppose the Han priests come through the portal and want it moved again?"

"The portal no longer exists. It was held open by Han; when Han dissolved, the portal closed... Is that the total of your desires?"

Kelly's mind raced, became a turmoil. This was his chance. Wealth, longevity, power, knowledge... Somehow thoughts would not form themselves — and there were curses attached to unnatural gifts —

"I'd like to get back to Bucktown safely..."

Kelly found himself in the glare of the outer world. He stood on the hill above Bucktown, and he breathed the salt air of the marshes. Above hung a hot white sun — Magra Taratempos.

He became aware of an object clenched in his hand. It was the jewel he had torn out of Han's neck. There were two others in his pocket.

Across the city he saw the light-blue and stainless-steel box of the station. What should he tell Herli and Mapes? Would they believe the truth? He looked at the three jewels. Two he could sell for a fortune on Earth. But one shone brilliantly in the bright sunlight and that was for Lynette Mason's tan and graceful neck.

TELEK

I

GESKAMP AND SHORN stood in the sad light of sundown, high on the rim of the new Telek-ordained arena, which seemed to them so eccentric and arbitrary. They were alone; no sound was to be heard but the murmur of their voices. Wooded hills rolled away to either side; behind them, far to the west, the towers of Tran cut sword-shaped notches into the sky.

Geskamp pointed east, up Swanscomb Valley, now glowing a thousand tones of gold and green in the long light of sunset. "That's where I was born, by that row of poplars. I knew the valley well in the old days." He spent a moment in far reflection. "I hate to see the changes, the old things wiped out. There —" he pointed "— by the stream was Pimssi's croft and stone barn. There, where you see the grove of oaks, that was the village Cobent. Can you believe it? There, by Poll Point, was the valley power tank. There, the Tran aquaport crossed the river, entered the tunnel. It was considered beautiful, the aquaport, antique, overgrown with ivy, stained with lichen. And only six months ago; already it seems a hundred years."

Shorn, intending to make a delicate request, considered how best to take advantage of Geskamp's nostalgia for the irretrievable past; he was faintly surprised to find Geskamp, a big jut-faced man with gray-blond hair, indulging in sentiment of any kind. "There certainly is no recognizing it now."

"No. It's all tidy and clean. Like a park. Look up that mile of clear lawn. I liked it better in the old days. Now it's waste, nothing else." Geskamp cocked his bristling eyebrows at Shorn. "Do you know, they hold me responsible, the farmers and villagers? Because I'm in charge, I gave the orders?"

"They strike out at what's closest."

"I merely earn my salary. I did what I could for them. Completely useless, of course; there never were people so obdurate as the Teleks. Level the valley, build a stadium. Hurry, in time for their midsummer get-together. I said, why not build in Mismarch Valley, around the mountain, where only sheepherders would be disturbed, no crofts and farms to be broken up, no village to be razed."

"What did they say to that?"

"It was Forence Nollinrude I spoke to; you know him?"

"I've seen him; one of their liaison committee. A young man, rather more lofty than the average."

Geskamp spat on the concrete under his feet. "The young ones are the worst. He asked, 'Do we not give you enough money? Pay them well, clear them out. Swanscomb Valley is where we will have our arena.' So —" Geskamp held out his hands in a quick gesticulation "— I bring out my machines, my men. We fly in material. For those who have lived here all their lives there is no choice; they take their money and go. Otherwise some morning perhaps they look out their door and find polar ice or mountains of the moon. I'd not put such refinement past the Teleks."

"Strange tales are told," Shorn agreed.

Geskamp pointed to the grove of oaks. His shadow, cast against the far side of the stadium by the level rays of the sun, followed the motion. "The oaks they brought, so much did they condescend. I explained that transplanting a forest was a job of great delicacy and expense. They were indifferent. 'Spend as much as you like.' I told them there wasn't enough time, if they wanted the stadium inside the month; finally they were aroused. Nollinrude and the one called Henry Motch stirred themselves, and the next day we had all our forest. But would they dispose of the waste from the aquaport, cast it in the sea? No. 'You hire four thousand men, let them move the rubble, brick by brick if need be; we have business elsewhere.' And they were gone."

"A peculiar people."

" 'Peculiar'?" Geskamp gathered his bushy eyebrows into arches of vast scorn. "Madmen. For a whim — a town erased, men and women sent forth homeless." He waved his hand around the stadium. "Two hundred million crowns spent to gratify irresponsible popinjays whose only —"

A droll voice above them said, "I hear myself bespoken."

The two men jerked around. A man stood in the air ten feet above them. His face was mercurial and lighthearted; a green cap clung waggishly to the side of his head; dark hair hung below, almost to his shoulders. He wore a flaring red cape, tight green trousers, black velvet shoes. "You speak in anger, with little real consideration. We are your benefactors; where would you be without us?"

"Living normal lives," growled Geskamp.

The Telek was disposed to facetiousness. "Who is to say that yours is a normal life? In any event, our whim is your employment; we formulate our idle dreams, you and your men enrich yourselves fulfilling them, and we're both the better for it."

"Somehow the money always ends up back with the Teleks. A mystery."

"No, no mystery whatever. It is the exercise of economic law. In any event, we procure the funds, and we would be fools to hoard. In our spending you find occupation."

"We would not be idle otherwise."

"Perhaps not. Perhaps... well, look." He pointed across the stadium to the shadows on the far wall. "Perhaps there is your bent." And as they watched their shadows became active. Shorn's shadow bent forward, Geskamp's shadow drew back, aimed and delivered a mighty kick, then turned, bent, and Shorn's shadow kicked.

The Telek cast no shadow.

Geskamp snorted, Shorn smiled grimly. They looked back overhead, but the Telek had moved high and was drifting south.

"Offensive creature," said Geskamp. "A law should be passed confiscating their every farthing."

Shorn shook his head. "They'd have it all back by nightfall. That's not the answer." He hesitated, as if about to add something further.

Geskamp, already irked by the Telek, did not take the contradiction kindly. Shorn, an architectural draughtsman, was his subordinate. "I suppose you know the answer?"

"I know several answers. One of them is that they should all be killed."

Geskamp's irritation had never carried him quite so far. Shorn was a strange, unpredictable fellow. "Rather bloodthirsty," he said heavily.

Shorn shrugged. "It might be best in the long run."

Geskamp's eyebrows lowered into a straight bar of gold-gray bristle across his face. "The idea is impractical. The creatures are hard to kill."

Shorn laughed. "It's more than impractical — it's dangerous. If you recall the death of Vernisaw Knerwig —"

Vernisaw Knerwig had been punctured by a pellet from a high-power rifle, fired from a window. The murderer, a wild-eyed stripling, was apprehended. But the jail had not been tight enough to keep him. He disappeared. For months misfortune dogged the town. Poison appeared in the water supply. A dozen fires roared up one night. The roof of the town school collapsed. And one afternoon a great meteor struck down from space and obliterated the central square.

"Killing Teleks is dangerous work," said Geskamp. "It's not a realistic thought. After all," he said hurriedly, "they're men and women like ourselves; nothing illegal has ever been proved."

Shorn's eyes glittered. "Illegality? When they dam the whole stream of human development?"

Geskamp frowned. "I'd hardly say —"

"The signs are clear enough when a person pulls his head up out of the sand."

The conversation had got out of hand; Geskamp had been left behind. Waste and excess he admitted, but there were so few Teleks, so many ordinary people. How could they be dangerous? It was strange talk for an architect. He looked sidewise in cautious calculation.

Shorn was faintly smiling. "Well, what do you make of it?"

"You take an extreme position. It's hardly conceivable —"

"The future is unknown. Almost anything is conceivable. We might become Teleks, all of us. Unlikely? I think so myself. The Teleks might die out, disappear. Equally unlikely. They've always been with us, all of history, latent in our midst. What are the probabilities for the future? Something like the present situation, a few Teleks among the great mass of common people?"

Geskamp nodded. "That's my opinion."

"Picture the future, then. What do you see?"

"Nothing extraordinary. I imagine things will move along much as they have been."

"You see no trend, no curve of shifting relationships?"

"The Teleks are an irritation, certainly, but they interfere very little in our lives. In a sense they're an asset. They spend their money like water; they contribute to the general prosperity." He looked anxiously into the sky through the gathering dusk. "Their wealth, it's honestly acquired; no matter where they find those great blocks of metal."

"The metal comes from the Moon, from the asteroids, from the outer planets."

Geskamp nodded. "Yes, that's the speculation."

"The metal represents restraint. The Teleks are giving value in return for what they could take."

"Of course. Why shouldn't they give value in return?"

"No reason at all. They should. But now — consider the trend. At the outset they were ordinary citizens. They lived by ordinary conventions; they were decent people. After the first Congress they made their fortunes by performing dangerous and unpleasant tasks. Idealism, public service was the keynote. They identified themselves with all of humanity, and very praiseworthy, too. Now, sixty years later! Consider the Teleks of today. Is there any pretension to public service? None. They dress differently, speak differently, live differently. They no longer load ships or clear jungles or build roads; they take an easier way, which makes less demands on their time. Humanity benefits; they bring us platinum, palladium, uranium, rhodium, all the precious metals, which they sell at half the old price, and they pour the money back into circulation." He gestured across the stadium. "And meanwhile the old ones are dying and the new Teleks have no roots, no connection with common man. They draw ever farther away, developing a way of living entirely different from ours."

Geskamp said half-truculently, "What do you expect? It's natural, isn't it?"

Shorn put on a patient face. "That's exactly the point I'm trying to make. Consider the trend, the curve. Where does this 'natural' behavior lead? Always away from common humanity, the old traditions, always toward an elite-herd situation."

Geskamp rubbed his heavy chin. "I think that you're — well, making a mountain out of a molehill."

"Do you think so? Consider the stadium, the eviction of the old property-owners. Think of Vernisaw Knerwig and the revenge they took."

"Nothing was proved," said Geskamp uneasily. What was the fellow up to? Now he was grinning, a superior sort of grin.

"In your heart you agree with what I say; but you can't bring yourself to face the facts — because then you'd be forced to take a stand. For or against."

Geskamp stared out across the valley, wholly angry, but unable to dispute Shorn's diagnosis. "I don't see the facts clearly."

"There are only two courses for us. We must either control the Teleks, that is, make them answerable to human law — or we must eliminate them entirely. In blunt words — kill them. If we don't — they become the masters; we the slaves. It's inevitable."

Geskamp's anger broke surface.

"Why do you tell me all these things? What are you driving at? This is strange talk to hear from an architect; you sound like one of the conspirators I've heard rumors of."

"I'm talking for a specific purpose — just as I worked on this job for a specific purpose. I want to bring you to our way of thinking."

"Oh. So that's the way of it."

"And with this accomplished, recruit your ability and your authority toward a definite end."

"Who are you? What is this group?"

"A number of men worried by the trend I mentioned."

"A subversive society?" Geskamp's voice held a tinge of scorn.

Shorn laughed. "Don't let the flavor of words upset you. Call us a committee of public-spirited citizens."

"You'd be in trouble if the Teleks caught wind of you," said Geskamp woodenly.

"They're aware of us. But they're not magicians. They don't know who we are."

"I know who you are," said Geskamp. "Suppose I reported this conversation to Nollinrude?"

Shorn grinned. "What would you gain?"

"A great deal of money."

"You'd live the rest of your life in fear of revenge."

"I don't like it," said Geskamp in a brutal voice, "I don't care to be involved in any undercover plots."

"Examine your conscience. Think it over."

II

The attack on Forence Nollinrude came two days later.

The construction office was a long L-shaped building to the west of the stadium. Geskamp stood in the yard angrily refusing to pay a trucker more than the agreed scale for his concrete aggregate.

"I can buy it cheaper in half a dozen places," roared Geskamp. "You only got the contract in the first place because I went to bat for you."

The trucker had been one of the dispossessed farmers. He shook his head mulishly. "You did me no favor. I'm losing money. It's costing me three crowns a meter."

Geskamp waved an arm angrily toward the man's equipment, a small hopper carried by a pair of ramcopters. "How do you expect to make out with that kind of gear? All your profit goes in running back and forth to the quarry. Get yourself a pair of Samson lifts; you'll cut your costs to where you can make a few crowns."

"I'm a farmer, not a trucker. I took this contract because I had what I have. If I go in the hole for heavy equipment, then I'm stuck with it. It'll do me no more good now, the job's three-quarters done. I want more money, Geskamp, not good advice."

"Well, you can't get it from me. Talk to the purchasing agent; maybe he'll break down. I got you the contract, that's as far as I go."

"I already talked to the purchasing agent; he said nothing doing."

"Strike up one of the Teleks then; they've got the money. I can't do anything for you."

The trucker spat on the ground. "The Teleks, they're the devils who started this whole thing. A year ago I had my dairy — right where that patch of water is now. I was doing good. Now I've got nothing; the money they gave me to get out, most of it's gone in this gravel. Now where do I go? I got my family."

Geskamp drew his bushy gray-blond eyebrows together. "I'm sorry, Hopson. But there's nothing I can do. There's the Telek now; tell him your troubles."

The Telek was Forence Nollinrude, a tall yellow-haired man, magnificent in a rust cape, saffron trousers, black velvet slippers. The trucker looked across the yard to where he floated a fastidious three feet above the ground, then resolved himself and trudged sullenly forward.

Shorn, inside the office, could hear nothing of the interview. The trucker stared up belligerently, legs spread out. Forence Nollinrude turned himself a little to the side, looked down with distaste deepening the lines at the corners of his mouth.

The trucker did most of the talking. The Telek replied in curt monosyllables, and the trucker became progressively more furious.

Geskamp had been watching with a worried frown. He started across the yard with the evident intention of calming the trucker. As he approached, Nollinrude pulled himself a foot or two higher, drew slightly away, turned toward Geskamp, motioned toward the trucker, as if requiring Geskamp to remove the annoyance.

The trucker suddenly seized a bar of reinforcing iron, swung mightily. Geskamp bawled hoarsely; Forence Nollinrude jerked away, but the iron caught him across the shins. He cried in agony, drew back, looked at the trucker. The trucker rose like a rocket a hundred feet into the air, turned end for end, dived head-first to the ground. He struck with crushing force, pulping his head, his shoulders. But, as if Nollinrude were not yet satisfied, the bar of iron rose and beat the limp body with enormous savage strokes.

Had Nollinrude been less anguished by the pain of his legs he would have been more wary. Almost as the trucker struck the ground, Geskamp seized a laborer's mattock. As Nollinrude plied the bar of iron, Geskamp stalked close behind, swung. The Telek collapsed to the ground.

"Now," said Shorn to himself, "there will be hell to pay." He ran from the office. Geskamp stood panting, looking down at the body huddled in the finery that suddenly seemed not chosen human vestments, but the gaudy natural growth of a butterfly or flash-beetle in pathetic disarray. He became aware of the mattock he still held, flung it away as if it were red-hot and stood wiping his hands nervously together.

Shorn knelt beside the body, searched with practiced swiftness. He found and pocketed a wallet, a small pouch, then rose to his feet.

"We've got to work fast." He looked around the yard. Possibly half a dozen men had witnessed the occurrence — a tool-room attendant, a form foreman, a couple of time-clerks, a laborer or two. "Get them all together, everyone who saw what happened; I'll take care of the body. Here, you!" He called to a white-faced lift operator. "Get a hopper down here."

They rolled the gorgeous hulk into the hopper. Shorn jumped up beside the operator, pointed. "Up there where they're pouring that abutment."

They swept diagonally up the great north wall, to where a pour-crew worked beside a receptor designed to receive concrete from loaded hoppers. Shorn jumped four feet from the hopper to the deck, went to the foreman. "There's a hold-up here; take your crew down to B-142 Pilaster and work there for a while."

The foreman grumbled, protested. The receptor was half full of concrete.

Shorn raised his voice impatiently. "Leave it set. I'll send a lift up to move the whole thing."

The foreman turned away, barked ill-naturedly to his men. They moved with exaggerated slowness. Shorn stood tautly while they gathered their equipment and trooped down the ramp.

He turned to the lift operator. "Now."

The bedizened body rolled into the pour.

Shorn guided the dump-hose into position, pulled the trigger. Gray slush pressed down the staring face that had known so much power.

Shorn sighed slightly. "That's good. Now — we'll get the crew back on the job."

At Pilaster B-142 Shorn signaled the foreman, who glowered belligerently. Shorn was a mere draughtsman, therefore a fumbler and impractical. "You can go back to work up above now."

Before the foreman could find words for an adequate retort, Shorn was back in the hopper.

In the yard he found Geskamp standing at the center of an apprehensive group.

"Nollinrude's gone." He looked at the body of the trucker who had caused the original outburst. "Somebody will have to take him home."

He surveyed the group, trying to gauge their strength, and found nothing to reassure him. Eyes shifted sullenly from his. With an empty feeling in his stomach Shorn knew that the fact of the killing could not be disposed of as easily as the body.

Shorn once more scanned the surroundings. A great blank wall rose immediately to the east; to the north were the Alban Hills, to the south the empty Swanscomb Valley.

Probably these few people were still alone in their knowledge of the killing. He looked from face to face. "A lot of people to keep a secret. If one of us talks — even to his brother or his friend or his wife — then there's no more secret. You all remember Vernisaw Knerwig?"

A nervous mutter assured him that they did: that their urgent hope was to disassociate themselves from any part of the episode.

Geskamp's face was working irritably. Shorn remembered that Geskamp was nominally in charge and was possibly sensitive to any usurpations of his authority. "Yes, Mr. Geskamp? Did you have something to add?"

Geskamp drew back his heavy lips, grinning like a big blond dog. With an effort he restrained himself. "You're doing fine."

Shorn turned back to the others. "You men are leaving the job now. You won't be questioned by the Teleks. Naturally they'll know that Nollinrude has disappeared, but I hope they won't know where. Just in case you are asked — Nollinrude came and went. That's all you know. Another thing." He paused weightily. "If any of us becomes wealthy and the Teleks become full of knowledge — this person will regret that he sold his voice." And he added, as if it were an inconsequential matter, "There's a group to cope with situations of this sort." He looked at Geskamp, but Geskamp kept stonily silent. "Now, I'll get your names — for future reference. One at a time —"

Twenty minutes later a carry-all floated off toward Tran.

"Well," said Geskamp bitterly, "I'm up to my neck in it now. Is that what you wanted?"

"I didn't want it this way. You're in a tough spot. So am I. With luck we'll come through. But — just in case — tonight we'll have to do what I was leading up to."

Geskamp squinted angrily. "Now I'm to be your cat's-paw. In what?"

"You can sign a requisition. You can send a pair of lifts to the explosives warehouse —"

Geskamp's bushy eyebrows took on an odd reverse tilt. "Explosives? How much?"

"A ton of mitrox."

Geskamp said in a tone of hushed respect: "That's enough to blow the stadium ten miles high!"

Shorn grinned. "Exactly. You'd better get that requisition off right now. Then you have the key to the generator room. Tomorrow the main pile is going in. Tonight you and I will arrange the mitrox under the piers."

Geskamp's mouth hung open. "But —"

Shorn's dour face became almost charming. "I know. Wholesale murder. Not sporting. I agree with you. A sneak attack. I agree. Stealth and sneak attacks and back-stabbing are our weapons. We don't have any others. None at all."

"But — why are you so confident of bloodshed?"

Shorn suddenly exploded in anger. "Man, get your head up out of the sand. When will we have another chance of getting every single one without exception?"

Geskamp jumped out of the company airboat assigned to his use, stalked with a set face around the arena toward the construction office. Above him rose two hundred feet of sheer concrete, glowing in the morning sun. In his mind's eye Geskamp saw the dark cartons that he and Shorn had carried below like moles on the night previous; he still moved with reluctance and uncertainty, carried only by Shorn's fire and direction.

Now the trap was set. A single coded radio signal would pulverize the new concrete, fling a molten gout miles into the air, pound a gigantic blow at the earth.

Geskamp's honest face became taut as he wrestled with his conscience. Had he been too malleable? Think what a revenge the Teleks would take for such a disaster! Still, if the Teleks were as terrible a threat to human freedom as Shorn had half made him believe, then the mass killing was a deed to be resolutely carried through, like the killing of dangerous beasts. And certainly the Teleks only paid lip-service to human laws. His mind went to the death of Forence Nollinrude. In ordinary events there would be an inquiry. Nollinrude had killed the trucker; Geskamp, swept by overwhelming rage and pity, had killed the Telek. At the worst a human court would have found him guilty of manslaughter, and no doubt would have granted probation. But with a Telek — Geskamp's blood chilled in his veins. Maybe there was something to Shorn's extreme methods after all; certainly the Teleks could be controlled by no normal methods of law.

He rounded the corner of the tool-room, noted an unfamiliar face within. Good. Home office had acted without inquisitiveness; the shifting of employees had interested no one with authority to ask questions.

He looked into the expediter's room. "Where's the draughtsman?" he asked Cole, the steel detailer.

"Never showed up this morning, Mr. Geskamp."

Geskamp cursed under his breath. Just like Shorn, getting him into trouble, then ducking out, leaving him to face it. Might be better to come clean with the whole incident; after all it had been an accident, a fit of blood-rage. The Teleks could understand so much, surely.

He turned his head. Something flickered at the edge of his vision. He looked sharply. Something like a big black bug whisked up behind a shelf of books. Big cockroach, thought Geskamp. A peculiar cockroach.

He attacked his work in a vicious humor, and foremen around the job asked themselves wonderingly what had got into Geskamp. Three times during the morning he looked into the office for Shorn, but Shorn had made no appearance.

And once, as he ducked under a low soffit on one of the upper decks, a black object darted up behind him. He jerked his eyes around, but the thing had disappeared under the beams.

"Funny bug," he said to the new form foreman, whom he was showing around the job.

"I didn't see it, Mr. Geskamp."

Geskamp returned to the office, obtained Shorn's home address — a
hotel in the Marmion Tower — and put in a visiphone call.

Shorn was not in.

Geskamp turned away, almost bumped into the feet of a Telek
standing in the air before him: a thin somber man with silver hair and
oil-black eyes. He wore two tones of gray, with a sapphire clasp at the
collar of his cape, and the usual Telek slippers of black velvet.

Geskamp's heart started thudding; his hands became moist. The
moment he had been dreading. Where was Shorn?

"You are Geskamp?"

"Yes," said Geskamp. "I —"

He was picked up, hurled through the air. Far, fleeting below, went
the stadium, Swanscomb Valley, the entire countryside. Tran was a gray
and black honeycomb, he was in the sunny upper air, hurtling with
unthinkable speed. Wind roared past his ears, but he felt no pressure
on his skin, no tear at his clothes.

The ocean spread blue below, and something glittered ahead — a
complex edifice of shiny metal, glass and bright color. It floated high in
the sunny air, with no support above or below.

Geskamp saw a glitter, a flash; he was standing on a floor of glass
threaded and drawn with strands of green and gold. The thin gray man
sat behind a table in a yellow chair. The room was flooded with sunlight; Geskamp was too dazed to notice further details.

The Telek said, "Geskamp, tell me what you know of Forence
Nollinrude."

It appeared to Geskamp that the Telek was watching him with
superior knowledge, as if any lie would be instantly known, dismissed
with grim humor. He was a poor liar to begin with. He looked around
for a place to rest his big body. A chair appeared.

"Nollinrude?" He seated himself. "I saw him yesterday. What about
him?"

"Where is he now?"

Geskamp forced a painful laugh. "How would I know?"

A sliver of glass darted through the air, stung the back of Geskamp's neck. He rose to his feet, startled and angry.

"Sit down," said the Telek, in a voice of unnatural coolness.

Geskamp slowly sat down. A kind of faintness dimmed his vision, his brain seemed to move away, seemed to watch dispassionately.

"Where is Nollinrude?"

Geskamp held his breath. A voice said, "He's dead. Down in the concrete."

"Who killed him?"

Geskamp listened to hear what the voice would say.

III

Shorn sat in a quiet tavern in that section of Tran where the old suddenly changes to the new. South were the sword-shaped towers, the neat intervening plazas and parks; north spread the ugly crust of three- and four-story apartments gradually blending into the industrial district.

A young woman with straight brown hair sat across the table from Shorn. She wore a brown cloak without ornament; looking into her face there was little to notice but her eyes — large, brown-black, somber; the rest of her face was without accent.

Shorn was drinking strong tea, his thin dark face in repose.

The young woman seemed to see an indication that the surface calm was false. She put out her hand, rested it on his, a quick exquisite gesture, the first time she had touched him in the three months of their acquaintance. "How could you have done differently?" Her voice became mildly argumentative. "What could you have done?"

"Taken the whole half-dozen underground. Kept Geskamp with me."

"How would that have helped? There'll be a certain number of deaths, a certain amount of destruction — how many and how much is out of our hands. Is Geskamp a valuable man?"

"No. He's a big hard-working likeable fellow, hardly devious or many-tracked enough to be of use. And I don't think he would have come with me. He was to the point of open rebellion as it was — the type who resents infringement."

"It's not impossible that your arrangements are still effective."

"Not a chance. The only matter for speculation is how many the Teleks destroy and whom."

The young woman leaned somberly back in her chair, stared straight ahead. "If nothing else, this episode marks a new place in the — in the — I don't know what to call it. Struggle? Campaign? War?"

"Call it war."

"We're almost out in the open. Public opinion may be aroused, swung to our side."

Shorn shook his head gloomily. "The Teleks have bought most of the police, and I suspect that they own the big newspapers, through fronts, of course. No, we can't expect much public support yet. We'll be called Nihilists, Totalitarists —"

The young woman quoted Turgenev. " 'If you want to annoy an opponent thoroughly or even harm him, you reproach him with every defect or vice you are conscious of in yourself.' "

"It's just as well." Shorn laughed bitterly. "Perhaps it's one of our big advantages, our freedom to merge into the masses. If everyone were anti-Telek, the Teleks would have an easy job. Kill everybody."

"Then they'd have to do all their own work."

"That's right, too."

She made a fluttering gesture, her voice was strained. "It's a blood penance on our century, on humanity —"

Shorn snorted. "Mysticism."

She went on as if she had not heard. "If men were to develop from sub-apes a thousand times — each of those thousand rises would show the same phases, and there would be a Telek phase in all of them. It's as much a part of humanity as hunger and fear and sex."

"And when the Teleks are out of the way — what's the next phase? Is history only a series of bloody phases? Where's the leveling-off point?"

She smiled wanly. "Perhaps when we're all Teleks."

Shorn gave her a strange look — calculation, curiosity, wonder. He returned to his tea as if to practical reality. "I suppose Geskamp has been trying to get hold of me all morning." He considered a moment, then rose to his feet. "I'll call the job and find out what's happened."

A moment later he returned. "Geskamp's nowhere around. A message just came in for me at the hotel, and it's to be delivered by hand only."

"Perhaps Geskamp went of his own accord."

"Perhaps."

"More likely—" she paused. "Anyway, the hotel is a good place to stay away from."

Shorn clenched and unclenched his hands. "It frightens me."

"What?" She seemed surprised.

"My own — vindictiveness. It's not right to hate anyone. A person is bad because exterior forces have hurt his essentially good brain. I realize this — and yet I hate."

"The Teleks?"

"No, not the Teleks." He spoke slowly. "I fear them, good healthy fear. I kill them for survival. Those I *want* to kill, for pleasure, are the men who serve the Teleks for money, who sell their own kind." He clenched, unclenched his hands. "It's unhealthy to think like that."

"You're too much the idealist, Will."

Shorn mused, talking in a monotone. "Our war is the war of ants against giants. They have the power — but they loom, we see them for miles. We're among the swarm. We move a hundred feet, into a new group of people, we're lost. Anonymity, that's our advantage. So we're safe — until a Judas-ant identifies us, drags us forth from the swarm. Then we're lost; the giant foot comes down, there's no escape. We —"

The young woman raised her hand. "Listen."

A voice from the sound-line running under the ceiling molding said, "The murder of a Telek, Forence Nollinrude, Liaison Lieutenant, by subversive conspiracy has been announced. The murderer, Ian Geskamp, superintendent of construction at the Swanscomb Valley Stadium, has disappeared. It is expected that he will implicate a number of confederates when captured."

Shorn sat quietly.

"What will they do if they catch him? Will they turn him over to the authorities?"

Shorn nodded. "They've announced the murder. If they want to maintain the fiction of their subservience to federal law, then they've got to submit to the regular courts. Once he's out of their direct custody, then no doubt he'll die — any one of a number of unpleasant deaths. And then there will be further Acts of God. Another meteor into Geskamp's home town, something of the sort…"

"Why are you smiling?"

"It just occurred to me that Geskamp's home town was Cobent Village, that used to be in Swanscomb Valley. They've already wiped that one off the map. But they'll do something significant enough to point up the moral — that killing Teleks is a very expensive process."

"It's odd that they bother with legality at all."

"It means that they want no sudden showdown. Whatever revolution there is to be, they want it to come gradually, with as little dislocation as possible, no sudden flood of annoying administrative detail." He sat tapping his fingers nervously. "Geskamp was a good fellow. I'm wondering about this message at the hotel."

"If he were captured, drugged, your name and address would come out. You would be a valuable captive."

"Not while I can bite down on my back tooth. Full of cyanide. But I'm curious about that message. If it's from Geskamp he needs help, and we should help him. He knows about the mitrox under the stadium. The subject might not arise during the course of questioning, especially under drugs, but we don't want to run the risk."

"Suppose it's a trick?"

"Well — we might learn something."

"I could get it," she said doubtfully.

Shorn frowned.

"No," she said, "I don't mean by walking in and asking for it; that would be foolish. You write a note authorizing delivery of the message to bearer."

The young woman said to the boy, "It's very important that you follow instructions exactly."

"Yes, miss."

The boy rode the slipway to the Marmion Tower, whose seventh and eighth floors were given over to the Cort Hotel. He rode the lift to the seventh floor, went quietly to the desk.

"Mr. Shorn sent me to pick up his mail." He passed the note across the desk.

The clerk hesitated, looked away in preoccupation, then without words handed the boy an envelope.

The boy returned to the ground floor, walked out on the street, where he paused, waited. Apparently no one followed him. He rode the slipway north, along the gray streets to the Tarrogat, stepped around the corner, jumped on the high-speed East Division slipway. Heavy commercial traffic growled through the street beside him, trucks and drays, a few surface cars. The boy spied a momentary gap, stepped to the outside band, jumped running into the street. He darted across, climbed on the slipway moving in the opposite direction, watching over his shoulder. No one followed. He rode a mile, past the Flatiron Y, turned into Grant Avenue, jumped to the stationary, crouched by the corner.

No one came hurrying after.

He crossed the street, entered the Grand Maison Café.

The food panel made an island down the center; to either side were tables. The boy walked around the food panel, ignoring a table where a young woman in a brown cloak sat by herself. He ducked out an entrance opposite to where he entered, rounded the building, entered once more.

The young woman rose to her feet, followed him out. At the exit they brushed together accidentally.

The boy went about his business, and the young woman turned, went back to the restroom. As she opened the door a black beetle buzzed through with her.

She ducked, looked around the ceiling, but the insect had disappeared. She went to a visiphone, paid for sonic, dialed.

"Well?"

"I've got it."

"Anyone follow?"

"No. I watched him leave Marmion Tower. I watched behind him in —" her voice broke off.

"What's the matter?"

She said in a strained voice, "Get out of there fast. Hurry. Don't ask questions. Get away — *fast*!"

She hung up, pretending that she had not noticed the black bug pressed against the glass, crystal eyes staring at the visiphone dial.

She reached in her pouch, selected one of the four weapons she carried, drew it forth, closed her eyes, snapped the release.

White glare flooded the room, seared behind her closed lids. She ran out the door, picked up the dazed bug in her handkerchief, stuffed it into her pouch. It was strangely heavy, like a slug of lead.

She must hurry. She ran from the restroom, up through the café, out into the street.

Safe among the crowds she watched six emergency vans vomit Black and Golds who rushed to the exits of the Grand Maison Café.

Bitterly she rode the slipway north. The Teleks controlled the police; it was no secret.

She wondered about the beetle in her pouch. It evinced no movement, no sign of life. If her supposition were correct, it would remain quiet so long as she kept light from its eyes, so long as she denied it reference points.

For an hour she wandered the city, intent on evading not only men, but also little black beetle-things. At last she ducked into a narrow passageway in the hard industry quarter, ran up a flight of wooden steps, entered a drab but neat sitting room.

She went to a closet, found a small cannister with a screw top, gingerly pushed the handkerchief and the beetle-thing inside, screwed down the lid.

She removed her long brown cloak, drew a cup of coffee from the dispenser, waited.

Half an hour passed. The door opened. Shorn looked in. His face was haggard and pale as a dog skull; his eyes glowed with an unhealthy yellow light.

She jumped to her feet. "What's happened?"

"Sit still, Laurie, I'm all right." He slumped into a seat.

She drew another cup of coffee, passed it to him. "What happened?"

His eyes burnt brighter. "As soon as I heard from you, I left the tavern. Twenty seconds later — no more — the place exploded. Flame shooting out the door, out the windows — thirty or forty people inside;

I can hear them yelling now —" His mouth sagged. He licked his lips. "I hear them —"

Laurie controlled her voice. "Just ants."

Shorn assented with a ghastly grin. "The giant steps on forty ants, but the guilty ant, the marked ant, the intended ant — he's gone."

She told him about the black bug. He groaned ironically. "It was bad enough dodging spies and Black and Golds. Now little bugs — can it hear?"

"I don't know. I suppose so. It's shut up tight in the can, but sound probably gets through."

"We'd better move it."

She wrapped the can in a towel, tucked it in a closet, shut the door. When she returned, Shorn was eying her with a new look in his eye. "You thought very swiftly, Laurie."

She turned away to hide her pleasure. "I had to."

"You still have the message?"

She handed the envelope across the table.

He read, " 'Get in touch with Clyborn at the Perendalia.' "

"Do you know him?"

"No. We'll make discreet inquiries. I don't imagine there'll be anything good come out of it."

"It's so much — work."

"Easy for the giants. One or two of them manage the entire project. I've heard that the one called Dominion is in charge, and the others don't even realize there's dissatisfaction. Just as we appoint a dog-catcher, then dismiss the problem of stray dogs from our minds. Probably not one Telek in a hundred realizes that we're fighting for our lives, our futures, our dignity as human beings."

After a moment she asked, "Do you think we'll win, Will?"

"I don't know. We have nothing to lose." He yawned, stretched. "Tonight I meet Circumbright; you remember him?"

"He's the chubby little biophysicist."

Shorn nodded. "If you'll excuse me, I think I'll take a nap."

IV

At eleven o'clock Shorn descended to the street. The sky was bright with glow from the lakeshore entertainment strip, the luxury towers of downtown Tran.

He walked along the dark street till he came to Bellman Boulevard, and stepped out on to the slipway.

There was a cold biting wind and few people were abroad; the hum of the rollers below was noticeable. He turned into Stockbridge Street, and as he approached the quarter-mile strip of night stores, the slipways became crowded and Shorn felt more secure. He undertook a few routine precautions, sliding quickly through doors, to break contact with any spy-beetles that might have fixed on him.

At midnight the fog blew thick in from the harbor, smelling of oil, mercaptan, ammonia. Pulling up his hood Shorn descended a flight of stairs, pushed into a basement recreation hall, sidled past the dull-eyed men at the mechanical games. He walked directly toward the men's room, turned at the last minute into a short side corridor, passed through a door marked 'Employees' into a workshop littered with bits and parts from the amusement machines.

Shorn waited a moment, ears alert for sound, then went to the rear of the room, unlocked a steel door, slipped through into a second workshop, much more elaborately fitted than the first. A short stout man with a big head and mild blue eyes looked up. "Hello, Will."

Shorn waved his hand. "Hello, Gorman."

He stood with his back to the door, looking around the molding for a black, apparently innocent, beetle. Nothing in sight. He crossed the room, scribbled on a bit of paper. *"We've got to search the room. Look for a flying spy-cell, like this."* He sketched the beetle he carried with him in the canister, then appended a postscript. *"I'll cover the ventilator."*

An hour's search revealed nothing.

Shorn sighed, relaxed. "Ticklish. If there was one of the things here, and it saw us searching, the Telek at the other end would have known the jig was up. We'd have been in trouble. A fire, an explosion. They missed me once already today by about ten seconds." He set the canister on a bench. "I've got one of the things in here. Laurie caught it; rare presence of mind. Her premise is, that if its eyes and ears are made useless — in other words, if it loses its identity on a spatial frame of reference — then it ceases to exist for the Teleks, and they can no longer manipulate it. I think she's right; the idea seems intuitively sound."

Gorman Circumbright picked up the canister, jiggled it. "Rather heavy. Why did you bring it down here?"

"We've got to figure out a counter to it. It must function like a miniature video transmitter. I suppose Alvac Corporation makes them. If we can identify the band it broadcasts on, we can build ourselves detectors, warning units."

Circumbright sat looking at the can. "If it's still in operation, if it's still broadcasting, I can find out very swiftly."

He set the can beside an all-wave tuner. Shorn unscrewed the lid, gingerly removed the bug, still wrapped in cloth, set it on the bench. Circumbright pointed to a scale, glowing at several points. He started to speak, but Shorn motioned for silence, pointed to the bug. Circumbright nodded, wrote, *"The lower lines are possibly static, from the power source. The sharp line at the top is the broadcast frequency — very sharp. Powerful."*

Shorn replaced the bug in the can. Circumbright turned away from the tuner. "If it's insensitive to infrared we can see to take it apart, disconnect the power."

Shorn frowned doubtfully. "How could we be sure?"

"Give it to me." Circumbright clipped leads from an oscillograph to the back of the tuner, dialed to the spy-beetle's carrier frequency.

The oscillograph showed a normal sine-curve.

"Now. Turn out the lights."

Shorn threw the switch. The room was dark except for the dancing yellow-green light of the oscillograph and the dull red murk from the infra-red projector.

Circumbright's bulk cut off the glow from the projector; Shorn watched the oscillograph face. There was no change in the wave.

"Good," said Circumbright. "And I think that if I strain my eyes I can — or better, reach in the closet and hand me the heat-conversion lenses. Top shelf."

He worked fifteen minutes, then suddenly the carrier wave on the face of the oscillograph vanished. "Ah," sighed Circumbright. "That's got it. You can turn the lights back on now."

Together they stood looking down at the bug — a little black torpedo two inches long with two crystalline eyes bulging at each side of the head.

"Nice job," said Circumbright. "It's an Alvac product all right. I'll say a word to Graythorne; maybe he can introduce a few disturbing factors."

"What about that detector unit?"

Circumbright pursed his lips. "For each of the bugs there's probably a different frequency; otherwise they'd get their signals mixed up. But the power-bank probably radiates about the same in all cases. I can fix up a jury-rig which you can use for a few days, then Graythorne can bring us down some tailor-made jobs from Alvac, using the design data."

He crossed the room, found a bottle of red wine which he set beside Shorn. "Relax a few minutes."

Half an hour passed. Shorn watched quietly while Circumbright soldered together stock circuits, humming in a continuous tuneless drone.

"There," said Circumbright finally. "If one of those bugs gets within a hundred yards, this will vibrate, thump."

"Good." Shorn tucked the device tenderly in his breast pocket, while Circumbright settled himself into an armchair, stuffed tobacco in a pipe. Shorn watched him curiously. Circumbright, placid and unemotional as a man could be, revealed himself to Shorn by various small signs, such as pressing the tobacco home with a thumb more vigorous than necessary.

"I hear another Telek was killed yesterday."

"Yes. I was there."

"Who is this Geskamp?"

"Big blond fellow. What's the latest on him?"

"He's dead."

"Hm-m-m." Shorn was silent a moment, a sick feeling at the pit of his stomach. "How?"

"The Teleks turned him over to the custody of the Federal Marshal at Knoll. He was shot trying to escape."

Shorn felt as if anger were being pumped inside him, as if he were swelling, as if the pressure against his taut muscles were too great to bear.

"Take it easy," said Circumbright mildly.

"I'll kill Teleks from a sense of duty," said Shorn. "I won't enjoy it. But — and I feel ashamed, I'll admit — I *want* to kill the Federal Marshal at Knoll."

"It wasn't the Federal Marshal himself," said Circumbright. "It was two of his deputies. And it's always possible that Geskamp actually did try to escape. We'll know for sure tomorrow."

"How so?"

"We're moving out a little bit. There'll be an example made of those two if they're guilty. We'll narcotize them tonight, find out the truth. If they're working for the Teleks — they'll go." Circumbright spat on the floor. "Although I dislike the label of a terrorist organization."

"What else can we do? If we got a confession, turned them over to the Section Attorney, they'd be reprimanded, turned loose."

"True enough." Circumbright puffed meditatively.

Shorn moved restlessly in his chair. "It frightens me, the imminence, the urgency of all this — and how few people are aware of it! Surely there's never been an emergency so ill-publicized before! In a week, a month, three months, there'll be more dead people on Earth than live ones, unless we get the entire shooting-match at once in the stadium."

Circumbright puffed at his pipe. "Will, sometimes I wonder whether we're not approaching the struggle from the wrong direction."

"How so?"

"Perhaps instead of attacking the Teleks, we should be learning more of the fundamental nature of telekinetics."

Shorn leaned back fretfully. "The Teleks don't know themselves."

"A bird can't tell you much about aerodynamics. The Teleks have a disadvantage which is not at all obvious — the fact that action comes too easy, that they are under no necessity to think. To build a dam, they look at a mountain, move it down into the valley. If the dam gives way, they move down another mountain, but they never look at a slide rule. In this respect, at least, they represent a retrogression rather than an advance."

Shorn slowly opened and closed his hands, watching as if it were the first time he had ever seen them. "They're caught in the stream of life, like the rest of us. It's part of the human tragedy that there can't be any compromise; it's them or us."

Circumbright heaved a deep sigh. "I've racked my brains…Compromise. Why can't two kinds of people live together? Our abilities complement each other."

"One time it was that way. The first generation. The Teleks were still common men, perhaps a little peculiar in that things always turned out lucky for them. Then Joffrey and his Telekinetic Congress, and the reinforcing, the catalysis, the forcing, whatever it was — and suddenly they're different."

"If there were no fools," said Circumbright, "either among us or among them, we could co-inhabit the earth. There's the flaw in any compromise negotiation — the fact of fools, both among the Teleks and the common men."

"I don't quite follow you."

Circumbright gestured with his pipe. "There will always be Telek fools to antagonize common-man fools; then the common-man fools will ambush the Teleks, and the Teleks will be very upset, especially since for every Telek, there are forty Earth fools eager to kill him. So they use force, terror. Inexorable, inevitable. But — they have a choice. They can leave Earth, find a home somewhere among the planets they claim they visit; they can impose this reign of power; or they can return to humanity, renounce telekinesis entirely. Those are the choices open to them."

"And our choices?"

"We submit or we challenge. In the first instance we become slaves. In the second we either kill the Teleks, drive them away, or we all become dead men."

Shorn sipped at his wineglass. "We might all become Teleks ourselves."

"Or we might find a scientific means to control or cancel out telekinesis." Circumbright poured a careful finger of wine for himself. "My own instinct is to explore the last possibility."

"There's nowhere to get a foothold in the subject."

"Oh I don't know. We have a number of observations. Telekinesis and teleportation have been known for thousands of years. It took the concentration of telekinetics at Joffrey's Congress to develop the power fully. We know that Telek children are telekinetic — whether by contagion or by genetics we can't be sure."

"Probably both. A genetic predisposition; parental training."

Circumbright nodded. "Probably both. Although as you know, in rare instances they reward a common man by making a Telek out of him."

"Evidently telekinesis is latent in everyone."

"There's a large literature of early experiments and observations. The so-called spiritualist study of poltergeists and house-demons might be significant."

Shorn remained silent.

"I've tried to systematize the subject," Circumbright continued, "deal with it logically. The first question seems to be, does the Law of Conservation of Energy apply or not? When a Telek floats a ton of iron across the sky by looking at it, is he creating energy or is he directing the use of energy from an unseen source? There is no way of knowing offhand."

Shorn stretched, yawned, settled back in his chair. "I have heard a metaphysical opinion, to the effect that the Telek uses nothing more than confidence. The universe that he perceives has reality only to the backdrop of his own brain. He sees a chair; the image of a chair exists in his mind. He orders the chair to move across the room. His confidence is so great that, in his mind, he believes he sees the chair move, and he bases his future actions on the perception. Somehow he is not disappointed. In other words, the chair has moved because he believes he has moved it."

Circumbright puffed placidly on his pipe.

Shorn grinned. "Go on; I'm sorry I interrupted you."

"Where does the energy come from? Is the mind a source, a valve or a remote control? There are the three possibilities. Force is applied; the mind directs the force. But does the force *originate* in the mind, is the force *collected, channeled through* the mind, or does the mind act like a modulator, a grid in a vacuum tube?"

Shorn slowly shook his head. "So far we have not even defined the type of energy at work. If we knew that, we might recognize the function of the mind."

"Or vice versa. It works either way. But if you wish, consider the force at work. In all cases, an object moves in a single direction. That is to say, there has been no observed case of an explosion or a compression. The object moves as a unit. How? Why? To say the mind projects a force-field is ignoring the issue, redefining at an equal level of abstraction."

"Perhaps the mind is able to control poltergeists — creatures like the old Persian genii."

Circumbright tapped the ash from his pipe. "I've considered the possibility. Who are the poltergeists? Ghosts? Souls of the dead? A matter for speculation. Why are the Teleks able to control them, and ordinary people not?"

Shorn grinned. "I assume these are rhetorical questions — because I don't have the answers."

"Perhaps a form of gravity is at work. Imagine a cup-shaped gravity screen around the object, open on the side the Telek desires motion. I have not calculated the gravitational acceleration generated by matter at its average universal density, from here to infinity, but I assume it would be insignificant. A millimeter a day, perhaps. Count the cup-shaped gravity screen out; likewise a method for rendering the object opaque to the passage of neutrinos in a given direction."

"Poltergeists, gravity, neutrinos — all eliminated. What have we left?"

Circumbright chuckled. "I haven't eliminated the poltergeists. But I incline to the Organic Theory. That is, the concept that all the minds and all the matter of the universe are interconnected, much like brain cells and muscular tissue of the body. When certain of these brain cells achieve a sufficiently close vinculum, they are able to control certain twitchings of the corporeal frame of the universe. How? Why? I don't know. After all, it's only an idea, a sadly anthropomorphic idea."

Shorn looked thoughtfully up at the ceiling. Circumbright was a three-way scientist. He not only proposed theories, he not only devised critical experiments to validate them, but he was an expert laboratory technician. "Does your theory suggest any practical application?"

Circumbright scratched his ear.

"Not yet. I need to cross-fertilize it with a few other notions. Like the metaphysics you brought up a few moments ago. If I only had a Telek who would submit himself to experiments, we might get somewhere — and I think I hear Dr. Kurgill."

He rose to his feet, padded to the door. He opened it; Shorn saw him stiffen.

A deep voice said, "Hello, Circumbright; this is my son. Cluche, meet Gorman Circumbright, one of our foremost tacticians."

The two Kurgills came into the laboratory. The father was short, spare, with simian length to his arms. He had a comical simian face with a high forehead, long upper lip, flat nose. The son resembled his father not at all: a striking young man with noble features, a proud crest of auburn hair, an extreme mode of dress, reminiscent of Telek style. The elder was quick of movement, talkative, warm; the younger was careful of eye and movement.

Circumbright turned toward Shorn. "Will —" he stopped short. "Excuse me," he said to the Kurgills. "If you'll sit down I'll be with you at once."

He hurried into the adjoining storeroom. Shorn stood in the shadows.

"What's the trouble?"

Shorn took Circumbright's hand, held it against the warning unit in his pocket.

Circumbright jerked. "The thing's vibrating!"

Shorn looked warily into the room beyond. "How well do you know the Kurgills?"

Circumbright said, "The doctor's my lifelong friend, I'd go my life for him."

"And his son?"

"I can't say."

They stared at each other, then by common accord, looked through the crack of the door. Cluche Kurgill had seated himself in the chair Shorn had vacated, while his father stood in front of him, teetering comfortably on his toes, hands behind his back.

"I'd swear that no bug slipped past us while I stood in the doorway," muttered Circumbright.

"No, I don't think it did."

"That means it's on one or the other of their persons."

"It might be unintentional — a plant. But how would the Teleks know the Kurgills intended to come down here?"

Shorn shook his head.

Circumbright sighed. "I guess not."

"The bug will be where it can see, but where it can't be seen — or at least, not noticed."

Their glances went to the ornate headdress Cluche Kurgill wore on one side of his head: a soft roll of gray-green leather, bound by a strip across his hair, trailing a dangle of moon-opals past his ear.

Circumbright said in a tight voice, "We can expect destruction at any time. Explosion —"

Shorn said slowly, "I doubt if they'll send an explosion. If they feel they are unsuspected, they'll prefer to bide their time."

Circumbright said huskily, "Well, what do you propose, then?"

Shorn hesitated a moment before replying. "We're in a devil of a ticklish position. Do you have a narco-hypnotic stinger handy?"

Circumbright nodded.

"Perhaps then —"

Two minutes later Circumbright rejoined the Kurgills. The old doctor was in a fine humor. "Gorman," he said to Circumbright, "I'm very proud of Cluche here. He's been a scapegrace all his life — but now he wants to make something of himself."

"Good," said Circumbright with hollow heartiness. "If he were of our conviction, I could use him right now — but I wouldn't want him to do anything against his —"

"Oh no, not at all," said Cluche. "What's your problem?"

"Well, Shorn just left for a very important meeting — the regional chiefs — and he's forgotten his code-book. I couldn't trust an ordinary messenger, but if you will deliver the code-book you'd be doing us a great service."

"Any little thing I can do to help," said Cluche. "I'll be delighted."

His father regarded him with fatuous pride. "Cluche has surprised me. He caught me out just the day before yesterday, and now nothing must do but that he plunges in after me. Needless to say, I'm very pleased; glad to see that he's a chip off the old block; nothing stands in his way."

Circumbright said, "I can count on you then? You'll have to follow instructions exactly."

"Quite all right, sir, glad to help."

"Good," said Circumbright. "First thing then — you'll have to change your clothes. You'd be too conspicuous as you are."

"Oh, now!" protested Cluche. "Surely a cloak —"

"No!" snapped Circumbright. "You'll have to dress as a dock worker from the skin out. No cloak would hide that headgear. In the next room you'll find some clothes. Come with me, I'll make a light."

He held open the door; reluctantly Cluche stepped through.

The door closed. Shorn expertly seized Cluche's neck, digging strong fingers into the motor nerves. Cluche stiffened, trembling.

Circumbright slapped the front of his neck with a barbful of drug, then fumbled for Cluche's headdress. He felt a smooth little object bulging with two eyes like a tadpole. He said easily, "Can't seem to find the light —" He tucked the bug into his pouch. "Here it is. Now — that fancy headgear. I'll put it into this locker; it'll be safe till you get back." He winked at Shorn, shoved the pouch into a heavy metal tool chest.

They looked down at the sprawled body. "There's not much time," said Circumbright. "I'll send Kurgill home and we'll have to get out ourselves." He looked regretfully around the room. "There's a lot of fine equipment here…We can get more, I suppose."

Shorn clicked his tongue. "What will you tell Kurgill?"

"Um-m-m. The truth would kill him."

"Cluche was killed by the Teleks. He died defending the code-book. The Teleks have his name; he'll have to go underground himself."

"He'll have to go under tonight. I'll warn him to lay low, say in Capistrano's, until we call him, then we can give him the bad news. As soon as he's gone we'll take Cluche out the back way, to Laurie's."

Cluche Kurgill sat in a chair, staring into space. Circumbright leaned back smoking his pipe. Laurie, in white pajamas and a tan robe, lay sidewise on a couch in the corner watching; Shorn sat beside her.

"How long have you been spying for the Teleks, Cluche?"

"Three days."

"Tell us about it."

"I found some writings of my father's which led me to believe he was a member of a sub-organization. I needed money. I reported to a police sergeant who I knew to be interested. He wanted me to furnish him the details; I refused. I demanded to speak to a Telek. I threatened the policeman —"

"What is his name?"

"Sergeant Cagolian Loo, of the Moxenwohl Precinct."

"Go on."

"Finally he arranged an appointment with Adlari Dominion. I met Dominion at the Pequinade, out in Vireburg. He gave me a thousand crowns and a spy-cell which I was to carry with me at all times. When anything interesting occurred I was to press an attention button."

"What were your instructions?"

"I was to become a conspirator along with my father, accompanying him as much as possible. If my efforts resulted in the arrest of important figures, he hinted that I might be made a Telek myself."

"Did he intimate how this metamorphosis is accomplished?"

"No."

"When are you to report to Dominion again?"

"I am to contact him by visiphone at 2 P.M. tomorrow, at Glarietta Pavilion."

"Is there any password or identification code?"

"No."

Silence held the room for several minutes. Shorn stirred, rose to his feet. "Gorman — suppose I were to be metamorphosed, suppose I were to become a Telek."

Circumbright chewed placidly on his pipestem. "It would be a fine thing. I don't quite understand how you'll manage. Unless," he added in a dry voice, "you intend to turn us all in to Adlari Dominion."

"No. But look at Cluche. Look at me."

Circumbright looked, grimaced, straightened up in his seat.

Shorn watched expectantly. "Could it be done?"

"Oh. I see. Give you more nose, a longer chin, fuller cheeks, a lot of red hair —"

"And Cluche's clothes."

"You'd pass."

"Especially if I come with information."

"That's what's puzzling me. What kind of information could you give Dominion that would please him but wouldn't hurt us?"

Shorn told him.

Circumbright puffed on his pipe. "It's a big decision. But it's a good exchange. Unless he's got the same thing already, from other sources."

"Such as Geskamp? In which case, we lose nothing."

"True." Circumbright went to the visiphone. "Tino? Bring your gear over to —" he looked at Laurie: "What's the address?"

"Two-nine two-four fourteen Martinvelt."

V

The red-haired man moved with a taut wiriness that had not been characteristic of Cluche Kurgill. Laurie inspected him critically.

"Walk slower, Will. Don't flail your arms so. Cluche was very languid."

"Check this." Shorn walked across the room.

"Better."

"Very well. I'm gone. Wish me luck. My first stop is the old workshop for Cluche's spy-cell. He'd hardly be likely to leave it there."

"But aren't you taking a chance, going back to the workshop?"

"I don't think so. I hope not. If the Teleks planned to destroy it, they would have done so last night." He waved his hand abruptly and was gone.

He rode the slipway, aping the languorous and lofty condescension he associated with Cluche. The morning had been overcast and blustery, with spatters of cold rain, but at noon the clouds broke. The sun surged through gaps in the hurrying wrack, and the great gray buildings of Tran stood forth like proud lords. Shorn tilted his head back; this was the grandeur of simple bulk, but nevertheless impressive. He himself preferred construction on a smaller scale, buildings to suit a lesser number of more highly individualized people. He thought of the antique Mediterranean temples, gaudy in their pinks and greens and blues, although now the marble had bleached white. Such idiosyncrasy was possible, even enforced, in the ancient monarchies. Today every man, in theory his own master, was required to mesh with his fellows, like a part in a great gear cluster. The culture-colors and culture-tones came out at the common denominator, the melange of all colors: gray. Buildings grew taller and wider from motives of economy — the volume increased by the cube but the enclosing surface only by the square. The motif was utilitarianism, mass policy, each tenant relinquishing edges and fringes of his personality, until only the common basic core — a sound roof, hot and cold water, good light, air-conditioning and good elevator service — remained.

People living in masses, thought Shorn, were like pebbles on a beach, each grinding and polishing his neighbor until all were absolutely uniform. Color and flair were to be found only in the wilderness and among the Teleks. Imagine a world populated by Teleks; imagine the four thousand expanded to four hundred million, four billion! First to go would be the cities. There would be no more concentrations, no more giant gray buildings, no directed rivers of men and women. Humanity would explode like a nova. The cities would corrode and crumble, great mournful hulks, the final monuments to medievalism. Earth would be too small, too limited. Out to the planets, where the Teleks claimed to roam at will. Flood Mars with blue oceans, filter the sky of Venus. Neptune, Uranus, Pluto — call them in, bestow warm new orbits upon them. Bring in even Saturn, so vast and yet with a surface gravity only a trifle more than Earth's... But these great works, suppose they exhausted the telekinetic energy, wherever it originated? Suppose some morning the Teleks awoke and found the power gone! Then — the crystal sky-castles falling! Food, shelter, warmth needed, and no secure gray cities, no ant-hill buildings, none of the pedestrian energies of metal and heat and electricity! Then what calamity! What wailing and cursing!

Shorn heaved a deep sigh. Speculation. Telekinetic energy might well be infinite. Or it might be at the point of exhaustion at this moment. Speculation, and not germane to his present goal.

He frowned. Perhaps it was important. Perhaps some quiet circuit in his mind was at work, aligning him into new opinions...

Ahead was the basement recreation hall. Shorn guiltily realized that he had been swinging along at his own gait, quite out of character with the personality of Cluche Kurgill. Best not forget these details; there would be opportunity for only one mistake.

He descended the stairs, strode through the hall, past the clicking, glowing, humming game machines, where men, rebelling at the predictability of their lives, came to buy synthetic adventure and surprise.

He walked unchallenged through the door marked 'Employees'; at the next door he paused, wondering whether he had remembered to bring the key, wondering if a spy-cell might be hidden in the shadows, watching the door.

If so, would Cluche Kurgill be likely to possess a key? It was in the bounds of possibility, he decided, and in any event would not be interpreted as suspicious.

Shorn groped into his pouch. The key was there. He opened the door, and assuming the furtive part of a spy, entered the workshop.

It was as they had left it the night before. Shorn went quickly to the tool chest, found Circumbright's pouch, brought forth the bug, set it carefully into his headdress.

Now — get out as fast as possible. He looked at his watch. Twelve noon. At two, Cluche's appointment with Adlari Dominion, chief of the Telek Liaison Committee.

Shorn ate an uncomfortable lunch in one corner of the Mercantile Mart Foodarium, a low-ceilinged acreage dotted with tables precisely as a tile floor, and served by a three-tier display of food moving slowly under a transparent case. His head itched furiously under the red toupee, and he dared not scratch lest he disturb Tino's elaborate effort. Secondly, he decided that the Foodarium, the noon resort of hurried day-workers, was out of character for Cluche Kurgill. Among the grays and dull greens and browns, his magnificent Telek-style garments made him appear like a flamingo in a chicken-run. He felt glances of dull hostility; the Teleks were envied but respected; one of their own kind aping the Teleks was despised with the animosity that found no release elsewhere.

Shorn ate quickly and departed. He followed Zyke Alley into Multiflores Park, where he sauntered back and forth among the dusty sycamores.

At two he sat himself deliberately in a kiosk, dialed Glarietta Pavilion on the visiphone. The connection clicked home; the screen glowed with a fanciful black and white drawing of Glarietta Pavilion, and a terse man's voice spoke. "Glarietta Pavilion."

"I want to speak to Adlari Dominion; Cluche Kurgill calling."

A thin face appeared, inquisitive, impertinent, with a lumpy nose, pale blue eyes set at a birdlike slant. "What do you want?"

Shorn frowned. He had neglected an important item of information; it would hardly do to ask the man in the visiphone if he were Adlari Dominion whom he was supposed to have met three days previously.

"I had an appointment for today at two," and cautiously he watched the man in the screen.

"You can report to me."

"No," said Shorn, now confident. The man was too pushing, too authoritative. "I want to speak to Adlari Dominion. What I have to say is not for your ears."

The thin man glared. "I'll be the judge of that; Dominion can't be bothered every five minutes."

"If Dominion learns that you are standing in my way, he will not be pleased."

The thin face flushed red. His hand swept up, the screen went pale-green. Shorn waited.

The screen lit once more, showing a bright room with high white walls. Windows opened on sun-dazzled clouds. A man, thin as the first to answer the screen, but somber, with gray hair and oil-black eyes, looked quietly at him. Under the bore of the sharp eyes, Shorn suddenly felt uneasy. Would his disguise hold up?

"Well, Kurgill, what do you have to tell me?"

"It's a face-to-face matter."

"Hardly wise," Dominion commented. "Don't you trust the privacy of the visiphone? I assure you it's not tapped."

"No. I trust the visiphone. But — I stumbled on something big. I want to be sure I get what's coming to me."

"Oh." Dominion made no play at misunderstanding. "You've been working — how long?"

"Three days."

"And already you expect the greatest reward it's in our power to bestow?"

"It's worth it. If I'm a Telek, it's to my advantage to help you. If I'm not — it isn't. Simple as that."

Dominion frowned slightly. "You're hardly qualified to estimate the value of your information."

"Suppose I knew of a brain disease which attacks only Teleks. Suppose I knew that inside of a year half or three-quarters of the Teleks would be dead?"

Dominion's face changed not a flicker. "Naturally I want to know about it."

Shorn made no reply.

Dominion said slowly, "If such is your information, and we authenticate it, you will be rewarded suitably."

Shorn shook his head. "I can't take the chance. This is my windfall. I've got to make sure I get what I'm after; I may not have another chance."

Dominion's mouth tightened, but he said mildly enough, "I understand your viewpoint."

"I want to come up to the Pavilion. But a word of warning to you; there's no harm in clear understanding between friends."

"None whatever."

"Don't try drugs on me. I've got a cyanide capsule in my mouth. I'll kill myself before you get something for nothing."

Dominion smiled grimly. "Very well, Kurgill. Don't execute yourself, swallow it by mistake."

Shorn smiled likewise. "Only as a gesture of protest. How shall I come up to Glarietta?"

"Hire a cab."

"Openly?"

"Why not?"

"You're not afraid of counter-espionage?"

Dominion's eyes narrowed; his head tilted slightly. "I thought we discussed that at our previous meeting."

Shorn took care not to protest his recollection too vehemently. "Very well, I'll be right up."

✳

Glarietta Pavilion floated high above the ocean, a fairy-book cloud-castle — shining white terraces, ranked towers with red and blue parasol roofs, gardens verdant with foliage and vines trailing down into the air.

The cab slid down on a landing flat. Shorn alighted. The driver looked at him without favor. "Want me to wait?"

"No, you can go." Shorn thought wryly, he'd either be leaving under his own power or not be leaving at all.

A door slid back before him; he entered a hall walled with russet, orange, purple and green prisms, glowing in the brilliant upper-air light. In a raised alcove sat a young woman, a beautiful creature with glossy butter-colored hair, a cream-smooth face.

"Yes, sir?" she asked, impersonally courteous.

"I want to see Adlari Dominion. I'm Cluche Kurgill."

She touched a key below her. "To your right."

He climbed a glass staircase which spiraled up a green glass tube, came out in a waiting room walled with gold-shot red rock that had never been quarried on Earth. Dark-green ivy veiled one wall; white columns opposite made a graceful frame into an herbarium full of green light and lush green growth, white and scarlet flowers.

Shorn hesitated, looked around him. A golden light blinked in the wall, an aperture appeared. Adlari Dominion stood in the opening. "Come in, Kurgill."

Shorn stepped into the wash of light, and for a moment lost Dominion in the dazzle. When vision returned, Dominion was lounging in a hammock-chair supported by a glistening rod protruding horizontally from the wall. A red-leather ottoman was the only other article of furniture visible. Three of the walls were transparent glass, giving on a magnificent vista: clouds bathed in sunlight, blue sky, blue sea.

Dominion pointed to the ottoman. "Have a seat."

The ottoman was only a foot high; sitting in it Shorn would be forced to crane his neck to see Dominion.

"No, thanks. I prefer to stand." He put a foot on the ottoman, inspected Dominion coolly, eye to eye.

Dominion said evenly, "What do you have to tell me?"

Shorn started to speak, but found it impossible to look into the smoldering black eyes and think at the same time. He turned his eyes out the window to a pinnacle of white cloud. "I've naturally considered this situation carefully. If you've done the same — as I imagine you have — then there's no point in each of us trying to outwit the other. I have information that's important, critically important, to a great number of Teleks. I want to trade this information for Telek status." He glanced toward Dominion whose eyes had never faltered, looked away once more.

"I'm trying to arrange this statement with absolute clarity, so there'll be complete understanding between us. First, I want to remind you, I have poison in my mouth. I'll kill myself before I part with what I know, and I guarantee you'll never have another chance to learn what I can tell you." Shorn glanced earnestly sidewise at Dominion. "No hypnotic drug can act fast enough to prevent me from biting open my cyanide — well, enough of that.

"Second: I can't trust any verbal or written contract you make; if I accepted such a contract I'd have no means to enforce it. You are in a stronger position. If you deliver your part of the bargain, and I fail to deliver my part, you can still arrange that I be — well, penalized. Therefore, to demonstrate your good faith, you must make delivery before I do.

"In other words, make me a Telek. Then I'll tell you what I know."

Dominion sat staring at him a full thirty seconds. Then he said softly, "Three days ago Cluche Kurgill was not so rigorous."

"Three days ago, Cluche Kurgill did not know what he knows now."

Dominion said abruptly, "I cannot argue with your exposition. If I were you, in your position, I would make the same stipulation. However —" he looked Shorn keenly up and down "— three days ago I would have considered you an undesirable adjunct."

Shorn assumed a lofty expression. "Judging from the Teleks I have known, I would not have assumed you to be so critical."

"You talk past your understanding," said Dominion crisply. "Do you think that men like Nollinrude, for instance, who was just killed, are typical of the Teleks? Do you think that we are all careless of our destiny?" His mouth twisted contemptuously. "There are forces at work which you do not know of, tremendous patterns laid out for the future. But enough; these are high-level ideas."

He floated clear of his chair, lowered to the floor. "I agree to your stipulation. Come with me, we'll get it over with. You see, we are not inflexible; we can move swiftly and decisively when we wish."

He led Shorn back into the green glass tube, jerked himself to the upper landing, watched impatiently while Shorn circled up the steps.

"Come." He stepped out on a wide white terrace bathed in afternoon sunlight, went directly to a low table on which rested a cubical block of marble.

He reached into a cabinet under the table, pulled out a small speaker, spoke into the mesh. "The top two hundred to Glarietta Pavilion." He turned back to Shorn. "Naturally there'll be certain matters you must familiarize yourself with."

"In order to become a Telek, you mean?"

"No, no," snapped Dominion. "That's a simple mechanical matter. Your perspective must be adjusted; you'll be living with a new orientation toward life."

"I had no idea it was quite so involved."

"There's a great deal you don't understand." He motioned brusquely. "Now to business. Watch that marble block on the table. Think of it as part of yourself, controlled by your own nervous impulses. No, don't look around; fix on the marble block. I'll stand here." He took a place near the table. "When I point to the left, move it toward the left; when I point to the right, move it to the right. Mind now, the cube is part of your organism, part of your flesh, like your hands and feet."

There was murmuring and a rustle behind Shorn; obedient to Dominion he fastened his eyes on the cube.

"Now." Dominion pointed to the left.

Shorn willed the cube to the left.

"The cube is part of you," said Dominion. "Your own body."

Shorn felt a cool tremor at his skin. The cube moved to the left.

Dominion pointed to the right. Shorn willed the cube to the right. The tingling increased. It was as if he were gradually finding himself immersed in cool carbonated water.

Left. Right. Left. Right. The cube seemed to be nearer to him, though he had not moved. As near as his own hand. His mind seemed to break through a tough sphincter into a new medium, cool and wide; he saw the world in a sudden new identity, something part of himself.

Dominion stepped away from the table; Shorn was hardly conscious that he no longer made directive gestures. He moved the cube right, left, raised it six feet into the air, twenty feet, sent it circling high around the sky. As he followed it with his eyes, he became aware of Teleks standing silently behind him, watching expressionlessly.

He brought the cube back to the table. Now he knew how to do it. He lifted himself into the air, moved across the terrace, set himself down. When he looked around the Teleks had gone.

Dominion wore a cool smile. "You take hold with great ease."

"It seems natural enough. What is the function of the others, the Teleks behind on the terrace?"

Dominion shrugged. "We know little of the actual mechanism. At the beginning, of course, I helped you move the cube, as did the others. Gradually we let our minds rest, and you did it all."

Shorn stretched. "I feel myself the center, the hub, of everything — as far as I can see."

Dominion nodded without interest. "Now — come with me." He sped through the air. Shorn followed, exulting in his new power and freedom. Dominion paused by the corner of the terrace, glanced over his shoulder. Shorn saw his face in the fore-shortened angle: white, rather pinched features, eyes subtly tilted, brows drawn down, mouth subtly down-curving. Shorn's elation gave way to sudden wariness. Dominion had arranged the telekinetic indoctrination with a peculiar facility. The easiest way to get the desired information, certainly; but was Dominion sufficiently free from vindictiveness to accept defeat? Shorn considered the expression he had surprised on Dominion's face.

It was a mistake to assume that any man, Telek or not, would accept with good grace the terms dictated by a paid turncoat.

Dominion would restrain himself until he learned what Shorn could tell him; then — and then?

Shorn slowed his motion. How could Dominion arrange a moment of gloating before he finally administered the *coup de grâce*? Poison seemed most likely. Shorn grinned. Dominion would consider it beautifully just if Shorn could be killed with his own poison. A sharp blow or pressure under the jaw would break the capsule in his tooth.

Somehow Dominion would manage.

They entered a great echoing hall, suffused with green-yellow light that entered through panes in the high-vaulted dome. The floor was silver-shot marble; dark-green foliage grew in formal raised boxes. The air was fresh and odorous with the scent of leaves.

Dominion crossed without pause. Shorn halted halfway across.

Dominion turned his head. "Come."

"Where?"

Dominion's mouth slowly bent into a grimace that was unmistakably dangerous. "Where we can talk."

"We can talk here. I can tell you what I want to tell you in ten seconds. Or if you like, I'll take you to the source of the danger."

"Very well," said Dominion. "Suppose you reveal the nature of the threat against the Teleks. A brain disease, you said?"

"No. I used the idea as a figure of speech. The danger I refer to is more cataclysmic than a disease. Let's go out in the open air. I feel constricted." He grinned at Dominion.

Dominion drew in a deep breath. It must infuriate him, thought Shorn, to be commanded and forced to obey a common man and a traitor to boot. Shorn made a careless gesture. "I intend to keep my part of the bargain; let's have no misunderstanding there. However — I want to escape with my winnings, if you understand me."

"I understand you," said Dominion. "I understand you very well." He made an internal adjustment, managed to appear almost genial. "However, perhaps you misjudge my motives. You are a Telek now; we conduct ourselves by a strict code of behavior which you must learn."

Shorn put on a face as gracious as Dominion's. "I suggest then that we hold our conference down on Earth."

Dominion pursed his lips. "You must acclimate yourself to Telek surroundings — think, act, like a Telek."

"In due time," said Shorn. "At the moment I'm rather confused; the sense of power comes as a great intoxication."

"It apparently has not affected your capacity for caution," Dominion observed dryly.

"I suggest that we at least go out into the open, where we can talk at leisure."

Dominion sighed. "Very well."

VI

Laurie went restlessly to the dispenser, drew tea for herself, coffee for Circumbright. "I just can't seem to sit still —"

Circumbright inspected the pale face with scientific objectivity. If Laurie condescended to even the slightest artifice or coquetry, he thought, she would become a creature of tremendous charm. He watched her appreciatively as she went to the window, looked up into the sky.

Nothing to see but reflected glow; nothing to hear but the hum of far traffic.

She returned to the couch. "Have you told Doctor Kurgill — of Cluche?"

Circumbright stirred his tea. "Naturally I couldn't tell him the truth."

"No." Laurie looked off into space. She shuddered. "I've never been so nervous before. Suppose —" her forebodings could find no words.

"You're very fond of Shorn, aren't you?"

The quick look, the upward flash of her eyes, was enough.

They sat in silence.

"*Sh*," said Laurie. "I think he's coming."

Circumbright said nothing.

Laurie rose to her feet. They both watched the door latch. It moved. The door slid back. The hall was empty.

Laurie gasped in something like terror. There came a tapping at the window.

They wheeled. Shorn was outside, floating in the air.

For a moment they stood paralyzed. Shorn rapped with his knuckles; they saw his mouth form the words, "Let me in."

Laurie walked stiffly to the window, swung it open. Shorn jumped down into the room.

"Why did you scare us like that?" she asked indignantly.

"I'm proud of myself. I wanted to demonstrate my new abilities."

He drew himself a cup of coffee. "I guess you'll want to know my adventures."

"Of course!"

He sat down at the table and described his visit to Glarietta Pavilion. Circumbright listened placidly. "And now what?"

"And now — you've got a Telek to experiment on. Unless Dominion conceives a long-distance method of killing me. He's spending a restless night, I should imagine."

Circumbright grunted.

"First," said Shorn, "they put a bug on me. I expected it. They knew I expected it. I got rid of it in the Beaux-Arts Museum. Then I began thinking, since they would expect me to dodge the bug and feel secure after I'd done so, no doubt they had a way to locate me again. Tracker material sprayed on my clothes, fluorescent in a non-visual frequency. I threw away Cluche's clothes, which I didn't like in the first place, washed in three changes of solvicine and water, disposed of the red wig. Cluche Kurgill has disappeared. By the way, where is Cluche's body?"

"Safe."

"We can let it be found tomorrow morning. With a sign on him reading, 'I am a Telek spy'. Dominion will certainly hear of it; he'll think I'm dead, and that will be one problem the less."

"Good idea."

"But poor old Doctor Kurgill," remonstrated Laurie.

"He'll never believe such a note."

"No...I suppose not." She looked Shorn over from head to feet. "Do you feel different from before?"

"I feel as if all of creation were part of me. Identification with the cosmos, I guess you'd call it."

"But how does it work?"

Shorn deliberated. "I'm really not sure. I can move the chair the same way I move my arm, with about the same effort."

"Evidently," said Circumbright, "Geskamp had told them nothing of the mitrox under the stadium."

"They never asked him. It was beyond their imagination that we could conceive such an atrocity." Shorn laughed. "Dominion was completely flabbergasted. Bowled over. For a few minutes I think he was grateful to me."

"And then?"

"And then, I suppose he remembered his resentment, and began plotting how best to kill me. But I told him nothing until we were in the open air; any weapon he held I could protect myself from. A bullet I could think aside, even back at him; a heat-gun I could deflect."

"Suppose his will on the gun and your will clashed?" Circumbright asked mildly.

"I don't know what would happen. Perhaps nothing. Like a man vacillating between two impulses. Or perhaps the clash and the subsequent lack of reaction would invalidate both our confidence, and down we'd fall into the ocean. Because now we were standing on nothing, a thousand feet over the ocean."

"Weren't you afraid, Will?" asked Laurie.

"At first — yes. But a person becomes accustomed to the sensation very quickly. It's a thing we've all experienced in our dreams. Perhaps it's only a trifling aberration that stands in the way of telekinesis for everyone."

Circumbright grunted, loaded his pipe. "Perhaps we'll find that out, along with the other things."

"Perhaps. Already I begin to look at life and existence from another viewpoint."

Laurie looked worried. "I thought things were just the same."

"Fundamentally, yes. But this feeling of power — of not being tied down —" Shorn laughed. "Don't look at each other like that. I'm not dangerous. I'm only a Telek by courtesy. And now, where can we get three pressure suits?"

"At this time of night? I don't know."

"No matter. I'm a Telek. We'll get them. Provided of course you'd like to visit the Moon. All-expense tour, courtesy of Adlari Dominion. Laurie, would you like to fly up, fast as light, fast as thought, stand in the Earthshine, on the lip of Eratosthenes, looking out over the Mare Imbrium —"

She laughed uneasily. "I'd love it, Will. But — I'm scared."

"What about you, Gorman?"

"No. You two go. There'll be other chances for me."

Laurie jumped to her feet. Her cheeks were pink, her mouth was red and half open in excitement. Shorn looked at her with a sudden new vision. "Very well, Gorman. Tomorrow you can start your experiments. Tonight —"

Laurie found herself picked up, carried out through the window.

"Tonight," said Shorn by her side, "we'll pretend that we're souls — happy souls — exploring the universe."

Circumbright lived in a near-abandoned suburb to the north of Tran. His house was a roomy old antique, rearing like a balky horse over the Meyne River. Big industrial plants blocked the sky in all directions; the air reeked with foundry fumes, sulfur, chlorine, tar, burnt-earth smells.

Within, the house was cheerful and untidy. Circumbright's wife was a tall strange woman who worked ten hours a day in her studio, sculpturing dogs and horses. Shorn had met her only once; so far as he knew she had no interest or even awareness of Circumbright's anti-Telek activities.

He found Circumbright basking in the sun, watching the brown river water roll past. He sat on a little porch he had built apparently for no other purpose but this.

Shorn dropped a small cloth sack in his lap. "Souvenirs."

Circumbright opened the bag unhurriedly, pulled out a handful of stones, each tagged with a card label. He looked at the first, hefted it. "Agate." He read the label. "Mars. Well, well." A bit of black rock was next. "Gabbro? From — let's see. Ganymede. My word, you wandered far afield." He shot a bland blue glance up at Shorn. "Telekinesis seems to have agreed with you. You've lost that haggard hunted expression. Perhaps I'll have to become a Telek myself."

"You don't look haggard and hunted. Quite the reverse."

Circumbright returned to the rocks. "Pumice. From the Moon, I suppose." He read the label. "No — Venus. You made quite a trip."

Shorn looked up into the sky. "Rather hard to describe. There's naturally a feeling of loneliness. Darkness. Something like a dream. Out on Ganymede we were standing on a ridge, obsidian, sharp as a razor. Jupiter filled a third of the sky, the red spot right in the middle, looking at us. There was a pink and blue dimness. Peculiar. Black rock, the big bright planet. It was — weird. I thought, suppose the power fails me now, suppose we can't get home? It gave me quite a chill."

"You seem to have made it."

"Yes, we made it." Shorn seated himself, thrust out his legs. "I'm not hunted and haggard, but I'm confused. Two days ago I thought I had a good grasp on my convictions —"

"And now?"

"Now — I don't know."

"About what?"

"About — our efforts. Their ultimate effect, assuming we're successful."

"Hm-m-m." Circumbright rubbed his chin. "Do you still want to submit to experiments?"

"Of course. I want to know why and how telekinesis works."

"When will you be ready?"

"Whenever you wish."

"Now?"

"Why not? Let's get started."

"As soon as you're ready, we'll try encephalograms as a starting point."

Circumbright was tired. His face, normally pink and cherubic, sagged; filling his pipe, his fingers trembled.

Shorn leaned back in the leather chaise longue, regarded Circumbright with mild curiosity. "Why are you so upset?"

Circumbright gave the litter of paper on the workbench a contemptuous flick of the fingers. "It's the cursed inadequacy of the technique, the instruments. Trying to paint miniatures with a whisk broom, fix a watch with a pipe wrench. There —" he pointed "— encephalograms. Every lobe of your brain. Photographs — by X-ray, by planar section, by metabolism triggering. We've measured your energy flow so closely that if you tossed me a paper clip I'd find it on paper somewhere."

"And there's what?"

"Nothing suggestive. Wavy lines on the encephalograms. Increased oxygen absorption. Pineal tumescence. All gross by-products of whatever is happening."

Shorn yawned and stretched. "About as we expected."

Circumbright nodded heavily. "As we expected. Although I hoped for—something. Some indication where the energy came from—whether through the brain, from the object itself, or from—nowhere."

Shorn caused water to leap from a glass, form a wet glistening hoop in the air. He set it around Circumbright's neck, started it contracting slowly.

"Hey," cried Circumbright reproachfully. "This is serious business."

Shorn snaked the water back in the glass.

Circumbright leaned forward. "Where do *you* feel the energy comes from?"

Shorn reflected. "It seems to be in matter itself—just as motion seems to be part of your hand."

Circumbright sighed in dissatisfaction. He continued half-querulously. "And at what speed does telekinesis work? If it's light-speed, then the action presumably occurs in our own space-time. If it's faster, then it's some other medium, and the whole thing's unknowable."

Shorn rose to his feet. "We can check the last with comparative facility."

Circumbright shook his head. "We'd need instruments of a precision I don't have on hand."

"No. Just a stop watch and—let's see. A flare, a timer, a couple of spacesuits."

"What's your idea?" Circumbright asked suspiciously.

"I'm taking you space-walking."

Circumbright rose uncertainly. "I'm afraid I'll be frightened."

"If you're an agoraphobe—don't try it."

Circumbright blew out his cheeks. "I'm not that."

"You wait here," said Shorn. "I'll be back in ten minutes with the spacesuits."

Half an hour later, they stumped out on Circumbright's little sun porch. Circumbright's outfit had been intended for a larger man; his head projected only half up into the head-bubble, to Shorn's amusement. "Ready?"

Circumbright, his blue eyes wide and solemn, nodded.

"Up we go."

Earth dwindled below, as if snatched out from under their feet. Speed without acceleration. To all sides was blackness, the black of vacancy, continuing emptiness. The moon rolled over their shoulders, a pretty pocked ball, black and silver.

The sun dwindled, became a disk of glare which seemed to cast no light, no heat. "We're seeing it by its high frequencies," Shorn observed. "A kind of reverse Doppler effect —"

"Suppose we run into an asteroid or meteorite?"

"Don't worry, we won't."

"How do you know? You couldn't stop in time."

Shorn ruminated. "No. It's something to think about. I'm not sure whether or not we have momentum. Another experiment for you to worry about. But after today I'll send some kind of shield out ahead of us, just in case."

"Where are we going?"

"Out to one of Jupiter's satellites. Look, there goes Mars." He dropped the telescopic lens in front of his eyes. "There's Io. We'll land on Io."

They stood on a dim gray table, a few feet above a tortured jumble of black scoriae. Frozen white stuff, like rock salt, lay in the crevices. The horizon was near, very sharp. Jupiter filled a quadrant of the sky to the left.

Shorn arranged the flare and the timer on a flat area. "I'll set it for ten minutes. Now — on the count of five I'll start the timer and you start your stopwatch."

"Ready."

"One — two — three — four — five." He looked at Circumbright, Circumbright nodded. "Good. Now we take ourselves out into space where we can watch."

Io dwindled to a tarnished metal disk, a bright spot.

"We're far enough, I think. Now we watch for the flare, and check the time by your stop watch. The increment over ten minutes will give us the light-distance from Io to where we're —" Shorn considered. "What are we doing? Standing? Floating?"

"Waiting."

"Waiting. After knowing the light distance, we can make our tests."

"Are we sure that we're not moving now? If we're moving, our observations will be inaccurate."

Shorn shook his head. "We're not moving. It's the way telekinesis works. I stop us dead, in relation to Io, the same way a man on roller skates stops by grabbing a post. He just — stops himself."

"You know more about it than I do."

"It's more intuition than knowledge — which is suggestive in itself. How's the time?"

"Nine minutes. Ten — twenty seconds. Thirty seconds. Forty. Fifty — one — two — three —"

They looked toward Io through the telescopic visors. Circumbright counted on in the same cadence. "Four — five — six — seven — eight — nine — ten minutes. One — two — three —"

A brief flicker appeared from the dull disk. Circumbright clamped down on the stem of his stop watch. "Three point six seconds. Allow two tenths of a second reaction time. That gives three point four seconds. Over six hundred thousand miles. Now what?"

"Let me have your stop watch. I'll set it to zero. Now." Shorn squared himself towards Io. "Now we'll try telekinesis on a whole world."

Circumbright blinked. "Suppose there's not enough energy available?"

"We'll soon know." He looked at Io, pressed the stop watch starter.

One second — two seconds — three seconds — Io jerked ahead in its orbit.

Shorn looked at the stop watch. "Three point seven. A tenth of a second, which might be an error. Apparently telekinesis works almost instantaneously."

Circumbright looked glumly out toward incandescent Sirius. "We'll play merry hell trying to get any significant results with my lab equipment. Somebody's got to invent some new tools —"

Shorn followed his gaze out toward Sirius. "I wonder what the limit of action is."

Circumbright asked doubtfully, "You're not going to try this — knack of yours on Sirius?"

"No. We'd have to wait eight years for the light to reach us. But —"

He contemplated the massive form of Jupiter. "There's a challenging subject right there."

Circumbright said uneasily, "Suppose the effort drains the source of telekinetic energy — like a short circuit drains a battery? We might be left out here helpless —"

Shorn shook his head. "It wouldn't work that way. My mind is the critical factor. Size doesn't mean much, so long as I can grasp it, take hold of all of it."

He stared at Jupiter. Seconds passed. "About now, if it's going to happen."

Jupiter quivered, floated up across twenty degrees of sky, dropped back into its former orbit.

Circumbright looked almost fearfully at Shorn. Shorn laughed shakily. "Don't worry, Gorman. I'm not out of my mind. But think of the future! All these wasted worlds moved in close, bathing in sunlight. Wonderful new planets for men to live on —"

They turned their faces toward the sun. Earth was a mist-white ball, growing larger. "Think," said Circumbright, "think of what a mad Telek could do. He could come out here as we did, pick up the moon, toss it into North America or Europe as easily as dropping a rock into the mud. Or he could look at Earth, and it would start to move toward the sun — through the corona, and Earth would be singed, seared clean; he could drop it into a sunspot."

Shorn kept his eyes turned away from Earth. "Don't put any ideas into my mind."

"It's a real problem," insisted Circumbright.

"I imagine that eventually there will be an alarm system of some kind; and as soon as it sounds, every mind will grab onto conditions as they are and hold tight. Or maybe a corps of guardians —"

VII

Back on Earth, in Laurie's apartment on upper Martinvelt, Shorn and Circumbright sat drinking coffee.

Circumbright was unaccustomedly nervous and consulted his watch at five-minute intervals.

Shorn watched quizzically. "Who are you expecting?"

Circumbright glanced quickly, guiltily, around the room. "I suppose there's no spy-beetle anywhere close."

"Not according to the detector cell."

"I'm waiting for the messenger. A man called Luby, from East Shore."

"I don't think I know him."

"You'd remember him if you did."

Laurie said, "I think I hear him now."

She went to the door, slid it back. Luby came into the room, quiet as a cat. He was a man of forty who looked no more than seventeen. His skin was clear gold, his features chiseled and handsome, his hair a close cap of tight bronze curls. Shorn thought of the Renaissance Italians — Cesare Borgia, Lorenzo Medici.

Circumbright made introductions which Luby acknowledged with a nod of the head and a lambent look; then he took Circumbright aside, muttered in a rapid flow of syllables.

Circumbright raised his eyebrows, asked a question; Luby shook his head, responded impatiently. Circumbright nodded, and without another word Luby left the room, as quietly as he had entered.

"There's a high-level meeting — policy-makers — out at Portinari Gate. We're wanted." He rose to his feet, stood indecisively a moment. "I suppose we had better be going."

Shorn went to the door, looked out into the corridor. "Luby moves quietly. Isn't it unusual to concentrate top minds in a single meeting?"

"Unprecedented. I suppose it's something important."

Shorn thought a moment. "Perhaps it would be better to say nothing of my new — achievements."

"Very well."

They flew north through the night, into the foothills, and Lake Paienza spread like a dark blot below, rimmed by the lights of Portinari.

Portinari Gate was a rambling inn six hundred years old, high on a hillside, overlooking lake and town. They dropped to the soft turf in the shadow of great pines, walked to the back entrance.

Circumbright knocked, and they felt a quiet scrutiny.

The door opened, an iron-faced woman with a halo of iron-gray hair stood facing them. "What do you want?"

Circumbright muttered a password; silently she stepped back. Shorn felt her wary scrutiny as he and Laurie entered the room.

A brown-skinned man with black eyes and gold rings in his ears flipped up a hand. "Hello, Circumbright."

"Hello…Thursby, this is Will Shorn, Laurita Chelmsford."

Shorn inspected the brown man with interest. The Great Thursby, rumored co-ordinator of the world-wide anti-Telek underground.

There were others in the room, sitting quietly, watchfully. Circumbright nodded to one or two, then took Shorn and Laurie to the side.

"I'm surprised," he said. "The brains of the entire movement are here." He shook his head. "Rather ticklish."

Shorn felt of the detector. "No spy-cells."

More people entered, until possibly fifty men and women occupied the room. Among the last group was the young-old Luby.

A stocky dark-skinned man rose to his feet. "This meeting is a departure from our previous methods, and I hope it won't be necessary again for a long time."

Circumbright whispered to Shorn, "That's Kasselbarg, European Post."

Kasselbarg swung a slow glance around the room. "We're starting a new phase of the campaign. Our first was organizational; we built a world-wide underground, a communication system, set up a ladder of command. Now — the second stage: preparation for our eventual action…which, of course, will constitute the third stage.

"We all know the difficulties under which we work; since we can't hold up a clear and present danger, our government is not sympathetic to us, and in many cases actively hostile — especially in the persons of suborned police officials. Furthermore we're under the compulsion of striking an absolutely decisive blow on our first sally. There won't be a second chance for us. The Teleks must be —" he paused "— they must be killed. It's a course toward which we all feel an instinctive revulsion, but any other course bares us to the incalculable power of the Teleks. Now, any questions, any comments?"

Shorn, compelled by a sudden pressure he only dimly understood, rose to his feet. "I don't want to turn the movement into a debating society — but there's another course where killing is unnecessary. It erases the need of the decisive blow, it gives us a greater chance of success."

"Naturally," said Kasselbarg mildly, "I'd like to hear your plan."

"No operation, plan it as carefully as you will, can guarantee the death of every Telek. And those who aren't killed may go crazy in anger and fear; I can picture a hundred million deaths, five hundred million, a billion deaths in the first few seconds after the operation starts — but does not quite succeed."

Kasselbarg nodded. "The need for a hundred per cent *coup* is emphatic. The formulation of such a plan will constitute Phase Two, of which I just now spoke. We certainly can't proceed on any basis other than a ninety-nine percent probability of fulfillment."

The iron-faced woman spoke. "There are four thousand Teleks, more or less. Here on Earth ten thousand people die every day. Killing the Teleks seems a small price to pay for security against absolute tyranny. It's either act now, while we have limited freedom of choice, or dedicate the human race to slavery for as long into the future as we can imagine."

Shorn looked around the faces in the room. Laurie was sympathetic; Circumbright looked away uncomfortably; Thursby frowned thoughtfully; Kasselbarg waited with courteous deference.

"Everything you say is true," Shorn said. "I would be the most ruthless of us all, if these four thousand deaths did not rob the human race of the most precious gift it possesses. Telekinesis to date has been misused; the Teleks have been remarkable for their selfishness and egotism. But in reacting to the Teleks' mistakes, we should not make mistakes of our own."

Thursby said in a cool clear voice, "What is your concrete proposal, Mr. Shorn?"

"I believe we should dedicate ourselves, not to killing Teleks, but to giving telekinesis to every sane man and woman."

A small red-haired man sneered. "The ancient fallacy, privilege for the chosen ones — in this case, the sane. And who, pray, determines their sanity?"

Shorn smiled. "Your fallacy is at least as ancient; surely there's nothing occult about sanity. But let me return to my fundamental proposition: that taking telekinesis out of monopoly and broadcasting it is a better solution to the problem than killing Teleks. One way is up, the other down; building versus destruction. In one direction we put mankind at its highest potential for achievement; in the other we have four thousand dead Teleks, if our plan succeeds. Always latent is the possibility of a devastated world."

Thursby said, "You're convincing, Mr. Shorn. But aren't you operating on the unproved premise that universal telekinesis is a possibility? Killing the Teleks seems to be easier than persuading them to share their power; we've got to do one or the other."

Shorn shook his head. "There are at least two methods to create Teleks. The first is slow and a long-range job: that is, duplicating the conditions which produced the first Teleks. The second is much easier, quicker, and, I believe, safer. I have good reason for —" he stopped short. A faint buzzing, a vibration in his pocket.

The detector.

He turned to Luby, who stood by the door. "Turn out the lights! There's a Telek spy-cell nearby! Out with the lights, or we're all done for."

Luby hesitated. Shorn cursed under his breath. Thursby rose to his feet, startled and tense. "What's going on?"

There was a pounding at the door. "Open up, in the name of the law."

Shorn looked at the windows: the tough vitripane burst out; the windows were wide open. "Quick, out the window!"

Circumbright said in a voice of deadly passion, "Somewhere there's a traitor —"

A man in black and gold appeared at the window with a heat-gun. "Out the door," he bellowed. "You can't get away, the place is surrounded. Move out the door in an orderly fashion; move out the door. You're all under arrest. Don't try to break for it; our orders are shoot to kill."

Circumbright sidled close to Shorn. "Can't you do something?"

"Not here. Wait till we're all outside; we don't want anyone shot."

Two burly troopers appeared in the doorway, gestured with pistols. "Outside, everybody. Keep your hands up."

Thursby led the way, his face thoughtful. Shorn followed; behind came the others. They marched into the parking area, now flooded with light from police lamps.

"Stop right there," barked a new voice.

Thursby halted. Shorn squinted against the searchlight; he saw a dozen men standing in a circle around them.

"This is a catch and no mistake," muttered Thursby.

"Quiet! No talking."

"Better search them for weapons," came another new voice. Shorn recognized the dry phrasing, the overtones of careless contempt. Adlari Dominion.

Two Black and Golds walked through the group, making a quick search.

A mocking voice came from behind the searchlights. "Isn't that Colonel Thursby, the people's hero? What's he doing in this nasty little conspiracy?"

Thursby stared ahead with an immobile face. The red-haired man who had challenged Shorn cried to the unseen voice: "You Telek boot-licker, may the money they pay rot the hands off your wrists!"

"Easy, Walter," said Circumbright.

Thursby spoke toward the lights. "Are we under arrest?"

There was no answer — a contemptuous silence.

Thursby repeated in a sharper tone: "Are we under arrest? I want to see your warrant; I want to know what we're charged with."

"You're being taken to headquarters for questioning," came the reply. "Behave yourselves; if you've committed no crime, there'll be no charge."

"We'll never reach headquarters," Circumbright muttered to Shorn. Shorn nodded grimly, staring into the lights, seeking Dominion. Would he recognize the Cluche Kurgill whom he had invested with Telek power?

The voice called out, "Were you contemplating resistance to arrest? Go ahead. Make it easy on us."

There was motion in the group, a swaying as if from the wind which moved the tops of the dark pine trees.

The voice said, "Very well, then, march forward, one at a time. You first, Thursby."

Thursby turned slowly, like a bull, followed the trooper who walked ahead waving a flashlight.

Circumbright muttered to Shorn, "Can't you do something?"

"Not while Dominion is out there —"

"Silence!"

One by one the group followed Thursby. An air barge loomed ahead, the rear hatch gaping like the mouth of a cave.

"Up the ramp; inside."

The hold was a bare, metal-walled cargo space. The door clanged shut, and the fifty captives stood in sweating silence.

Thursby's voice came from near the wall. "A clean sweep. Did they get everybody?"

Circumbright answered in a carefully toneless voice. "So far as I know."

"This will set the movement back ten years," said another voice, controlled but tremulous.

"More likely destroy it entirely."

"But — what can they convict us of? We're guilty of nothing they can prove."

Thursby snorted. "We'll never get to Tran. My guess is gas."

"Gas?" — a horrified whisper.

"Poison gas pumped through the ventilator. Then out to sea, drop us, and no one's the wiser. Not even 'killed while escaping'. Nothing."

The aircraft vibrated, rose into the air; under their feet was the soft feeling of air-borne flight.

Shorn called out softly, "Circumbright?"

"Right here."

"Make a light."

A paper torch ignited by a cigarette lighter cast a yellow flicker around the hold; faces glowed pale and damp as toad-bellies; eyes glared and reflected in the flare of the torch.

The row of ports was well shuttered, the hand-keys were replaced by bolts. Shorn turned his attention to the door. He had moved the planet Jupiter; he should be able to break open a door. But the problem was different; in a sense this bulging open of a door was a concept several times more advanced than movement of a single object, no matter how large. There was also a psychological deterrent in the fact that the door was locked. What would happen if he attempted to telekinecize and nothing happened? Would he retain his power?

Thursby was standing with his ear to the ventilator. He turned, nodded. "Here it comes. I can hear the hiss —"

The paper torch was guttering; in darkness Shorn was as helpless as the others. Desperately he plunged his mind at the door; the door burst open, out into the night. Shorn caught it before it fluttered away into the dark air, brought it edgewise back through the door opening.

The wind had blown out the torch; Shorn could only vaguely feel the black bulk of the door. He yelled, to be heard over the roar of the wind rushing past the door, "Stand back, stand back —" He could wait no longer; he felt reality slipping in the darkness; the door was only a vague blot. He concentrated on it, strained his eyes to see, hurled it against the metal hull, stove out a great rent. Air swept through the hold, whisked out any gas which might have entered.

Shorn took himself out the door, rose above the cabin, looked through the sky dome. A dozen Black and Golds sat in the forward compartment looking uneasily back toward the cargo hold whence had come the rending jar. Adlari Dominion was not visible. Luby, the bronze-haired courier with the medallion face, sat statue-quiet in a corner. Luby was to be preserved, thought Shorn. Luby was the traitor.

He had neither time nor inclination for half-measures. He tore a strip off the top of the ship; the troopers and Luby looked up in terror. If they saw him at all, he was a white-faced demon of the night, riding the wind above them. They were shucked out of the cabin like peas from a pod, flung out into the night, and their cries came thinly back to Shorn over the roar of the wind.

He jumped down into the cabin, cut off the motors, jerked the cylinder of gas away from the ventilation system, then whisked the craft east, toward the Monaghill Mountains.

Clouds fell away from the moon; he saw a field below. Here was as good a spot as any to land and reorganize.

The aircraft settled to the field. Dazed, trembling, buffeted, fifty men and women crept from the hold.

Shorn found Thursby leaning against the hull. Thursby looked at him through the moonlight as a child might watch a unicorn. Shorn grinned. "I know you must be puzzled; I'll tell you all about it as soon as we're settled. But now —"

Thursby squinted. "It's hardly practical our going home, acting as if nothing had happened. The Black and Golds took photographs; and there's a number of us that — are not unknown to them."

Circumbright appeared out of the darkness like a pink and brown owl. "There'll be a great deal of excitement at the Black and Gold head-quarters when there's no news of this hulk."

"There'll be a great deal of irritation at Glarietta Pavilion."

Shorn counted the days on his fingers. "Today is the twenty-third. Nine days to the first of the month."

"What happens on the first of the month?"

"The First Annual Telekinetic Olympiad, at the new stadium in Swanscomb Valley. In the meantime — there's an old mine back of Mount Mathias. The bunkhouses should hold two or three hundred."

"But there's only fifty of us —"

"We'll want others. Two hundred more. Two hundred good people. And to avoid any confusion —" he looked around to find the red-haired man who thought that sanity was no more than a function of individual outlook "— we will equate goodness to will to survive for self, the family group, human culture and tradition."

"That's broad enough," said Thursby equably, "to suit almost anyone. As a practical standard — ?" In the moonlight Shorn saw him cock his eyebrows humorously.

"Practically," said Shorn, "we'll pick out people we like."

VIII

Sunday morning, June the first, was dull and overcast. Mist hung along the banks of the Swanscomb River as it wound in its new looping course down the verdant valley; the trees dripped with clammy condensations.

At eight o'clock a man in rich garments of purple, black and white dropped from the sky to the rim of the stadium. He glanced up at the overcast, the cloud-wrack broke open like a scum, slid across the sky.

Horizon to horizon the heavens showed pure and serene blue; the sun poured warmth into Swanscomb Valley.

The man looked carefully around the stadium, his black eyes keen, restless. At the far end stood a man in a black and gold police uniform; he brought the man through the air to the rim of the stadium beside him.

"Good morning, Sergeant. Any disturbance?"

"None at all, Mr. Dominion."

"How about below?"

"I couldn't say, sir. I'm only responsible for the interior, and I've had the lights on all night. Not a fly has showed itself."

"Good." Dominion glanced around the great bowl. "If there are no trespassers now, there won't be any, since there's no ground level entrance."

He took himself and the trooper to the ground. Two other men in uniform appeared.

"Good morning," said Dominion. "Any disturbance?"

"No sir. Not a sound."

"Curious." Dominion rubbed his pale peaked chin. "Nothing below the stadium?"

"Nothing, sir. Not a nail. We've searched every nook and cranny, down to bedrock, inch by inch."

"Nothing on the detectors?"

"No, sir. If a gopher had tunneled under the stadium, we'd have known it."

Dominion nodded. "Perhaps there won't be any demonstration after all." He stroked his chin. "My intuition is seldom at fault. But never mind. Take all your men, station them at the upper and lower ends of the valley. Allow no one to enter. No one, on any pretext whatever. Understand me?"

"Yes, sir."

"Good."

Dominion returned to the rim of the stadium, gazed around the sunny bowl. The grass was green and well cropped; the colored upholstery of the chairs made circular bands of pastel around the stadium.

He took himself through the air to the director's cupola, an enclosed booth hanging in a vantage point over the field on a long transparent spar. He entered, seated himself at the table, switched on the microphone. "One — two — three." He stopped, listened. His voice, channeled to speakers in the arms of each of the seats, came back to him as a husky murmur.

Other Teleks began to arrive, dropping like brilliant birds from the sky, settling to bask in the sunlight. Refreshment trays floated past; they sipped fruit juice, tea, and ate mint cakes.

Dominion presently left the high cupola, drifted low over the stadium. There was no expectation of filling it; thirty thousand seats would allow room for future increase. Thirty thousand Teleks was the theoretical limit that the economy of Earth could maintain at the present standard of living. And after thirty thousand? Dominion shrugged aside the question; the problem had no contemporary meaning. The solution should prove simple enough; there had been talk of swinging Venus out into a cooler orbit, moving in Neptune, and creating two habitable worlds by transferring half of Neptune's mantle of ice to dusty Venus. A problem for tomorrow. Today's concern was the creation of the Telek Earth State, the inculcation of religious awe into the common folk of Earth — the only means, as it had been decided, to protect Teleks from witless assassination.

He dropped into a group of friends, seated himself. His work was done for the day; now, with security achieved, he could relax, enjoy himself.

Teleks came in greater numbers. Here was a large group — fifty together. They settled into a section rather high up on the shady side, somewhat apart from the others. A few minutes later another group of fifty joined them, and later there were other similar groups.

At nine o'clock the program of events got under way. A whirlpool of jewel colors glinted high in the sky — A dozen great ice prisms appeared, each frozen from water of a different color.

They commenced to revolve in a circle, rotating at the same time; shafts of colored light — red, gold-yellow, emerald, blue — played around the stadium. Then each of the prisms broke into twenty sections, and the pieces swung, swirled like a swarm of polychrome fireflies. With a great swoop they disappeared into the sky.

The voice of Lemand De Troller, the Program Director, sounded from the speakers:

"Sixty years ago, at the original Telekinetic Congress, our race was born. Today is the first annual convention of the issue of these early giants, and I hope the custom will persist down the stream of history, down the million years that is our destined future, ten million times a million years.

"Now — the program for the day. Immediately following will be a game of bump-ball, for the world championship, between the Crimean Blues and the Oslandic Vikings. Then there will be a water-sculpture contest and display, and next — arrow-dueling, followed by an address by Miss Gloriana Hallen, on the Future of Telekinesis, and then lunch will be served on the turf—"

Circumbright and Shorn listened with dissatisfaction as De Troller announced the program. He finished with "— the final valediction by Graycham Gray, our chairman for the year."

Circumbright said to Shorn, "There's nothing there, no mass telekinesis in the entire program."

Shorn said nothing. He leaned back in his seat, looked up to the director's cupola.

"Ample opportunity for mass exercise," complained Circumbright, "and they overlook it entirely."

Shorn brought his attention back down from the cupola. "It's an obvious stunt — perhaps too obvious for such a sophisticated people."

Circumbright scanned the two hundred and sixty-five men and women in radiant Telek costumes that Shorn had brought into the stadium, fifty at a time. "Do you suppose that the program as it stands will do the trick?"

Shorn shook his head fretfully. "Doesn't seem possible. Not enough mass participation." He looked over his shoulder to Thursby, in the seat behind him. "Any ideas?"

Thursby in brown and yellow said tentatively, "We can't very well force them to indoctrinate us."

Laurie, beside Shorn, laughed nervously. "Let's send Circumbright out to plead with them."

Shorn moved restlessly in his seat. Two hundred and sixty-five precious lives, dependent for continued existence on his skill and vigilance. "Maybe something will turn up."

The game of bump-ball was underway. Five men lying prone in eight-foot red torpedoes competed against five men in blue torpedoes, each team trying to bump a floating three-foot ball into the opposition goal. The game was lightning swift, apparently dangerous. The ten little boats moved so fast as to be mere flickers; the ball slammed back and forth like a ping-pong ball.

Shorn began to notice curious glances cast up toward his group. There was no suspicion, only interest; somehow they were attracting attention. He looked around and saw his group sitting straight and tense as vestrymen at a funeral — obviously uneasy and uncomfortable. He rose to his feet, spoke in an angry undertone, "Show a little life; act as if you're enjoying yourselves!"

He turned back to the field, noticed a service wagon not in use, pulled it up, moved it past his charges. Gingerly they took tea, rum punch, cakes, fruit. Shorn set the case back on the turf.

The bump-ball game ended; now began the water sculpture. Columns of water reared into the air: glistening soft forms, catching the sunlight glowing deep from within.

Event followed event: compositions and displays in color, skill, ingenuity, swift reaction; arrows were pitted against arrows each trying to pierce the bladder trailed by the other. Colored spheres were raced through an obstacle course; there was an exhibition in which sparrows were released and after an interval herded into a basket by a small white tambourine.

There were other displays: the air over the stadium swam with fascinating colors, shapes, tapes, screens, and so passed the morning. At twelve, laden buffet tables dropped from the sky to the stadium turf. And now Shorn found himself on the horns of a dilemma. By remaining aloof from the tables his group made themselves conspicuous; but they risked quick detection by mingling with the Teleks.

Thursby resolved the problem. He leaned forward. "Don't you think we'd better go down to lunch? Maybe a few at a time. We stick out like a sore thumb sitting up here hungry."

Shorn acquiesced. By ones and twos he set the members of his company down to the sward. Laurie nudged him. "Look. There's Dominion. He's talking to old Poole."

Circumbright in unusual agitation said, "I hope Poole keeps his wits about him."

Shorn smiled grimly. "If Dominion makes one move —" Circumbright saw one of the dueling arrows lift easily into the air. Dominion turned away. Shorn sighed. The arrow returned to the turf.

A moment later Shorn brought Poole back to his seat. "What did Dominion want?"

Poole was a scholarly-looking man of middle age, mild and myopic. "Dominion? Oh, the gentleman who spoke to me. He was very pleasant. Asked if I were enjoying the spectacles, and said that he didn't think he recognized me."

"And what did you say?"

"I said I didn't get out very much, and that there were many here I hardly knew."

"And then?"

"He just moved away."

Shorn sighed. "Dominion is very sharp."

Thursby wore a worried frown. "Things haven't gone so well this morning."

"No. But there's still the afternoon."

The afternoon program began with a score of young Telek girls performing an air ballet.

IX

Three o'clock.

"There's not much more," said Circumbright.

Shorn sat hunched forward. "No."

Circumbright clenched the arms of his seat. "We've got to do something, and I know what to do."

"What?"

"Drop me down to the field. I'll pick up the arrows, and you start picking off the Teleks. Dominion first. Then they'll all —"

Shorn shook his head. "It wouldn't work. You'd be throwing away your life for nothing."

"Why wouldn't it work?" Circumbright demanded belligerently.

Shorn gestured to the two hundred and sixty-five. "Do you think we could arouse a real rapport in the business of pulverizing you? No." He looked up at the director's cupola. "It's got to come from there. And I've got to arrange it." He reached over, clasped Laurie's hand, nodded to Thursby, rose to his feet, took himself by an inconspicuous route along the back wall, up to the transparent spar supporting the cupola. Inside he glimpsed the shapes of two men.

He slid back the door, entered quietly, froze in his footprints. Adlari Dominion, lounging back in an elastic chair, smiled up at him, ominous as a cobra. "Come in. I've been expecting you."

Shorn looked quickly to Lemand De Troller, the program director, a bulky blond man with lines of self-indulgence clamping his mouth.

"How so?"

"I have a pretty fair idea of your intentions, and I admit their ingenuity. Unluckily for you, I inspected the body of Cluche Kurgill, assassinated a short time ago, and it occurred to me that this was not the man whom I entertained at Glarietta; I have since reprimanded myself for not scrutinizing the catch at Portinari Gate more carefully. In any event, today will be a complete debacle, from your standpoint. I have excised from the program any sort of business which might have helped you."

Shorn said thickly, "You showed a great deal of forbearance in allowing us to enjoy your program."

Dominion made a lazy gesture. "It's just as well not to bring our problems too sharply to the attention of the spectators; it might lay a macabre overtone upon the festival for them to observe at close hand two hundred and sixty-five condemned anarchists and provocateurs."

"You would have been made very uncomfortable if I had not come up here to the cupola."

Dominion shook his head indulgently. "I asked myself, what would I do in your position? I answered, I would proceed to the cupola and myself direct such an event to suit my purposes. So — I preceded you." He smiled. "And now — the sorry rebellion is at its end. The entire nucleus of your gang is within reach, helpless; if you recall, there is no exit, they have no means to scale the walls."

Shorn felt thick bile rising in his throat; his voice sounded strange to his ears. "It's not necessary to revenge yourself on all these people; they're merely decent individuals, trying to cope with —" He spoke on, pleading half-angrily for the two hundred and sixty-five. Meanwhile his mind worked at a survival sub-level. Dominion, no matter how lazy-seeming and catlike, was keyed-up, on his guard; there would be no surprising him. In any struggle Lemand De Troller, the program director, would supply the decisive force. Shorn might be able to parry the weapons of one man, but two cores of thought would be too much for him.

Decision and action came to him simultaneously. He gave the cupola a great shake; startled, De Troller seized the desk. Shorn threw a coffee mug at his head. Instantly, before the mug had even struck, he flung himself to the floor. Dominion, seizing the instant of Shorn's distraction, aimed a gun at him, fired an explosive pellet. Shorn hit the floor, saw De Troller slump, snatched the weapon from Dominion's hand, all at once.

The gun clattered to the deck, and Shorn found himself looking into Dominion's pale glowing eyes.

Dominion spoke in a low voice, "You're very quick. You've effectively reduced the odds against yourself."

Shorn smiled tightly. "What odds do you give me now?"

"Roughly, a thousand to one."

"Seems to me they're even. You against me."

"No. I can hold you helpless, at the very least, until the program property man returns."

Shorn slowly rose to his feet. Careful. Let no movement escape his eye. Without moving his eyes from Dominion's he lifted the coffee mug, hurled it at Dominion's head. Dominion diverted it, accelerated it toward Shorn. Shorn bounced it back, into Dominion's face. It stopped only an inch short, then sprang back at Shorn's head with tremendous speed. Shorn flicked it with a thought, he felt the breath of its passage and it shattered against the wall.

"You're fast," said Dominion lightly. "Very fast indeed. In theory, your reactions should have missed that."

Shorn stared at him thoughtfully. "I've got a theory of my own."

"I'd like to hear it."

"What happens when two minds try to teleport an object in opposing directions?"

Dominion frowned slightly. "A very exhausting matter, if carried to the limit. The mind with the greater certainty wins, the other mind — sometimes — lapses."

Shorn stared at Dominion. "My mind is stronger than yours."

Dominion's eye lit up with a peculiar inner glow, then filmed over. "Very well, suppose it is? What do I gain in proving otherwise?"

Shorn said, "If you want to save your life — you'll have to." With his eyes still on Dominion, he took a knife from his pocket, flicked open the blade.

It leaped from his hand at his eyes. He frantically diverted it, and in the instant his defense was distracted, the gun darted to Dominion's hand. Shorn twisted up the muzzle by a hair's-breadth; the pellet sang past his ear.

Fragments of the coffee mug pelted the back of his head, blinding him with pain. Dominion, smiling and easy, raised the gun. It was all over, Shorn thought. His mind, wilted and spent, stood naked and bare of defense — for the flash of an instant. Before Dominion could pull the trigger Shorn flung the knife at his throat. Dominion turned his attention away from the gun to divert the knife; Shorn reached out, grabbed the gun with his bare hands, tossed it under the table out of sight.

Dominion and Shorn glared eye to eye. Both of them thought of the knife. It lay on the table, and now under the impulse of both minds, slowly trembled, rose quivering into the air, hilt up, blade down, swinging as if hung by a short string. Gradually it drifted to a position midway between their eyes.

The issue was joined. Sweating, breathing hard, they glared at the knife, and it vibrated, sang to the induced quiver from the opposing efforts. Eye to eye stared Dominion and Shorn, faces red, mouths open, distorted. No opportunity now for diversionary tactics; relax an instant and the knife would stab; blunt force strained against force.

Dominion said slowly, "You can't win, you who have only known telekinesis a few days; your certainty is as nothing compared to mine.

I've lived my lifetime in certainty; it's part of my living will, and now see — your reality is weakening, the knife is aiming at you, to slash your neck."

Shorn watched the knife in fascination, and indeed it slowly turned toward him like the clock-hand of Fate. Sweat streamed into his eyes; he was aware of Dominion's grimace of triumph.

No. Allow no words to distract you; permit no suggestion; bend down Dominion's own resolution. His vocal chords were like rusty wire, his voice was a croak.

"My certainty is stronger than yours because —" as he said the words the knife halted its sinister motion toward his throat "— time has no effect upon telekinesis! Because I've got the will of all humanity behind me, and you've got only yourself!"

The knife trembled, twisted, as if it were a live thing, tortured by indecision.

"I'm stronger than you are, because — I've *got to be*!" He sank the words into Dominion's mind.

Dominion said quickly, "Your neck hurts, your mind hurts, you cannot see."

Shorn's neck hurt indeed, his head ached, sweat stung his eyes, and the knife made a sudden lurch toward him. This can't go on, thought Shorn. "I don't need tricks, Dominion; you need them only because your confidence is going and you're desperate." He took a deep breath, reached out, seized the knife, plunged it into Dominion's breast.

Shorn stood looking down at the body. "I won — and by a trick. He was so obsessed by the need for defeating me mentally that he forgot the knife had a handle."

Panting he looked out over the stadium. Events had come to a halt. The spectators restively waited for word from the program director.

Shorn picked up the microphone.

"Men and women of the future —" as he spoke he watched the little huddle of two hundred and sixty-five. He saw Laurie stir, look up; he saw Circumbright turn, clap Thursby's knee. He felt the wave of thankfulness, of hero-worship, almost insane in its fervor that welled up from their minds. At that moment he could have commanded any of them to their death.

An intoxicated elation came to him; he fought to control his voice. "This is an event improvised to thank Lemand De Troller, our program director, for his work in arranging the events. All of us will join our telekinetic powers together; we will act as one mind. I will guide this little white ball —" he lifted a small ball used in the obstacle race "— through the words 'Thank you, Lemand De Troller'. You, with your united wills, will follow with the large bump-ball." He rolled it out into the center of the stadium. "With more preparation we would have achieved something more elaborate, but I know Lemand will be just as pleased if he feels all of us are concentrating on the big ball, putting our hearts into the thanks. So — now. Follow the little white ball."

Slowly he guided the white ball along imaginary block letters in the air; faithfully, the big bump-ball followed.

It was finished.

Shorn looked anxiously toward Circumbright. No signal.

Once again.

"Now — there is one other whom we owe a vote of thanks: Adlari Dominion, the capable liaison officer. This time we will spell out, 'Thank you and good luck, Adlari Dominion'."

The white ball moved. The big ball followed. Four thousand minds impelled, two hundred and sixty-five minds sought to merge into the pattern: each a new Prometheus trying to steal a secret more precious than fire from a race more potent than the Titans.

Shorn finished the last N, glanced toward Circumbright. Still no signal. Anxiety beset him; was this the right indoctrination technique? Suppose it was only effective under special conditions, suppose he had been operating on a misapprehension the entire time?

"Well," said Shorn doggedly, "once again." But the spectators would be growing restless. Who to thank this time?

The ball was moving of its own volition. Shorn, fascinated, followed its path. It was spelling a word.

W – I – L – L — then a space — S – H – O – R – N — another space — T – H – A – N – K – S.

Shorn sank back into the elastic seat, his eyes brimming with tears of release and thankfulness. "Someone is thanking Will Shorn," he said into the microphone. "It's time for them to leave." He paused. Two hundred and sixty-five new telekinetics lifted themselves from the stadium, flew west toward Tran, disappeared into the afternoon.

Shorn returned to the microphone. "There're a few more words I want to say; please be patient a moment or two longer.

"You have just been witnesses — unwitting witnesses — to an event as important as Joffrey's original Congress. The future will consider the sixty-year interval only a transition, humanity's final separation from the beast.

"We have completely subdued the material world; we know the laws governing all the phenomena that our senses can detect. Now we turn ourselves into a new direction; humanity enters a new stage, and wonderful things lie before us." He noticed a ripple of uneasiness running along the ranks of the Teleks. "This new world is on us, we can't evade it. For sixty years the Teleks have rejoiced in a state of special privilege, and this is the last shackle humanity throws off: the idea that one man may dominate or control another man."

He paused; the uneasiness was ever more marked.

"There are trying times to come — a period of severe readjustment. At the moment you are not quite certain to what I am referring, and that is just as well. Thank you for your attention and good-bye. I hope you enjoyed the program as much as I did."

He rose to his feet, stepped over Dominion's body, slid back the door, stepped out of the cupola.

Teleks leaving the stadium rose up past him like May flies, some turning him curious glances as they flew. Shorn, smiling, watched them flit past, toward their glittering pavilions, their cloud-castles, their sea-bubbles. The last one was gone; he waved an arm after them as if in valediction.

Then he himself rose, plunged westward toward the sword-shaped towers of Tran, where two hundred and sixty-five men and women were already starting to spread telekinesis through all of mankind.

NOISE

I

CAPTAIN HESS PLACED a notebook on the desk and hauled a chair up under his sturdy buttocks. Pointing to the notebook, he said, "That's the property of your man Evans. He left it aboard the ship."

Galispell asked in faint surprise, "There was nothing else? No letter?"

"No, sir, not a thing. That notebook was all he had when we picked him up."

Galispell rubbed his fingers along the scarred fibers of the cover. "Understandable, I suppose." He flipped back the cover. "Hmmmm."

Hess said tentatively, "What's been your opinion of Evans? Rather a strange chap?"

"Howard Evans? No, not at all. He's been a very valuable man to us." He considered Captain Hess reflectively. "Exactly how do you mean 'strange'?"

Hess frowned, searching for the precise picture of Evans' behavior. "I guess you might say erratic, or maybe emotional."

Galispell was genuinely startled. "Howard Evans?"

Hess' eyes went to the notebook. "I took the liberty of looking through his log, and — well —"

"And you got the impression he was — strange."

Hess flushed stubbornly. "Maybe everything he writes is true. But I've been poking into odd corners of space all my life and I've never seen anything like it."

"Peculiar situation," said Galispell in a neutral voice. He looked thoughtfully at the notebook.

II

Journal of Howard Charles Evans

I commence this journal without pessimism but certainly without optimism. I feel as if I have already died once. My time in the lifeboat was at least a foretaste of death. I flew on and on through the dark, and a coffin could be only slightly more cramped. The stars were above, below, ahead, astern. I have no clock, and I can put no duration to my drifting. It was more than a week, it was less than a year.

So much for space, the lifeboat, the stars. There are not too many pages in this journal. I will need them all to chronicle my life on this world which, rising up under me, gave me life.

There is much to tell and many ways in the telling. There is myself, my own response to this rather dramatic situation. But lacking the knack for tracing the contours and contortions of my psyche, I will try to detail events as objectively as possible.

I landed the lifeboat on as favorable a spot as I had opportunity to select. I tested the atmosphere, temperature, pressure and biology; then I ventured outside. I rigged an antenna and despatched my first SOS.

Shelter is no problem; the lifeboat serves me as a bed, and, if necessary, a refuge. From sheer boredom later on I may fell a few of these trees and build a house. But I will wait; there is no urgency.

A stream of pure water trickles past the lifeboat; I have abundant concentrated food. As soon as the hydroponic tanks begin to produce there will be fresh fruits and vegetables and yeast proteins —

Survival seems no particular problem.

The sun is a ball of dark crimson, and casts hardly more light than the full moon of Earth. The lifeboat rests on a meadow of thick black-green creeper, very pleasant underfoot. A hundred yards distant in the direction I shall call south lies a lake of inky water, and the meadow slopes smoothly down to the water's edge. Tall sprays of rather pallid vegetation — I had best use the word 'trees' — bound the meadow on either side.

Behind is a hillside, which possibly continues into a range of mountains; I can't be sure. This dim red light makes vision uncertain after the first few hundred feet.

The total effect is one of haunted desolation and peace. I would enjoy the beauty of the situation if it were not for the uncertainties of the future.

The breeze drifts across the lake, smelling pleasantly fragrant, and it carries a whisper of sound from off the waves.

I have assembled the hydroponic tanks and set out cultures of yeast. I shall never starve nor die of thirst. The lake is smooth and inviting; perhaps in time I will build a little boat. The water is warm, but I dare not swim. What could be more terrible than to be seized from below and dragged under?

There is probably no basis for my misgivings. I have seen no animal life of any kind: no birds, fish, insects, crustacea. The world is one of absolute quiet, except for the whispering breeze.

The scarlet sun hangs in the sky, remaining in place during many of my sleeps. I see it is slowly westering; after this long day how long and how monotonous will be the night!

I have sent off four SOS sequences; somewhere a monitor station must catch them.

A machete is my only weapon, and I have been reluctant to venture far from the lifeboat. Today (if I may use the word) I took my courage in my hands and started around the lake. The trees are rather like birches, tall and supple. I think the bark and leaves would shine a clear silver in light other than this wine-colored gloom. Along the lakeshore they stand in a line, almost as if long ago they had been planted by a wandering gardener. The tall branches sway in the breeze, glinting scarlet with purple overtones, a strange and wonderful picture which I am alone to see.

I have heard it said that enjoyment of beauty is magnified in the presence of others: that a mysterious rapport comes into play to reveal subtleties which a single mind is unable to grasp. Certainly as I walked along the avenue of trees with the lake and the scarlet sun behind, I would have been grateful for companionship — but I believe that something of peace, the sense of walking in an ancient abandoned garden, would be lost.

The lake is shaped like an hour-glass; at the narrow waist I could look across and see the squat shape of the lifeboat. I sat down under a bush, which continually nodded red and black flowers in front of me.

Mist fibrils drifted across the lake and the wind made low musical sounds.

I rose to my feet, continued around the lake.

I passed through forests and glades and came once more to my lifeboat.

I went to tend my hydroponic tanks, and I think the yeast had been disturbed, prodded at curiously.

The dark red sun is sinking. Every day — it must be clear that I use 'day' as the interval between my sleeps — finds it lower in the sky. Night is almost upon me, long night. How shall I spend my time in the dark?

I have no gauge other than my mind, but the breeze seems colder. It brings long mournful chords to my ears, very sad, very sweet. Mist-wraiths go fleeting across the meadow.

Wan stars already show themselves, nameless ghost-lamps without significance.

I have been considering the slope behind my meadow; tomorrow I think I will make the ascent.

I have plotted the position of every article I possess. I will be gone some hours; and — if a visitor meddles with my goods, I will know his presence for certain.

The sun is low, the air pinches at my cheeks. I must hurry if I wish to return while light still shows me the landscape. I picture myself lost; I see myself wandering the face of this world, groping for my precious lifeboat, my tanks, my meadow.

Anxiety, curiosity, obstinacy all spurring me, I set off up the slope at a half-trot.

Becoming winded almost at once, I slowed my pace. The turf of the lakeshore had disappeared; I was walking on bare rock and lichen. Below me the meadow became a patch, my lifeboat a gleaming spindle. I watched for a moment. Nothing stirred anywhere in my range of vision.

I continued up the slope and finally breasted the ridge. A vast rolling valley fell off below me. Far away a range of great mountains stood into the dark sky. The wine-colored light slanting in from the west lit the prominences, the frontal sallies and bluffs, left the valleys in gloom: an alternate sequence of red and black beginning far in the west, continuing past, far to the east.

I looked down behind me, down to my own meadow, and was hard put to find it in the fading light. Ah, there it was! And there, the lake, a sprawling hour-glass. Beyond was dark forest, then a strip of old rose savannah, then a dark strip of woodland, then delicate laminae of colorings to the horizon.

The sun touched the edge of the mountains, and with what seemed almost a sudden lurch, fell half below the horizon. I turned down-slope; a terrible thing to be lost in the dark. My eye fell upon a white object, a hundred yards along the ridge. I stared, and walked nearer. Gradually it assumed form: a thimble, a cone, a pyramid — a cairn of white rocks. I walked forward with feet achingly heavy.

A cairn, certainly. I stood looking down on it.

I turned, looked over my shoulder. Nothing in view. I looked down to the meadow. Swift shapes? I strained through the gathering murk. Nothing.

I tore at the cairn, threw rocks aside. What was below?

Nothing.

In the ground a faintly-marked rectangle three feet long was perceptible. I stood back. No power I knew of could induce me to dig into that soil.

The sun was disappearing. Already at the south and north the afterglow began, lees of wine: the sun moved with astounding rapidity; what manner of sun was this, dawdling at the meridian, plunging below the horizon?

I turned down-slope, but darkness came faster. The scarlet sun was gone; in the west was the sad sketch of departed flame. I stumbled, I fell. I looked into the east. A marvellous zodiacal light was forming, a strengthening blue triangle.

I watched, from my hands and knees. A cusp of bright blue lifted into the sky. A moment later a flood of sapphire washed the landscape. A new sun of intense indigo rose into the sky.

The world was the same and yet different; where my eyes had been accustomed to red and the red subcolors, now I saw the intricate cycle of blue.

When I returned to my meadow the breeze carried a new sound: bright chords that my mind could almost form into melody. For a moment I so amused myself, and thought to see dance-motion in the wisps of vapor which for the last few days had been noticeable over my meadow.

In what I will call a peculiar frame of mind I crawled into the lifeboat and went to sleep.

I crawled blinking out of the lifeboat into an electric world. I listened. Surely that was music — faint whispers drifting in on the wind like a fragrance.

I went down to the lake, as blue as a ball of that cobalt dye so aptly known as bluing.

The music came louder; I could catch snatches of melody — sprightly quick-step phrases carried like colored tinsel on a flow of cream.

I put my hands to my ears; if I were experiencing hallucinations, the music would continue. The sound diminished, but did not fade entirely; my test was not definitive. But I felt sure it was real. And where music was there must be musicians... I ran forward, shouted, "Hello!"

"Hello!" came the echo from across the lake.

The music faded a moment, as a cricket chorus quiets when disturbed, then gradually I could hear it again — distant music, 'horns of elf-land faintly blowing'.

It went completely out of perception. I was left standing haggard in the blue light, alone on my meadow.

I washed my face, returned to the lifeboat, sent out another set of SOS signals.

Possibly the blue day is shorter than the red day; with no clock I can't be sure. But with my new fascination, the music and its source, the blue day seems to pass swifter.

Never have I caught sight of the musicians. Is the sound generated by the trees, by diaphanous insects crouching out of my vision?

One day I glanced across the lake, and wonder of wonders! a gay town spread along the opposite shore. After a first dumbfounded gaze, I ran down to the water's edge, stared as if it were the most precious sight of my life.

Pale silk swayed and rippled: pavilions, tents, fantastic edifices... Who inhabited these places? I waded knee-deep into the lake, the breath catching and creaking in my throat, and thought to see flitting shapes.

I ran like a madman around the shore. Plants with pale blue blossoms succumbed to my feet; I left the trail of an elephant through a patch of delicate reeds.

And when I came panting and exhausted to the shore opposite my meadow, what was there? Nothing.

The city had vanished like a dream, like spectres blown on a wind. I sat down on a rock. Music came clear for an instant, as if a door had momentarily opened.

I jumped to my feet. Nothing to be seen. I looked back across the lake. There — on my meadow — a host of gauzy shapes moved like May-flies over a still pond.

When I returned, my meadow was vacant. The shore across the lake was bare.

So goes the blue day; and now there is amazement to my life. Whence comes the music? Who and what are these flitting shapes, never quite real but never entirely out of mind? Four times an hour I press a hand to my forehead, fearing the symptoms of a mind turning in on itself... If music actually exists on this world, actually vibrates the air, why should it come to my ears as Earth music? These chords I hear might be struck on familiar instruments; the harmonies are not at all alien... And these pale plasmic wisps that I forever seem to catch from the corner of my eye: the style is that of gay and playful humanity. The tempo of their movement is the tempo of the music: tarantella, sarabande, farandole...

So goes the blue day. Blue air, blue-black turf, ultramarine water, and the bright blue star bent to the west... How long have I lived on this planet? I have broadcast the SOS sequence until now the batteries hiss with exhaustion; soon there will be an end to power. Food, water are no problem to me, but what use is a lifetime of exile on a world of blue and red?

The blue day is at its close. I would like to mount the slope and watch the blue sun's passing — but the remembrance of the red sunset still provokes a queasiness in my stomach. So I will watch from my meadow, and then, if there is darkness, I will crawl into the lifeboat like a bear into a cave, and wait the coming of light.

The blue day goes. The sapphire sun wanders into the western forest, the sky glooms to blue-black, the stars show like unfamiliar home-places.

For some time now I have heard no music; perhaps it has been so all-present that I neglect it.

The blue star is gone, the air chills. I think that deep night is on me indeed...I hear a throb of sound, plangent, plaintive; I turn my head. The east glows pale pearl. A silver globe floats up into the night like a lotus drifting on a lake: a great ball like six of Earth's full moons. Is this a sun, a satellite, a burnt-out star? What a freak of cosmology I have chanced upon!

The silver sun — I must call it a sun, although it casts a cool satin light — moves in an aureole like oyster-shell. Once again the color of the planet changes. The lake glistens like quicksilver, the trees are ham-mered metal...The silver star passes over a high wrack of clouds, and the music seems to burst forth as if somewhere someone flung wide curtains: the music of moonlight, medieval marble, piazzas with slim fluted colonnades, soft sighing strains...

I wander down to the lake. Across on the opposite shore once more I see the town. It seems clearer, more substantial; I note details that shim-mered away to vagueness before — a wide terrace beside the lake, spiral columns, a row of urns. The silhouette is, I think, the same as when I saw it under the blue sun: great silken tents; shimmering, reflecting cusps of light; pillars of carved stone, lucent as milk-glass; fantastic fixtures of no obvious purpose...Barges drift along the dark quicksilver lake like moths, great sails bellying idly, the rigging a mesh of cobweb. Nodules of light, like fairy lanterns, hang on the stays, along the masts...On sudden thought, I turn, look up to my own meadow. I see a row of booths as at an old-time fair, a circle of pale stone set in the turf, a host of filmy shapes.

Step by step I edge toward my lifeboat. The music waxes, chords and structures of wonderful sweetness. I peer at one of the shapes, but the outlines waver. It moves to the emotion of the music — or does the motion of the shape generate the music?

I run forward, shouting hoarsely. One of the shapes slips past me, and I look into a blur where a face might be. I come to a halt, panting hard; I stand on the marble circle. I stamp; it rings solid. I walk toward the booths, they seem to display complex things of pale cloth and dim metal — but as I look my eyes mist over as with tears. The music goes far far away, my meadow lies bare and quiet. My feet press into silver-black turf; in the sky hangs the silver-black star.

I am sitting with my back to the lifeboat, staring across the lake, which is still as a mirror. I have arrived at a set of theories.

My primary proposition is that I am sane — a necessary article of faith; why bother even to speculate otherwise? So — events occurring outside my own mind cause everything I have seen and heard. But — note this! — these sights and sounds do not obey the laws of classical science; in many respects they seem particularly subjective.

It must be, I tell myself, that both objectivity and subjectivity enter into the situation. I receive impressions which my brain finds unfamiliar, and so translates to the concept most closely related. By this theory the inhabitants of this world are constantly close; I move unknowingly through their palaces and arcades; they dance incessantly around me. As my mind gains sensitivity, I verge upon rapport with their way of life and I see them. More exactly, I sense something which creates an image in the visual region of my brain. Their emotions, the pattern of their life sets up a kind of vibration which sounds in my brain as music... The reality of these creatures I am sure I will never know. They are diaphane, I am flesh; they live in a world of spirit, I plod the turf with my heavy feet.

These last days I have neglected to broadcast the SOS. Small lack; the batteries are about done.

The silver sun is at the zenith, and leans westward. What comes next? Back to the red sun? Or darkness? Certainly this is no ordinary planetary system; the course of this world along its orbit must resemble one of the pre-Copernican epicycles.

I believe that my brain is gradually tuning into phase with this world, reaching a new high level of sensitivity. If my theory is correct, the *élan vital* of the native beings expresses itself in my brain as music. On Earth we would perhaps use the word 'telepathy'... So I am practicing, concentrating, opening my consciousness wide to these new perceptions. Ocean mariners know a trick of never looking directly at a far light lest it strike the eyes' blind spot. I am using a similar device of never staring directly at one of the gauzy beings. I allow the image to establish itself, build itself up, and by this technique they appear quite definitely human. I sometimes think I can glimpse the features. The women are like sylphs, achingly beautiful; the men — I have not seen one in detail, but their carriage, their form is hauntingly familiar.

The music is always part of the background, just as rustling of leaves is part of a forest. The mood of these creatures seems to change with their sun, so I hear music to suit. The red sun gave them passionate melancholy, the blue sun merriment. Under the silver star they are delicate, imaginative, wistful, and in my mind sounds Debussy's *La Mer* and *Les Sirènes*.

The silver day is on the wane. Today I sat beside the lake with the trees a screen of silver filigree, watching the moth-barges drift back and forth. What is their function? Can life such as this be translated in terms of economies, ecology, sociology? I doubt it. The word intelligence may not even enter the picture; is not our brain a peculiarly anthropoid characteristic, and is not intelligence a function of our peculiarly anthropoid brain?... A portly barge sways near, with swamp-globes of orange and blue in the rigging, and I forget my hypotheses. I can never know the truth, and it is perfectly possible that these creatures are no more aware of me than I originally was aware of them.

Time goes by; I return to the lifeboat. A young woman-shape whirls past. I pause, peer into her face; she tilts her head, her eyes burn into mine as she passes, mocking topaz, not unkindly... I try an SOS — listlessly, because I suspect the batteries to be dank and dead.

And indeed they are.

*

The silver star is like an enormous Christmas tree bauble, round and glistening. It floats low, and once more I stand irresolute, half-expecting night.

The star falls; the forest receives it. The sky dulls, and night has come.

I face the east, my back pressed to the pragmatic hull of my lifeboat. Nothing.

I have no conception of the passage of time. Darkness, timelessness. Somewhere clocks turn minute hands, second hands, hour hands — I stand staring into the night, perhaps as slow as a sandstone statue, perhaps as feverish as a salamander.

In the darkness there is a peculiar cessation of sound. The music has dwindled; down through a series of wistful chords, a forlorn last cry...

A glow in the east, a green glow, spreading. Up rises a magnificent green sphere, the essence of all green, the tincture of emeralds, glowing as grass, fresh as mint, deep as the sea.

A throb of sound: rhythmical strong music, swinging and veering.

The green light floods the planet, and I prepare for the green day.

I am almost one with the native things. I wander among their pavilions, I pause by their booths to ponder their stuffs and wares: silken medallions, spangles and circlets of woven metal, cups of fluff and iridescent puff, puddles of color and wafts of light-shot gauze. There are chains of green glass; captive butterflies; spheres which seem to hold all the heavens, all the clouds, all the stars.

And to all sides of me go the flicker and flit of the dream-people. The men are all vague, but familiar; the women turn me smiles of ineffable provocation. But I will drive myself mad with temptations; what I see is no more than the formulation of my own brain, an interpretation... And this is tragedy, for there is one creature so unutterably lovely that whenever I see the shape that is she, my throat aches and I run forward, to peer into her eyes that are not eyes...

Today I clasped my arms around her, expecting yielding wisp. Surprisingly there was the feel of supple flesh. I kissed her, cheek, chin, mouth. Such a look of perplexity on the sweet face as I have never seen; Heaven knows what strange act the creature thought me to be performing.

She went her way, but the music is strong and triumphant: the voice of cornets, the shoulder of resonant bass below.

A man comes past; something in his stride, his posture, plucks at my memory. I step forward; I will gaze into his face, I will plumb the vagueness.

He whirls past like a figure on a carousel; he wears flapping ribbons of silk and pompoms of spangled satin. I pound after him, I plant myself in his path. He strides past with a side-glance, and I stare into the rigid mask-like face.

It is my own face.

He wears my face, he walks with my stride. He is I.

Already is the green day gone?

The green sun goes, and the music takes on depth. No cessation now; there is preparation, imminence…What is that other sound? A far spasm of something growling and clashing like a broken gear-box.

It fades out.

The green sun goes down in a sky like a peacock's tail. The music is slow, exalted.

The west fades, the east glows. The music goes toward the east, to the great bands of rose, yellow, orange, lavender. Cloud-flecks burst into flame. A golden glow consumes the sky, north and south.

The music takes on volume, a liturgical chanting.

Up rises the new sun — a gorgeous golden ball. The music swells into a paean of light, fulfillment, regeneration…Hark! A second time the harsh sound grates across the music.

Into the sky, across the sun, drifts the shape of a spaceship. It hovers over my meadow, the landing jets come down like plumes.

The ship lands.

I hear the mutter of voices — men's voices.

The music is vanished; the marble carvings, the tinsel booths, the wonderful silken cities are gone.

III

Galispell looked up, rubbed his chin.

Captain Hess asked anxiously, "What do you think of it?"

For a moment Galispell made no reply; then he said, "It's a strange document…" He looked for a long moment out the window. "What happened after you picked him up? Did you see any of these phenomena he talks about?"

"Not a thing." Captain Hess solemnly shook his big round head. "Sure, the system was a fantastic gaggle of dark stars and fluorescent planets and burnt-out old suns; maybe all these things played hob with his mind. He didn't seem too overjoyed to see us, that's a fact — just stood there, staring at us as if we were trespassers. 'We got your SOS,' I told him. 'Jump aboard, wrap yourself around a good meal!' He came walking forward as if his feet were dead.

"Well, to make a long story short, he finally came aboard. We loaded on his lifeboat and took off.

"During the voyage back he had nothing to do with anybody — just kept to himself, walking up and down the promenade.

"He had a habit of putting his hands to his head; one time I asked him if he was sick, if he wanted the medic to look him over. He said no, there was nothing wrong with him. That's about all I know of the man.

"We made Sun, and came down toward Earth. Personally, I didn't see what happened because I was on the bridge, but this is what they tell me:

"As Earth got bigger and bigger Evans began to act more restless than usual, wincing and turning his head back and forth. When we were about a thousand miles out, he gave a kind of furious jump.

"'The noise!' he yelled. 'The horrible *noise*!' And with that he ran astern, jumped into his lifeboat, cast off, and they tell me disappeared back the way we came.

"And that's all I got to tell you, Mr. Galispell. It's too bad, after our taking all that trouble to get him, Evans decided to pull up stakes — but that's the way it goes."

"He took off back along your course?"

"That's right. If you're wanting to ask, could he have made the planet where we found him, the answer is, not likely."

"But there's a chance?" persisted Galispell.

"Oh, sure," said Captain Hess. "There's a chance."

Seven Exits from Bocz

To the shrouded shape in the back of the car, Nicholas Trasek said, "You understand, then? Three buzzes means come in."

The figure moved.

Trasek turned away slowly, hesitated, looked back. "You're sure you can make it? It's about twenty yards, along a gravel path."

A whirring sound came from the huddled shape.

"Very well," said Trasek. "I'm going in."

But he paused another moment, listening.

Everything was breathlessly quiet. The house stood ghostly white in the moonlight among old trees, three stories of archaic elegance, with lights showing dim yellow along the bottom floor.

Trasek walked up the path, the gravel crunching under his feet. He stopped at the marble porch, and the entry light shone on his face — a harsh tense face with brooding black eyes, a peculiar leaden skin. He mounted the steps gingerly, like a cat on a strange roof, pressed the button.

Presently the door was opened, by a fat middle-aged woman in a pink robe.

"I've come to see Dr. Horzabky," said Trasek.

The woman uncertainly surveyed the pale face. "Couldn't you call some other time? I don't think he'd like to be disturbed this time of night."

"He'll see me," said Trasek.

The woman peered at him. "An old friend?"

"No," said Trasek. "We have — mutual acquaintances."

"Well, I'll see. You'll have to wait a minute." She closed the door, and Trasek was left alone on the moonlit marble.

A few moments later, the door opened, and the woman motioned him in. "This way, if you please."

Trasek followed her down a hall, the woman's slippers scuffing along the dark red carpet. She opened the door and Trasek passed into a long room, lit with golden light from a great crystal chandelier.

The floor was covered by an oriental rug — sumptuous orange, mulberry, indigo — and the furniture was massive antique hardwood. Books in old walnut racks lined one wall — heavy volumes, all sizes, all shapes and colors. Across the room a number of large paintings hung, and a mirror on the far wall reflected the door Trasek had entered.

Dr. Horzabky stood holding a book. He wore a red velveteen smoking jacket over black trousers — a tall narrow-shouldered man with a thin neck, a wide flat head. His chin was small and pointed, his hair sparse. He wore thick-lensed spectacles, under which his eyes showed large and mild blue.

Trasek closed the door behind him, advanced slowly into the room, harsh and fierce as a black wolf.

"Yes?" inquired Dr. Horzabky. "What can I do for you?"

Trasek smiled. "I doubt if you'll do it."

Horzabky raised his eyebrows slightly. "In that case, there was small reason for you to call."

"I might be an art fancier," said Trasek, nodding toward the pictures on the wall. "Although they're something queer for my taste…Mind if I look at them?"

"Not at all." Horzabky lay down his book. "The pictures however are not for sale."

Trasek approached the first, rather more closely than a connoisseur would recommend. It appeared, at first glance, merely a shading of blacks, dull browns and purples. "This one seems dull."

"According to your taste," said Horzabky, looking quizzically back and forth from the picture to Trasek.

"Who is the artist?"

"His name is unknown."

"Ah," and Trasek passed on to the second, an abstraction. "Now this is a nightmare." Indeed, the shapes were unreal, and when the mind reached to grasp them, they slipped away from comprehension; and the colors were equally strange — nameless off-tones, bright tints the eye saw but could not name. Trasek shook his head disapprovingly, to Horzabky's amusement, and passed on to the third, likewise an abstraction, but composed in a quieter spirit — horizontal lines and stripes of gold, silver, copper, and other metallic colors.

Trasek examined this closely. "There's a clever illusion of space and distance here," he said, watching Horzabky from the corner of his eye. "Almost you would think you could reach in, gather up the gold."

"Many have thought so," assented Horzabky, eyes owlish behind the spectacles.

Trasek examined the fourth picture with even greater care. "Another one I can't understand," he said at last. "Are those trees?"

Horzabky nodded. "The artist has painted everything as it would appear inside out."

"Ah, ah..." Trasek nodded wisely and passed on to the fifth picture. Here he found depicted an intricate framework of luminous yellow-white bars on a black background, the framework filling all of space with a cubical lattice, the parallel members meeting at the picture's vanishing point. Without comment Trasek turned to the last picture on the wall, merely a grayish-pink blur, and shook his head silently, then turned away.

"Perhaps now you will reveal your reason for calling," Horzabky put forward, gently.

Trasek looked fiercely toward Horzabky, who blinked in discomfort.

"A friend asked me to find you," said Trasek.

Horzabky shook his flat head. "You still have the advantage of me. Who is the friend?"

"I doubt if you'd recognize his name. He knew yours, though — from the Bocz death-camp, in Kunvasy."

"Ah," said Horzabky softly. "I begin to understand."

Trasek's eyes glowed like eyes seen in the darkness from beside a campfire. "There were sixty-eight thousand devil-ridden slaves. All starved, jellied with beatings, rotten with frost-bite — things that monkeys and jackals would turn away from."

"Come, come," Horzabky protested mildly, lowering his spindly figure into a chair. "Surely —"

"One of the Kunvasian scientists asked for them, was told to do anything he liked; they were too sick and weak to be worked profitably and had been sent to Bocz to be killed." Trasek leaned forward. "Do I interest you?"

"I'm listening," replied Horzabky without emotion.

"The scientist was a man of vision, no question about it. He wished to probe into other dimensions, other universes, but there was no known tool or contrivance to give him a purchase. Any earthly force acted in the bounds of earth dimensions, and he needed a force beyond these bounds. He thought of mental power — of telepathy. All the evidence seemed to indicate that telepathy acted through non-earthly dimensions. Suppose this force were magnified tremendously? Might it not twist open a path into the unknown? Possibly the concentrated effort of a great number of minds might be effective. So he obtained the sixty-eight thousand slaves. He dosed them with drugs that stimulated their concentration but numbed their wills, made them pliable. Into the compound he herded them, massed them cheek on shoulder facing a target painted on a panel of plywood. He told them to will! will! will! To go in but not beyond! Three directions, then a fourth! To imagine the unimaginable!

"The slaves stood there panting, sweating, eyes popping in their efforts. Mist gathered on the target. 'In! In!' yelled the scientist. 'In but not out!' And the target burst open — a three-foot hole into nowhere.

"He let them rest a day, then he brought them out again, and again they broke a way into another space. Seven times he did this, and then catastrophe interrupted him. The Kunvasian General Staff decided that the time had come. On I Day they turned loose their air force, but the United defenses smashed the armada over the Balt Bay; the war was lost the same day it was started.

"The scientist at Bocz was in a quandary. Sixty-eight thousand slaves knew of his seven holes, in addition to a few guards. Silence must be arranged, and death was an excellent arranger. An idea came to him. Why not put all this dying to some use — if only to gratify a whimsical curiosity? So he divided the sixty-eight thousand into seven groups, and on succeeding nights he herded a group through one of the holes.

"By this time the United Army of Occupation was approaching, but when Bocz was liberated, the scientist had disappeared, together with his seven holes. Strangely, all the guards who had aided the scientist were housed in the same barracks, and this barracks was fumigated one night with nocumene. Seems as if the case were closed, doesn't it?"

"I would think so," said Horzabky, casually displaying a small automatic, "but this is your story. Please continue."

"I've about finished my part of it," said Trasek, grinning obliquely at the gun.

"Perhaps you are right." Horzabky rose to his feet. "The accuracy of your knowledge puzzles me, I admit. Possibly you will reveal its source?"

"That's a rather valuable bit of information," said Trasek. "Suppose you talk for a while."

"Hm..." Horzabky hesitated. "Very well. Why not?" He pulled the robe closer around his thin shoulders, as if he were cold. "As you say, it was a grand conception, noble indeed, and no ordinary person can conceive my exultation when success came on the first night of trial... Long after the prisoners had retired to their barracks I stood on the platform, staring into my new universe. I asked myself, what now? I thought, if the hole were fixed in space, the earth's motion would have left it far behind in an instant; evidently it was fixed, part of the plywood panel. And true, when I lifted the panel — cautiously, inch by inch — the hole moved along as well. I carried it to my quarters, and soon I had six others: seven wonderful new universes I could carry around almost in a portfolio." Horzabky gazed at the pictures on the wall. Trasek, if he had leapt at this instant, could have seized the gun; however he chose to keep his distance. "And the prisoners, they had been condemned to die; now wasn't it better that they participated in my grand experiment?"

"Their opinion was not asked," remarked Trasek. "However, I think it likely that they would have preferred to live."

"Pah!" Horzabky pursed his lips, flung his thin arm wide. "Creatures such as they —"

Trasek cut him short, lowered himself into a chair. "Tell me about your universes."

"Ah, yes," said Horzabky. "They're a strange collection, all different, every one, though two of them appear to act by the same set of fundamental laws as our own. This one —" he indicated Picture No. 4 "— is identical to ours, except that it's seen from a versi-dimensional angle. Everything appears inside out. Universe No. 5 now —" this was the space cut into innumerable cubes by the luminous webbing "— is built of the same sort of stuff as our own, but it developed differently. Those bars are actually lines of ions; the whole universe is a tremendous dynamo." He stood back, hands buried in the big pockets of his jacket. "Those two are the only ones susceptible to discussion in our words. Look at No. 1. It appears a mottled crust of black, rusty-purple. The colors are an illusion; there is no light in that universe, and the color is light reflected from our own. What actually is past that blur I don't know. Our words are useless. No word, no thought in our language can possibly be of any use, even ideas like space, time, distance, hard, soft, here, there ... A new language, a new set of abstracts is necessary to deal with that universe, and I suspect that, almost by definition, our brains are incapable of dealing with it."

Trasek nodded with genuine admiration. "Well put, doctor. You interest me."

Horzabky smiled slightly. "We have the same difficulty with No. 2, which looks like a particularly frenetic modern painting; also No. 3 and No. 6."

"That's six," Trasek remarked. "Where's the seventh?"

Horzabky smiled again, a small trembling-lipped kewpie-smile. He rubbed his sharp chin, nodded at the mirror. "There."

"Of course," muttered Trasek.

"No. 7 —" Horzabky shook his flat bald head "— so alien to our world that light refuses to penetrate it."

"Is it not grotesque," Trasek commented, "that the prisoners of Bocz were denied that option?"

"Only superficially," replied his host. "A moment's reflection solves the paradox. However," he added sadly, "the inflexible nature of light made it impossible for me to observe the experiences of the more obliging prisoners."

"What happens to a stick you push in?"

"It dissolves. Melts to nothing, like tissue paper in a furnace.

Conservation of energy falls down in the other universes, where matter and energy are equally unacceptable, and where our laws have no authority."

"And the others?"

"In No. 1 a stick, a bar of iron, crumbles, falls to dust. In No. 2, you can't hold it; it's wrenched from your hands, by whom or what I don't know. In No. 3, the stick may be withdrawn unchanged, and likewise in No. 4. In No. 5 the stick acquires an electric charge, and if released flies off at tremendous speed down one of the corridors. In No. 6 — that's the blurred, pinkish-gray place — the stick becomes a new material, though it's structurally the same. The different space alters the electrons and protons, makes the wood as hard as iron, though chemically the substance is still wood. And, in No. 7, as I said, the material merely melts."

Trasek stood up; Horzabky's hand leapt out of the pocket of the robe like a snake, and with it the gun.

"A pity," sighed Horzabky, "that in the discussion these reminders of our tangled lives must intrude. But you appear a passionate man, a bitter man, Mr. Whatever-your-name, and my little weapon, though blunt and unsubtle, is an effectual ally. It is necessary that I be careful. At this moment a number of so-called war-criminals are being rounded up. My innocent activities at Bocz would be misconstrued and I'd suffer a great deal of inconvenience. Perhaps now you had better tell me what you seek here."

Trasek's hand went to his pocket. "Easy!" hissed Horzabky.

Trasek smiled his hard smile. "I have no weapon. I need none. I merely wish to withdraw a small article...This." He displayed a small round box with a button on the lid. "I press this small button three times — so. And presently the reason for my visit will appear."

A long moment the two stared at each other, motionless, as if frozen in crystal; the one suspicious, the other mocking.

"We turn our attention to Universe No. 4," said Trasek, "where recently you commended ten thousand guests. Examine the scene. Does it suggest nothing to you?"

Horzabky forbore to answer, watched Trasek balefully.

"Those are trees, it's evident that they are trees, although the foliage appears to be growing inside the tube of the trunk. We can see we're on dry land, though that's about all we can be sure of, with that lighting...Would you like to know the actual whereabouts of the scene? I'll tell you. It's Arnhem Land, the most isolated part of Australia. It's our own Earth."

The faint buzz of the door-bell sounded.

"You better answer it," said Trasek. "You'll save your housekeeper the worst fright of her life."

Horzabky motioned with his gun. "Go ahead of me, open the door."

As they marched down the hall, the fat woman in the pink robe appeared. "Go back to bed, Martha," said Horzabky. "I'll take care of it." The woman turned, retired.

The bell rang again. Trasek put his hand on the door. "A warning, Doctor. Be careful with that gun. I don't mind a bullet or two at me — but if you injure my brother, the relatively easy death I plan for you will be postponed indefinitely."

"Open the door!" croaked Horzabky.

Trasek threw it wide.

The thing lurched in from the darkness, stood swaying in the hall. Horzabky's breath came as if someone had kicked him in the belly.

"That's a man," said Trasek. "A man inside out."

Horzabky pushed the glasses back up on the ridge of his nose. "Is this — is this one of —"

Trasek had been brightly watching Horzabky's gun. "It's one of your victims, Doctor. You sent him through your No. 4 hole. That's a plastic coverall he's wearing to keep the flies off him, or rather, from inside him, because to himself he's still a normal man, and it's the universe that's backwards."

"How many more are there like him?" inquired Horzabky, casually.

"None. Flies got some, sunburn most of the others, and the natives shot a lot full of reed arrows. A government cattle inspector came along and wanted to know what was going on. How he ever recognized —" Trasek nodded toward his brother "— for a man is a mystery. But he took care of him, as well as he was able, and I finally got a letter..."

Horzabky pursed his small pink mouth. "And what was your plan, relative to him?"

"You and I are going to help him back through Hole No. 4. That should put him right side out again, in relation to the world."

Horzabky smiled thinly. "You're an amazing fellow. You must know that both you and your brother are threats to the quiet life I plan to live here, that I can't possibly permit you to leave alive."

Trasek sprang forward so fast his figure blurred. Before Horzabky could blink, Trasek seized his wrist, jerked the gun free. He turned his head to his brother.

"This way, Emmer." Then to Horzabky: "Back with you, Doctor, back to your art gallery."

They returned down the hall to the library. Trasek motioned to picture No. 4. "Remove the glass, if you please."

Horzabky complied slowly, and with a surly expression. Trasek leaned slightly through the hole, surveyed the country, pulled back. "If this is how things look to you, Emmer, I fail to understand your continued sanity…Well, here's the hole. It's about a six foot drop, but at least you'll be right side to the world. First you'd better take off that plastic playsuit, or you'll have it all wound up in your bowels."

Trasek unzipped the covering, wadded it up, tossed it through the hole. He dragged a chair close under the hole. Emmer climbed awkwardly up, inserted himself, dropped through.

Trasek and Horzabky watched him a moment — still inside out, but one with his environment.

"That's a bad month out of anyone's life," said Trasek. His mouth jerked. "I was forgetting the years he spent as a Kunvasian slave…" A hand was at his pocket; Horzabky seized the gun, stepped away, the weapon leveled.

"You won't snatch it this time, my friend."

Trasek's harsh smile came. "No, you're right there. You may keep the gun."

Horzabky stood staring, half-at, half-past Trasek. "You have given me an upsetting evening," he muttered. "I was sure the entire number had been disposed of." He glanced down the line of pictures.

"Now you're not sure, eh Doctor?" Trasek jeered. "Maybe not all of them died when they passed through…Maybe they're waiting just out of sight, like rats in a hole —"

"Impossible."

"— maybe you've carried them with you everywhere, maybe they steal out during the night to eat and return to hide."

"Nonsense," blurted Horzabky. "I saw them die. In No. 1 they turned stiff and crumbled, vanished off in the murk. In No. 2 they struggled and kicked and finally came all apart and the parts jerked off in all directions. In No. 3 they expanded, exploded. In No. 4 — well, as you know. In No. 5 they were picked up and whisked like chaff along the corridors, far down and out of sight. In No. 6 — it's impossible to see into the blur, but any object pushed in and withdrawn is changed in every atom, petrified, every bit made part of the new space. In No. 7, matter just melts."

Trasek had been musing. "No. 2 seems disagreeable…No. 4 — no, Horzabky, not even for you. I don't believe in torture, for which you can thank your stars…Well, No. 2, shall we say? Will you climb through by yourself, or shall I help you?"

Horzabky's mouth twisted like a mottled rose-bud; his eyes sparked. "You miserable…Insolent…" He spat the words, and they darted through the air like white serpents. He raised his arm; the gun roared — once, twice.

Trasek, still grinning, went to the wall, took down No. 2, propped it against one of the massive tables. The violent shapes of the world within swam, shifted, outraged the mind.

Horzabky was whining in a high-pitched tone. He ran a few steps closer to Trasek, pushed the gun almost into his face, fired again — again — again.

White marks appeared on Trasek's forehead, cheek. Horzabky floundered back.

"You can't kill me," said Trasek. "Not with matter from this world. I'm one of your alumni, too. You sent me through No. 6; I'm like that stick of wood — impervious!"

Horzabky leaned against the table, the gun dangling from his hand. "But — but —"

"The rest of them are dead, Doctor. There is no bottom to this hole; you just fall forever — unless you happen to catch the edge of the opening. I finally climbed back in while you were out gassing the guards. Now, Doctor," he took a soft step closer to the palsied Horzabky, "No. 2 is waiting for you…"

DP!

An old woodcutter woman, hunting mushrooms up the north fork of the Kreuzberg, raised her eyes and saw the strangers. They came step by step through the ferns, arms extended, milk-blue eyes blank as clam shells. When they chanced into patches of sunlight, they cried out in hurt voices and clutched at their naked scalps, which were white as ivory, and netted with pale blue veins.

The old woman stood like a stump, the breath scraping in her throat. She stumbled back, almost falling at each step, her legs moving back to support her at the last critical instant. The strange people came to a wavering halt, peering through sunlight and dark-green shadow. The woman took an hysterical breath, turned, and put her gnarled old legs to flight.

A hundred yards downhill she broke out on a trail; here she found her voice. She ran, uttering cracked screams and hoarse cries, lurching from side to side. She ran till she came to a wayside shrine, where she flung herself into a heap to gasp out prayer and frantic supplication.

Two woodsmen, in leather breeches and rusty black coats, coming up the path from Tedratz, stared at her in curiosity and amusement. She struggled to her knees, pointed up the trail. "Fiends from the pit! Walking in all their evil; with my two eyes I've seen them!"

"Come now," the older woodsman said indulgently. "You've had a drop or two, and it's not reverent to talk so at a holy place."

"I saw them," bellowed the old woman. "Naked as eggs and white as lard; they came running at me waving their arms, crying out for my very soul!"

"They had horns and tails?" the younger man asked jocularly. "They prodded you with their forks, switched you with their whips?"

"Ach, you blackguards! You laugh, you mock; go up the slope, and see for yourself…Only five hundred meters, and then perhaps you'll mock!"

"Come along," said the first. "Perhaps someone's been plaguing the old woman; if so, we'll put him right."

They sauntered on, disappeared through the firs. The old woman rose to her feet, hobbled as rapidly as she could toward the village.

Five quiet minutes passed. She heard a clatter; the two woodsmen came running at breakneck speed down the path. "What now?" she quavered, but they pushed past her and ran shouting into Tedratz.

Half an hour later fifty men armed with rifles and shotguns stalked cautiously back up the trail, their dogs on leash. They passed the shrine; the dogs began to strain and growl.

"Up through here," whispered the older of the two woodsmen. They climbed the bank, threaded the firs, crossed sun-flooded meadows and balsam-scented shade.

From a rocky ravine, tinkling and chiming with a stream of glacier water, came the strange, sad voices.

The dogs snarled and moaned; the men edged forward, peered into the meadow. The strangers were clustered under an overhanging ledge, clawing feebly into the dirt.

"Horrible things!" hissed the foremost man, "Like great potato-bugs!" He aimed his gun, but another struck up the barrel. "Not yet! Don't waste good powder; let the dogs hunt them down. If fiends they be, their spite will find none of us!"

The idea had merit; the dogs were loosed. They bounded forward, full of hate. The shadows boiled with fur and fangs and jerking white flesh.

One of the men jumped forward, his voice thick with rage. "Look, they've killed Tupp, my good old Tupp!" He raised his gun and fired, an act which became the signal for further shooting. And presently, all the strangers had been done to death, by one means or another.

Breathing hard, the men pulled off the dogs and stood looking down at the bodies. "A good job, whatever they are, man, beast, or fiend," said Johann Kirchner, the innkeeper. "But there's the point! What are they? When have such creatures been seen before?"

"Strange happenings for this earth; strange events for Austria!"

The men stared at the white tangle of bodies, none pushing too close, and now with the waning of urgency their mood became uneasy. Old Alois, the baker, crossed himself and, furtively examining the sky, muttered about the Apocalypse. Franz, the village atheist, had his reputation to maintain. "Demons," he asserted, "presumably would not succumb so easily to dog-bite and bullet; these must be refugees from the Russian zone, victims of torture and experimentation." Heinrich, the village Communist, angrily pointed out how much closer lay the big American lager near Innsbruck; this was the effect of Coca-Cola and comic books upon decent Austrians.

"Nonsense," snapped another. "Never an Austrian born of woman had such heads, such eyes, such skin. These things are something else. Salamanders!"

"Zombies," muttered another. "Corpses, raised from the dead."

Alois held up his hand. "Hist!"

Into the ravine came the pad and rustle of aimless steps, the forlorn cries of the troglodytes.

The men crouched back into the shadows; along the ridge appeared silhouettes, crooked, lumpy shapes feeling their way forward, recoiling from the shafts of sunlight.

Guns cracked and spat; once more the dogs were loosed. They bounded up the side of the ravine and disappeared.

Panting up the slope, the men came to the base of a great overhanging cliff, and here they stopped short. The base of the cliff was broken open. Vague pale-eyed shapes wadded the gap, swaying, shuddering, resisting, moving forward inch by inch, step by step.

"Dynamite!" cried the men. "Dynamite, gasoline, fire!"

These measures were never put into effect. The commandant of the French occupation garrison arrived with three platoons. He contemplated the fissure, the oyster-pale faces, the oyster-shell eyes and threw up his hands. He dictated a rapid message for the Innsbruck headquarters, then required the villagers to put away their guns and depart the scene.

The villagers sullenly retired; the French soldiers, brave in their sky-blue shorts, gingerly took up positions; and with a hasty enclosure of barbed wire and rails restrained the troglodytes to an area immediately in front of the fissure.

The April 18 edition of the *Innsbruck Kurier* included a skeptical paragraph: "A strange tribe of mountainside hermits, living in a Kreuzberg cave near Tedratz, was reported today. Local inhabitants profess the deepest mystification. The Tedratz constabulary, assisted by units of the French garrison, is investigating."

A rather less cautious account found its way into the channels of the wire services: "Innsbruck, April 19. A strange tribe has appeared from the recesses of the Kreuzberg near Innsbruck in the Tyrol. They are said to be hairless, blind, and to speak an incomprehensible language.

"According to unconfirmed reports, the troglodytes were attacked by terrified inhabitants of nearby Tedratz, and after bitter resistance were driven back into their caves.

"French occupation troops have sealed off the entire Kreuzertal. A spokesman for Colonel Courtin refuses either to confirm or deny that the troglodytes have appeared."

Bureau chiefs at the wire services looked long and carefully at the story. Why should French occupation troops interfere in what appeared on the face a purely civil disturbance? A secret colony of war criminals? Unlikely. What then? Mysterious race of troglodytes? Clearly hokum. What then? The story might develop, or it might go limp. In any case, on the late afternoon of April 19, a convoy of four cars started up the Kreuzertal, carrying reporters, photographers, and a member of the U.N. Minorities Commission, who by chance happened to be in Innsbruck.

The road to Tedratz wound among grassy meadows, story-book forests, in and out of little Alpine villages, with the massive snow-capped knob of the Kreuzberg gradually pushing higher into the sky.

At Tedratz, the party alighted and started up the now notorious trail, to be brought short almost at once at a barricade manned by French soldiers. Upon display of credentials the reporters and photographers were allowed to pass; the U.N. commissioner had nothing to show, and the NCO in charge of the barricade politely turned him back.

"But I am an official of the United Nations!" cried the outraged commissioner.

"That may well be," assented the NCO. "However, you are not a journalist, and my orders are uncompromising." And the angry commissioner was asked to wait in Tedratz until word would be taken to Colonel Courtin at the camp.

The commissioner seized on the word. "'Camp'? How is this? I thought there was only a cave, a hole in the mountainside?"

The NCO shrugged. "Monsieur le Commissionnaire is free to conjecture as he sees best."

A private was told off as a guide; the reporters and photographers started up the trail, with the long, yellow afternoon light slanting down through the firs.

It was a jocular group; repartee and wise cracks were freely exchanged. Presently the party became winded, as the trail was steep and they were all out of condition. They stopped by the wayside shrine to rest. "How much farther?" asked a photographer.

The soldier pointed through the firs toward a tall buttress of granite. "Only a little bit; then you shall see."

Once more they set out and almost immediately passed a platoon of soldiers stringing barbed wire from tree to tree.

"This will be the third extension," remarked their guide over his shoulder. "Every day they come pushing up out of the rock. It is —" he selected a word "—*formidable.*"

The jocularity and wise cracks died; the journalists peered through the firs, aware of the sudden coolness of the evening.

They came to the camp, and were taken to Colonel Courtin, a small man full of excitable motion. He swung his arm. "There, my friends, is what you came to see; look your fill, since it is through your eyes that the world must see."

For three minutes they stared, muttering to one another, while Courtin teetered on his toes.

"How many are there?" came an awed question.

"Twenty thousand by latest estimate, and they issue ever faster. All from that little hole." He jumped up on tiptoe, and pointed. "It is incredible; where do they fit? And still they come, like the objects a magician removes from his hat."

"But — do they eat?"

Courtin held out his hands. "Is it for me to ask? I furnish no food; I have none; my budget will not allow it. I am a man of compassion. If you will observe, I have hung the tarpaulins to prevent the sunlight."

"With that skin, they'd be pretty sensitive, eh?"

"Sensitive!" Courtin rolled up his eyes. "The sunlight burns them like fire."

"Funny that they're not more interested in what goes on."

"They are dazed, my friend. Dazed and blinded and completely confused."

"But — what *are* they?"

"That, my friend, is a question I am without resource to answer."

The journalists regained a measure of composure, and swept the enclosure with studiously impassive glances calculated to suggest, *we have seen so many strange sights that now nothing can surprise us.* "I suppose they're men," said one.

"But of course. What else?"

"What else indeed? But where do they come from? Lost Atlantis? The land of Oz?"

"Now then," said Colonel Courtin, "you make jokes. It is a serious business, my friends; where will it end?"

"That's the big question, Colonel. Whose baby is it?"

"I do not understand."

"Who takes responsibility for them? France?"

"No, no," cried Colonel Courtin. "You must not credit me with such a statement."

"Austria, then?"

Colonel Courtin shrugged. "The Austrians are a poor people. Perhaps — of course I speculate — your great country will once again share of its plenitude."

"Perhaps, perhaps not. The one man of the crowd who might have had something to say is down in Tedratz — the chap from the Minorities Commission."

✳

The story pushed everything from the front pages, and grew bigger day by day.

From the U.P. wire:

> *Innsbruck*, April 23 (UP): The Kreuzberg miracle continues to confound the world. Today a record number of troglodytes pushed through the gap, bringing the total surface population up to forty-six thousand...

From the syndicated column, *Science Today* by Ralph Dunstaple, for April 28:

> The scientific world seethes with the troglodyte controversy. According to the theory most frequently voiced, the trogs are descended from cavemen of the glacial eras, driven underground by the advancing wall of ice. Other conjectures, more or less scientific, refer to the lost tribes of Israel, the fourth dimension, Armageddon, and Nazi experiments.
>
> Linguistic experts meanwhile report progress in their efforts to understand the language of the trogs. Dr. Allen K. Mendelson of the Princeton Institute of Advanced Research, spokesman for the group, classifies the trog speech as "one of the agglutinatives, with the slightest possible kinship to the Basque tongue — so faint as to be highly speculative, and it is only fair to say that there is considerable disagreement among us on this point. The trogs, incidentally, have no words for 'sun', 'moon', 'fight', 'bird', 'animal', and a host of other concepts we take for granted. 'Food' and 'fungus', however, are the same word.

From the *New York Herald Tribune*:

TROGS HUMAN, CLAIM SAVANTS;
INTERBREEDING POSSIBLE
by Mollie Lemmon
Milan, April 30: Trogs are physiologically identical with

surface humanity, and sexual intercourse between man and trog might well be fertile. Such was the opinion of a group of doctors and geneticists at an informal poll I conducted yesterday at the Milan Genetical Clinic, where a group of trogs are undergoing examination.

———————

From *The Trog Story*, a daily syndicated feature by Harlan B. Temple, April 31:

"Today I saw the hundred thousandth trog push his way up out of the bowels of the Alps; everywhere in the world people are asking, where will it stop? I certainly have no answer. This tremendous migration, unparalleled since the days of Alaric the Goth, seems only just now shifting into high gear. Two new rifts have opened into the Kreuzberg; the trogs come shoving out in close ranks, faces blank as custard, and only God knows what is in their minds.

"The camps — there are now six, interconnected like knots on a rope — extend down the hillside and into the Kreuzertal. Tarpaulins over the treetops give the mountainside, seen from a distance, the look of a lawn with handkerchiefs spread out to dry.

"The food situation has improved considerably over the past three days, thanks to the efforts of the Red Cross, CARE, and FAO. The basic ration is a mush of rice, wheat, millet or other cereal, mixed with carrots, greens, dried eggs, and reinforced with vitamins; the trogs appear to thrive on it.

"I cannot say that the trogs are a noble, enlightened, or even ingratiating race. Their cultural level is abysmally low; they possess no tools, they wear neither clothing nor ornaments. To their credit it must be said that they are utterly inoffensive and mild; I have never witnessed a quarrel or indeed seen a trog exhibit anything but passive obedience.

"Still they rise in the hundreds and thousands. What brings them forth? Do they flee a subterranean Attila, some pandemonic Stalin? The linguists who have been studying the trog speech are close-mouthed, but I have it from a highly informed source that a report will be published within the next day or so…"

———————

Report to the Assembly of the U.N., May 4, by V.G. Hendlemann, Coordinator for the Committee of Associated Anthropologists:

"I will state the tentative conclusions to which this committee has arrived. The processes and inductions which have led to these conclusions are outlined in the appendix to this report.

"Our preliminary survey of the troglodyte language has convinced a majority of us that the trogs are probably the descendants of a group of European cave-dwellers who either by choice or by necessity took up underground residence at least fifty thousand, at most two hundred thousand, years ago.

"The trog which we see today is a result of evolution and mutation, and represents adaptation to the special conditions under which the trogs have existed. He is quite definitely of the species *homo sapiens,* with a cranial capacity roughly identical to that of surface man.

"In our conversations with the trogs we have endeavored to ascertain the cause of the migration. Not one of the trogs makes himself completely clear on the subject, but we have been given to understand that the great caves which the race inhabited have been stricken by a volcanic convulsion and are being gradually filled with lava. If this be the case the trogs are seen to become literally 'displaced persons'.

"In their former home the trogs subsisted on fungus grown in shallow 'paddies', fertilized by their own wastes, finely pulverized coal, and warmed by volcanic heat.

"They have no grasp of 'time' as we understand the word. They have only the sparsest traditions of the past and are unable to conceive of a future further removed than two minutes. Since they exist in the present, they neither expect, hope, dread, nor otherwise take cognizance of what possibly may befall them.

"In spite of their deficiencies of cultural background, the trogs appear to have a not discreditable native intelligence. The committee agrees that a troglodyte child reared in ordinary surface surroundings, and given a typical education, might well become a valuable citizen, indistinguishable from any other human being except by his appearance."

———————

Excerpt from a speech by Porfirio Hernandez, Mexican delegate to the U.N. Assembly, on May 17:

"...We have ignored this matter too long. Far from being a scientific curiosity or a freak, this is a very human problem, one of the biggest problems of our day and we must handle it as such. The trogs are pressing from the ground at an ever-increasing rate; the Kreuzertal, or Kreuzer Valley, is inundated with trogs as if by a flood. We have heard reports, we have deliberated, we have made solemn noises, but the fact remains that every one of us is sitting on his hands. These people — we must call them people — must be settled somewhere permanently; they must be made self-supporting. This hot iron must be grasped; we fail in our responsibilities otherwise..."

———————

Excerpt from a speech, May 19, by Sir Lyandras Chandryasam, delegate from India:

"...My esteemed colleague from Mexico has used brave words; he exhibits a humanitarianism that is unquestionably praiseworthy. But he puts forward no positive program. May I ask how many trogs have come to the surface, thus to be cared for? Is not the latest figure somewhere short of a million? I would like to point out that in India alone five million people yearly die of malnutrition or preventable disease; but no one jumps up here in the assembly to cry for a crusade to help these unfortunate victims of nature. No, it is this strange race, with no claim upon anyone, which has contributed nothing to the civilization of the world, which now we feel has first call upon our hearts and purse-strings. I say, is not this a paradoxical circumstance..."

———————

From a speech, May 20, by Dr. Karl Byrnisted, delegate
from Iceland:

"...Sir Lyandras Chandryasam's emotion is understandable,
but I would like to remind him that the streets of India swarm
with millions upon millions of so-called sacred cattle and apes,
who eat what and where they wish, very possibly the food to keep
five million persons alive. The recurrent famines in India could
be relieved, I believe, by a rationalistic dealing with these para-
sites, and by steps to make the new birth-control clinics popular,
such as a tax on babies. In this way, the Indian government, by
vigorous methods, has it within its power to cope with its terrible
problem. These trogs, on the other hand, are completely unable
to help themselves; they are like babies flung fresh into a world
where even the genial sunlight kills them..."

From a speech, May 21, by Porfirio Hernandez, delegate
from Mexico:

"I have been challenged to propose a positive program for
dealing with the trogs...I feel that as an activating principle, each
member of the U.N. agree to accept a number of trogs propor-
tionate to its national wealth, resources, and density of population...Obviously the exact percentages will have to be thrashed
out elsewhere...I hereby move the President of the Assembly
appoint such a committee, and instruct them to prepare such a
recommendation, said committee to report within two weeks."
(Motion defeated, 20 to 35)

The Trog Story, June 2, by Harlan B. Temple:

"No matter how many times I walk through Trog Valley, the
former Kreuzertal, I never escape a feeling of the profoundest
bewilderment and awe. The trogs number now well over a million; yesterday they chiseled open four new openings into the
outside world, and they are pouring out at the rate of thousands

every hour. And everywhere is heard the question, where will it stop? Suppose the earth is a honeycomb, a hive, with more trogs than surface men?

"Sooner or later our organization will break down; more trogs will come up than it is within our power to feed. Organization already has failed to some extent. All the trogs are getting at least one meal a day, but not enough clothes, not enough shelter is being provided. Every day hundreds die from sunburn. I understand that the Old-Clothes-for-Trogs drive has nowhere hit its quota; I find it hard to comprehend. Is there no feeling of concern or sympathy for these people merely because they do not look like so many chorus boys and screen starlets?"

From the *Christian Science Monitor*:

CONTROVERSIAL TROG BILL
PASSES U.N. ASSEMBLY

New York, June 4: By a 35 to 20 vote — exactly reversing its first tally on the measure — the U.N. Assembly yesterday accepted the motion of Mexico's Hernandez to set up a committee for the purpose of recommending a percentage-wise distribution of trogs among member states.

Tabulation of voting on the measure found the Soviet bloc lined up with the United States and the British Commonwealth in opposition to the measure — presumably the countries which would be awarded large numbers of the trogs.

Handbill passed out at rally of the Socialist Reich (Neo-Nazi) party at Bremen, West Germany, June 10:

A NEW THREAT

COMRADES! It took a war to clean Germany of the Jews; must we now submit to an invasion of troglodyte filth? All Germany cries *no!* All Germany cries, hold our borders firm against these cretin moles! Send them to Russia; send them to the Arctic wastes! Let them return to their burrows; let them perish! But guard the Fatherland; guard the sacred German Soil!

(Rally broken up by police, handbills seized.)

Letter to the *London Times*, June 18:

To the Editor:

I speak for a large number of my acquaintances when I say that the prospect of taking to ourselves a large colony of 'troglodytes' awakens in me no feeling of enthusiasm. Surely England has troubles more than enough of its own, without the added imposition of an unassimilable and non-productive minority to eat our already meager rations and raise our already sky-high taxes.

Yours, etc.,

Sir Clayman Winifred, Bart.

Lower Ditchley, Hants.

Letter to the *London Times*, June 21:

To the Editor:

Noting Sir Clayman Winifred's letter of June 18, I took a quick check-up of my friends and was dumbfounded to find how closely they hew to Sir Clayman's line. Surely this isn't our tradition, not to get under the load and help lift with everything we've got? The troglodytes are human beings, victims of a disaster we have no means of appreciating. They must be cared for, and if a qualified committee of experts sets us a quota, I say, let's bite the bullet and do our part.

The Ameriphobe section of our press takes great delight in baiting our cousins across the sea for the alleged denial of civil rights to the Negroes — which, may I add, is present in its most violent and virulent form in a country of the British Commonwealth: the Union of South Africa. What do these journalists say to evidences of the same unworthy emotion here in England?

Yours, etc.,

J.C.T. Harrodsmere

Tisley-on-Thames, Sussex.

DP!

Headline in the *New York Herald Tribune*, June 22:

FOUR NEW TROG CAMPS OPENED;
POPULATION AT TWO MILLION

Letter to the *London Times*, June 24:

To the Editor:

I read the letter of J.C.T. Harrodsmere in connection with the trog controversy with great interest. I think that in his praiseworthy efforts to have England do its bit, he is overlooking a very important fact: namely, we of England are a close-knit people, of clear clean vigorous blood, and admixture of any nature could only be for the worse. I know Mr. Harrodsmere will be quick to say, no admixture is intended. But mistakes occur, and as I understand a man-trog union to be theoretically fertile, in due course there would be a number of little half-breeds scampering like rats around our gutters, a bad show all around. There are countries where this type of mongrelization is accepted: the United States, for instance, boasts that it is the 'melting pot'. Why not send the trogs to the wide open spaces of the U.S. where there is room and to spare, and where they can 'melt' to their heart's content?

Yours, etc.,
Col. G.P. Barstaple (Ret.), Queens Own Hussars.
Mide Hill, Warwickshire.

Letter to the *London Times*, June 28:

To the Editor:

Contrasting the bank accounts, the general air of aliveness of mongrel U.S.A. and non-mongrel England, I say maybe it might do us good to trade off a few retired colonels for a few trogs extra to our quota. Here's to more and better mongrelization!

Yours, etc.,
(Miss) Elizabeth Darrow Brown
London, S.W.

The Trog Story, June 30, by Harlan B. Temple:

> "Will it come as a surprise to my readers if I say the trog situation is getting out of hand? They are coming not slower but faster; every day we have more trogs and every day we have more at a greater rate than the day before. If the sentence sounds confused it only reflects my state of mind.
>
> "Something has got to be done.
>
> "Nothing is being done.
>
> "The wrangling that is going on is a matter of public record. Each country is liberal with advice but with little else. Sweden says, send them to the center of Australia; Australia points to Greenland; Denmark would prefer the Ethiopian uplands; Ethiopia politely indicates Mexico; Mexico says, much more room in Arizona; and at Washington senators from below the Mason-Dixon Line threaten to filibuster from now till Kingdom Come rather than admit a single trog to the continental limits of the U.S. Thank the Lord for an efficient food administration! The U.N. and the world at large can be proud of the organization by which the trogs are being fed.
>
> "Incidental Notes: trog babies are being born — over fifty yesterday."

From the *San Francisco Chronicle:*

REDS OFFER HAVEN TO TROGS
PROPOSAL STIRS WORLD

New York, July 3: Ivan Pudestov, the USSR's chief delegate to the U.N. Assembly, today blew the trog question wide open with a proposal to take complete responsibility for the trogs.

The offer startled the U.N. and took the world completely by surprise, since heretofore the Soviet delegation has held itself aloof from the bitter trog controversy, apparently in hopes that the free world would split itself apart on the problem...

DP!

Editorial in the *Milwaukee Journal*, July 5, headed
"A Question of Integrity":

> At first blush the Russian offer to take the trogs appears to ease our shoulders of a great weight. Here is exactly what we have been grasping for, a solution without sacrifice, a sop to our consciences, a convenient carpet to sweep our dirt under. The man in the street, and the responsible official, suddenly are telling each other that perhaps the Russians aren't so bad after all, that there's a great deal of room in Siberia, that the Russians and the trogs are both barbarians and really not so much different, that the trogs were probably Russians to begin with, etc.
>
> Let's break the bubble of illusion, once and for all. We can't go on forever holding our Christian integrity in one hand and our inclinations in the other...Doesn't it seem an odd coincidence that while the Russians are desperately short of uranium miners at the murderous East German and Ural pits, the trogs, accustomed to life underground, might be expected to make a good labor force?...In effect, we would be turning over to Russia millions of slaves to be worked to death. We have rejected forced repatriation in West Europe and Korea, let's reject forced patriation and enslavement of the trogs.

Headline in the *New York Times*, July 20:

REDS BAN U.N. SUPERVISION OF TROG COMMUNITIES
SOVEREIGNTY ENDANGERED, SAYS PUDESTOV
ANGRILY WITHDRAWS TROG OFFER

Headline in the *New York Daily News*, July 26:

BELGIUM OFFERS CONGO FOR TROG HABITATION
ASKS FUNDS TO RECLAIM JUNGLE
U.N. GIVES QUALIFIED NOD

From *The Trog Story*, July 28, by Harlan B. Temple:

"Four million (give or take a hundred thousand) trogs now breathe surface air. The Kreuzertal camps now constitute one of the world's largest cities, ranking under New York, London, Tokyo. The formerly peaceful Tyrolean valley is now a vast array of tarpaulins, circus tents, Quonset huts, water tanks, and general disorder. Trog City doesn't smell too good either.

"Today might well mark the high tide in what the Austrians are calling 'the invasion from hell'. Trogs still push through a dozen gaps ten abreast, but the pressure doesn't seem so intense. Every once in a while a space appears in the ranks, where formerly they came packed like asparagus in crates. Another difference: the first trogs were meaty and fairly well nourished. These late arrivals are thin and ravenous. Whatever strange subterranean economy they practiced, it seems to have broken down completely..."

From *The Trog Story*, August 1, by Harlan B. Temple:

"Something horrible is going on under the surface of the earth. Trogs are staggering forth with raw stumps for arms, with great wounds..."

From *The Trog Story*, August 8, by Harlan B. Temple:

"Operation Exodus got underway today. One thousand trogs departed the Kreuzertal bound for their new home near Cabinda, at the mouth of the Congo River. Trucks and buses took them to Innsbruck, where they will board special trains to Venice and Trieste. Here ships supplied by the U.S. Maritime Commission will take them to their new home.

"As one thousand trogs departed Trog City, twenty thousand pushed up from their underground homeland, and camp officials are privately expressing concern over conditions. Trog City has expanded double, triple, ten times over the original estimates.

The machinery of supply, sanitation and housing is breaking down. From now on, any attempts to remedy the situation are at best stopgaps, like adhesive tape on a rotten hose, when what is needed is a new hose or, rather, a four-inch pipe.

"Even to maintain equilibrium, thirty thousand trogs per day will have to be siphoned out of the Kreuzertal camps, an obvious impossibility under present budgets and efforts..."

From *Newsweek*, August 14:

Camp Hope, in the bush near Cabinda, last week took on the semblance of the Guadalcanal army base during World War II. There was the old familiar sense of massive confusion, the grind of bulldozers, sweating white, beet-red, brown and black skins, the raw earth dumped against primeval vegetation, bugs, salt tablets, Atabrine...

From the U.P. wire:

Cabinda, Belgian Congo, August 20 (UP): The first contingent of trogs landed last night under shelter of dark, and marched to temporary quarters, under the command of specially trained group captains.

Liaison officers state that the trogs are overjoyed at the prospect of a permanent home, and show an eagerness to get to work. According to present plans, they will till collective farms, and continuously clear the jungle for additional settlers.

On the other side of the ledger, it is rumored that the native tribesmen are showing unrest. Agitators, said to be Communist-inspired, are preying on the superstitious fears of a people themselves not far removed from savagery...

Headline in the *New York Times*, August 22:

CONGO WARRIORS RUN AMOK AT CAMP HOPE
KILL 800 TROG SETTLERS IN SINGLE HOUR

Military Law Established
Belgian Governor Protests
Says Congo Unsuitable

From the U.P. Wire:

Trieste, August 23 (UP): Three shiploads of trogs bound for Trogland in the Congo today marked a record number of embarkations. The total number of trogs to sail from European ports now stands at 24,965...

Cabinda, August 23 (UP): The warlike Matemba Confederation is practically in a state of revolt against further trog immigration, while Resident-General Bernard Cassou professes grave pessimism over eventualities.

Mont Blanc, August 24 (UP): Ten trogs today took up experimental residence in a ski-hut to see how well trogs can cope with the rigors of cold weather.

Announcement of this experiment goes to confirm a rumor that Denmark has offered Greenland to the trogs if it is found that they are able to survive Arctic conditions.

Cabinda, August 28 (UP): The Congo, home of witch-doctors, tribal dances, cannibalism and Tarzan, seethes with native unrest. Sullen anger smolders in the villages, riots are frequent and dozens of native workmen at Camp Hope have been killed or hospitalized.

Needless to say, the trogs, whose advent precipitated the crisis, are segregated far apart from contact with the natives, to avoid a repetition of the bloodbath of August 22...

Cabinda, August 29 (UP): Resident-General Bernard Cassou today refused to allow debarkation of trogs from four ships standing off Cabinda roadstead.

Mont Blanc, September 2 (UP): The veil of secrecy at the experimental trog home was lifted a significant crack this morning, when the bodies of two trogs were taken down to Chamonix via the ski-lift...

From *The Trog Story*, September 10, by Harlan B. Temple:

"It is one a.m.; I've just come down from Camp No. 4. The trog columns have dwindled to a straggle of old, crippled, diseased. The stench is frightful... But why go on? Frankly, I'm heartsick. I wish I had never taken on this assignment. It's doing something terrible to my soul; my hair is literally turning gray. I pause a moment, the noise of my typewriter stops, I listen to the vast murmur through the Kreuzertal; despondency, futility, despair come at me in a wave. Most of us here at Trog City, I think, feel the same.

"There are now five or six million trogs in the camp; no one knows the exact count; no one even cares. The situation has passed that point. The flow has dwindled, one merciful dispensation — in fact, at Camp No. 4 you can hear the rumble of the lava rising into the trog caverns.

"Morale is going from bad to worse here at Trog City. Every day a dozen of the unpaid volunteers throw up their hands, and go home. I can't say as I blame them. Lord knows they've given the best they have, and no one backs them up. Everywhere in the world it's the same story, with everyone pointing at someone else. It's enough to make a man sick. In fact it has. I'm sick — desperately sick.

"But you don't read *The Trog Story* to hear me gripe. You want factual reporting. Very well, here it is. Big news today was that movement of trogs out of the camp to Trieste has been held up pending clarification of the Congo situation. Otherwise, everything's the same here — hunger, smell, careless trogs dying of sunburn..."

Headline in the *New York Times*, September 20:

TROG QUOTA PROBLEM RETURNED TO
STUDY GROUP FOR ADJUSTMENT

From the U.P. Wire:

> *Cabinda*, September 25 (UP): Eight ships, loaded with 9,462 trog refugees, still wait at anchor, as native chieftains reiterated their opposition to trog immigration...
>
> *Trog City*, October 8 (UP): The trog migration is at its end. Yesterday for the first time no new trogs came up from below, leaving the estimated population of Trog City at six million.
>
> *New York*, October 13 (UP): Deadlock still grips the Trog Resettlement Committee, with the original positions, for the most part, unchanged. Densely populated countries claim they have no room and no jobs; the underdeveloped states insist that they have not enough money to feed their own mouths. The U.S., with both room and money, already has serious minority head-aches and doesn't want new ones...
>
> *Chamonix*, France, October 18 (UP): The Trog Experimen-tal Station closed its doors yesterday, with one survivor of the original ten trogs riding the ski-lift back down the slopes of Mont Blanc.
>
> Dr. Sven Emeldson, director of the station, released the following statement: "Our work proves that the trogs, even if provided shelter adequate for a European, cannot stand the rigors of the North; they seem especially sensitive to pulmonary ailments..."
>
> *New York*, October 26 (UP): After weeks of acrimony, a revised set of trog immigration quotas was released for action by the U.N. Assembly. Typical figures are: USA 31%, USSR 16%, Canada 8%, Australia 8%, France 6%, Mexico 6%.
>
> *New York*, October 30 (UP): The USSR adamantly rejects the principle of U.N. checking of the trog resettlement areas inside the USSR...
>
> *New York*, October 31 (UP): Senator Bullrod of Mississippi today promised to talk till his "lungs came out at the elbows" before he would allow the Trog Resettlement Bill to come to a vote before the Senate. An informal check revealed insufficient strength to impose cloture...

St. Arlberg, Austria, November 5 (UP): First snow of the season fell last night...

Trog City, November 10 (UP): Last night, frost lay a sparkling sheath across the valley...

Trog City, November 15 (UP): Trog sufferers from influenza have been isolated in a special section...

Buenos Aires, November 23 (UP): Dictator Peron today flatly refused to meet the Argentine quota of relief supplies to Trog City until some definite commitment has been made by the U.N....

Trog City, December 2 (UP): Influenza following the snow and rain of the last week has made a new onslaught on the trogs; camp authorities are desperately trying to cope with the epidemic...

Trog City, December 8 (UP): Two crematoriums, fired by fuel oil, are roaring full time in an effort to keep ahead of the mounting influenza casualties...

———

From *The Trog Story*, December 13, by Harlan B. Temple:

"This is it..."

———

From the U.P. Wire:

Los Angeles, December 14 (UP): The Christmas buying rush got under way early this year, in spite of unseasonably bad weather...

Trog City, December 15 (UP): A desperate appeal for penicillin, sulfa, blankets, kerosene heaters, and trained personnel was sounded today by Camp Commandant Howard Kerkovits. He admitted that disease among the trogs was completely out of control, beyond all human power to cope with...

———

From *The Trog Story*, December 23, by Harlan B. Temple:

"I don't know why I should be sitting here writing this, because — since there are no more trogs — there is no more trog story."

The Absent Minded Professor

I stood in the dark in front of the observatory, watching the quick fiery meteor trails streaking down from Perseus. My plans were completed. I had been meticulous, systematic.

The night was remarkable: clear and limpid … a perfect night for what we had arranged, the cosmos and I. And here came Dr. Patcher — old "Dog" Patcher, as the students called him — the lights of his staid sedan sniffing out the road up the hill. I looked at my watch: ten-fifteen. The old rascal was late, probably had spent an extra three minutes shining his high-top shoes, or punctiliously brushing the coarse white plume of his hair.

The car nosed up over the hill, the head-lights sent scurrying yellow shapes and shadows past my feet. I heard the motor thankfully gasp and die, and, after a sedate moment, the slam of the door, then the *crush-crush* of Dr. Patcher's feet across the gravel. He seemed surprised to see me standing in the doorway, and looked at me sharply as much as to say, "Nothing better to do, Sisley?"

"Good evening, Dr. Patcher," I said smoothly. "It's a lovely night. The Perseids are showing very well … Ah! There's one now." I pointed at one of the instant white meteor streaks.

Dr. Patcher shook his head with that mulish nicety which has infuriated me since I first laid eyes on him. "Sorry, Sisley, I can't waste a moment of this wonderful seeing." He pushed past me, remarking over his shoulder, "I hope that everything is in order."

I remained silent. I could hardly say "no"; if I said "yes", he would pry and poke until he found something — anything — at which he could raise his eyebrows: a smudge of oil, the roof opening not precisely symmetrical to the telescope, a cigarette butt on the floor. Anything. Then I would hear a snort of disparagement; a quick gleam of a glance would flick in my direction; the deficiency would be ostentatiously remedied. And at last he would get busy with his work — if work it could be called. Myself, I considered it trivial, a piddling waste of time, a repetition of what better men at better instruments had already accomplished. Dr. Patcher was seeking novae. He would not be satisfied until a nova bore his name — "Patcher's Nova". And night after night, when the seeing was best, Dr. Patcher had crowded me away from the telescope, I who had research that was significant and important. Tonight I would show Dr. Patcher a nova indeed.

He was inside now, rustling and probing; tonight he would find nothing a millimeter out of place. I was wrong. "Oh, Sisley," came his voice, "are you busy?"

I hurried inside. Patcher was standing by the senior faculty closet with his old tweed coat already carefully arranged on a hanger. Instantly I knew his complaint. Patcher affected a white laboratory coat, which he called his "duster". About twice a month the janitor, in cleaning out the senior faculty closet, would remove the duster and replace it in the junior closet — whether as an act of crafty malice or sheer wool-gathering I had never made up my mind. In any event the ritual ran its course as usual. "Have you seen my duster, Sisley? It's not in the clothes closet where it should be."

It was on the tip of my tongue to retort, "Dr. Patcher, I am a professor of astronomy, not your valet." To which he would make the carping correction: "*Assistant* professor, my dear Sisley," thus enraging me. But tonight of all nights a state of normality must be assured, since what was to happen would be so curious and unique that only a framework of absolute humdrum routine would make the circumstances convincing.

So I swallowed my temper and, opening the junior closet, handed Patcher his duster. "Well, well," said Patcher as usual, "what on earth is it doing in there?"

"I suppose the janitor has been careless."

"We'll have to bring him up short," said Patcher. "One place where carelessness can never be tolerated is an observatory."

"I agree whole-heartedly," I said, as indeed I did. I am a systematic man, with every aspect of my life conducted along lines of the most rigorous efficiency.

Buttoning his duster, Dr. Patcher looked me up and down. "You seem restless tonight, Sisley."

"I? Certainly not. Perhaps a little tired, a little fatigued. I was prospecting up Mount Tinsley today and found several excellent specimens of sphalerite." Perhaps I should mention that my hobby is mineralogy, that I am an assiduous "rock-hound", and devote a good deal of time to my collection of rocks, minerals and crystals.

Dr. Patcher shook his head a little. "I personally could not afford to dilute my energy to such an extent. I feel that every ounce of attention belongs to my work."

This was a provocative misstatement. Dr. Patcher was an ardent horticulturalist and had gone so far as to plant a border of roses around the observatory.

"Well, well," I said, perhaps a trifle heavily, "I suppose each of us must go his own way." I glanced at my watch. Twenty-five minutes. "I'll leave the place in your hands, Doctor. If the visibility is good I'll be here about three —"

"I'm afraid I'll be using the instrument," said Patcher. "This is a perfect night in spite of the breeze —"

I thought: it is a perfect night *because* of the breeze.

"— I can't afford to waste a minute."

I nodded. "Very well; you can telephone me if you change your mind."

He looked at me queerly; I seldom showed such good grace. "Goodnight, Sisley."

"Good-night, Dr. Patcher. Perhaps I'll watch the Perseids for a bit."

He made no reply. I went outside, strolled around the observatory, re-entered. I cried, "Dr. Patcher, Dr. Patcher!"

"Yes, yes, what is it?"

"Most extraordinary! Of course I'm no gardener, but I've never seen anything like it before, a luminescent rose!"

"What's that?"

"One of the rose bushes seems to be bearing luminescent blossoms."

"Oh, nonsense," muttered Patcher. "It's a trick of vision."

"A remarkable illusion, if so."

"Never heard of such a thing," said Patcher. "I can't see how it's possible. Where is this 'luminescent rose-bush'?"

"It's right around here," I said. "I could hardly believe my eyes." I led him a few feet around the observatory, to where the bed of roses rustled and swayed in the breeze. "Just in there."

Dr. Patcher spoke the last words of his existence on earth. "I don't see any —"

I hurried to my car, which I had parked headed down-slope. I started the motor, roared down the hill as fast as the road and my excellent reflexes allowed. Three days ago I had timed myself: six minutes from the observatory to the outskirts of town. Tonight I made it in five.

Slowing to my usual pace, I rounded the last turn and pulled into Sam's Service Station, stopping the car at a spot which I had calculated to a nicety several weeks earlier. And now I had a stroke of rather good luck. Pulled up in the inside lane was a white police car, with a trooper leaning against the fender.

"Hello, Mr. Sisley," said Sam. "How's all the stars in their courses tonight?"

At any other time I might have treated the pleasantry to the cool rejoinder it deserved. Sam, a burly young man with a perpetual smut on his nose, was a typical layman, in a total fog concerning the exacting and important work that we do at the observatory. Tonight, however, I welcomed his remark. "The stars are about as usual, Sam, but if you keep your eyes open, you'll see any number of shooting stars tonight."

"Honest to Pete?" Sam glanced politely around the sky.

"Yes." I looked at my watch. "Astronomers call them the Perseids. Every year about this time we run into a meteoric shower which seems to come from the constellation of Perseus — right up there. A little later in the year come the Leonids, from Leo."

Sam shook his head admiringly. "My mother's nuts on that stuff, but I didn't know she got it from you guys." He turned to the trooper. "How about that! All the time I thought these guys up at the observatory was — well, kinda passing the time, but now Professor Sisley tells me that they put out these Sign of the Zodiac books — you know, don't-invest-money-with-a-blonde-woman-today stuff. Real practical dope."

The trooper said, "What do you know? I always figured that stuff for so much hogwash."

"Of course it is," I said heatedly. "All foolishness. I said that was the constellation Leo up there, not the 'sign of Leo'!" I checked the time. About thirty seconds. "I'll have five gallons of ethyl, Sam."

"Right," said Sam. "Can you back up a bit? Wait! I guess the hose will reach…" He stood facing the direction I wished him to face.

Glare lit the sky; a flaming gout of white fire plunged down from the heavens, followed an instant later by a flat orange smear of light.

"Heavens to Betsy," cried Sam, standing with his mouth open and the hose in his hand, "what was that?"

"A meteor," I said. "A shooting star."

"That was a humdinger," the trooper said. "You don't see many that close!"

Out of the sky came a sharp report, an explosion.

Sam shook his head and numbly valved gas into the tank. "Looked like that one struck ground right up close to the observatory too."

"Yes," I said, "it certainly did. I think I'll telephone Dr. Patcher and ask if he noticed it."

"Notice it!" said Sam. "He's lucky if he got out of the way!"

I went into the station, dropped a dime into the box, called the observatory.

"Sorry," the operator said a moment later. "There's no reply."

I returned outside. "He doesn't answer. He's probably up in the cage and can't be bothered."

"Cantankerous old devil," said Sam. "But then — excuse me, Professor — all you astronomers act a little bit odd, one way or another. I don't mean screwy or anything like that — but just, well, odd. Absent-minded like."

"Ha, ha," I said. "That's where you're mistaken. I imagine that very few people are as methodical and systematic as I am."

Sam shrugged. "I can't argue with you, Doc."

I got into my car and drove through town toward the University;

I parked in front of the Faculty Club, walked into the lounge, and ordered a pot of tea.

John Dalrymple of the English Department joined me. "I say, Sisley, something in your line — saw a whacking great fire-ball a moment or two ago. Lit up the entire sky, marvellous thing."

"Yes, I saw it at the service station. It apparently struck ground somewhere up near the observatory. This is the time of year for them, you know."

Dalrymple rubbed his chin. "Seems to me I see 'em all the time."

"Oh indeed! But these are the Perseids, a special belt of meteorites, or perhaps, a small comet traversing a regular orbit. The earth, entering this orbit, collides with the rocks and pebbles that make up the comet. When we watch, it seems as if the meteors are coming from the constellation of Perseus — hence we call them Perseids."

Dalrymple rose to his feet. "Well put, old man, awfully interesting and all that, but I've got something to say to Benjamin. See you again."

"Good evening, Dalrymple."

I read a magazine, played a game of chess with Hodges of the Economics Department, and discovered it was twelve-thirty. I rose to my feet. "Excuse me; Dr. Patcher's alone at the observatory. I think I'll call and find out how long he's going to be."

I called the observatory once more, and was told, "Sorry, sir, no answer."

"He's probably up in the cage," I told Hodges. "If he gets busy, he refuses to move."

"Rather crusty old bird, isn't he?"

"Not the easiest person in the world to work with. No doubt but what he has his good points. Well, good-night, Hodges; thanks for the game. I think I'll snooze a bit in one of the chairs before heading up the hill. I'm due at three or thereabouts."

At two o'clock Jake the night janitor aroused me. "Everybody's gone home, sir, and the heat's been turned off. Don't know as you'd want to catch your death of cold sitting here."

"No, by all means. Thank you, Jake." I looked at my watch. "I must be off to work."

"You and me," said Jake, "we keep strange hours."

"The best time of the day is night," I said. "By day, of course, I mean the sidereal day."

"Oh, I understand you, sir. I'm used to hearing all manner of strange talk, and I understand lots better than some of 'em think."

"I'm sure you do, Jake."

"The things I've heard, Mr. Sisley."

"Yes, interesting indeed. Well, good-night, Jake. I must be off to work."

"Getcher coat, Mr. Sisley?"

"Thank you, Jake."

The night was glorious beyond description. Stars, stars, stars — magnificent flowers of heaven, spurting pips of various lights down from their appointed places. I know the night skies as I know my face; I know all the lore, the fable, the mystery. I know where to expect Arcturus, in one corner of the Great Diamond, with Denebola to the side, Spica below, Cor Caroli above. I know Argo Navis and the Northern Cross, sometimes called Cygnus, and the little rocking-horse of Lyra, with Vega at the head. I know how to sight down the three stars in Aquila, with Altair at the center, to find Fomalhaut, when it comes peering briefly over the southern horizon. I know the Lair of the Howling Dog, with Vindemiatrix close by; I can find Algol the demon star and Mira the Wonderful on the spine of Cetus the whale. I know Orion and his upraised arm, with the river Eridanus winding across twenty million light-years of desolation. Ah, the stars! Poetry the poor day-dweller never dreams of! Poetry in the star names: Alpheta, Achernar, Alpheratz; Canopus, Antares, Markab; Sirius, Rigel, Bellatrix; Aldebaran, Betelgeuse, Fomalhaut; Alphard, Spica, Procyon; Deneb Kaitos, Alpha Centauri: rolling magnificent sounds, each king of a myriad worlds. And now, with old Dog Patcher gone to his reward, the heavens were mine, to explore at my leisure; possibly with the help of young Katkus, who would be promoted to my place, when I became head of the department.

I drove up the familiar road, winding among aromatic eucalyptus, and breasted over the edge of the parking area.

The observatory was as I had left it, with Patcher's shiny old sedan pressed close to the wall, much more lonesome and pathetic than ever Patcher's body would look.

But I must not cry out the alarm too quickly; first I had one or two matters to take care of.

I found my flashlight and walked out on the slope behind the observatory. I knew approximately where to look and exactly what I was looking for — and there it was: a bit of cardboard, a scrap of red paper, a length of stick. Everything was proceeding as I had planned, and after all, why should it not? It is very easy to kill a man, so I find. I merely had chosen one of many ways, perhaps a trifle more elaborate than necessary, but it seemed such a fitting end for old Dog Patcher. I could have arranged for his car to have left the road; there would have been precedent in the death of Professor Harlow T. Kane, Patcher's predecessor as Senior Astronomer, who had lost his life in just such a manner... So the thoughts ran through my head as I burned the stick and cardboard and paper, and scattered the ashes.

I returned to the observatory, sauntered inside, looked over the big reflector with a sense of proprietorship... About time now for the alarm.

I wandered outside, turned my flashlight on the body. Everything just so. I ran back in, telephoned the sheriff's office, since the observatory is outside city limits. "Sheriff?"

A sleepy voice grumbled, "What in Sam Hill's the idea, waking me up this time of night?"

"This is Professor Sisley up at the observatory. Something terrible has happened! I've just discovered the body of Dr. Patcher!"

The sheriff was a fat and amiable man, much more concerned with his take from slot machines and poker rooms than the prevention of crime. He arrived at the observatory with a doctor. They stood looking down at the body, the sheriff holding a flashlight, neither one showing zest or enthusiasm.

"Looks like he's been beaned with a rock," said the sheriff. "Find out how long he's been dead, will you, Doc?"

He turned to me. "Just what happened, Professor?"

"It looks to me," I said, "as if he's been struck by a meteorite."

"A meteorite, hey?" He pulled at his chin doubtfully. "Ain't that a little far-fetched? One chance in a thousand, you might say?"

"I can't be sure, naturally. You'll have to get an expert to check on that piece of metal or rock, whatever it is."

The sheriff was still rubbing his chin.

"When I left him at about ten-thirty, he said he was going to watch the meteors — we're passing through the Perseids, you know — and shortly after — I was in town by then at Sam's Service Station — we saw a very large shooting star, meteor, fire-ball, whatever you want to call it, come down from the sky. Sam saw it, the state trooper saw it —"

"Yeah," said the sheriff, "I saw it myself. Monstrous thing…" He bent over Dr. Patcher's dead body. "You think this might be a meteorite, hey?"

"I certainly couldn't say at a glance, but Professor Doheny of the Geology Department could tell you in jig-time."

"Humph," said the sheriff. To the doctor, "Any idea when he died, Doc?"

"Oh, roughly five or six hours ago."

"Humph. That's ten-thirty to eleven-thirty…That meteor came down at, let's see —"

"At exactly twelve minutes to eleven."

"Well, well," said the sheriff, looking at me with mild speculation. After this, I told myself, I would volunteer no more information. But no matter, no harm done.

"I suppose," said the sheriff, "we'd better wait till it's light, and then we can look around a little bit more."

"If you will come into the observatory," I said, "I'll brew up a pot of coffee. This night air is a trifle brisk."

Dawn came; the sheriff called his office; an ambulance climbed the hill. I was asked a few more questions, photographs were taken, and the body was moved.

Newspapers from coast to coast featured accounts of the "freak accident". The "man bites dog" angle was played up heavily; the astronomer who made a career of hunting down "comets" had got a taste of his own medicine. Of course a meteor is by no means a comet, and Dr. Patcher was uninterested in comets, but in the general hullabaloo no one cared very much, and I suppose that insofar as the public is concerned it is all one and the same.

The president of the University telephoned his sympathy. "You'll take Patcher's place, of course; I hope you won't refuse out of any misplaced feelings of delicacy. I've approached young Katkus, and he'll move up to your previous place."

"Thank you, sir," said I, "I'll do my best. With your encouragement and the help of young Katkus I'll see that Patcher's work goes on; indeed, I think it would be a fitting memorial if the first nova we found we named for poor old Patcher."

"Excellent," said the president. "I'll put through your appointment at once."

So events went their course. I cleaned Patcher's notes and books out of the study and moved my own in. Young Katkus made his appearance, and I was pleased by the modest manner in which he accepted his good fortune.

A week passed and the sheriff called at my apartment. "Come in, sheriff, come in. Glad to see you. Here —" I moved some journals "— have a chair."

"Thanks, thanks very much." He eased his fat little body gingerly into the seat.

I had not quite finished my breakfast. "Will you have a cup of coffee?"

He hesitated. "No, think I'd better not. Not today."

"What's on your mind, sheriff?"

He put his hands on his knees. "Well, Professor, it's that Patcher accident. I'd like to talk it over with you."

"Why certainly, if you wish... but I thought that was all water under the bridge."

"Well — not entirely. We've been lying low, you might say. Maybe it's an accident — and again, maybe it's not."

I said with great interest, "What do you mean, sheriff? Surely...?"

As I have mentioned, the sheriff is a mild man, and looks more like an insurance salesman than a law-enforcement officer. But at the moment a rather dogged and unpleasant expression stiffened his features.

"I've been doing a bit of investigating, and a bit of thinking. And I've got to admit I'm puzzled."

"How so?"

"Well, there's no question but what Dr. Patcher was killed with a meteorite. That chunk of rock was a funny kind of nickel–iron mixture, and showed a peculiar set of marks under the microscope. Professor Doheny said meteorite it was, and no doubt about it."

"Oh?" I said, sipping my coffee.

"There's no question but what a streak of fire was seen shooting down out of the sky at about the time Dr. Patcher was killed."

"Yes, I believe so. In fact, I saw it myself. Quite an impressive phenomenon."

"I thought at first that a meteorite would be hot, and I wondered why Patcher's hair wasn't singed, but I find that when a meteor comes down, only a little bit of the surface heats up and glows off, but the rest stays icy-cold."

"Right," I said cordially. "Exactly right."

"But let's suppose," said the sheriff, looking at me sidewise with an expression I can only call crafty, "let's suppose that someone wanted to kill poor old Dr. Patcher —"

I shook my head doubtfully. "Far-fetched."

"— and wanted to fake the murder so that it looked like an accident, how would he go about it?"

"But — who would want to do away with Patcher?"

The sheriff laughed uneasily. "That's what's got us stumped. There's no one with a speck of motive — except, possibly, yourself."

"Ridiculous."

"Of course, of course. But we were just —"

"Why should I want to kill Dr. Patcher?"

"I hear," said the sheriff, watching me sidelong, "that he was a hard man to get along with."

"Not when you understood his foibles."

"I hear that you and he had a few bust-ups over the work up at the observatory?"

"Now that," I said with feeling, "is pure taradiddle. Naturally, we had our differences. I felt, as many of my colleagues did, that Patcher was entering upon his dotage, and it shows in the rather trivial nature of the work he was doing."

"Exactly what was the work, Professor? In words of one syllable?"

"Well," and I laughed, "he was actually going over the sky with a fine-tooth comb, looking for novae, and I'll admit that occasionally it was a vexation, when I had important work to do —"

"Er, what is your work, Professor?"

"I am conducting a statistical count of the Cepheid variables in the Great Nebula of Andromeda."

"Ah, I see," said the sheriff. "Pretty tough job, sounds like."

"The work is progressing now, of course. But certainly you don't think — you can't assume —"

The sheriff waved his hand. "We don't assume anything. We just, well, call it figure a little."

"How could I, how could anyone, control what might literally be called a bolt from the blue?"

"Ah, now we're getting down to brass tacks. How could you, indeed? I admit I racked my brains, and I think I've got it puzzled out."

"My dear sheriff, are you accusing —"

"No, no, sit still. We're just talking things over. I was telling you how you could — if you wanted, mind you, *if* you wanted — fake a meteor."

"Well," I asked in fine scorn, "how could I fake a meteor?"

"You'd need something to make a good streak of light. You'd need something to get it up there. You'd need a way of setting it off at the right time."

"And?"

"Well, the first could be a good strong old-fashioned sky-rocket."

"Why — theoretically, I suppose so. But —"

"I thought of all kinds of things," said the sheriff. "Airplanes, balloons, birds — everything except flying fish. The answer has to be one thing: a kite. A big box kite."

"I admire your ingenuity, sheriff. But —"

"Then you'd need some way to send this thing off, and aim it right. Now I may be all wet on this — but I imagine that you had the rocket fixed with a couple of wire loops over the string, so that it would follow the string to the ground."

"Sheriff, I —"

"Now as for setting it off — why that's a simple matter. I could probably rig up something of the sort myself. A wrist-watch with the glass off, a flashlight battery, a contact stuck on the dial, insulated from the rest of the watch, so that when the minute hand met it, the circuit would open. Then you'd use magnesium floss and magnesium tape to start the fuse of your rocket, and that's practically the whole of it."

"My dear sheriff," I said with all my dignity, "if I were guilty of such a pernicious offense, how in the world would I dispose of the kite?"

"Well," said the sheriff, scratching his chin, "I hadn't thought of that. I suppose you could haul it down and burn it, together with the string."

I was taken aback. Actually, I hadn't thought of anything so simple. The kite I had blown up with half a stick of dynamite, fused to explode after the rocket had started down; the string I had soaked in a solution of potassium chlorate; it had burned to dust like a train of gunpowder. "Humph. Well, if you are accusing me of this crime you have conceived —"

"No, no, no!" cried the sheriff. "I'm not accusing anybody. We're just sitting here chewing this thing over. But I admit I am wondering why you bought all that kite-string from Fuller's Hardware about three weeks ago."

I stared at him indignantly. "Kite-string? Nonsense. I bought that string at the request of Dr. Patcher himself, with which to tie up his sweet peas, and if you check at his home they'll tell you the same story."

The sheriff nodded. "I see. Well, just a point I'm glad to have cleared up. I understand you're an amateur rock-hunter?"

"That's perfectly true," I said. "I have a small but not unrepresentative collection."

"Any meteorites in the bunch?" the sheriff asked carelessly.

Just as carelessly I replied, "Why I believe so. One or two."

"I wonder if I could see them."

"Certainly, if you wish. I keep my collection out here, in the back rooms. I'm very methodical about all this; I don't let the rocks intrude into the astronomy, or vice versa."

"That's how hobbies should be," said the sheriff.

We went out upon the back-porch, which I have converted to a display room. On all sides are chests of narrow drawers, glass-topped tables where my choicest pieces are on view, geological charts, and the like. At the far end is my little laboratory, with my reagents, scales,

and furnace. Midway is the file cabinet where I have indexed and cata-
logued each piece in my collection.

The sheriff glanced with an unconvincing show of interest along the
trays and shelves. "Now, let's see them meteorites."

Although I knew their whereabouts to the inch, I made a move of
indecision. "I'll have to check in the catalogue; I'm afraid it's slipped
my mind."

I pulled open the filing cabinet, flipped the dividers to M. "Meteorites — RG-17. Ah yes, right on here, sheriff. Case R, tray G, space 17. As
you see, I'm nothing if not systematic…"

"What's the matter?" asked the sheriff.

I suppose I was staring at the sheet of paper. It read:

RG-17-A — Meteorite — Nickel–iron
Weight — 171 grams
Origin   — Burnt Rock Ranch, Arizona

RG-17-B — Meteorite — Granitic stone
Weight — 216 grams
Origin   — Kelsey, Nevada

RG-17-C — Meteorite — Nickel–iron
Weight — 1,842 grams
Origin   — Kilgore, Mojave Desert

Meticulously, systematically, I had typed in red against RG-17-C:
Removed from collection, August 9. Three days before Dr. Patcher had
been killed by a meteorite weighing 1,842 grams.

"What's the matter?" asked the sheriff. "Not feeling so good?"

"The meteorites," I croaked, "are over here."

"Let's see that sheet of paper."

"No — it's just a memorandum."

"Sure — but I want to see it."

"I'll show you the meteorites."

"Show me that paper."

"Do you want to see the meteorites or don't you?"

"I want to see that paper."

"Go to blazes."

"Professor Sisley —"

I went to the tray, pulled it open. "The meteorites. Look at them!"

The sheriff stepped over, bent his head. "Hm. Yeah. Just rocks." He cocked an eye at the sheet of paper I gripped in my hand. "Are you going to show me that paper or not?"

"No. It's got nothing to do with this business. It's a record of where I obtained these rocks. They're valuable, and I promised not to reveal the source."

"Well, well." The sheriff turned away. I walked quickly to the toilet, locked the door, quickly tore the paper to shreds, flushed it down the drain.

"There," I said, emerging, "the paper is gone. If it was evidence, it's gone too."

The sheriff shook his head a little mournfully. "I should have known better than to come calling so friendly-like. I should have had a gun and a search-warrant and my two big deputies. But now —" he paused, chewed thoughtfully at something inside his mouth.

"Well," I asked impatiently, "are you going to arrest me or not?"

"Arrest you? No, Professor Sisley. We know what we know, you and I, but how will we get a jury to see it? You claim a meteorite killed Dr. Patcher, and a thousand people saw a meteor head toward him. I'll say, Professor Sisley was mad at Dr. Patcher; Professor Sisley could have whopped Dr. Patcher with a rock, then fired his sky-rocket down from a kite. You'll say, prove it. And I'll say, Professor Sisley flushed a piece of paper down the toilet. And then the judge will bang his gavel a couple of times and that's all there is to it. No, Professor, I'm not going to arrest you. My job wouldn't be worth a plugged nickel. But I'll tell you what I'm going to do — just like I told Doc Patcher when the head man before him died so sudden."

"Well, go ahead, say it! What are you going to do?"

"It's really not a great lot," the sheriff said modestly. "I'm just going to let events take their course."

"I can't say as I understand your meaning."

But the sheriff had gone. I blew my nose, mopped my brow, and considered the file which had so nearly betrayed me. Even at this juncture, I took a measure of satisfaction in the fact that it was system and method which had come so close to undoing me, and not the absent-mindedness which an ignorant public ascribes to men of learning.

I am senior astronomer at the observatory. My work is progressing. I have control of the telescope. I have the vastness of the universe under my finger-tips.

Young Katkus is developing well, although he currently displays a particularly irritating waywardness and independence. The young idiot thinks he is hot on the track of an undiscovered planet beyond Pluto, and if I gave him his head, he'd waste every minute of good seeing peering back and forth along the ecliptic. He sulks now and again, but he'll have to wait his chance, as I did, as Dr. Patcher did before me, and, presumably, Dr. Kane before him.

Dr. Kane — I have not thought of him since the day his car went out of control and took him over the cliff. I must learn who preceded him as senior astronomer. A telephone call to Nolbert at Administration Hall will do the trick...I find that Dr. Kane succeeded a Professor Maddox, who drowned when a boat he and Dr. Kane were paddling capsized on Lake Niblis. Nolbert says the tragedy weighed on Dr. Kane to the day of his death, which came as an equally violent shock to the department. He had been computing the magnetic orientation of globular clusters, a profoundly interesting topic, although it was no secret that Dr. Patcher considered the work fruitless and didactic. It is sometimes tempting to speculate — but no, they all are decently in their graves, and I have more serious demands upon my attention. Such as Katkus, who comes demanding the telescope at the very moment when air and sky are at their best. I tell him quite decisively that off-trail investigations such as his must be conducted when the telescope is otherwise idle. He goes off sulking. I can feel no deep concern for his hurt feelings; he must learn to fit himself to the schedule of research as mapped out by the senior astronomer.

I saw the sheriff today; he nodded quite politely. I wonder what he meant, letting events take their course? Cryptic and not comfortable; it has put me quite out of sorts. Perhaps, after all, I was overly sharp with Katkus. He is sitting at his desk, pretending to check the new plates into the glossary, watching me from the corner of his eye.

I wonder what is passing through his mind.

The Devil on Salvation Bluff

A FEW MINUTES BEFORE noon the sun took a lurch south and set.

Sister Mary tore the solar helmet from her fair head and threw it at the settee — a display that surprised and troubled her husband, Brother Raymond.

He clasped her quivering shoulders. "Now, dear, easy does it. A blow-up can't help us at all."

Tears were rolling down Sister Mary's cheeks. "As soon as we start from the house the sun drops out of sight! It happens every time!"

"Well — we know what patience is. There'll be another soon."

"It may be an hour! Or ten hours! And we've got our jobs to do!"

Brother Raymond went to the window, pulled aside the starched lace curtains, peered into the dusk. "We could start now, and get up the hill before night."

" 'Night'?" cried Sister Mary. "What do you call this?"

Brother Raymond said stiffly, "I mean night by the Clock. *Real* night."

"The Clock ..." Sister Mary sighed, sank into a chair. "If it weren't for the Clock we'd all be lunatics."

Brother Raymond, at the window, looked up toward Salvation Bluff, where the great clock bulked unseen. Mary joined him; they stood gazing through the dark. Presently Mary sighed. "I'm sorry, dear. But I get so upset."

Raymond patted her shoulder. "It's no joke living on Glory."

Mary shook her head decisively. "I shouldn't let myself go. There's the Colony to think of. Pioneers can't be weaklings."

They stood close, drawing comfort from each other.

"Look!" said Raymond. He pointed. "A fire, and up in Old Fleet-ville!"

In perplexity they watched the far spark.

"They're all supposed to be down in New Town," muttered Sister Mary. "Unless it's some kind of ceremony... The salt we gave them..."

Raymond, smiling sourly, spoke a fundamental postulate of life on Glory. "You can't tell anything about the Flits. They're liable to do most anything."

Mary uttered a truth even more fundamental. "*Anything* is liable to do anything."

"The Flits most liable of all... They've even taken to dying without our comfort and help!"

"We've done our best," said Mary. "It's not our fault!" — almost as if she feared that it was.

"No one could possibly blame us."

"Except the Inspector... The Flits were thriving before the Colony came."

"We haven't bothered them; we haven't encroached, or molested, or interfered. In fact we've knocked ourselves out to help them. And for thanks they tear down our fences and break open the canal and throw mud on our fresh paint!"

Sister Mary said in a low voice, "Sometimes I hate the Flits... Sometimes I hate Glory. Sometimes I hate the whole Colony."

Brother Raymond drew her close, patted the fair hair that she kept in a neat bun. "You'll feel better when one of the suns comes up. Shall we start?"

"It's dark," said Mary dubiously. "Glory is bad enough in the day-time."

Raymond shot his jaw forward, glanced up toward the Clock. "It *is* daytime. The Clock says it's daytime. That's Reality; we've got to cling to it! It's our link with truth and sanity!"

"Very well," said Mary, "we'll go."

Raymond kissed her cheek. "You're very brave, dear. You're a credit to the Colony."

Mary shook her head. "No, dear. I'm no better or braver than any of the others. We came out here to found homes and live the Truth. We

— 213 —

knew there'd be hard work. So much depends on everybody; there's no room for weakness."

Raymond kissed her again, although she laughingly protested and turned her head. "I still think you're brave — and very sweet."

"Get the light," said Mary. "Get several lights. One never knows how long these — these insufferable darknesses will last."

They set off up the road, walking because in the Colony private power vehicles were considered a social evil. Ahead, unseen in the darkness, rose the Grand Montagne, the preserve of the Flits. They could feel the harsh bulk of the crags, just as behind them they could feel the neat fields, the fences, the roads of the Colony. They crossed the canal, which led the meandering river into a mesh of irrigation ditches. Raymond shone his light into the concrete bed. They stood looking in a silence more eloquent than curses.

"It's dry! They've broken the banks again."

"Why?" asked Mary. "*Why?* They don't use the river water!"

Raymond shrugged. "I guess they just don't like canals. Well," he sighed, "all we can do is the best we know how."

The road wound back and forth up the slope. They passed the lichen-covered hulk of a star-ship which five hundred years ago had crashed on Glory. "It seems impossible," said Mary. "The Flits were once men and women just like us."

"Not like *us*, dear," Raymond corrected gently.

Sister Mary shuddered. "The Flits and their goats! Sometimes it's hard to tell them apart."

A few minutes later Raymond fell into a mudhole, a bed of slime, with enough water-seep to make it sucking and dangerous. Floundering, panting, with Mary's desperate help, he regained solid ground, and stood shivering — angry, cold, wet.

"That blasted thing wasn't there yesterday!" He scraped slime from his face, his clothes. "It's these miserable things that makes life so trying."

"We'll get the better of it, dear." And she said fiercely: "We'll fight it, subdue it! Somehow we'll bring order to Glory!"

While they debated whether or not to proceed, Red Robundus belled up over the northwest horizon, and they were able to take stock of the situation. Brother Raymond's khaki puttees and his white shirt of course were filthy. Sister Mary's outfit was hardly cleaner.

Raymond said dejectedly, "I ought to go back to the bungalow for a change."

"Raymond — do we have time?"

"I'll look like a fool going up to the Flits like this."

"They'll never notice."

"How can they help?" snapped Raymond.

"We haven't time," said Mary decisively. "The Inspector's due any day, and the Flits are dying like flies. They'll say it's our fault — and that's the end of Gospel Colony." After a pause she said carefully, "Not that we wouldn't help the Flits in any event."

"I still think I'd make a better impression in clean clothes," said Raymond dubiously.

"Pooh! A fig they care for clean clothes, the ridiculous way they scamper around."

"I suppose you're right."

A small yellow-green sun appeared over the southwest horizon. "Here comes Urban... If it isn't dark as pitch we get three or four suns at once!"

"Sunlight makes the crops grow," Mary told him sweetly.

They climbed half an hour, then, stopping to catch their breath, turned to look across the valley to the colony they loved so well. Seventy-two thousand souls on a checkerboard green plain, rows of neat white houses, painted and scrubbed, with snowy curtains behind glistening glass; lawns and flower gardens full of tulips; vegetable gardens full of cabbages, kale and squash.

Raymond looked up at the sky. "It's going to rain."

Mary asked, "How do you know?"

"Remember the drenching we had last time Urban and Robundus were both in the west?"

Mary shook her head. "That doesn't mean anything."

"Something's got to mean something. That's the law of our universe — the basis for all our thinking!"

A gust of wind howled down from the ridges, carrying great curls and feathers of dust. They swirled with complicated colors, films, shades, in the opposing lights of yellow-green Urban and Red Robundus.

"There's your rain," shouted Mary over the roar of the wind. Raymond pressed on up the road. Presently the wind died.

Mary said, "I believe in rain or anything else on Glory when I see it."

"We don't have enough facts," insisted Raymond. "There's nothing magic in unpredictability."

"It's just — unpredictable." She looked back along the face of the Grand Montagne. "Thank God for the Clock — something that's dependable."

The road wandered up the hill, through stands of horny spile, banks of gray scrub and purple thorn. Sometimes there was no road; then they had to cast ahead like surveyors; sometimes the road stopped at a bank or at a blank wall, continuing on a level ten feet above or below. These were minor inconveniences which they overcame as a matter of course. Only when Robundus drifted south and Urban ducked north did they become anxious.

"It wouldn't be conceivable that a sun should set at seven in the evening," said Mary. "That would be too normal, too matter-of-fact."

At seven-fifteen both suns set. There would be ten minutes of magnificent sunset, another fifteen minutes of twilight, then night of indeterminate extent.

They missed the sunset because of an earthquake. A tumble of stones came pelting across the road; they took refuge under a jut of granite while boulders clattered into the road and spun on down the mountainside.

The shower of rocks passed, except for pebbles bouncing down as an afterthought. "Is that all?" Mary asked in a husky whisper.

"Sounds like it."

"I'm thirsty."

Raymond handed her the canteen; she drank.

"How much further to Fleetville?"

"Old Fleetville or New Town?"

"I don't care," she said wearily. "Either one."

Raymond hesitated. "As a matter of fact, I don't know the distance to either."

"Well, we can't stay here all night."

"It's day coming up," said Raymond as the white dwarf Maude began to silver the sky to the northeast.

"It's night," Mary declared in quiet desperation. "The Clock says it's night; I don't care if every sun in the galaxy is shining, including Home Sun. As long as the Clock says it's night, it's night!"

"We can see the road anyway…New Town is just over this ridge; I recognize that big spile. It was here last time I came."

Of the two, Raymond was the more surprised to find New Town where he placed it. They trudged into the village. "Things are awful quiet."

There were three dozen huts, built of concrete and good clear glass, each with filtered water, a shower, wash-tub and toilet. To suit Flit prejudices the roofs were thatched with thorn, and there were no interior partitions. The huts were all empty.

Mary looked into a hut. "Mmmph — horrid!" She puckered her nose at Raymond. "The smell!"

The windows of the second hut were innocent of glass. Raymond's face was grim and angry. "I packed that glass up here on my blistered back! And that's how they thank us."

"I don't care whether they thank us or not," said Mary. "I'm worried about the Inspector. He'll blame us for —" she gestured "— this filth. After all it's supposed to be our responsibility."

Seething with indignation Raymond surveyed the village. He recalled the day New Town had been completed — a model village, thirty-six spotless huts, hardly inferior to the bungalows of the Colony. Arch-Deacon Burnette had voiced the blessing; the volunteer workers knelt to pray in the central compound. Fifty or sixty Flits had come down from the ridges to watch — a wide-eyed ragged bunch: the men all gristle and unkempt hair; the women sly, plump and disposed to promiscuity, or so the colonists believed.

After the invocation Arch-Deacon Burnette had presented the chief of the tribe a large key of gilded plywood. "In your custody, Chief — the future and welfare of your people! Guard it — cherish it!"

The chief stood almost seven feet tall; he was lean as a pike, his profile cut in and out, sharp and hard as a turtle's. He wore greasy black rags and carried a long staff, upholstered with goat-hide. Alone in the tribe he spoke the language of the colonists, with a good accent that always came as a shock. "They are no concern of mine," he said in a casual, hoarse voice. "They do as they like. That's the best way."

Arch-Deacon Burnette had encountered this attitude before. A large-minded man, he felt no indignation, but rather sought to argue away what he considered an irrational attitude. "Don't you want to be civilized? Don't you want to worship God, to live clean, healthy lives?"

"No."

The Arch-Deacon grinned. "Well, we'll help anyway, as much as we can. We can teach you to read, to cipher; we can cure your disease. Of course you must keep clean and you must adopt regular habits — because that's what civilization means."

The chief grunted. "You don't even know how to herd goats."

"We are not missionaries," Arch-Deacon Burnette continued, "but when you choose to learn the Truth, we'll be ready to help you."

"Mmph-mmph — where do you profit by this?"

The Arch-Deacon smiled. "We don't. You are fellow-humans; we are bound to help you."

The chief turned, called to the tribe; they fled up the rocks pell-mell, climbing like desperate wraiths, hair waving, goat-skins flapping.

"What's this? What's this?" cried the Arch-Deacon. "Come back here," he called to the chief, who was on his way to join the tribe.

The chief called down from a crag. "You are all crazy people."

"No, no," exclaimed the Arch-Deacon, and it was a magnificent scene, stark as a stage-set: the white-haired Arch-Deacon calling up to the wild chief with his wild tribe behind him; a saint commanding satyrs, all in the shifting light of three suns.

Somehow he coaxed the chief back down to New Town. Old Fleetville lay half a mile farther up, in a saddle funnelling all the winds and clouds of the Grand Montagne, until even the goats clung with difficulty to the rocks. It was cold, dank, dreary. The Arch-Deacon hammered home each of Old Fleetville's drawbacks. The chief insisted he preferred it to New Town.

Fifty pounds of salt made the difference, with the Arch-Deacon compromising his principles over the use of bribes. About sixty of the tribe moved into the new huts with an air of amused detachment, as if the Arch-Deacon had asked them to play a foolish game.

The Arch-Deacon called another blessing upon the village; the colonists knelt; the Flits watched curiously from the doors and windows of their new homes. Another twenty or thirty bounded down from the crags with a herd of goats which they quartered in the little chapel. Arch-Deacon Burnette's smile became fixed and painful, but to his credit he did nothing to interfere.

After a while the colonists filed back down into the valley. They had done the best they could, but they were not sure exactly what it was they had done.

Two months later New Town was deserted. Brother Raymond and Sister Mary Dunton walked through the village; and the huts showed dark windows and gaping doorways.

"Where have they gone?" asked Mary in a hushed voice.

"They're all mad," said Raymond. "Stark staring mad." He went to the chapel, pushed his head through the door. His knuckles shone suddenly white where they gripped the door frame.

"What's the trouble?" Mary asked anxiously.

Raymond held her back. "Corpses... There's — ten, twelve, maybe fifteen bodies in there."

"Raymond!" They looked at each other. "How? Why?"

Raymond shook his head. With one mind they turned, looked up the hill toward Old Fleetville.

"I guess it's up to us to find out."

"But this is — is such a nice place," Mary burst out. "They're — they're *beasts!* They should *love* it here!" She turned away, looked out over the valley, so that Raymond wouldn't see her tears. New Town had meant so much to her; with her own hands she had white-washed rocks and laid neat borders around each of the huts. The borders had been kicked askew, and her feelings were hurt. "Let the Flits live as they like, dirty, shiftless creatures. They're irresponsible," she told Raymond, "just completely *irresponsible!*"

Raymond nodded. "Let's go on up, Mary; we have our duty."

Mary wiped her eyes. "I suppose they're God's creatures, but I can't see why they should be." She glanced at Raymond. "And don't tell me about God moving in a mysterious way."

"Okay," said Raymond. They started to clamber up over the rocks, up toward Old Fleetville. The valley became smaller and smaller below. Maude swung up to the zenith and seemed to hang there.

They paused for breath. Mary mopped her brow. "Am I crazy, or is Maude getting larger?"

Raymond looked. "Maybe it is swelling a little."

"It's either a nova or we're falling into it!"

"I suppose anything could happen in this system," sighed Raymond. "If there's any regularity in Glory's orbit it's defied analysis."

"We might very easily fall into one of the suns," said Mary thoughtfully.

Raymond shrugged. "The system's been milling around for quite a few million years. That's our best guarantee."

"Our only guarantee." She clenched her fists. "If there were only some certainty somewhere — something you could look at and say, this is immutable, this is changeless, this is something you can count on. But there's nothing! It's enough to drive a person crazy!"

Raymond put on a glassy smile. "Don't, dear. The Colony's got too much trouble like that already."

Mary sobered instantly. "Sorry... I'm sorry, Raymond. Truly."

"It's got me worried," said Raymond. "I was talking to Director Birch at the Rest Home yesterday."

"How many now?"

"Almost three thousand. More coming in every day." He sighed. "There's something about Glory that grinds at a person's nerves — no question about it."

Mary took a deep breath, pressed Raymond's hand. "We'll fight it, darling, and beat it! Things will fall into routine; we'll straighten everything out."

Raymond bowed his head. "With the Lord's help."

"There goes Maude," said Mary. "We'd better get up to Old Fleetville while there's still light."

A few minutes later they met a dozen goats, herded by as many scraggly children. Some wore rags; some wore goat-skin clothes; others ran around naked, and the wind blew on their washboard ribs.

On the other side of the trail they met another herd of goats — perhaps a hundred, with one urchin in attendance.

"That's the Flit way," said Raymond, "twelve kids herd twelve goats and one kid herds a hundred."

"They're surely victims of some mental disease... Is insanity hereditary?"

"That's a moot point... I can smell Old Fleetville."

Maude left the sky at an angle which promised a long twilight. With aching legs Raymond and Mary plodded up into the village. Behind came the goats and the children, mingled without discrimination.

Mary said in a disgusted voice, "They leave New Town — pretty, clean New Town — to move up into this filth."

"Don't step on that goat!" Raymond guided her past the gnawed carcass which lay on the trail. Mary bit her lip.

They found the chief sitting on a rock, staring into the air. He greeted them with neither surprise nor pleasure. A group of children were building a pyre of brush and dry spile.

"What's going on?" asked Raymond with forced cheer. "A feast? A dance?"

"Four men, two women. They go crazy, they die. We burn them."

Mary looked at the pyre. "I didn't know you cremated your dead."

"This time we burn them." He reached out, touched Mary's glossy golden hair. "You be my wife for a while."

Mary stepped back, and said in a quivering voice, "No, thanks. I'm married to Raymond."

"All the time?"

"All the time."

The chief shook his head. "You are crazy. Pretty soon you die."

Raymond said sternly, "Why did you break the canal? Ten times we've fixed it; ten times the Flits came down in the dark and pulled down the banks."

The chief deliberated. "The canal is crazy."

"It's not crazy. It helps irrigate, helps the farmers."

"It goes too much the same."

"You mean, it's straight?"

"Straight? Straight? What word is that?"

"In *one* line — in one direction."

The chief rocked back and forth. "Look — mountain. Straight?"

"No, of course not."

"Sun — straight?"

"Look here —"

"My leg." The chief extended his left leg, knobby and covered with hair. "Straight?"

"No," sighed Raymond. "Your leg is not straight."

"Then why make canal straight? Crazy." He sat back. The topic was disposed of. "Why do you come?"

"Well," said Raymond. "Too many Flits die. We want to help you."

"That's all right. It's not me, not you."

"We don't want you to die. Why don't you live in New Town?"

"Flits get crazy, jump off the rocks." He rose to his feet. "Come along, there's food."

Mastering their repugnance, Raymond and Mary nibbled on bits of grilled goat. Without ceremony, four bodies were tossed into the fire. Some of the Flits began to dance.

Mary nudged Raymond. "You can understand a culture by the pattern of its dances. Watch."

Raymond watched. "I don't see any pattern. Some take a couple hops, sit down; others run in circles; some just flap their arms."

Mary whispered, "They're all crazy. Crazy as sandpipers."

Raymond nodded. "I believe you."

Rain began to fall. Red Robundus burnt the eastern sky but never troubled to come up. The rain became hail. Mary and Raymond went into a hut. Several men and women joined them, and with nothing better to do, noisily began loveplay.

Mary whispered in agony. "They're going to do it right in front of us! They don't have any shame!"

Raymond said grimly, "I'm not going out in that rain. They can do anything they want."

Mary cuffed one of the men who sought to remove her shirt; he jumped back. "Just like dogs!" she gasped.

"No repressions there," said Raymond apathetically. "Repressions mean psychoses."

"Then I'm psychotic," sniffed Mary, "because I have repressions!"

"I have too."

The hail stopped; the wind blew the clouds through the notch; the sky was clear. Raymond and Mary left the hut with relief.

The pyre was drenched; four charred bodies lay in the ashes; no one heeded them.

Raymond said thoughtfully, "It's on the tip of my tongue — the verge of my mind…"

"What?"

"The solution to this whole Flit mess."

"Well?"

"It's something like this: The Flits are crazy, irrational, irresponsible."

"Agreed."

"The Inspector's coming. We've got to demonstrate that the Colony poses no threat to the aborigines — the Flits, in this case."

"We can't force the Flits to improve their living standards."

"No. But if we could make them sane; if we could even make a start against their mass psychosis…"

Mary looked rather numb. "It sounds like a terrible job."

Raymond shook his head. "Use rigorous thinking, dear. It's a real problem: a group of aborigines too psychotic to keep themselves alive. But we've *got* to keep them alive. The solution: remove the psychoses."

"You make it sound sensible, but how in heaven's name shall we begin?"

The chief came spindle-legged down from the rocks, chewing at a bit of goat-intestine. "We've got to begin with the chief," said Raymond.

"That's like belling the cat."

"Salt," said Raymond. "He'd skin his grandmother for salt."

Raymond approached the chief, who seemed surprised to find him still in the village. Mary watched from the background.

Raymond argued; the chief looked first shocked, then sullen. Raymond expounded, expostulated. He made his telling point: salt — as much as the chief could carry back up the hill. The chief stared down at Raymond from his seven feet, threw up his hands, walked away, sat down on a rock, chewed at the length of gut.

Raymond rejoined Mary. "He's coming."

Director Birch used his heartiest manner toward the chief. "We're honored! It's not often we have visitors so distinguished. We'll have you right in no time!"

The chief had been scratching aimless curves in the ground with his staff. He asked Raymond mildly, "When do I get the salt?"

"Pretty soon now. First you've got to go with Director Birch."

"Come along," said Director Birch. "We'll have a nice ride."

The chief turned and strode off toward the Grand Montagne. "No, no!" cried Raymond. "Come back here!" The chief lengthened his stride.

Raymond ran forward, tackled the knobby knees. The chief fell like a loose sack of garden tools. Director Birch administered a shot of sedative, and presently the shambling, dull-eyed chief was secure inside the ambulance.

Brother Raymond and Sister Mary watched the ambulance trundle down the road. Thick dust roiled up, hung in the green sunlight. The shadows seemed tinged with bluish-purple.

Mary said in a trembling voice, "I do so hope we're doing the right thing…The poor chief looked so — *pathetic*. Like one of his own goats trussed up for slaughter."

Raymond said, "We can only do what we think best, dear."

"But *is* it the best?"

The ambulance had disappeared; the dust had settled. Over the Grand Montagne lightning flickered from a black-and-green thunderhead. Faro shone like a cat's-eye at the zenith. The Clock — the staunch Clock, the good, sane Clock — said twelve noon.

"The best," said Mary thoughtfully. "A relative word…"

Raymond said, "If we clear up the Flit psychoses — if we can teach them clean, orderly lives — surely it's for the best." And he added after a moment, "Certainly it's best for the Colony."

Mary sighed. "I suppose so. But the chief looked so stricken."

"We'll go see him tomorrow," said Raymond. "Right now, sleep!"

When Raymond and Mary awoke, a pink glow seeped through the drawn shades: Robundus, possibly with Maude. "Look at the clock," yawned Mary. "Is it day or night?"

Raymond raised up on his elbow. Their clock was built into the wall, a replica of the Clock on Salvation Bluff, and guided by radio pulses from the central movement. "It's six in the afternoon — ten after."

They rose and dressed in their neat puttees and white shirts. They ate in the meticulous kitchenette, then Raymond telephoned the Rest Home.

Director Birch's voice came crisp from the sound box. "God help you, Brother Raymond."

"God help you, Director. How's the chief?"

Director Birch hesitated. "We've had to keep him under sedation. He's got pretty deep-seated troubles."

"Can you help him? It's important."

"All we can do is try. We'll have a go at him tonight."

"Perhaps we'd better be there," said Mary.

"If you like... Eight o'clock?"

"Good."

The Rest Home was a long, low building on the outskirts of Glory City. New wings had recently been added; a set of temporary barracks could also be seen to the rear.

Director Birch greeted them with a harassed expression.

"We're so pressed for room and time; is this Flit so terribly important?"

Raymond gave him assurance that the chief's sanity was a matter of grave concern for everyone.

Director Birch threw up his hands. "Colonists are clamoring for therapy. They'll have to wait, I suppose."

Mary asked soberly, "There's still — the trouble?"

"The Home was built with five hundred beds," said Director Birch. "We've got thirty-six hundred patients now; not to mention the eighteen hundred colonists we've evacuated back to Earth."

"Surely things are getting better?" asked Raymond. "The Colony's over the hump; there's no need for anxiety."

"Anxiety doesn't seem to be the trouble."

"What *is* the trouble?"

"New environment, I suppose. We're Earth-type people; the surroundings are strange."

"But they're not really!" argued Mary. "We've made this place the exact replica of an Earth community. One of the nicer sort. There are Earth houses and Earth flowers and Earth trees."

"Where is the chief?" asked Brother Raymond.

"Well — right now, in the maximum-security ward."

"Is he violent?"

"Not unfriendly. He just wants to get out. Destructive! I've never seen anything like it!"

"Have you any ideas — even preliminary?"

Director Birch shook his head grimly. "We're still trying to classify him. Look." He handed Raymond a report. "That's his zone survey."

"Intelligence zero." Raymond looked up. "I *know* he's not that stupid."

"You'd hardly think so. It's a vague referent, actually. We can't use the usual tests on him — thematic perception and the like; they're weighted for our own cultural background. But these tests here —" he tapped the report "— they're basic; we use them on animals — fitting pegs into holes; matching up colors; detecting discordant patterns; threading mazes."

"And the chief?"

Director Birch sadly shook his head. "If it were possible to have a negative score, he'd have it."

"How so?"

"Well, for instance, instead of matching a small round peg into a small round hole, first he broke the star-shaped peg and forced it in sideways, and then he broke the board."

"But why?"

Mary said, "Let's go see him."

"He's safe, isn't he?" Raymond asked Birch.

"Oh, entirely."

The chief was confined in a pleasant room exactly ten feet on a side. He had a white bed, white sheets, gray coverlet. The ceiling was restful green, the floor was quiet gray.

"My!" said Mary brightly, "you've been busy!"

"Yes," said Director Birch between clenched teeth. "He's been busy."

The bedclothes were shredded, the bed lay on its side in the middle of the room, the walls were befouled. The chief sat on the doubled mattress.

Director Birch said sternly, "Why do you make this mess? It's really not clever, you know!"

"You keep me here," spat the chief. "I fix the way I like it. In your house you fix the way *you* like." He looked at Raymond and Mary. "How much longer?"

"In just a little while," said Mary. "We're trying to help you."

"Crazy talk, everybody crazy." The chief was losing his good accent; his words rasped with fricatives and glottals. "Why you bring me here?"

"It'll be just for a day or two," said Mary soothingly, "then you get salt — lots of it."

"Day — that's while the sun is up."

"No," said Brother Raymond. "See this thing?" He pointed to the clock in the wall. "When this hand goes around twice — that's a day."

The chief smiled cynically.

"We guide our lives by this," said Raymond. "It helps us."

"Just like the big Clock on Salvation Bluff," said Mary.

"Big Devil," the chief said earnestly. "You good people; you all crazy. Come to Fleetville. I help you; lots of good goat. We throw rocks down at Big Devil."

"No," said Mary quietly, "that would never do. Now you try your best to do what the doctor says. This mess for instance — it's very bad."

The chief took his head in his hands. "You let me go. You keep salt; I go home."

"Come," said Director Birch kindly. "We won't hurt you." He looked at the clock. "It's time for your first therapy."

Two orderlies were required to conduct the chief to the laboratory. He was placed in a padded chair, and his arms and legs were constricted so that he might not harm himself. He set up a terrible, hoarse cry. "The Devil, the Big Devil — it comes down to look at my life…"

Director Birch said to the orderly, "Cover over the wall clock; it disturbs the patient."

"Just lie still," said Mary. "We're trying to help you — you and your whole tribe."

The orderly administered a shot of D-beta hypnidine. The chief relaxed, his eyes open, vacant, his skinny chest heaving.

Director Birch said in a low tone to Mary and Raymond, "He's now entirely suggestible — so be very quiet; don't make a sound."

Mary and Raymond eased themselves into chairs at the side of the room.

"Hello, Chief," said Director Birch.

"Hello."

"Are you comfortable?"

"Too much shine — too much white."

The orderly dimmed the lights.

"Better?"

"That's better."

"Do you have any troubles?"

"Goats hurt their feet, stay up in the hills. Crazy people down the valley; they won't go away."

"How do you mean 'crazy'?"

The chief was silent. Director Birch said in a whisper to Mary and Raymond, "By analyzing his concept of sanity we get a clue to his own derangement."

The chief lay quiet. Director Birch said in his soothing voice, "Suppose you tell us about your own life."

The chief spoke readily. "Ah, that's good. I'm chief. I understand all talks; nobody else knows about things."

"A good life, eh?"

"Sure, everything good." He spoke on, in disjointed phrases, in words sometimes unintelligible, but the picture of his life came clear. "Everything go easy — no bother, no trouble — everything good. When it rain, fire feels good. When suns shine hot, then wind blow, feels good. Lots of goats, everybody eat."

"Don't you have troubles, worries?"

"Sure. Crazy people live in valley. They make town: New Town. No good. Straight — straight — straight. No good. Crazy. That's bad. We get lots of salt, but we leave New Town, run up hill to old place."

"You don't like the people in the valley?"

"They good people, they all crazy. Big Devil bring them to valley. Big Devil watch all time. Pretty soon all go tick-tick-tick — like Big Devil."

Director Birch turned to Raymond and Mary, his face in a puzzled frown. "This isn't going so good. He's too assured, too forthright."

Raymond said guardedly, "Can you cure him?"

"Before I can cure a psychosis," said Director Birch, "I have to locate it. So far I don't seem to be even warm."

"It's not sane to die off like flies," whispered Mary. "And that's what the Flits are doing."

The Director returned to the chief. "Why do your people die, Chief? Why do they die in New Town?"

The chief said in a hoarse voice, "They look down. No pretty scenery. Crazy cut-up. No river. Straight water. It hurts the eyes; we open canal, make good river... Huts all same. Go crazy looking at all same. People go crazy; we kill 'em."

Director Birch said, "I think that's all we'd better do just now till we study the case a little more closely."

"Yes," said Brother Raymond in a troubled voice. "We've got to think this over."

They left the Rest Home through the main reception hall. The benches bulged with applicants for admission and their relatives, with custodian officers and persons in their care. Outside the sky was wadded with overcast. Sallow light indicated Urban somewhere in the sky. Rain spattered in the dust, big, syrupy drops.

Brother Raymond and Sister Mary waited for the bus at the curve of the traffic circle.

"There's something wrong," said Brother Raymond in a bleak voice. "Something very very wrong."

"And I'm not so sure it isn't in us." Sister Mary looked around the landscape, across the young orchards, up Sarah Gulvin Avenue into the center of Glory City.

"A strange planet is always a battle," said Brother Raymond. "We've got to bear faith, trust in God — and fight!"

Mary clutched his arm. He turned. "What's the trouble?"

"I saw — or thought I saw — someone running through the bushes."

Raymond craned his neck. "I don't see anybody."

"I thought it looked like the chief."

"Your imagination, dear."

They boarded the bus, and presently were secure in their white-walled, flower-gardened home.

The communicator sounded. It was Director Birch. His voice was troubled. "I don't want to worry you, but the chief got loose. He's off the premises — where we don't know."

Mary said under her breath, "I knew, I knew!"

Raymond said soberly, "You don't think there's any danger?"

"No. His pattern isn't violent. But I'd lock my door anyway."

"Thanks for calling, Director."

"Not at all, Brother Raymond."

There was a moment's silence. "What now?" asked Mary.

"I'll lock the doors, and then we'll get a good night's sleep."

Sometime in the night Mary woke up with a start. Brother Raymond rolled over on his side. "What's the trouble?"

"I don't know," said Mary. "What time is it?"

Raymond consulted the wall clock. "Five minutes to one."

Sister Mary lay still.

"Did you hear something?" Raymond asked.

"No. I just had a — twinge. Something's wrong, Raymond!"

He pulled her close, cradled her fair head in the hollow of his neck. "All we can do is our best, dear, and pray that it's God's will."

They fell into a fitful doze, tossing and turning. Raymond got up to go to the bathroom. Outside was night — a dark sky except for a rosy glow at the north horizon. Red Robundus wandered somewhere below.

Raymond shuffled sleepily back to bed.

"What's the time, dear?" came Mary's voice.

Raymond peered at the clock. "Five minutes to one."

He got into bed. Mary's body was rigid. "Did you say — five minutes to one?"

"Why yes," said Raymond. A few seconds later he climbed out of bed, went into the kitchen. "It says five minutes to one in here, too. I'll call the Clock and have them send out a pulse."

He went to the communicator, pressed buttons. No response.

"They don't answer."

Mary was at his elbow. "Try again."

Raymond pressed out the number. "That's strange."

"Call Information," said Mary.

Raymond pressed for Information. Before he could frame a question, a crisp voice said, "The Great Clock is momentarily out of order. Please have patience. The Great Clock is out of order."

Raymond thought he recognized the voice. He punched the visual button. The voice said, "God keep you, Brother Raymond."

"God keep you, Brother Ramsdell…What in the world has gone wrong?"

"It's one of your protégés, Raymond. One of the Flits — raving mad. He rolled boulders down on the Clock."

"Did he — did he —"

"He started a landslide. We don't have any more Clock."

Inspector Coble found no one to meet him at the Glory City spaceport. He peered up and down the tarmac; he was alone. A scrap of paper blew across the far end of the field; nothing else moved.

Odd, thought Inspector Coble. A committee had always been on hand to welcome him, with a program that was flattering but rather wearing. First to the Arch-Deacon's bungalow for a banquet, cheerful speeches and progress reports, then services in the central chapel, and finally a punctilious escort to the foot of the Grand Montagne.

Excellent people, by Inspector Coble's lights, but too painfully honest and fanatical to be interesting.

He left instructions with the two men who crewed the official ship, and set off on foot toward Glory City. Red Robundus was high, but sinking toward the east; he looked toward Salvation Bluff to check local time. A clump of smoky lace-veils blocked his view.

Inspector Coble, striding briskly along the road, suddenly jerked to a halt. He raised his head as if testing the air, looked about him in a complete circle. He frowned, moved slowly on.

The colonists had been making changes, he thought. Exactly what and how, he could not instantly determine: the fence there — a section had been torn out. Weeds were prospering in the ditch beside the road. Examining the ditch, he sensed movement in the harp-grass behind, the sound of young voices. Curiosity aroused, Coble jumped the ditch, parted the harp-grass.

A boy and girl of sixteen or so were wading in a shallow pond; the girl held three limp water-flowers, the boy was kissing her. They turned up startled faces; Inspector Coble withdrew.

Back on the road he looked up and down. Where in thunder was everybody? The fields — empty. Nobody working. Inspector Coble shrugged, continued.

He passed the Rest Home, and looked at it curiously. It seemed considerably larger than he remembered it: a pair of wings, some temporary barracks had been added. He noticed that the gravel of the driveway was hardly as neat as it might be. The ambulance drawn up to the side was dusty. The place looked vaguely run down. The inspector for the second time stopped dead in his tracks. Music? From the Rest Home?

He turned down the driveway, approached. The music grew louder. Inspector Coble slowly pushed through the front door. In the reception hall were eight or ten people — they wore bizarre costumes: feathers, fronds of dyed grass, fantastic necklaces of glass and metal. The music sounded loud from the auditorium, a kind of wild jig.

"Inspector!" cried a pretty woman with fair hair. "Inspector Coble! You've arrived!"

Inspector Coble peered into her face. She wore a kind of patchwork jacket sewn with small iron bells. "It's — it's Sister Mary Dunton, isn't it?"

"Of course! You've arrived at a wonderful time! We're having a carnival ball — costumes and everything!"

Brother Raymond clapped the inspector heartily on the back. "Glad to see you, old man! Have some cider — it's the early press."

Inspector Coble backed away. "No, no thanks." He cleared his throat. "I'll be off on my rounds…and perhaps drop in on you later."

Inspector Coble proceeded to the Grand Montagne. He noted that a number of the bungalows had been painted bright shades of green, blue, yellow; that fences in many cases had been pulled down, that gardens looked rather rank and wild.

He climbed the road to Old Fleetville, where he interviewed the chief. The Flits apparently were not being exploited, suborned, cheated, sickened, enslaved, forcibly proselyted or systematically irritated. The chief seemed in a good humor.

"I kill the Big Devil," he told Inspector Coble. "Things go better now."

Inspector Coble planned to slip quietly to the space-port and depart, but Brother Raymond Dunton hailed him as he passed their bungalow.

"Had your breakfast, Inspector?"

"Dinner, darling!" came Sister Mary's voice from within. "Urban just went down."

"But Maude just came up."

"Bacon and eggs anyway, Inspector!"

The inspector was tired; he smelled hot coffee. "Thanks," he said, "don't mind if I do."

After the bacon and eggs, over the second cup of coffee, the inspector said cautiously, "You're looking well, you two."

Sister Mary looked especially pretty with her fair hair loose.

"Never felt better," said Brother Raymond. "It's a matter of rhythm, Inspector."

The inspector blinked. "Rhythm, eh?"

"More precisely," said Sister Mary, "a lack of rhythm."

"It all started," said Brother Raymond, "when we lost our Clock."

Inspector Coble gradually pieced out the story. Three weeks later, back at Surge City he put it in his own words to Inspector Keefer.

"They'd been wasting half their energies holding onto — well, call it a false reality. They were all afraid of the new planet. They pretended it was Earth — tried to whip it, beat it, and just plain hypnotize it into being Earth. Naturally they were licked before they started. Glory is about as completely random a world as you could find. The poor devils were trying to impose Earth rhythm and Earth routine upon this magnificent disorder; this monumental chaos!"

"No wonder they all went nuts."

Inspector Coble nodded. "At first, after the Clock went out, they thought they were goners. Committed their souls to God and just about gave up. A couple of days passed, I guess — and to their surprise they found they were still alive. In fact, even enjoying life. Sleeping when it got dark, working when the sun shone."

"Sounds like a good place to retire," said Inspector Keefer. "How's the fishing out there on Glory?"

"Not so good. But the goat-herding is great!"

THE PHANTOM MILKMAN

I'VE HAD ALL I can stand. I've got to get out, away from the walls, the glass, the white stone, the black asphalt. All of a sudden I see the city for the terrible place that it is. Lights burn my eyes, voices crawl on my skin like sticky insects, and I notice that the people look like insects too. Burly brown beetles, wispy mosquito-men in tight black trousers, sour sow-bug women, mantids and scorpions, fat little dung-beetles, wasp-girls gliding with poisonous nicety, children like loathsome little flies... This isn't a pleasant thought; I must not think of people so; the picture could linger to bother me. I think I'm a hundred times more sensitive than anyone else in the world, and I'm given to very strange fancies. I could list some that would startle you, and it's just as well that I don't. But I do have this frantic urge to flee the city; it's settled. I'm going.

I consult my maps — there's the Andes, the Atlas, the Altai; Mt. Godwin-Austin, Mt. Kilimanjaro; Stromboli and Etna. I compare Siberia above Baikal Nor with the Pacific between Antofagasta and Easter Island. Arabia is hot; Greenland is cold. Tristan da Cunha is very remote; Bouvet even more so. There's Timbuktu, Zanzibar, Bali, the Great Australian Bight.

I am definitely leaving the city. I have found a cabin in Maple Valley, four miles west of Sunbury. It stands a hundred feet back from Maple Valley Road, under two tall trees. It has three rooms and a porch, a fireplace, a good roof, a good well and windmill.

Mrs. Lipscomb is skeptical, even a little shocked. "A good-looking girl like you shouldn't go off by yourself; time to hide away when you're old and nobody wants you." She predicts hair-raising adventures, but I don't care. I was married to Poole for six weeks; nothing could happen that would be any worse.

I'm in my new house. There's lots of work ahead of me: scrubbing, chopping wood. I'll probably bulge with muscles before the winter's over.

My cats are delighted. They are Homer and Moses. Homer is yellow; Moses is black and white. Which reminds me: milk. I saw a Sunbury Dairy delivery truck on the highway. I'll write them an order now.

> Sunbury Dairy   November 14
> Sunbury
>
> Dear Sirs:
>   Please leave me a quart of milk three times a week on whatever days are convenient. Please bill me.
>
>   Isabel Durbrow
>   RFD Route 2, Box 82
>   Sunbury

My mailbox is battered and dusty; one day I'll paint it: red, white and blue, to cheer the mailman. He delivers at ten in the morning, in an old blue panel truck.

When I mail the letter, I see that there's already one in the box. It's for me — forwarded from the city by Mrs. Lipscomb. I take it slowly. I don't want it; I recognize the handwriting: it's from Poole, the dark-visaged brute I woke up from childhood to find myself married to. I tear it in pieces; I'm not even curious. I'm still young and very pretty, but right now there's no one I want, Poole least of all. I shall wear blue jeans and write by the fireplace all winter; and in the spring, who knows?

During the night the wind comes up; the windmill cries from the cold. I lie in bed, with Homer and Moses at my feet. The coals in the fireplace flicker…Tomorrow I'll write Mrs. Lipscomb; by no means must she give Poole my address.

✳

I have written the letter. I run down the slope to the mailbox. It's a glorious late autumn day. The wind is crisp, the hills are like an ocean of gold with scarlet and yellow trees for surf.

I pull open the mailbox...Now, this is odd! My letter to Sunbury Dairy — gone. Perhaps the carrier came early? But it's only nine o'clock. I put in the letter to Mrs. Lipscomb and look all around...Nothing. Who would want my letter? My cats stand with tails erect, looking keenly up the road, first in one direction, then the other, like surveyors planning a new highway. Well, come kittens, you'll drink canned milk today.

At ten o'clock the carrier passes, driving his dusty blue panel truck. He did not come early. That means — someone took my letter.

It's all clear; I understand everything. I'm really rather angry. This morning I found milk on my porch — a quart, bottled by the Maple Valley Dairy. They have no right to go through my mailbox; they thought I'd never notice...I won't use the milk; it can sit and go sour; I'll report them to the Sunbury Dairy and the post office besides...

I've worked quite hard. I'm not really an athletic woman, much as I'd like to be. The pile of wood that I've chopped and sawed is quite disproportionate to the time I've spent. Homer and Moses help me not at all. They sit on the logs, wind in and out underfoot. It's time for their noon meal. I'll give them canned milk, which they detest.

On investigation I see that there's not even canned milk; the only milk in the house is that of the Maple Valley Dairy...Well, I'll use it, if only for a month.

I pour milk into a bowl; the cats strop their ribs on my shins.

I guess they're not hungry. Homer takes five or six laps, then draws back, making a waggish face. Moses glances up to see if I'm joking. I know my cats very well; to some extent I can understand their language. It's not all in the 'meows' and 'maroos'; there's the slope of the whiskers and set of the ear. Naturally they understand each other better than I do, but I generally get the gist.

Neither one likes his milk.

"Very well," I say severely, "you're not going to waste good milk; you won't get any more."

They saunter across the room and sit down. Perhaps the milk is sour; if so, that's the last straw. I smell the milk, and very nice milk it smells: like hay and pasturage. Surely this isn't pasteurized milk! And I look at the cap. It says: "Maple Valley Dairy. Fresh milk. Sweet and clean, from careless cows."

I presume that 'careless' is understood in the sense of 'free from care', rather than 'slovenly'.

Well, careless cows or not, Homer and Moses have turned up their noses. What a wonderful poem I could write, in the Edwardian manner.

> Homer and Moses have turned up their noses;
> They're quite disappointed with tea.
> Their scones are like stones, the fish is all bones;
> The milk that they've tasted, it's certainly wasted,
> But they're getting no other from me.

They'll just learn to like fresh milk or do without, ungrateful little scamps.

I have been scrubbing floors and white-washing the kitchen. No more chopping and sawing. I've ordered wood from the farmer down the road. The cabin is looking very cheerful. I have curtains at the windows, books on the mantel, sprays of autumn leaves in a big blue bottle I found in the shed.

Speaking of bottles: tomorrow morning the milk is delivered. I must put out the bottle.

Homer and Moses still won't drink Maple Valley Dairy milk...They look at me so wistfully when I pour it out, I suppose I'll have to give in and get something else. It's lovely milk; I'd drink it myself if I liked milk.

Today I drove into Sunbury, and just for a test I brought home a bottle of Sunbury Dairy Milk. Now we'll see...I fill a bowl. Homer and Moses are wondering almost audibly if this is the same distasteful stuff I've been serving the last week. I put down the bowl; they fall to with such gusto that milk splashes on to their whiskers and drips all over the floor. That settles it. Tonight I'll put a note in the bottle, stopping delivery from Maple Valley Dairy.

I don't understand it! I wrote very clearly. "Please deliver no more milk." Lo and behold, the driver has the gall to leave me two bottles. I certainly won't pay for it. The ineffable, unutterable nerve of the man!

Sunbury Dairy doesn't deliver up Maple Valley. I'll just buy milk with my groceries. And tonight I'll write a firm note to Maple Valley Dairy.

> November 21
>
> Dear Sirs:
> Leave no more milk! I don't want it. My cats won't drink it. Here is fifty cents for the two bottles I have used.
>
> Isabel Durbrow

I am perplexed and angry. The insolence of the people is incredible. They took the two bottles back, then left me another. And a note. It's on rough gray paper, and it reads:

YOU ASKED FOR IT; YOU ARE GOING TO GET IT.

The note has a rather unpleasant ring to it. It certainly couldn't be a threat...I don't think I like these people...They must deliver very early; I've never heard so much as a step.

The farmer down the road is delivering my wood. I say to him, "Mr. Gable, this Maple Valley Dairy, they have a very odd way of doing business."

"Maple Valley Dairy?" Mr. Gable looks blank. "I don't think I know them."

"Oh," I ask him, "don't you buy their milk?"

"I've got four cows of my own to milk."

"Maple Valley Dairy must be further up the road."

"I hardly think so," says Mr. Gable. "I've never heard of them."

I show him the bottle; he looks surprised, and shrugs.

Many of these country people don't travel more than a mile or two from home the whole of their lives.

Tomorrow is milk day; I believe I'll get up early and tell the driver just what I think of the situation.

It is six o'clock; very gray and cold. The milk is already on the porch. What time do they deliver, in Heaven's name?

Tomorrow is milk day again. This time I'll get up at four o'clock and wait till he arrives.

The alarm goes off. It startles me. The room is still dark. I'm warm and drowsy. For a moment I can't remember why I should get up... The milk, the insufferable Maple Valley Dairy. Perhaps I'll let it go till next time... I hear a thump on the porch. There he is now! I jump up, struggle into a bathrobe, run across the room.

I open the door. The milk is on the porch. I don't see the milkman. I don't see the truck. I don't hear anything. How could he get away so fast? It's incredible. I find this whole matter very disturbing.

To make matters worse there's another letter from Poole in the mail. This one I read, and am sorry that I bothered. He is planning to fight the divorce. He wants to come back and live with me. He explains at great length the effect I have on him; it's conceited and parts are rather disgusting. Where have I disappeared to? He's sick of this stalling around. The letter is typical of Poole, the miserable soul in the large flamboyant body. I was never a person to him; I was an ornamental vessel into which he could spend his passion — a lump of therapic clay he could knead and pound and twist. He is a very ugly man; I was his wife all of six weeks... I'd hate to have him find me out here. But Mrs. Lipscomb won't tell...

Farmer Gable brought me another load of wood. He says he smells winter in the air. I suppose it'll snow before long. Then won't the fire feel good!

The Phantom Milkman

The alarm goes off. Three-thirty. I'm going to catch that milkman if it's the last thing I do.

I crawl out on the cold floor. Homer and Moses wonder what the hell's going on. I find my slippers, my bathrobe. I go to the porch.

No milk yet. Good. I'm in time. So I wait. The east is only tinged with gray; a pale moon shines on the porch. The hill across the road is tarnished silver, the trees black.

I wait... It is four o'clock. The moon is setting.

I wait... It is four-thirty.

Then five.

No milkman.

I am cold and stiff. My joints ache. I cross the room and light a fire in the wood stove. I see Homer looking at the door. I run to the window. The milk is in its usual place.

There is something very wrong here. I look up the valley, down the valley. The sky is wide and dreary. The trees stand on top of the hills like people looking out to sea. I can't believe that anyone is playing a joke on me... Today I'll go looking for the Maple Valley Dairy.

I haven't found it. I've driven the valley one end to the other. No one's heard of it.

I stopped the Sunbury Dairy delivery truck. He never heard of it.

The telephone book doesn't list it.

No one knows them at the post office... Or the police station... Or the feed store.

It would almost seem that there is no Maple Valley Dairy. Except for the milk that they leave on my porch three times a week.

I can't think of anything to do — except ignore them... It's interesting if it weren't so frightening... I won't move; I won't return to the city...

Tonight it's snowing. The flakes drift past the window, the fire roars up the flue. I've made myself a wonderful hot buttered rum. Homer and Moses sit purring. It's very cozy — except I keep looking at the window, wondering what's watching me.

Tomorrow there'll be more milk. They can't be doing this for nothing! Could it be that — no… For a moment I felt a throb. Poole. He's cruel enough, and he's subtle enough, but I don't see how he could have done it.

I'm lying awake. It's early morning. I don't think the milk has come; I've heard nothing.

It's stopped snowing; there's a wonderful hush outside.

A faint thud. The milk. I'm out of bed, but I'm terribly frightened. I force myself to the window. I've no idea what I'll see.

The milk is there; the bottle shining, white… Nothing else. I turn away. Back to bed. Homer and Moses look bored.

I swing back in sudden excitement; my flashlight, where is it? There'll be tracks.

I open the door. The snow is an even blanket everywhere — shimmering, glimmering, pale and clear. No tracks… Not a mark!

If I have any sense I'll leave Maple Valley, I'll never come back…

Around the neck of the bottle hangs a printed form.

I reach out into the cold.

> DEAR CUSTOMER:
> DOES OUR SERVICE SATISFY YOU?
> HAVE YOU ANY COMPLAINTS?
> CAN WE LEAVE YOU ANY OTHER COMMODITIES?
> JUST LET US KNOW; WE WILL DELIVER AND YOU WILL BE BILLED.

I write on the card:

> My cats don't like your milk and I don't like you. The only thing I want you to leave is your footprints. No more milk! I won't pay for it!
>
> Isabel Durbrow

I can't get my car started; the battery's dead. It's snowing again. I'll wait till it stops, then hike up to Gable's for a push.

It's still snowing. Tomorrow the milk. I've asked for his footprints. Tomorrow morning…

✳

I haven't slept. I'm still awake, listening. There are noises off in the woods, and windmill creaks and groans, a dismal sound.

Three o'clock. Homer and Moses jump down to the floor — two soft thuds. They pad back and forth, then jump back up on the bed. They're restless tonight. Homer is telling Moses, "I don't like this at all. We never saw stuff like this going on in the city."

Moses agrees without reservation.

I lie quiet, huddled under the blankets, listening. The snow crunches a little. Homer and Moses turn to look.

A thud. I am out of bed; I run to the door.

The milk.

I run out in my slippers.

The footprints.

There are two of them in the snow just under the milk bottle. Two footprints, the mark of two feet. Bare feet!

I yell. "You cowards! You miserable sneaks! I'm not afraid of you!"

I am though. It's easy to yell when you know that no one will answer... But I'm not sure... Suppose they do?

There is a note on the bottle. It reads:

YOU ORDERED MILK; YOU'LL BE BILLED. YOU ORDERED FOOTPRINTS; YOU'LL BE BILLED. ON THE FIRST OF THE MONTH ALL ACCOUNTS ARE DUE AND PAYABLE.

I sit in the chair by the fire.

I don't know what to do. I'm terribly scared. I don't dare to look at the window for fear of seeing a face. I don't dare to wander up into the woods.

I know I should leave. But I hate to let anyone or anything drive me away. Someone must be playing a joke on me... But they're not... I wonder how they expect me to pay; in what coin?... What is the value of a footprint? Of six quarts of goblin milk the cats won't drink? Today is the 30th of November.

Tomorrow is the first.

At ten o'clock the mailman drives past. I run down and beg him to help me start my car. It takes only a minute; the motor catches at once.

I drive into Sunbury and put in a long distance call, to Howard Mansfield. He's a young engineer I knew before I was married. I tell him everything in a rush. He is interested but he takes the practical viewpoint. He says he'll come tomorrow and check the situation. I think he's more interested in checking me. I don't mind; he'll behave himself if I tell him to. I do want someone here the next time the milk comes…Which should be the morning of the day after tomorrow.

It's clear and cool. I've recharged the battery; I've bought groceries; I drive home. The fire in the stove has gone down; I build it up and make a fire in the fireplace.

I fry two lamb chops and make a salad. I feed Homer and Moses and eat my dinner.

Now it's very quiet. The cold makes small creaking noises outside; about ten o'clock the wind starts to come up. I'm tired, but I'm too nervous to go to sleep. These are the last hours of November 30th, they're running out…

I hear a soft sound outside, a tap at the door. The knob turns, but the door is bolted. For some reason I look at the clock. Eleven-thirty. Not yet the first. Howard has arrived?

I slowly go to the door. I wish I had a gun.

"Who's there?" My voice sounds strange.

"It's me." I recognize the voice.

"Go away."

"Open up. Or I'll bust in."

"Go away." I'm suddenly very frightened. It's so dark and far away; how could he have found me? Mrs. Lipscomb? Or through Howard?

"I'm coming in, Isabel. Open up, or I'll tear a hole in the wall!"

"I'll shoot you…"

He laughs. "You wouldn't shoot me…I'm your husband."

The door creaks as he puts his shoulder to it. The screws pull out of old wood; the bolt snaps loose, the door bursts open.

He poses for a moment, half-smiling. He has very black hair, a sharp thin nose, pale skin. His cheeks are red with the cold. He has the look of a decadent young Roman senator, and I know he's capable of anything queer and cruel.

"Hello, honey. I've come to take you back."

I know I'm in for a long hard pull. Telling him to get out, to go away, is a waste of breath.

"Shut the door." I go back to the fire. I won't give him the satisfaction of seeing that I'm frightened.

He comes slowly across the room. Homer and Moses crouch on the bed hoping he won't notice them.

"You're pretty well hid out."

"I'm not hiding." And I wonder if after all he's behind the Maple Valley Dairy. It must be.

"Have you come to collect for the milk, Poole?" I try to speak softly, as if I've known all the time.

He looks at me half-smiling. I see he's puzzled. He pretends that he understands. "Yeah. I've been missing my cream."

I sit looking at him, trying to convey my contempt. He wants me to fear him. He knows I don't love him. Fear or love — one suits him as well as the other. Indifference he won't take.

His mouth starts to droop. It looks as if he's thinking wistful thoughts, but I know he is becoming angry.

I don't want him angry. I say, "It's almost my bed-time, Poole."

He nods. "That's a good idea."

I say nothing.

He swings a chair around, straddles it with his arms along the back, his chin on his arms. The firelight glows on his face.

"You're pretty cool, Isabel."

"I've no reason to be otherwise."

"You're my wife."

"No."

He jumps up, grabs my wrists, looks down into my eyes. He's playing with me. We both know what he's planning; he advances to it by easy stages.

"Poole," I say in a cool voice, "you make me sick."

He slaps my face. Not hard. Just enough to indicate that he's the master. I stare at him; I don't intend to lose control. He can kill me; I won't show fear, nothing but contempt.

He reads my mind, he takes it as a challenge; his lips droop softly. He drops my arms, sits down, grins at me. Whatever he felt when he came here, now it's hate. Because I see through his poses, past his good looks, his black, white and rose beauty.

"The way I see it," says Poole, "you're up here playing around with two or three other men."

I blush; I can't help it. "Think what you like."

"Maybe it's just one man."

"If he finds you here — he'll give you a beating."

He looks at me interestedly; then laughs, stretches his magnificent arms, writhes his shoulder muscles. He is proud of his physique.

"It's a good bluff, Isabel. But knowing you, your virginal mind..."

The clock strikes twelve. Someone taps at the door. Poole jerks around, looks at the door, then at me.

I jump to my feet. I look at the door.

"Who's that?"

"I — really don't — know." I'm not sure. But it's twelve o'clock; it's December first. Who else could it be? "It's — it's the milkman." I start for the door — slowly. Of course I don't intend to open it.

"Milkman, eh? At midnight?" He jumps up, catches my arm. "Come to collect the milk bill, I suppose."

"That's quite right." My voice sounds weird and dry.

"Maybe he'd like to collect from me."

"I'll take care of him, Poole." I try to pull away, knowing that whatever I seem to want he won't allow. "Let me go."

"I'll pay your milk bill... After all, dear," he says silkily, "I'm your husband."

He shoves me across the room, goes to the door. I bury my face in my arms.

The door swings wide. "So you're the milkman," he says. His voice trails away. I hear a sudden gasp. I don't look.

Poole is paying the milk bill.

The door creaks slowly shut. A quick shuffle of steps on the porch, a crunching of snow.

After a while I get up, prop a chair under the door knob, build up the fire. I sit looking at the flames. I don't go near the window.

The cold yellow dawn-sun is shining through the window. The room is cold. I build a roaring fire, put on the coffee, look around the cabin. I've put in lots of work, but I don't have much to pack. Howard is coming today. He can help me.

The sun shines bright through the window. At last — I open the door, step out on the porch. The sun is dazzling on the snow. I wonder where Poole is. There's a shuffle of prints around the door, but away from the porch the snow is pure and clean. His convertible sits in the road.

A milk bill is stuck in a bottle and it's marked,

PAID IN FULL.

I go inside the house, where I drink coffee, pet Homer and Moses, and try to stop my hands from shaking.

WHERE HESPERUS FALLS

MY SERVANTS WILL NOT ALLOW me to kill myself. I have sought self-extinction by every method, from throat-cutting to the intricate routines of Yoga, but so far they have thwarted my most ingenious efforts.

I grow ever more annoyed. What is more personal, more truly one's own, than a man's own life? It is his basic possession, to retain or relinquish as he sees fit. If they continue to frustrate me, someone other than myself will suffer. I guarantee this.

My name is Henry Revere. My appearance is not remarkable, my intelligence is hardly noteworthy, and my emotions run evenly. I live in a house of synthetic shell, decorated with wood and jade, and surrounded by a pleasant garden. The view to one side is the ocean, the other, a valley sprinkled with houses similar to my own. I am by no means a prisoner, although my servants supervise me with the most minute care. Their first concern is to prevent my suicide, just as mine is to achieve it.

It is a game in which they have all the advantages — a detailed knowledge of my psychology, corridors behind the walls from which they can observe me, and a host of technical devices. They are men of my own race, in fact my own blood. But they are immeasurably more subtle than I.

My latest attempt was clever enough — although I had tried it before without success. I bit deeply into my tongue and thought to infect the cut with a pinch of garden loam. The servants either noticed me placing the soil in my mouth or observed the tension of my jaw.

They acted without warning. I stood on the terrace, hoping the soreness in my mouth might go undetected. Then, without conscious hiatus, I found myself reclining on a pallet, the dirt removed, the wound healed. They had used a thought-damping ray to anaesthetize me, and their sure medical techniques, aided by my almost invulnerable constitution, defeated the scheme.

As usual, I concealed my annoyance and went to my study. This is a room I have designed to my own taste, as far as possible from the complex curvilinear style which expresses the spirit of the age.

Almost immediately the person in charge of the household entered the room. I call him Dr. Jones because I cannot pronounce his name. He is taller than I, slender and fine-boned. His features are small, beautifully shaped, except for his chin which to my mind is too sharp and long, although I understand that such a chin is a contemporary criterion of beauty. His eyes are very large, slightly protuberant; his skin is clean of hair, by reason both of the racial tendency toward hairlessness, and the depilation which every baby undergoes upon birth.

Dr. Jones' clothes are vastly fanciful. He wears a body mantle of green film and a dozen vari-colored disks which spin slowly around his body like an axis. The symbolism of these disks, with their various colors, patterns, and directions of spin, are discussed in a chapter of my *History of Man* — so I will not be discursive here. The disks serve also as gravity deflectors, and are used commonly in personal flight.

Dr. Jones made me a polite salute, and seated himself upon an invisible cushion of anti-gravity. He spoke in the contemporary speech, which I could understand well enough, but whose nasal trills, gutturals, sibilants and indescribable fricatives, I could never articulate.

"Well, Henry Revere, how goes it?" he asked.

In my pidgin-speech I made a non-committal reply.

"I understand," said Dr. Jones, "that once again you undertook to deprive us of your company."

I nodded. "As usual I failed," I said.

Dr. Jones smiled slightly. The race had evolved away from laughter, which, as I understand, originated in the cave-man's bellow of relief at the successful clubbing of an adversary.

"You are self-centered," Dr. Jones told me. "You consider only your own pleasure."

"My life is my own. If I want to end it, you do great wrong in stopping me."

Dr. Jones shook his head. "But you are not your own property. You are the ward of the race. How much better if you accepted this fact!"

"I can't agree," I told him.

"It is necessary that you so adjust yourself." He studied me ruminatively. "You are something over ninety-six thousand years old. In my tenure at this house you have attempted suicide no less than a hundred times. No method has been either too crude or too painstaking."

He paused to watch me but I said nothing. He spoke no more than the truth, and for this reason I was allowed no object sharp enough to cut, long enough to strangle, noxious enough to poison, heavy enough to crush — even if I could have escaped surveillance long enough to use any deadly weapon.

I was ninety-six thousand, two hundred and thirty-two years old, and life long ago had lost that freshness and anticipation which makes it enjoyable. I found existence not so much unpleasant, as a bore. Events repeated themselves with a deadening familiarity. It was like watching a rather dull drama for the thousandth time: the boredom becomes almost tangible and nothing seems more desirable than oblivion.

Ninety-six thousand, two hundred and two years ago, as a student of bio-chemistry, I had offered myself as a guinea pig for certain tests involving glands and connective tissue. An incalculable error had distorted the experiment, with my immortality as the perverse result. To this day I appear not an hour older than my age at the time of the experiment, when I was so terribly young.

Needless to say, I suffered tragedy as my parents, my friends, my wife, and finally my children grew old and died, while I remained a young man. So it has been. I have seen untold generations come and go; faces flit before me like snowflakes as I sit here. Nations have risen and fallen, empires extended, collapsed, forgotten. Heroes have lived and died; seas drained, deserts irrigated, glaciers melted, mountains levelled. Almost a hundred thousand years I have persisted, for the most part effacing myself, studying humanity. My great work has been the *History of Man*.

Although I have lived unchanging, across the years the race evolved.

Men and women grew taller, and more slender. Every century saw features more refined, brains larger, more flexible. As a result, I, Henry Revere, *homo sapiens* of the twentieth century, today am a freakish survival, somewhat more advanced than the Neanderthal, but essentially a precursor to the true Man of today.

I am a living fossil, a curio among curios, a public ward, a creature denied the option of life or death. This was what Dr. Jones had come to explain to me, as if I were a retarded child. He was as kindly as he knows how, but unusually emphatic. Presently he departed and I was left to myself, in whatever privacy the scrutiny of a half a dozen pairs of eyes allows.

It is harder to kill one's self than one might imagine. I have considered the matter carefully, examining every object within my control for lethal potentialities. But my servants are preternaturally careful. Nothing in this house could so much as bruise me. And when I leave the house, as I am privileged to do, gravity deflectors allow me no profit from high places, and in this exquisitely organized civilization there are no dangerous vehicles or heavy machinery in which I could mangle myself.

In the final analysis I am flung upon my own resources. I have an idea. Tonight I shall take a firm grasp on my head and try to break my neck...

Dr. Jones came as always, and inspected me with his usual reproach. "Henry Revere, you trouble us all with your discontent. Why can't you reconcile yourself to life as you have always known it?"

"Because I am bored! I have experienced everything. There is no more possibility of novelty or surprise! I feel so sure of events that I could predict the future!"

He was rather more serious than usual. "You are our guest. You must realize that our only concern is to ensure your safety."

"But I don't want safety! Quite the reverse!"

Dr. Jones ignored me. "You must make up your mind to cooperate. Otherwise —" he paused significantly "— we will be forced into a course of action that will detract from the dignity of us all."

"Nothing could detract any further from my dignity," I replied bitterly. "I am hardly better than an animal in a zoo."

"That is neither your fault nor ours. We all must fulfill our existences to the optimum. Today your function is to serve as vinculum with the past."

He departed. I was left to my thoughts. The threats had been veiled but were all too clear. I was to desist from further attempts upon my life or suffer additional restraint.

I went out on the terrace, and stood looking across the ocean, where the sun was setting into a bed of golden clouds. I was beset by a dejection so vast that I felt stifled. Completely weary of a world to which I had become alien, I was yet denied freedom to take my leave. Everywhere I looked were avenues to death: the deep ocean, the heights of the palisade, the glitter of energy in the city. Death was a privilege, a bounty, a prize, and it was denied to me.

I returned to my study and leafed through some old maps. The house was silent — as if I were alone. I knew differently. Silent feet moved behind the walls, which were transparent to the eyes above these feet, but opaque to mine. Gauzy webs of artificial nerve tissue watched me from various parts of the room. I had only to make a sudden gesture to bring an anaesthetic beam snapping at me.

I sighed, slumped into my chair. I saw with the utmost clarity that never could I kill myself by my own instrumentality. Must I then submit to an intolerable existence? I sat looking bleakly at the nacreous wall behind which eyes noted my every act.

No, I would never submit. I must seek some means outside myself, a force of destruction to strike without warning: a lightning bolt, an avalanche, an earthquake.

Such natural cataclysms, however, were completely beyond my power to ordain or even predict.

I considered radioactivity. If by some pretext I could expose myself to a sufficient number of roentgens…

I sat back in my chair, suddenly excited. In the early days atomic wastes were sometimes buried, sometimes blended with concrete and dropped into the ocean. If only I were able to — but no. Dr. Jones would hardly allow me to dig in the desert or dive in the ocean, even if the radioactivity were not yet vitiated.

Some other disaster must be found in which I could serve the role of a casualty. If, for instance, I had foreknowledge of some great meteor, and where it would strike...

The idea awoke an almost forgotten association. I sat up in my chair. Then, conscious that knowledgeable minds speculated upon my every expression, I once again slumped forlornly.

Behind the passive mask of my face, my mind was racing, recalling ancient events. The time was too far past, the circumstances obscured. But details could be found in my great *History of Man*.

I must by all means avoid suspicion. I yawned, feigned acute ennui. Then with an air of surly petulance, I secured the box of numbered rods which was my index. I dropped one of them into the viewer, focused on the molecule-wide items of information.

Someone might be observing me. I rambled here and there, consulting articles and essays totally unrelated to my idea: *The Origin and Greatest Development of the Dithyramb; The Kalmuk Tyrants; New Camelot, 18119 A.D.; Oestheotics; The Caves of Phrygia; The Exploration of Mars; The Launching of the Satellites.* I undertook no more than a glance at this last; it would not be wise to show any more than a flicker of interest. But what I read corroborated the inkling which had tickled the back of my mind.

The date was during the twentieth century, during what would have been my normal lifetime.

The article read in part:

> Today *Hesperus*, last of the unmanned satellites, was launched into orbit around Earth. This great machine will swing above the equator at a height of a thousand miles, where atmospheric resistance is so scant as to be negligible. Not quite negligible, of course; it is estimated that in something less than a hundred thousand years *Hesperus* will lose enough momentum to return to Earth.
>
> Let us hope that no citizen of that future age suffers injury when *Hesperus* falls.

I grunted and muttered. A fatuous sentiment! Let us hope that one person, at the very least, suffers injury. Injury enough to erase him from life!

I continued to glance through the monumental work which had occupied so much of my time. I listened to aquaclave music from the old Poly-Pacific Empire; read a few pages from *The Revolt of the Manitobans*. Then, yawning and simulating hunger, I called for my evening meal.

Tomorrow I must locate more exact information, and brush up on orbital mathematics.

The *Hesperus* will drop into the Pacific Ocean at Latitude 0° 0' 0.0" ± 0.1", Longitude 141° 12' 36.9" ± 0.2" at 2 hours 22 minutes 18 seconds after standard noon on January 13 of next year. It will strike with a velocity of approximately one thousand miles an hour, and I hope to be on hand to absorb a certain percentage of its inertia.

I have been occupied seven months establishing these figures. Considering the necessary precautions, the dissimulation, the delicacy of the calculations, seven months is a short time to accomplish as much as I have. I see no reason why my calculations should not be accurate. The basic data were recorded to the necessary refinement and there have been no variables or fluctuations to cause error.

I have considered light pressure, hysteresis, meteoric dust; I have reckoned the calendar reforms which have occurred over the years; I have allowed for any possible Einsteinian, Gambade, or Kolbinski perturbation. What is there left to disturb the *Hesperus*? Its orbit lies in the equatorial plane, south of spaceship channels; to all intents and purposes it has been forgotten.

The last mention of the *Hesperus* occurs about eleven thousand years after it was launched. I find a note to the effect that its orbital position and velocity were in exact accordance with theoretical values. I believe I can be certain that the *Hesperus* will fall on schedule.

The most cheerful aspect to the entire affair is that no one is aware of the impending disaster but myself.

The date is *January 9*. To every side long blue swells are rolling, rippled with cat's-paws. Above are blue skies and dazzling white clouds. The yacht slides quietly south-west in the general direction of the Marquesas Islands.

Dr. Jones had no enthusiasm for this cruise. At first he tried to dissuade me from what he considered a whim but I insisted, reminding him that I was theoretically a free man and he made no further difficulty.

The yacht is graceful, swift, and seems as fragile as a moth. But when we cut through the long swells there is no shudder or vibration — only a gentle elastic heave. If I had hoped to lose myself overboard, I would have suffered disappointment. I am shepherded as carefully as in my own house. But for the first time in many years I am relaxed and happy. Dr. Jones notices and approves.

The weather is beautiful — the water so blue, the sun so bright, the air so fresh that I almost feel a qualm at leaving this life. Still, now is my chance and I must seize it. I regret that Dr. Jones and the crew must die with me. Still — what do they lose? Very little. A few short years. This is the risk they assume when they guard me. If I could allow them survival I would do so — but there is no such possibility.

I have requested and have been granted nominal command of the yacht. That is to say, I plot the course, I set the speed. Dr. Jones looks on with indulgent amusement, pleased that I interest myself in matters outside myself.

January 12. Tomorrow is my last day of life. We passed through a series of rain squalls this morning, but the horizon ahead is clear. I expect good weather tomorrow.

I have throttled down to Dead-Slow, as we are only a few hundred miles from our destination.

January 13. I am tense, active, charged with vitality and awareness. Every part of me tingles. On this day of my death it is good to be alive. And why? Because of anticipation, eagerness, hope.

I am trying to mask my euphoria. Dr. Jones is extremely sensitive; I would not care to start his mind working at this late date.

The time is noon. I keep my appointment with *Hesperus* in two hours and twenty-two minutes. The yacht is coasting easily over the water. Our position, as recorded by a pin-point of light on the chart, is only a few miles from our final position. At this present rate we will arrive in about two hours and fifteen minutes. Then I will halt the yacht and wait...

The yacht is motionless on the ocean. Our position is exactly at Latitude 0° 0' 0.0", Longitude 141° 12' 36.9". The degree of error represents no more than a yard or two. This graceful yacht with the unpronounceable name sits directly on the bull's-eye. There is only five minutes to wait.

Dr. Jones comes into the cabin. He inspects me curiously. "You seem very keyed up, Henry Revere."

"Yes, I feel keyed up, stimulated. This cruise is affording me much pleasure."

"Excellent!" He walks to the chart, glances at it. "Why are we halted?"

"I took it into mind to drift quietly. Are you impatient?"

Time passes — minutes, seconds. I watch the chronometer. Dr. Jones follows my glance. He frowns in sudden recollection, goes to the telescreen. "Excuse me; something I would like to watch. You might be interested."

The screen depicts an arid waste. "The Kalahari Desert," Dr. Jones tells me. "Watch."

I glance at the chronometer. Ten seconds — they tick off. Five — four — three — two — one. A great whistling sound, a roar, a crash, an explosion! It comes from the telescreen. The yacht rides on a calm sea.

"There went Hesperus," said Dr. Jones. "Right on schedule!"

He looks at me, where I have sagged against a bulkhead. His eyes narrow, he looks at the chronometer, at the chart, at the telescreen, back to me. "Ah, I understand you now! All of us you would have killed!"

"Yes," I mutter, "all of us."

"Aha! You savage!"

I pay him no heed. "Where could I have miscalculated? I considered everything. Loss of entropic mass, lunar attractions — I know the orbit of *Hesperus* as I know my hand. How did it shift, and so far?"

Dr. Jones' eyes shine with a baleful light. "You know the orbit of *Hesperus* then?"

"Yes. I considered every aspect."

"And you believe it shifted?"

"It must have. It was launched into an equatorial orbit; it falls into the Kalahari."

"There are two bodies to be considered."

"Two?"

"*Hesperus* and Earth."

"Earth is constant…Unchangeable." I say this last word slowly, as the terrible knowledge comes.

And Dr. Jones, for the first time in my memory, laughs, an unpleasant harsh sound. "Constant — unchangeable. Except for libration of the poles. *Hesperus* is the constant. Earth shifts below."

"Yes! What a fool I am!"

"An insensate murdering fool! I see you cannot be trusted!"

I charge him. I strike him once in the face before the anaesthetic beam hits me.

A Practical Man's Guide

RALPH BANKS, EDITOR of *Popular Crafts Monthly*, was a short stocky man with a round pink face, a crisp crew-cut, an intensely energetic manner. He wore gabardine suits and bow-ties; he lived in Westchester with a wife, three children, an Irish Setter, a pair of Siamese cats. He was respected by his underlings, liked not quite to the same extent.

The essence of Ralph Banks was practicality — an unerring discrimination between sound and sham, feasible and foolish. The faculty was essential to his job; in its absence he could not have functioned a day. Across his desk flowed a tide of articles, ideas, sketches, photographs, working models, each of which he must evaluate at a glance. Looking at blueprints for houses, garages, barbeque pits, orchidariums, off-shore cruisers, sailplanes and catamarans, he saw the completed project, functional or not, as the case might be — a feat which he similarly performed with technical drawings for gasoline turbines, hydraulic rams, amateur telescopes, magnetic clutches, monorail systems and one-man submarines. Given a formula for weed-killer, anti-freeze compound, invisible ink, fine-grain developer, synthetic cattle-fodder, stoneware glaze or rubber-base paint, he could predict its efficacy. At his fingertips were specifications and performance data for Stutz Bearcat, Mercer, S.G.V., Doble and Stanley Steamer; also Bugatti, Jaguar, Porsche, Nash–Healey and Pegaso; not to mention Ford, Chevrolet, Cadillac, Packard, Chrysler Imperial. He could build lawn furniture, hammer copper, polish agate, weave Harris tweed, repair watches, photograph amoebae, lithograph, dye *batik*, etch glass, detect forgeries with infra-red light, and seriously disable a heavier opponent. True, Banks farmed out much of his work to experts and department editors, but responsibility was his. Blunders evoked quiet ridicule from the competitors and sardonic letters from the readers; Banks made few blunders. Twelve years he had ridden the tiger, and in the process had developed a head for his job which amounted to second-sight; by now he was able to relax, enjoy his work, and indulge himself in his hobby, which was the collecting of freakish inventions.

Every morning his secretary sifted the mail, and when Ralph Banks arrived he would find the material arranged by categories. A special large basket was labelled SCREWBALL ALLEY — and here Editor Banks found the rarest gems of his collection.

The morning of Tuesday, October 27, was like any other. Ralph Banks came to his office, hung up his hat and coat, seated himself, hitched up his chair, loosened his belt, put a winter-green Lifesaver into his mouth. He consulted his appointments: at 10, Seth R. Framus, a highly-placed consultant to the AEC who had agreed to write an article on atomic power-plants. Framus had obtained a special clearance and proposed to hint at some new and rather startling developments — something in the nature of a planned leak. The article would enhance *Popular Crafts'* prestige, and put a handsome feather in Editor Banks' cap.

Banks pressed the intercom key.

"Lorraine."

"Yes, Mr. Banks."

"Seth R. Framus is calling this morning at ten. I'll see him as soon as he gets here."

"Very well."

Banks turned to his mail. First he checked SCREWBALL ALLEY. Nothing very much this morning. A perpetual-motion device, but he was tired of these. Replete... This was better. A timepiece for blind invalids, to be strapped against the temple. Needle pricks notified of the passing quarter-hours, while a small hammer tapped strokes of the hour against the skull... Next was a plan to irrigate Death Valley by installing cloud-condensing equipment along the ridge of the Panamint Mountains... Next — a manuscript on pebbled beige paper, entitled "Behind the Masque: A Practical Man's Guide".

Ralph Banks raised his eyebrows, glanced at the note clipped to the title-page.

Dear Sir:

I have learned in the course of a long life that exaggerated modesty brings few rewards. Hence I will put on no face of humility — I will not "pull my punches" as the expression goes. The following document is a tremendous contribution to human knowledge. In fact it knocks the props from under the entire basis of our existence, the foundation of our moral order. The implications — indeed the bald facts — will come as a shock supreme in its devastation to all but a few. You will observe, and I need hardly emphasize, that this is a *field not to be pursued lightly*! I have therefore prefaced description of techniques with a brief account of my own findings in order to warn any who seek to satisfy a dilettante's curiosity. You will wonder why I have chosen your periodical as an outlet for my work. I will be frank. Yours is a practical magazine; you are a practical man — and I submit the following as a practical guide. I may add, that certain other journals, edited by men less able than yourself, have returned my work with polite but obtuse notes.

Yours sincerely,

Angus McIlwaine,

c/o Archives, Smithsonian Institution,

Washington D.C.

An interesting letter, thought Banks. The work of a crack-pot — but it gave off an interesting flavor… He glanced at the manuscript, thumbed through the pages. McIlwaine's typography made a pretty show. The margins allowed two inches of pebbled beige space at either side. Passages in red interspersed the black paragraphs, and some of these were underlined in purple ink. Small green stars appeared in the left-hand margin from time to time, indicating further emphasis. The effect was colorful and dramatic.

He turned pages, reading sentences, paragraphs.

I have had serious misgivings [read Banks] but I cannot countenance cowardice or retreat. It is no argument to say that Masquerayne is unrelieved evil. Masquerayne is knowledge and men must never shrink from knowledge. And who knows, it may lead to ultimate good. Fire has done more good than harm for mankind; so have explosives, and so ultimately, we may hope, will atomic energy. Therefore, as Einstein steeled himself against his qualms to write the equation $E = mc^2$, so I will record my findings.

Banks grinned. A bona fide crack-pot, straight from the nut-hatch. He frowned. "c/o Archives, Smithsonian Institution". An incongruity...He read on, skimming down the paragraphs, assimilating a line here, a sentence there.

— a process of looking in, in, still further in; straining, forcing; then at the limits turning, as if in one's tracks, and looking out...

Banks looked up suddenly; the intercom buzzer. He pressed the key. "Mr. Seth R. Framus is here, Mr. Banks," came Lorraine's voice.

"Ask him to have a seat, please," said Banks. "I'll be with him in just one minute."

Lorraine, who had, "Please go right in, Mr. Framus," formed on her lips, was startled. Mr. Framus himself looked a little surprised; nevertheless he took a seat with good grace, tapping at his knee with a folded newspaper.

Banks returned to the manuscript.

Sometimes it is very quiet [he read] but only when the Ego can dodge behind these viscous milky pillars I have mentioned. It is easily possible to become lost here, in a very mundane manner. What could be more ludicrous, more tragic? A prisoner of self, so to speak!

Banks called through the intercom to Lorraine, "Get me the Smithsonian Institution."

"Yes, Mr. Banks," said Lorraine, glancing to see if Seth R. Framus had heard. He had, and the tempo at which he tapped his knee with the newspaper increased.

Banks leafed on through the pages.

> Naturally this never halted me. I steeled myself; I composed my nerves, my stomach. I continued. And here, as a footnote, may I mention that it is quite possible to come and go, returning with several of the red devices, many of them still warm.

The telephone startled Banks. He answered with a trace of irritation: "Yes, Lorraine?"

"The Smithsonian Institution, Mr. Banks."

"Oh...Hello? I'd like to speak to someone in the Department of Archives. Er — perhaps Mr. McIlwaine?"

"Just a minute," replied a female voice, "I'll give you Mr. Crispin."

Mr. Crispin came on the line; Banks introduced himself. Mr. Crispin inquired how he could be of service.

"I'd like to speak to Angus McIlwaine," said Banks.

Crispin asked in a puzzled voice, "McIlwaine? In what department?"

"Archives, I believe."

"That's odd...Of course we have a number of special projects going on — research teams and the like."

"Could you possibly make a check for me?"

"Well, certainly, Mr. Banks, if it's necessary."

"Will you do that please, and call me back collect? Or perhaps I can just hold the line."

"It'll take five or ten minutes."

"That's perfectly all right."

Banks turned the key on the intercom. "Keep an ear on the line, Lorraine, let me know when Crispin gets back on."

Lorraine glanced sideways at Seth R. Framus, whose mouth was showing taut lines of petulance. "Very well, Mr. Banks."

Seth R. Framus spoke in a polite voice, "What's Mr. Banks got on with Smithsonian, if I may ask?"

Lorraine said helplessly, "I'm really not sure, Mr. Framus...I guess it's something pretty important; he gave me orders to show you right in."

"Mumph." Mr. Framus opened his newspaper.

Banks was now skimming the final pages: "And now — the inescapable conclusion. It is very simple; it can be seen that we are all victims of a gruesome joke —"

He turned to the last page: "To demonstrate for yourself —"

Lorraine buzzed him on the intercom. "Mr. Crispin is back on the line; and I think Mr. Framus is in a hurry, Mr. Banks."

"I'll be right with Mr. Framus," said Banks. "Ask him to be good enough to wait just a moment." He spoke into the telephone: "Hello, Mr. Crispin?"

"I'm sorry, Mr. Banks; we just don't have an Angus McIlwaine with us."

Banks thoughtfully scratched his head. "There's the possibility he's using a pseudonym."

"In that case, I assume that he wishes to preserve his anonymity," Crispin responded politely.

"Tell me this: suppose I wrote to Angus McIlwaine, care of Archives, Smithsonian Institution. Who would get the letter?"

Crispin laughed. "No one, Mr. Banks! You'd get it back! Because we just don't have any McIlwaines. Unless, of course, whoever it is has made special arrangements...Now just a minute; maybe I know your man. That is, if it's really a pseudonym."

"Fine. Will you connect me?"

"Well, Mr. Banks, I think I'd better check first...Perhaps — Well, after all, perhaps he wants to retain his anonymity."

"Would you be good enough to find if Angus McIlwaine is his pseudonym; and if so, have him call me collect?"

"Yes. I can do that, Mr. Banks."

"Thank you very much."

Banks hesitated by the intercom. He really should see Mr. Framus... but there wasn't much left to the manuscript; he might as well skim

through it … McIlwaine, whoever he was, was ripe for the booby-hatch —
but he had a flair; a compelling urgent style. Banks had read a little — a
very little — of abnormal psychology; he knew that hallucinations generated a frightening reality. McIlwaine doubtless had a dose of everything
in the book … Well, thought Banks, just for ducks, let's see how he rec-
ommends unmasking this "grisly joke on humanity"; let's check the
directions for exploring Masquerayne …

> To demonstrate the whole shoddy terrible trick is the
> task of few minutes — simple and certain. If you are dar-
> ing — let us say, reckless — if you would tear the silken
> tissue that binds your eyes, do then as I say.
> First, obtain the following: a basin or carafe of clear
> water; six tumblers; six pins; a steel knitting needle; a
> four-foot square of dull black cardboard —

Lorraine called in through the intercom. "Mr. Banks, Mr. Framus
says —"

"Ask him to wait," said Banks rapidly. "Take a list, Lorraine. I want a
quart of water in a glass jug — six glasses — a steel knitting needle — a
sheet of black cardboard; get this from Art, dull, not gloss — a piece of
white chalk — a can of ether —"

"Did you say *ether*, Mr. Banks?"

"Yes, I said *ether*."

Lorraine made a hasty notation; Banks continued down the list of
his needs. "I need some red oil and some yellow oil. Get these from Art
too. A dozen new nails; big ones. A bottle of perfume good and strong.
And a pound of rice. Got that?"

"A pound of rice, yes sir."

"What in thunder does he want with all that junk?" growled Framus.

"I'm sure I don't know," said Lorraine a little breathlessly. "Will you
excuse me, Mr. Framus? I've got to get this stuff."

She ran out of the room. Framus half-rose to his feet, undecided
whether to stay or whether to stalk from the office. He slowly settled
back, now slapping his knee with measured resonant blows. Fifteen
more minutes!

In the inner office, Banks came to the final sentence.

> Following these instructions will take you past the barriers of Sight, Direction, Confusion, and the Fallacy of Pain. You will find twin channels — advisedly I call them arteries — and either one will bring you safely inside the Cordon, and here you can watch the progressions, these events that fill you with disgust at the thought of returning, but from which you recoil in worse disgust.

That was all. The finish.

Lorraine came in with the equipment. A boy from the Art Department assisted her.

"Mr. Banks," said Lorraine, "maybe I shouldn't mention this, but Mr. Framus is acting awful impatient."

"I'll see him in just a minute," muttered Banks. "One minute."

Lorraine returned to the outer office. Looking over her shoulder on the way out the door, she saw Banks pouring water into each of the glasses.

Fifteen minutes were up. Seth R. Framus rose to his feet. "I'm sorry, Miss — I simply can't wait any longer."

"Mr. Banks said he'd only be a minute, Mr. Framus," said Lorraine anxiously. "I think it's some kind of demonstration…"

Framus said with quiet force, "I'll wait exactly one more minute." He took his place, and sat gripping the paper.

The minute passed.

"There's a funny smell in here," said Seth R. Framus.

Lorraine sniffed the air, and looked embarrassed. "It must be something on the wind — from the river…"

"What's that noise?" asked Framus, staring at Banks' door.

"I don't know," said Lorraine. "It doesn't sound like Mr. Banks."

"Whatever it is," said Framus, "I can't wait." He clapped his hat on his head. "Mr. Banks can call me when he's free."

He left the office.

Lorraine sat listening to the sounds from Banks' office: a gurgling of water, mingled with a hissing, frying sound. Then came Banks' voice, subdued and muffled; then a vague roaring sound, as if someone momentarily had opened the door into the engine room of a ship.

Then a murmur, then quiet.

The telephone rang. "Mr. Banks' office," said Lorraine.

Mr. Crispin spoke. "Hello, please put Mr. Banks on the line. I've got the man he was looking for."

Lorraine buzzed Mr. Banks.

"Hello, Mr. Banks?" a voice from Crispin's end, the deepest, most melancholy voice Lorraine had ever heard.

"He's not on the line yet," said Lorraine.

"Tell him it's Angus McIlwaine Hunter speaking."

"I will, Mr. Hunter, as soon as he comes on." She buzzed again. "He doesn't answer... I guess he's stepped out for a minute."

"Well, it's not too important. I wonder if he's read my manuscript."

"I believe so, Mr. Hunter. He seemed fascinated with it."

"Good. Will you tell him that the last two pages will be along tomorrow? I foolishly omitted them, and they're very important to the article — crucial, if I may say so... In the nature of an antidote..."

"I'll tell him, Mr. Hunter."

"Thank you very much."

Lorraine once more buzzed Mr. Banks' office, then went to the door, knocked, looked in. The stuff Mr. Banks had ordered was scattered around in an awful mess. Mr. Banks was gone. Probably stepped out for a cup of coffee.

Lorraine went back to her desk, and sat waiting for Mr. Banks to return. After a while she brought out a file and began to work on her nails.

THE HOUSE LORDS

I

THE TWO MEN, with not a word spoken, had become very disturbed. Caffridge, the host, rose to his feet, took quick steps back and forth across the room. He went to the window, looked into the sky toward the distant star BGD 1169. The guest, Richard Emerson, was affected to an even greater degree. He sat back in his chair, face white, mouth loose, eyes wide and glistening.

Nothing had been said and there was nothing visible to explain their emotion. They sat in an ordinary suburban living room, notable only for a profusion of curios, oddities and trinkets hanging on the walls, filling shelves, suspended from the ceiling.

At a scratching sound, Caffridge turned from the window. He called sharply: "Sarvis!"

The black and white cat, sharpening its claws on a carved column of exotic wood, laid its ears back, but continued to scratch.

"You rascal!" Caffridge picked up the cat, hustled him outside through the cat's special door. He returned to Emerson. "We seem to be thinking the same thought."

Emerson was gripping the arms of his chair. "How did I miss it before?" he muttered.

"It's a strange business," said Caffridge. "I don't know what we should do."

"It's out of my hands now, thank heaven!" said Emerson in a hollow voice. And after a moment he added, "I won't be going back into space. Not for many years."

Caffridge picked up the small white box which contained Emerson's report. "Do you want to come along with me?"

Emerson shook his head. "I've nothing more to say. I don't want to see that again." He nodded toward the box.

"Very well," said Caffridge gloomily. "I'll show this to the Board to-night. After that —"

Emerson smiled, weary and skeptical. "After that?"

"Hanged if I can see what can be done. Or even what ought to be done. I suppose I'd better take it to someone in the government."

Sarvis the cat returned through its special door and sat quietly while Caffridge and Emerson considered their problem.

II

The Astrographical Society functioned as a non-profit organization, devoted to ex-terrestrial research and exploration. The dues paid in by a million active members were augmented by revenue from special patents and grants, licenses and counseling fees, with the result that over the years the Society had become very wealthy. A dozen spaceships carried the blue and green Astrographical chevron to remote places; the monthly publication was studied by school-children and savants alike; the Astrographical Museum housed a wonderful melange of objects gathered across the universe.

In a specially equipped cupola on the roof of the museum the Board of Directors met once a month, to transact business and to watch and hear vitaliscope reports from research teams. Theodore Caffridge, Chairman of the Board, arriving at the meeting, dropped the box containing Team Commander Richard Emerson's report into the vitaliscope mechanism. He stood silently, a tall somber figure, waiting while conversation around the table died.

"Gentlemen," said Caffridge in a dull monotone, "I have already examined this report. It is the strangest matter of my experience. I am seriously disturbed, and I may remark that Commander Emerson shares my feeling."

He paused. The Directors looked at him curiously. "Good Heavens, Caffridge," spoke one, "you sound positively lugubrious."

Another attempted jocularity. "What's the trouble? An invasion of Earth by robots?"

"I wish it were as simple," said Caffridge.

"What, then?" "Come, Caffridge, don't be mysterious!" "Let's hear it, Theodore!"

Caffridge smiled the faintest, most remote smile possible. "The report is here; you can see for yourselves."

He touched a switch; the walls of the room dissolved into gray mist; colors swirled and cleared. The Board of Directors became a cluster of invisible eyes and ears in the cabin of the spaceship *Gaea*. Their vantage point was the recording globe at the peak of Emerson's helmet. They saw what he saw, heard what he heard.

Emerson's voice came from a speaker. "We are in orbit over Planet 2 of Star BGD 1169, in Argo Navis IV. We were attracted here by a series of pulses radiating in the c^3 phase. These would seem to indicate a highly organized technical civilization, so naturally we stopped to investigate."

The images around the walls of the Directors' Room shifted, as Emerson stepped up into the control pulpit. Through the observation port the Directors could see a world swinging below, in the full light of an invisible sun.

Emerson detailed the physical characteristics of the world, which resembled those of Earth. "The atmosphere seems breathable; there is vegetation roughly comparable to our own."

Emerson approached the telescreen; again the images around the walls shifted. "The signals had led us to expect some sort of intelligent occupancy. We were not disappointed. The autochthones live, not in organized settlements, but in isolated dwellings. For lack of a better word, we've been calling them palaces." Emerson adjusted a dial on the console; the view on the telescreen expanded enormously; the Directors were looking into a forest dense as a jungle. The view shifted across the treetops to a clearing about a mile in diameter. The 'palace' occupied the center of the clearing — a dozen tall walls, steep and high as cliffs, joining apparently at random. They were constructed of some shimmering metalloid substance, and open to the sky. No portals or apertures were visible.

"That's about all the detail I can pick up from this altitude," came Emerson's voice. "Notice the absence of roof, the apparent lack of interior furnishing. It hardly seems a dwelling. Notice also how the clearing is landscaped — like a formal garden."

He backed away from the telescreen; the Directors once more sat in the cabin of the *Gaea*. "We have been broadcasting international symbols on all bands," said Emerson. "So far there has been no response. I think that we will set down in that clearing. There is an element of risk attached, but I believe that a race apparently so sophisticated will neither be surprised nor shocked by the appearance of a strange spaceship."

III

The *Gaea* settled into the atmosphere of BGD 1169-2, and the hull shivered to the slur of the thin gas whipping past.

Emerson spoke into the vitaliscope pickup, noting that the ship hovered above the area previously observed and was about to land.

The bumpers struck solid ground; there was a momentary fluctuation as the stabilizers took hold, then a sense of anchorage. Automatic switches cut off impulsion; the half-heard whine died down the scale into silence. The crew stood at the observation posts, staring out over the clearing.

At the center rose the 'palace' — the tall planes of glistening metalloid. Even from this close view, no openings, no windows, doors, vents could be seen.

The grounds surrounding the palace were carefully tended. Avenues of white-trunked trees held square black leaves large as trays turned up to the sun. There were irregular beds of black moss, feathery maroon ferns, fluffy pink and white growths like cotton candy. In the background rose the forest — a tangle of blue-green trees and broad-leaved shrubs, red, black, gray, and yellow.

Inside the *Gaea* the crew stood by the ports, ready to depart at any sign of hostility.

The palace remained quiet.

Half an hour passed. A small shape appeared briefly outside the wall of the palace. Cope, the young third officer, saw it first and called to Emerson. "Look there!"

Emerson focussed the telescopic bull's eye. "It's a child — a human child!"

The crew came to stare. Intelligent life among the stars was a rarity; to find such life in the human mold was cause for astonishment.

Emerson increased magnification of the telescopic pane.

"It's a boy, about seven or eight," he said. "He's looking at us — but he doesn't seem particularly interested."

The child turned back to the palace, and disappeared. Emerson uttered a soft ejaculation. "Did you see that?"

"What happened?" asked Wilhelm, the big blond second officer.

"He walked through the wall! As if it were air!"

Time passed; there was no further show of life. The crew fidgeted. "Why don't they show some interest?" complained Swett the steward. "Even the kids walk away."

Emerson shook his head in puzzlement. "Spaceships certainly don't drop down every day."

Wilhelm suddenly called out, "There's more of them — two, three, six — a whole confounded tribe!"

They came from the forest, quietly, almost stealthily — by ones and twos, until a dozen stood near the ship. They wore smocks woven of coarse fiber, crude leather shoes with flaring tops. At their belts hung daggers of several sizes and complicated little devices built of wood and twisted gut. They were a hard-bitten lot, with heavy-boned faces and glinting eyes. They walked with a careful bend to the knee, which gave them a furtive aspect. They kept the ship between themselves and the palace at all times, as if anxious to escape observation.

Emerson said, "I can't understand it. These aren't just humanoid types; they're human in every respect!" He looked across to where Boyd the biologist was finishing his final test. "What's the story?"

"Clean bill of health," said Boyd. "No dangerous pollen, no air-borne proteids, nothing remarkable in any way."

"I'm going outside," said Emerson.

Wilhelm protested, "They look untrustworthy and they're armed."

"I'll take a chance," said Emerson. "If they were hostile, I don't think they'd expose themselves."

Wilhelm was not convinced. "You never can tell what a strange race has in mind."

"Nevertheless," said Emerson, "I'm going out. You fellows cover me from the gun blisters. Also stand by the engines, in case we want to leave in a hurry."

"Are you going out alone?" Wilhelm asked dubiously.

"There's no point in risking two lives."

Wilhelm's square raw-boned face took on a mulish set. "I'll go out with you. Two eyes see better than one."

Emerson laughed. "I've already got two eyes. Besides, you're second in command; your place is here in the ship."

Cope, the young third officer, slender and dark, hardly out of his teens, spoke. "I'd like to go out with you."

"Very well, Cope," said Emerson. "Let's go."

Ten minutes later the two men stepped out of the ship, descended the ramp, stood on the soil of BGD 1169-2. The men and women from the forest still stood behind the ship, peering from time to time toward the palace. When Emerson and Cope appeared, they drew together, ready for either attack, defense or flight. Two of them fingered the wooden contrivances at their belts, which Emerson saw to be dart catapults. But otherwise there was no motion, friendly or otherwise.

The spacemen halted twenty feet distant. Emerson raised his hand, smiled in what he hoped to be a friendly manner. "Hello."

They stared at him, then began muttering among themselves. Emerson and Cope moved a step or two closer; the voices became audible. A lank gray-haired man, who seemed to wield a degree of authority, spoke with peevish energy, as if refuting nonsense. "No, no — impossible for them to be Free-men!"

The gnarled, beady-eyed man to whom he spoke retorted, "Impossible? What do you take them for, then, if not Free-men?"

Emerson and Cope stared in amazement. These men spoke English!

Someone else remarked, "They're not House Lords! Who ever saw House Lords like these!"

A fourth voice was equally definite. "And it's a certainty that they're not servants."

"All of you talk in circles," snapped one of the women. "Why don't you ask them and be done with it?"

English! The accent was blurred, the intonation unusual; the language, nonetheless, was their own! Emerson and Cope came a step closer; the forest people fell silent, and shifted their feet nervously.

Emerson spoke. "I am Richard Emerson," he said. "This is Howard Cope. Who are you people?"

The gray-haired chief surveyed them with crafty impudence. "Who are we? We're Free-men, as you must know very well. What do you here? What House are you from?"

Emerson said, "We're from Earth."

" 'Earth'?"

Emerson looked around the blank faces. "You don't know of Earth?"

"No."

"But you speak an Earth language!"

The chief grinned. "How else can men speak?"

Emerson laughed weakly. "There are a number of other languages."

The chief shook his head skeptically. "I can't believe that."

Emerson and Cope exchanged glances of bewildered amusement. "Who lives in the palace?" Emerson asked.

The chief seemed incredulous at Emerson's ignorance. "The House Lords, naturally. Genarro, Hesphor and the rest."

Emerson considered the tall walls, which seemed, on the whole, ill-adapted to human requirements. "They are men, like ourselves?"

The chief laughed jeeringly. "If you would call such luxurious creatures men! We tolerate them only for their females." From the men of the group came a lascivious murmur. "The soft sweet House Lord girls!"

The forest women hissed in anger. "They're as worthless as the men!" exclaimed one leathery old creature.

There was a sudden nervous motion at the outskirts of the group. "Here they come! The House Lords!"

Quickly, with long, bent-kneed strides, the savages retreated, and were gone into the forest.

Emerson and Cope walked around the ship. Crossing the clearing in leisurely fashion were a young man and woman, a girl and the boy they had seen before. They were the most handsome beings the Earthmen had ever seen. The young man wore a skin-tight garment of emerald-green sequins, a complicated head-dress of silver spines; the boy wore red trousers, a dark blue jacket and a long-billed blue cap. The young woman and the girl wore simple sheaths of white and blue, stretching with easy elasticity as they walked. They were bare-headed; their pale hair fell flowing to their shoulders.

They halted a few yards from the ship, considered the spacemen with sober curiosity. Their expressions were identical: intent, intelligent, with a vague underlying hauteur. The young man glanced casually toward the forest, held up a small rod. A puff of blackness came forth, a black bubble wafted toward the forest, expanding enormously as it went.

From the forest came yelps of fear, the stumble of racing feet. The black bubble exploded among the trees, scattering hundreds of smaller black bubbles, which grew and exploded in their turn.

The sound of flight diminished in the distance. The four young House Lords, smiling a little, returned to Emerson and Cope.

"And who may you be? Surely not Wild Men?"

"No, we're not Wild Men," said Emerson.

The boy said, "But you're not House Lords."

"And certainly you're not servants," said the girl, who was several years older than the boy, perhaps fourteen or fifteen.

Emerson explained patiently, "We are astrographers, scientists, from Earth."

Like the forest people, the House Lords were puzzled. "'Earth'?"

"Good Heavens!" exclaimed Emerson. "Surely you know of Earth!"

They shook their heads.

"But you're human beings — Earth people!"

"No," said the young man, "We are House Lords. 'Earth' is nothing to us."

"But — you speak our language — an Earth language!"

They shrugged and smiled. "There are a hundred ways in which your people might have learned our speech."

The matter seemed to interest them very little. The young woman looked toward the forest. "Best be careful of the Wild Men; they'll do you harm if they can." She turned. "Come, let us go back."

"Wait!" cried Emerson.

They observed him with austere politeness. "Yes?"

"Aren't you curious about us — interested in where we came from?"

The young man smilingly shook his head, and the silver spines of his headgear chimed like bells. "Why should we be interested?"

Emerson laughed in mingled astonishment and irritation.

"We're strangers from space — from Earth, which you claim you never heard of."

"Exactly. If we have never heard of you, how can we be interested?"

Emerson threw up his hands. "Suit yourself. However, we're interested in you."

The young man nodded, accepting this as a matter of course. The boy and girl were already walking away; the young woman had half-turned and was waiting. "Come, Hesphor," she called softly.

"I'd like to talk to you," Emerson said. "There's a mystery here — something we should straighten out."

"No mystery. We are House Lords, and this our House."

"May we come into your house?"

The young man hesitated, glanced at the young woman. She pursed her lips, shook her head. "Lord Genarro."

The young man made a small grimace. "The servants are gone; Genarro sleeps. They may come for a short time."

The young woman shrugged. "If Genarro wakes, he will not be pleased."

"Ah, but Genarro —"

"But Genarro," the woman interrupted quickly, "is the First Lord of the House!"

Hesphor seemed momentarily sulky. "Genarro sleeps, and the servants are gone. These outland wild-things may enter."

He signaled to Cope and Emerson. "Come."

The House Lords strolled back through the garden, talking quietly together. Emerson and Cope followed, half-angry, half-sheepish. "This is fantastic," Emerson muttered. "Snubbed by the aristocracy half an hour after we arrive."

"I guess we'll have to put up with it," said Cope. "They know things we've never even thought of. That black bubble, for instance."

The boy and girl reached the wall of the palace. Without hesitation they walked through the glistening surface. The young man and woman followed. When Emerson and Cope reached the wall, it was solid, super-normally cold. They felt along the smooth surface, pushing, groping in exasperation.

The boy came back through the wall. "Are you coming in?"

"We'd like to," said Emerson.

"That's solid there." The boy watched them in amusement. "Can't you tell where it's permeable?"

"No," said Emerson.

"Neither can the Wild Men," said the boy. He pointed. "Go through there."

Emerson and Cope passed through, and the wall felt like a thin film of cool water.

They stood on a dull blue floor, with silver filaments tracing a looped pattern. The walls rose high all around them. A hundred feet above, bars of black substance protruded from the metal, and the air around the tips seemed to quiver, like the air over a hot road.

There was no furniture in the room, no trace of human habitation.

"Come," said the boy. He crossed the room, walked through the wall opposite. Emerson and Cope followed. "I hope we can find our way out," said Cope. "I wouldn't want to climb these walls."

They stood in a hall similar to the first, but with a floor of a resilient white material. Their bodies felt light, their steps took them farther than they expected. The young man and woman were waiting for them. The boy had stepped back through the wall; the girl was nowhere in sight.

"We can stay with you a moment or two," said the young man. "Our servants are gone; the house is quiet. Perhaps you'd care to eat?" Without waiting for response he reached forward. His hands disappeared into nowhere. He drew them back, pulling forth a rack supporting trays and bowls of food-stuffs — wedges of red jelly, tall white cones, black wafers, small green globular fruits, flagons containing liquids of various colors.

"You may eat," said the young woman, motioning with her hand.

"Thank you," said Emerson. He and Cope gingerly sampled the

food. It was strange and rich, and tingled in the mouth like carbonated water.

"Where does this food come from?" asked Emerson. "How can you pull it out of the air like that?"

The young House Lord looked at his hands. "The servants put it there."

"Where do the servants get it?"

The young man shrugged. "Why should we trouble ourselves, so long as it's there?"

Cope asked quizzically, "What would you do if your servants left you?"

"Such a thing could never happen."

"I'd like to see your servants," said Emerson.

"They're not here now." The young man removed his headgear, tucked it into an invisible niche. "Tell us about this 'Earth' of yours."

"It's a planet like this one," said Emerson, "although men and women live much differently."

"Do you have servants?"

"None of us have servants now."

"Mmmph," said the young woman in barely dissembled scorn. "Like the Wild Men."

Cope asked, "How long have you lived here?"

The question seemed to puzzle the House Lords. "'How long?' What do you mean?"

"How many years."

"What is a 'year'?"

"A unit of time — the interval a planet takes to make a revolution around its sun. Just as a day is the time a planet takes to rotate on its axis."

The House Lords were amused. "That's a queer thought: magnificently arbitrary. What possible use is such an idea?"

Emerson said dryly, "We find time measurements useful."

The House Lords smiled at each other. "That well may be," Hesphor remarked.

"Who are the Wild Men?" asked Cope.

"Just riff-raff," said the young woman with a shudder. "Outcasts from Houses where there was no room."

"They harass us; they try to steal our women," said the young man. He held up his hand. "Listen." He and the young woman looked at each other.

Emerson and Cope could hear nothing.

"Lord Genarro," said the young woman. "He comes."

Hesphor looked uneasily at the wall, glanced at Emerson and Cope, then planted himself obstinately in the middle of the hall.

There was a slight sound. A tall man strode through the wall. He wore shining black, a black helm. His hair was copper-gold, his eyes frost-blue. He saw Emerson and Cope; he took a great stride forward. "What are these wild things doing here! Are you all mad? Out, out with them!"

Hesphor interposed. "They are strangers, from another world; they mean no harm."

"Out with them! Eating our food! Ogling the Lady Faelm!" He advanced menacingly; Emerson and Cope stepped back. "Wild things, go!"

"Just as you like," said Emerson. "Show us the way out."

"One moment!" said Hesphor. "I invited them here; they are my charges."

Genarro turned his displeasure against the young House Lord. "Do you wish to join the Wild Men?"

Hesphor stared at him; their eyes locked, then Hesphor wilted, turned away.

"Very well," he muttered. "They shall leave." He whistled; through the wall came the boy. "Take the strangers to their ship."

"Quickly!" roared Genarro. "The air reeks; they are covered with filth!"

"This way!" The boy scampered out of the wall; Emerson and Cope followed with alacrity.

Through two walls they passed and once more stood in the open air. Cope heaved a deep sigh. "Genarro's hospitality leaves much to be desired."

The girl came out of the palace and joined the boy.

"Come," said the boy. "We'll take you to your ship; you'd best be away before the servants return."

Emerson looked back toward the palace, shrugged. "Let's go."

They followed the boy and girl through the formal garden, past the white-trunked trees, the beds of black moss, the pink and white candy floss. The *Gaea*, at the far end of the clearing, seemed familiar and homelike; Emerson and Cope hurried their steps.

They passed a clump of gray-stalked bamboo. There was a rustle of movement, a quick rush; they were surrounded by Wild Men. Hands gripped Emerson and Cope, their weapons were snatched.

The boy and girl, struggling, kicking, screaming, were seized; nooses were dropped around their bodies, they were tugged toward the jungle.

"Loose us!" yelled the boy. "The servants will pulverize you."

"The servants are gone," cried the wild chief happily. "And I've got what I've wanted for many years — a fresh beautiful House Lord girl."

The girl sobbed and screamed and tore at her bonds; the boy struggled and kicked. "Easy, boy," the chief warned. "We're close enough to cutting your throat as it is."

Arms shoved; the party moved at a trot across the garden, toward the jungle. "Why are you taking us?" panted Emerson. "We're no good to you."

"Only in what your friends will give to have you back." The chief grinned knowingly over his shoulder. "Weapons! Good cloth! Good shoes!"

"We don't carry such things with us!"

"You'll wait till we get them!"

The forest was only fifty yards away. The boy flung himself flat on the ground, the girl did likewise. Emerson felt the grasp on his arms relax; he broke loose, swinging his fists. He struck a Wild Man, who fell to the ground. The chief snatched out his catapult, aimed it. "One move and you're dead!"

Emerson stood rigid. The Wild Men seized the boy and girl; the party moved ahead.

But now the raid had been noticed at the palace; the air pulsed to a weird high whistle. The Wild Men increased their pace.

From the palace came a fan of black, shearing down like a great dark vane, striking the ground at the forest's edge.

The Wild Men stopped short. Escape was blocked at this point. They turned, ran parallel to the edge of the clearing.

Out of the palace came Genarro and Hesphor, and behind them, Faelm and another woman. Across the clearing came the sound of Genarro's voice, full of passion and threat.

The Wild Men began to pant, to make hoarse sounds. "Hurry, hurry, hurry!" croaked the chief. "That's Genarro, the House Lord."

"Kill them," cried one of the men. "Kill them, and run!"

Emerson jerked himself loose, jumped on the chief. They rolled on the turf like tumble-bugs.

Cope likewise had won free; his captor danced away, snatched out his catapult. Cope fell flat; the dart whistled over his head.

The other Wild Men hesitated, milled irresolutely.

Genarro and Hesphor were close; the Wild Men aimed their catapults, fired a volley of darts. Genarro staggered, clawed at his neck. Hesphor aimed a hand-weapon, then dared not use it for fear of striking the boy and girl. Genarro sank to his knees, fell slowly forward. Hesphor stared in wonder.

The Wild Men dropped new darts in their catapults, raised them. Then they dropped their arms limply. Their faces were aghast. "The servants!"

They scuttled for the forest. Emerson rose from the limp body of the chief; he looked toward the palace.

Over the walls was a flicker of monstrous shadows.

Emerson grabbed Cope's arm. "Let's get out of here!"

"I'm with you!"

They ran like rabbits for the *Gaea*, which was not far distant. The air behind them quivered, they heard a vast furious murmur.

Emerson dared only a single glance over his shoulder; he caught a confused impression of Wild Men running crazily helter-skelter. As he watched, one of them crumpled, smashed into the ground, as if struck by a vast hammer. Emerson and Cope ran like men in a nightmare. The *Gaea* loomed before them; they pounded up the ramp, plunged into the hull.

"Take-off!" cried Emerson. "Let's get out of here!"

The crew, white-faced and anxious, had been waiting. There was not a second's delay. The door slid shut, power roared through the tubes; the *Gaea* rose from the clearing.

A dark shadow enveloped the ports; the ship quivered, gave a tremendous lurch, wheeled through a dozen impossible directions. The men aboard felt blinding pain, a sick wrench at the brain, a period of confusion.

Then there was easy motion and peace.

The *Gaea* was in space, far from any star.

The crew gradually recovered their faculties, stared into each other's white faces.

Emerson took a star-fix. They were far, far from Star BGD 1169.

Without comment he set a course for Earth.

IV

The vitaliscope images vanished. The Directors of the Astrographical Society sat stiff in their seats.

Theodore Caffridge spoke. His voice sounded flat and prosaic.

"As you have seen, Commander Emerson and crew underwent a most peculiar experience."

"Peculiar!" Ben Haynault whistled. "That's an understatement if there ever was one."

"But what's it mean?" demanded Pritchard. "Those people speaking English!"

"And knowing nothing of Earth!"

Caffridge said in his flat voice, "Emerson and I have formed a tentative hypothesis."

There was silence in the room.

"Come, come, Caffridge," called Ben Haynault, "don't keep us dangling."

Caffridge smiled grimly. "I was trying to order my thoughts... Chronologically what happened was this. Like you, we were mystified. Who were these House Lords? How could they speak an Earth language, but still know nothing of Earth? How did the House Lords control their servants, these tremendous creatures which could be seen only as flickers of light and shadow?"

Caffridge paused. No one spoke; he went on. "Commander Emerson had no answer to these questions. Neither did I. We were both completely at a loss. Then something very ordinary occurred, an event quite insignificant in itself. But it set off a charge in both our minds.

"What happened was that my cat Sarvis came into the house. He used his special little swinging door. My small House Lord, Sarvis. He came into his palace, he went to his dish and looked for his dinner."

There was frozen silence in the Board Room, the arrestment in time which comes of surprise and shock.

Then someone coughed; there was the hiss of breath, a bit of nervous laughter, general uneasy motion.

"Theodore," Ben Haynault asked in a husky voice, "what are you implying?"

"I've given you the facts. You must draw your own inferences."

Paul Pritchard muttered, "It was a hoax, surely. There's no other explanation. A society of crackpots...Escapists..."

Caffridge smiled. "You might discuss that theory with Emerson."

Pritchard fell silent.

"Emerson considers himself lucky," Caffridge went on reflectively. "I'm inclined to agree. If some wild thing came into my house and killed Sarvis, I'd consider it a domestic disturbance of the highest order. I might not have been quite so forbearing."

"What can we do?" asked Haynault quietly.

Caffridge went to the window and stood looking up into the southern sky. "We can hope that they already have all the House Lords they want. Otherwise — none of us are safe."

THE SECRET

SUNBEAMS SLANTED THROUGH CHINKS in the wall of the hut; from
the lagoon came shouts and splashing of the village children. Rona
ta Inga at last opened his eyes. He had slept far past his usual hour
of arising, far into the morning. He stretched his legs, cupped hands
behind his head, stared absently up at the ceiling of thatch. In actuality
he had awakened at the usual hour, to drift off again into a dreaming
doze — a habit to which lately he had become prone. Only lately. Inga
frowned and sat up with a jerk. What did this mean? Was it a sign?
Perhaps he should inquire from Takti Tai... But it was all so ridiculous.
He had slept late for the most ordinary of reasons: he enjoyed lazing
and drowsing and dreaming.

On the mat beside him were crumpled flowers, where Mai Mio
had lain. Inga gathered the blossoms and laid them on the shelf which
held his scant possessions. An enchanting creature, this Mai Mio.
She laughed no more and no less than other girls; her eyes were like
other eyes, her mouth like all mouths; but her quaint and charming
mannerisms made her absolutely unique: the single Mai Mio in all
the universe. Inga had loved many maidens. All in some way were
singular, but Mai Mio was a creature delightfully, exquisitely apart
from the others. There was considerable difference in their ages. Mai
Mio only recently had become a woman — even now from a distance
she might be mistaken for a boy — while Inga was older by at least five
or six seasons. He was not quite sure. It mattered little in any event. It
mattered very little, he told himself again, quite emphatically. This was
his village, his island; he had no desire to leave. Ever!

The children came up the beach from the lagoon. Two or three darted under his hut, swinging on one of the poles, chanting nonsense-words. The hut trembled; the outcry jarred upon Inga's nerves. He shouted in irritation. The children became instantly silent, in awe and astonishment, and trotted away looking over their shoulders.

Inga frowned; for the second time this morning he felt dissatisfied with himself. He would gain an unenviable reputation if he kept on in such a fashion. What had come over him? He was the same Inga that he was yesterday... Except for the fact that a day had elapsed and he was a day older.

He went out on the porch before his hut, stretched in the sunlight. To right and left were forty or fifty other such huts as his own, with intervening trees; ahead lay the lagoon blue and sparkling in the sunlight. Inga jumped to the ground, walked to the lagoon, swam, dived far down among the glittering pebbles and ocean growths which covered the lagoon floor. Emerging he felt relaxed and at peace — once more himself: Rona ta Inga, as he had always been, and always would be!

Squatting on his porch he breakfasted on fruit and cold baked fish from last night's feast and considered the day ahead. There was no urgency, no duty to fulfil, no need to satisfy. He could join the party of young bucks now on their way into the forest, hoping to snare fowl. He could fashion a brooch of carved shell and goana-nut for Mai Mio. He could lounge and gossip; he could fish. Or he could visit his best friend Takti Tai, who was building a boat. Inga rose to his feet. He would fish. He walked along the beach to his canoe, checked equipment, pushed off, paddled across the lagoon to the opening in the reef. The winds blew to the west as always. Leaving the lagoon Inga turned a swift glance downwind — an almost furtive glance — then bent his neck into the wind and paddled east.

Within the hour he had caught six fine fish, and drifted back along the reef to the lagoon entrance. Everyone was swimming when he returned. Maidens, young men, children. Mai Mio paddled to the canoe, hooked her arms over the gunwales, grinned up at him, water glistening on her cheeks. "Rona ta Inga! did you catch fish? Or am I bad luck?"

"See for yourself."

She looked. "Five — no, six! All fat silver-fins! I am good luck! May I sleep often in your hut?"

"So long as I catch fish the following day."

She dropped back into the water, splashed him, sank out of sight. Through the undulating surface Inga could see her slender brown form skimming off across the bottom. He beached the canoe, wrapped the fish in big sipi-leaves and stored them in a cool cistern, then ran down to the lagoon to join the swimming.

Later he and Mai Mio sat in the shade; she plaiting a decorative cord of coloured bark which later she would weave into a basket; he leaning back, looking across the water. Artlessly Mai Mio chattered — of the new song Ama ta Lalau had composed, of the odd fish she had seen while swimming underwater, of the change which had come over Takti Tai since he had started building his boat.

Inga made an absent-minded sound, but said nothing.

"We have formed a band," Mai Mio confided. "There are six of us: Ipa, Tuiti, Hali sai Iano, Zoma, Oiu Ngo and myself. We have pledged never to leave the island. Never, never, never. There is too much joy here. Never will we sail west — never. Whatever the secret, we do not wish to know."

Inga smiled, a rather wistful smile. "There is much wisdom in the pledge you have made."

She stroked his arm. "Why do you not join us in our pledge? True, we are six girls — but a pledge is a pledge."

"True."

"Do you want to sail west?"

"No."

Mai Mio excitedly rose to her knees. "I will call together the band, and all of us, all together: we will recite the pledge again, never will we leave our island! And to think, you are the oldest of all the village!"

"Takti Tai is older," said Inga.

"But Takti Tai is building his boat! He hardly counts any more!"

"Vai Ona is as old as I. Almost as old."

"Do you know something? Whenever Vai Ona goes out to fish, he always looks to the west. He wonders."

"Everyone wonders."

"Not I!" Mai Mio jumped to her feet. "Not I — not any of the band. Never, never, never — never will we leave the island! We have pledged

— 285 —

ourselves!" She reached down, patted Inga's cheek, ran off to where a group of her friends were sharing a basket of fruit.

Inga sat quietly for five minutes. Then he made an impatient gesture, rose and walked along the shore to the platform where Takti Tai worked on his boat. This was a catamaran with a broad deck, a shelter of woven withe thatched with sipi-leaf, a stout mast. In silence Inga helped Takti Tai shape the mast, scraping a tall well-seasoned pasiao-tui sapling with sharp shells. Inga presently paused, laid aside the shell. He said, "Long ago there were four of us. You, me, Akara and Zan. Remember?"

Takti Tai continued to scrape. "Of course I remember."

"One night we sat on the beach around a fire — the four of us. Remember?"

Takti Tai nodded.

"We pledged never to leave the island. We swore never to weaken, we spilled blood to seal the pact. Never would we sail west."

"I remember."

"Now you sail," said Inga. "I will be the last of the group."

Takti Tai paused in his scraping, looked at Inga, as if he would speak, then bent once more over the mast. Inga presently returned up the beach to his hut, where squatting on the porch he carved at the brooch for Mai Mio.

A youth came to sit beside him. Inga, who had no particular wish for companionship, continued with his carving. But the youth, absorbed in his own problems, failed to notice. "Advise me, Rona ta Inga. You are the oldest of the village and very sage."

Inga raised his eyebrows, then scowled, but said nothing.

"I love Hali sai Iano, I long for her desperately, but she laughs at me and runs off to throw her arms about the neck of Hopu. What should I do?"

"The situation is quite simple," said Inga. "She prefers Hopu. You need merely select another girl. What of Talau Io? She is pretty and affectionate, and seems to like you."

The youth vented a sigh. "Very well. I will do as you suggest. After all, one girl is much like another." He departed, unaware of the sardonic look Inga directed at his back. He asked himself, why do they come to me for advice? I am only two or three, or at most four or five, seasons their senior. It is as if they think me the fount and source of all sagacity!

During the evening a baby was born. The mother was Omei Ni Io, who for almost a season had slept in Inga's hut. Since it was a boy-child she named it Inga ta Omei. There was a naming ceremony at which Inga presided. The singing and dancing lasted until late, and if it were not for the fact that the child was his own, with his name, Inga would have crept off early to his hut. He had attended many naming ceremonies.

A week later Takti Tai sailed west, and there was a ceremony of a different sort. Everyone came to the beach to touch the hull of the boat and bless it with water. Tears ran freely down all cheeks, including Takti Tai's. For the last time he looked around the lagoon, into the faces of those he would be leaving. Then he turned, signaled; the young men pushed the boat away from the beach, then jumping into the water, towed it across the lagoon, guided it out into the ocean. Takti Tai cut brails, tightened halyards; the big square sail billowed in the wind. The boat surged west. Takti Tai stood on the platform, gave a final flourish of the hand, and those on the beach waved farewell. The boat moved out into the afternoon, and when the sun sank, it could be seen no more.

During the evening meal the talk was quiet; everyone stared into the fire. Mai Mio finally jumped to her feet. "Not I," she chanted. "Not I — ever, ever, ever!"

"Nor I," shouted Ama ta Lalau, who of all the youths was the most proficient musician. He reached for the guitar which he had carved from a black soa-gum trunk, struck chords, began to sing.

Inga watched quietly. He was now the oldest on the island, and it seemed as if the others were treating him with a new respect. Ridiculous! What nonsense! So little older was he that it made no difference whatever! But he noticed that Mai Mio was laughingly attentive to Ama ta Lalau, who responded to the flirtation with great gallantry. Inga watched with a heavy feeling around the heart, and presently went off to his hut. That night, for the first time in weeks Mai Mio did not sleep beside him. No matter, Inga told himself: one girl is much like another.

The following day he wandered up the beach to the platform where Takti Tai had built his boat. The area was clean and tidy, and tools were hung carefully in a nearby shed. In the forest beyond grew fine makara trees, from which the staunchest hulls were fashioned.

Inga turned away. He took his canoe out to catch fish, and leaving the lagoon looked to the west. There was nothing to see but empty horizon, precisely like the horizon to east, to north and to south — except that the western horizon concealed the secret...The rest of the day he felt uneasy. During the evening meal he looked from face to face. None were the faces of his dear friends; they all had built their boats and had sailed. His friends had departed; his friends knew the secret.

The next morning, without making a conscious decision, Inga sharpened the tools and felled two fine makara trees. He was not precisely building a boat — so he assured himself — but it did no harm for wood to season.

Nevertheless the following day he trimmed the trees, cut the trunks to length, and the next day assembled all the young men to help carry the trunks to the platform. No one seemed surprised; everyone knew that Rona ta Inga was building his boat. Mai Mio had now frankly taken up with Ama ta Lalau and as Inga worked on his boat he watched them play in the water, not without a lump of bitterness in his throat. Yes, he told himself, it would be pleasure indeed to join his true friends — the youths and maidens he had known since he dropped his milk-name, whom he had sported with, who now were departed, and for whom he felt an aching loneliness. Diligently he hollowed the hulls, burning, scraping, chiseling. Then the platform was secured, the little shelter woven and thatched to protect him from rain. He scraped a mast from a flawless pasiao-tui sapling, stepped and stayed it. He gathered bast, wove a coarse but sturdy sail, hung it to stretch and season. Then he began to provision the boat. He gathered nutmeats, dried fruit, smoked fish wrapped in sipi-leaf. He filled blow-fish bladders with water. How long was the trip to the west? No one knew. Best not to go hungry, best to stock the boat well: once down the wind there was no turning back.

One day he was ready. It was a day much like all the other days of his life. The sun shone warm and bright, the lagoon glittered and rippled up and down the beach in little gushes of play-surf. Rona ta Inga's throat felt tense and stiff; he could hardly trust his voice. The young folk came to line the beach; all blessed the boat with water. Inga gazed into each face, then along the line of huts, the trees, the beaches, the scenes he loved with such intensity… Already they seemed remote. Tears were coursing his cheeks. He held up his hand, turned away. He felt the boat leave the beach, float free on the water. Swimmers thrust him out into the ocean. For the last time he turned to look back at the village, fighting a sudden maddening urge to jump from the boat, to swim back to the village. He hoisted the sail, the wind thrust deep into the hollow. Water surged under the hulls and he was coasting west, with the island astern.

Up the blue swells, down into the long troughs, the wake gurgling, the bow rising and falling. The long afternoon waned and became golden; sunset burned and ebbed and became a halcyon dusk. The stars appeared, and Inga, sitting silently by his rudder, held the sail full to the wind. At midnight he lowered the sail and slept, the boat drifting quietly.

In the morning he was completely alone, the horizons blank. He raised the sail and scudded west, and so passed the day, and the next, and others. And Inga became thankful that he had provisioned the boat with generosity. On the sixth day he seemed to notice that a chill had come into the wind; on the eighth day he sailed under a high overcast, the like of which he had never seen before. The ocean changed from blue to grey and presently took on a green tinge. Now the water was cold. The wind blew with great force, bellying his bast sail, and Inga huddled in the shelter to avoid the harsh spray. On the morning of the ninth day he thought to see a dim dark shape loom ahead, which at noon became a line of tall cliffs with surf beating against jagged rocks, roaring back and forth across coarse shingle. In mid-afternoon he ran his boat up on one of the shingle beaches, jumped gingerly ashore. Shivering in the whooping gusts, he took stock of the situation. There was no living thing to be seen along the foreshore but three or four grey gulls. A hundred yards to his right lay a battered hulk of another boat, and beyond was a tangle of wood and fibre which might have been still another.

Inga carried ashore what provisions remained, bundled them together, and by a faint trail climbed the cliffs. He came out on an expanse of rolling grey-green downs. Two or three miles inland rose a line of low hills, toward which the trail seemed to lead.

Inga looked right and left; again there was no living creature in sight other than gulls. Shouldering his bundle he set forth along the trail.

Nearing the hills he came upon a hut of turf and stone, beside a patch of cultivated soil. A man and a woman worked in the field. Inga peered closer. What manner of creatures were these? They resembled human beings; they had arms and legs and faces — but how seamed and seared and grey they were! How shrunken were their hands, how they bent and hobbled as they worked! He walked quickly by, and they did not appear to notice him.

Now Inga hastened, as the end of the day was drawing on and the hills loomed before him. The trail led along a valley grown with gnarled oak and low purple-green shrubs, then slanted up the hillside through a stony gap, where the wind generated whistling musical sounds. From the gap Inga looked out over a flat valley. He saw copses of low trees, plots of tilled land, a group of huts. Slowly he walked down the trail. In a nearby field a man raised his head. Inga paused, thinking to recognize him. Was this not Oma ta Akara who had sailed west ten or twelve seasons back? It seemed impossible. This man was fat, the hair had almost departed his head, his cheeks hung loose at the jawline. No, this could not be lithe Oma ta Akara! Hurriedly Inga turned away, and presently entered the village. Before a nearby hut stood one whom he recognized with joy. "Takti Tai!"

Takti Tai nodded. "Rona ta Inga. I knew you'd be coming soon."

"I'm delighted to see you! But let us leave this terrible place; let us return to the island!"

Takti Tai smiled a little, shook his head.

Inga protested heatedly, "Don't tell me you prefer this dismal land? Come! My boat is still seaworthy. If somehow we can back it off the beach, gain the open sea..."

The wind sang down over the mountains, strummed through the trees. Inga's words died in his throat. It was clearly impossible to work the boat off the foreshore.

"Not only the wind," said Takti Tai. "We could not go back now. We know the secret."

Inga stared in wonderment. "The secret? Not I."

"Come. Now you will learn."

Takti Tai took him through the village to a structure of stone, with a high-gabled roof shingled with slate. "Enter, and you will know the secret."

Hesitantly Rona ta Inga entered the stone structure. On a stone table lay a still figure surrounded by six tall candles. Inga stared at the shrunken white face, at the white sheet which lay motionless over the narrow chest. "Who is this? A man? How thin he is. Does he sleep? Why do you show me such a thing?"

"This is the secret," said Takti Tai. "It is called 'death'."

About the Author

JACK VANCE was born in 1916 to a well-off California family that, as his childhood ended, fell upon hard times. As a young man he worked at a series of unsatisfying jobs before studying mining engineering, physics, journalism and English at the University of California Berkeley. Leaving school as America was going to war, he found a place as an ordinary seaman in the merchant marine. Later he worked as a rigger, surveyor, ceramicist, and carpenter before his steady production of sf, mystery novels, and short stories established him as a full-time writer.

His output over more than sixty years was prodigious and won him three Hugo Awards, a Nebula Award, a World Fantasy Award for lifetime achievement, as well as an Edgar from the Mystery Writers of America. The Science Fiction and Fantasy Writers of America named him a grandmaster and he was inducted into the Science Fiction Hall of Fame.

His works crossed genre boundaries, from dark fantasies (including the highly influential *Dying Earth* cycle of novels) to interstellar space operas, from heroic fantasy (the *Lyonesse* trilogy) to murder mysteries featuring a sheriff (the Joe Bain novels) in a rural California county. A Vance story often centered on a competent male protagonist thrust into a dangerous, evolving situation on a planet where adventure was his daily fare, or featured a young person setting out on a perilous odyssey over difficult terrain populated by entrenched, scheming enemies.

Late in his life, a world-spanning assemblage of Vance aficionados came together to return his works to their original form, restoring material cut by editors whose chief preoccupation was the page count of a pulp magazine. The result was the complete and authoritative *Vance Integral Edition* in 44 hardcover volumes. Spatterlight Press is now publishing the VIE texts as ebooks, and as print-on-demand paperbacks.

Colophon

This book was printed using Adobe Arno Pro as the primary text font, with NeutraFace used on the cover.

This title was created from the digital archive of the Vance Integral Edition, a series of 44 books produced under the aegis of the author by a worldwide group of his readers. The VIE project gratefully acknowledges the editorial guidance of Norma Vance, as well as the cooperation of the Department of Special Collections at Boston University, whose John Holbrook Vance collection has been an important source of textual evidence.

Special thanks to R.C. Lacovara, Patrick Dusoulier, Koen Vyverman, Paul Rhoads, Chuck King, Gregory Hansen, Suan Yong, and Josh Geller for their invaluable assistance preparing final versions of the source files.

Source: John Rick; Digitize: Derek W. Benson, Richard Chandler, Mike Dennison, Herve Goubin, Joel Hedlund, Damien G. Jones, Charles King, Sean Rainey, Chris Reid, Axel Roschinski, Thomas Rydbeck, John A. Schwab, Peter Strickland, Gan Uesli Starling, Hans van der Veeke, Dave Worden, Suan Hsi Yong; Format: Joel Riedesel, Suan Hsi Yong; Diff: Damien G. Jones, David A. Kennedy, Charles King, David Reitsema, Steve Sherman, Hans van der Veeke; Diff-Merge: Suan Hsi Yong; Tech Proof: Bob Moody, Michael Duncan, Ed Gooding, Peter Ikin, Karl Kellar, Turlough O'Connor, Joel Riedesel, Hans van der Veeke, Matt Westwood, Dave Worden; Text Integrity: Derek W. Benson, Ron Chernich, Patrick Dusoulier, Rob Friefeld, Alun Hughes, Charles King, Paul Rhoads, Kenneth Roberts, Robin L. Rouch, Jeffrey Ruszczyk, Thomas Rydbeck, John A. Schwab, Steve Sherman, Tim Stretton, Koen Vyverman, Dave Worden; Implement: Donna Adams, Derek W. Benson, Mike Dennison, Patrick Dusoulier, Joel Hedlund, Damien G. Jones, David Reitsema, Hans van der Veeke; Security: David A. Kennedy, Paul Rhoads, Suan Hsi Yong; Compose: Paul Rhoads, John A. Schwab; Comp Review: Mark Adams, Christian J. Corley, Marcel van Genderen, Brian Gharst, Karl Kellar, Charles King, Bob Luckin, Robin L. Rouch, Billy Webb; Update Verify: Joel Anderson, John A.D. Foley, Rob Friefeld, Marcel van Genderen, Charles King, Bob Luckin, Robert Melson, Paul Rhoads, Robin L. Rouch, Steve Sherman; RTF-Diff: Mark Bradford, Deborah Cohen, Patrick Dusoulier, Charles King, Errico Rescigno, Bill Schaub; Proofread: Michael Abramoff, Mark Adams, Joel Anderson, Neil Anderson, Nicola de Angeli, Neville Angove, Erik Arendse, Charles Ashford, Mike Barrett, Michel Bazin, Richard Behrens, Scott Benenati, Brian Bieniowski, Arjan Bokx, Malcolm Bowers, Mark Bradford, Dominic Brown, Angus Campbell-Cann, Jeremy Cavaterra, Deborah Cohen, Matthew Colburn, Robert Collins, Jeff Cook, Greg Delson, Dirk-Jan van der Duim, Michael Duncan, Patrick

Dusoulier, Patrick Dymond, Andrew Edlin, Kimmo Eriksson, Harry Erwin, Linda Escher, John A. D. Foley, Rob Friefeld, Marcel van Genderen, Rob Gerrand, Carl Goldman, Ed Gooding, Yannick Gour, Tony Graham, Martin Green, Erec Grim, Jasper Groen, Evert Jan de Groot, John Hawes, Linda Heaphy, Joel Hedlund, Wayne Henry, Marc Herant, Helmut Hlavacs, Peter Ikin, Jason Ives, Ralph Jas, Lucie Jones, Jurriaan Kalkman, Karl Kellar, Charles King, Per Kjellberg, Rob Knight, R.C. Lacovara, Chris LaHatte, Gabriel Landon, Stephane Leibovitsch, Bob Luckin, Roderick MacBeath, S.A. Manning, Betty Mayfield, John McDonough, Robert Melson, Michael Mitchell, Bob Moody, Eric Newsom, Till Noever, Michael Nolan, Joe Ormond, Jim Pattison, Eric Petersen, Michael Rathbun, Glenn Raye, Simon Read, David Reitsema, Errico Rescigno, Paul Rhoads, Joel Riedesel, Axel Roschinski, Robin L. Rouch, Jeffrey Ruszczyk, Thomas Rydbeck, Bill Schaub, Mike Schilling, Bill Sherman, Steve Sherman, Mark Shoulder, Lyall Simmons, Rudi Staudinger, Gabriel Stein, Mark J. Straka, Per Sundfeldt, Andrew Thompson, Anthony Thompson, Willem Timmer, Hans van der Veeke, John Velonis, Dirk Jan Verlinde, Paul Wedderien, Richard White, Dave Worden, Fred Zoetemeyer

Artwork (maps based on original drawings by Jack and Norma Vance):

Paul Rhoads, Christopher Wood

Book Composition and Typesetting: Joel Anderson

Art Direction and Cover Design: Howard Kistler

Proofing: Steve Sherman, Dave Worden

Jacket Blurb: Steve Sherman, John Vance

Management: John Vance, Koen Vyverman

Made in the USA
Middletown, DE
19 June 2020